Topper ran to the door and started growling. Sidney peeked out the window, saw the empty stairs, the still driveway below. "There's no one there, Toppie."

Topper growled again, and this time she heard a car door slamming shut.

Her Glock sat on the counter next to her purse, and she walked over, slid it from its holster, then shut off the light. "Topper," she whispered. "Quiet." She returned to the door, tried to listen past her quickening pulse. The sound of someone talking, an accent she couldn't decipher, saying, "Be careful. Don't kill—" Another car door closing. She told herself it was nothing, just a couple guys. She tightened her grip on her Glock, looked out the peephole.

And saw the silhouette of a man walking toward the steps . . .

By Robin Burcell

WHEN MIDNIGHT COMES
EVERY MOVE SHE MAKES
FATAL TRUTH
DEADLY LEGACY
COLD CASE
FACE OF A KILLER

FACE
OF A
KILLER

ROBIN BURCELL

HARPER

An Imprint of HarperCollinsPublishers

This is a work of fiction. Names, characters, places, and incidents are drawn from the author's imagination or are used fictitiously and are not to be construed as real. Any resemblance to actual events, locales, organizations, or persons, living or dead, is entirely coincidental.

HARPER

An Imprint of HarperCollins*Publishers*
10 East 53rd Street
New York, New York 10022-5299

Copyright © 2008 by Robin Burcell
ISBN 978-1-60751-427-5

Printed in the United States of America

To my father
Thank you for the music.
And to Joan
Thank you for taking care of my father.

Acknowledgments

For Their Expertise and Guidance

I truly owe thanks to a number of people who tirelessly answered my questions to ensure that this book gives an accurate yet fictional account of federal and local law enforcement beyond my own experience, as well as to those who brought their expertise in other areas. If any errors are made, I'm pleading this for my excuse: It's fiction.

To Supervisory Special Agent George Fong, FBI, for always answering my questions, and for arranging for the tour of the San Francisco FBI office. To Inspector Pat Correa, SFPD, for her help with my crime scene at Golden Gate Park. To Sheridan Rowe, officer from the Lone Star State, for assistance on HPD's crime scene unit. To Mary Young and Bill Young, retired San Quentin employees, for helping me with my prison scenes.

To Dr. Cherie Fiscus, for that ring of authenticity to my dental scenes. To Greg Weaver (and his wife, Juli), for interrupting his dinner plans to help with all things nautical.

To Susan Crosby, for reminding me that, since I was a forensic artist, I should write a book about one. To Georgia Bockoven, for helping me plot a particular testy scene.

Last but not least, to my agent, Jane Chelius, who cheered me on when I needed it most; to my editor, Lyssa Keusch, who helped me see the bigger picture; and to Barbara Peters at Poisoned Pen, for her infinite patience.

For Literacy

I'd also like to acknowledge the generous charitable donations in exchange for character names: To Gerald Shedden, for his late friend, Dave Dixon, on behalf of the Solano County Library. To Dr. Michael Jacob Schermer, on behalf of the Sacramento County Library. To Sandy Sechrest, on behalf of the literacy auction Bouchercon 2004. To Ren Pham-Peck and to Chuck Hilleary on behalf of their donations to Larson Elementary. Thank you each and every one of you.

Success breeds complacency. Complacency breeds failure. Only the paranoid survive.

Andrew Grove, founder, Intel Corporation

FACE

OF A

KILLER

1

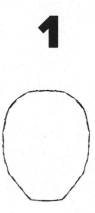

Sydney Fitzpatrick eyed the bottle of scotch, watched the bartender pour the amber liquid into her glass, and wondered how much of it she'd have to drink to forget it had been twenty years since her father had been killed.

"Leave the bottle," she told the bartender.

"Don't think so."

"You're only going to have to come back."

"Maybe," he said, returning the whiskey to its place among the other bottles, all backlit, shining, each advertising its own brand of panacea.

All false advertising, she thought, finishing her second shot. She would've ordered a third—except her cell phone started vibrating an alert.

Only one sort of call comes in at one in the morning, never mind that Sydney recognized the number: her boss, Dave Dixon. "Fitzpatrick," she announced into the phone. "And I'm supposed to have the day off."

"*Day* being the operative word. It's dark out, which makes it night, which you didn't request off."

"*And* I've been drinking."

"Since when do you drink?"

"Since an hour ago," she said, and let him wonder.

Apparently he didn't wonder long. "We need you down here. A Seven matter," he said, giving the Bureau program designator for initiating a kidnap investigation.

Her stomach knotted. She did not need this. Not tonight.

"Did you hear me, Fitzpatrick? Got a kidnap-rape."

"You assigning me the case?"

"No. Just a sketch."

Sydney eyed the bottle of whiskey that seemed to beckon, thinking that even on a good day it was hard enough to interview victims for drawings, hard to get past the mental exhaustion of being inside her victims' heads, knowing the pain and terror they felt . . .

Maybe she should tell Dixon no, but that would require an explanation, and she wasn't sure she wanted to go into that. It wasn't that Dixon didn't know her history. They'd worked together in D.C., used to be friends, at least up until he was promoted and all friendships were checked at the door. The last thing Sydney wanted was for him to worry about her. "I'm just a few blocks away. I'll be right there."

She took some money out of her wallet, paid for her drinks, then walked to the door and opened it. What had been a light sprinkle when she'd left her car at home that October night to drink herself into oblivion, had now turned into a heavy downpour that hammered the sidewalk with a deafening blast. And lucky her, not a cab in sight.

With no umbrella, she'd be soaked, and she was tempted to see if the rain might slow. But then she thought of the waiting that her victim had already endured. In the grand scheme of things, getting wet was the least of her worries, and she stepped out into the driving rain. She hadn't walked more than half a block when the odd feeling of being watched came over her. She stopped, turned, eyed the street up and down, saw nothing but a few parked cars, seemingly unoccupied. Across the street, a couple of women huddled beneath an overhang, smoking a cigarette. Other than that, the streets seemed deserted.

Hearing nothing but the rain, the water sluicing down the gutters into the storm drains, she pulled her coat tighter against the autumn chill. But the farther she walked, the stronger the feeling came that she was being followed. *It's only your imagination*, she told herself. Even so, she quickened her pace and pressed her right elbow into her hip, wanting to feel the reassuring presence of her holstered Glock—then remembered she'd left it in her desk drawer.

She normally carried the damned thing night and day, but she'd intended to spend the night drinking in a vain attempt to erase not only the anniversary of her father's murder, but also the bitter fight she'd had with her mother over her plans for the upcoming day. It was the same fight they'd had last year and the two years before that. At thirty-three years old, a girl should be able to make up her own damned mind on how she spent her day. Her mother had nothing to do with this, she thought, as a movement caught her eye. Definitely someone back there. She doubled her pace, didn't get far, when a man stepped out in front of her, blocked her path.

She jumped back, her pulse slamming in her veins. The man towered a good eight inches over her, his craggy face barely visible beneath his knit cap and a scarf wrapped around his neck and mouth. A sharp smell of body odor, unwashed clothes, wet, stale, and sour, assaulted her nose.

"Got some change?" he asked, opening his hand, palm up. His other was shoved in the pocket of an army coat, ragged, buttons dangling, held closed with another scarf tied around his waist.

Recognition hit her. Private Cooper was a regular on this block, chased off by the cops on a continual basis, only to return the moment they left. Right now she was grateful for his presence. "Yeah," she said, digging into her purse. She handed him a few bills, then looked back, saw a figure darting into the shadows. Someone was following her, no doubt. The federal building was only two blocks away, and she crossed to the other side of the street, where the building facades were more modern, better lit. If whoever it was thought she was going to be an easy mark, he'd have to come out and get her.

A few minutes later, she waved her access identification across the pad, punched in her code, and with one last look behind her, entered the door of the San Francisco FBI field office. A purse snatcher had been hitting women in the area for a couple of weeks now, and she wondered if that was who'd been tailing her. Not that she could offer any description, she thought, walking down the hall to her office.

Supervisory Special Agent Dave Dixon was talking on the phone when she reached her desk. He was a good supervisor, one who spoke his mind, whether it was politically correct or not. Like the time he told her that dumping her fiancé, also an FBI agent, was the smartest thing she'd done all year, and that transferring from Washington, D.C., to the San Francisco office was her next smartest move. The fiancé thing, Sydney was sure about; the move to the city, she wasn't so sure. Too many memories.

Dixon was still talking, and Sydney shrugged out of her sopping overcoat, then stopped to listen to her voice mail while she waited for him. The first message happened to be from her thank-God-he's-her-*ex*-fiancé, Scotty Ryan. "Hey, Syd. I know. I promised. But this isn't about us this time. It's important. Call me. No matter the hour." She'd get right on that. Not. Erasing it, she listened to the next. "This is Officer Kim Glynnis, Hill City PD. I was, uh, hoping to come by and talk to you about a case. A possible sketch on a Jane Doe. I work midnights, so if I don't answer, leave a message." Hill City PD was a small department in the South Bay, and Sydney jotted down the number, just as Dixon walked out of his office.

"You look like a drowned rat," he said, eyeing her.

"Yeah, well, I was shooting for the drunk-drowned-rat look, but I answered my cell phone. What's going on?"

"We were notified by SFPD about a kidnapping. Said they took it as far as they could and wanted us to take it from here. According to preliminary reports, our victim, Tara Brown, was kidnapped out of Reno, raped numerous times on the Nevada side, driven to California and raped again. She's pretty banged up. Stabbed, then dumped at Golden Gate Park. Smart kid, though. Pretended she was dead, and I'm thinking that's what saved her. She's out at General right now."

Sydney went to her desk, unlocked it, and picked up her leather case with her credentials, better known as "creds" in Bureau-speak. Just her luck, Dixon glanced over, saw her gun in the drawer. He gave her a hard glare. "Why aren't you armed?"

"I was out drinking."

"God granted you the power to carry. Do it."

"Actually it was J. Edgar Hoover."

"Same thing. Put it on." Dixon didn't believe in unarmed agents. But he'd always been a Bureau man. She'd started off as a cop, and cops weren't supposed to drink and wear firearms, though Sydney was probably the only cop who thought so. But that was one of her quirks; she followed rules. After her scare tonight, she was going to have to rethink the whole unarmed-while-drinking thing, she thought, as she strapped on her pistol, picked up her gold shield, and tucked her creds securely inside her back pocket. She grabbed the briefcase next to her desk, the one that contained her traveling art studio used for forensic drawings and suspect sketches. San Francisco PD had their own police artist, but this case was no longer theirs. It belonged to the Bureau now, and Sydney was the resident artist.

"Ready," she said. Everything in hand, she looked around to make sure she hadn't forgotten anything.

Dixon eyed her, his brows raised.

"What?" she asked.

"Drowned rat?"

"Does it work for me? Or make me look fat?"

"You couldn't ask me that *before* you put on your gun?"

"You are such a chicken."

"Yeah, yeah. Heard it before from my wife, who, if anyone inquires, looks like a supermodel," he said, pulling his car keys from his pocket. He eyed her, thoughtful. Since she tended to be reserved at work, he was no doubt noticing. "Just how much *have* you had to drink?"

"Not nearly enough. Give me two minutes. I'll meet you downstairs."

Sydney took her things into the restroom; combed her soaked, shoulder-length brown hair into a ponytail; wiped the rain-smeared mascara from beneath her eyes; decided she looked presentable. After popping a mint, she met Dixon in the parking garage. By the time they left, the rain had finally stopped, and she hoped it wouldn't return for the night. The hospital's parking lot was filled to capacity, and they had to drive around a couple of times in search of a parking space, since those reserved for law enforcement were full. Busy night. As usual.

"Over there." Sydney pointed toward the glow of red brake lights at the far end of the lot, as someone began to back up.

Dixon pulled around, and when it was apparent some guy in a red Ford Tempo was already headed for the same spot, Dixon gunned it a bit harder, winning the space by a matter of seconds. "That's why they spend the big bucks on driver training at the academy," he said, angling in.

"Dang. And I thought it was to teach you how not to spill your coffee on high-speed chases." She stepped out of the car, then opened the back door to retrieve her briefcase.

"Asshole!"

Sydney glanced up, saw the red Ford Tempo, the driver shoving his hand out the open window, his middle finger pointed skyward. Jerk, she thought looking past him to the next row over, where a newer model white delivery utility truck cruised slowly. The driver wore a yellow ball cap, pulled low, and even though Sydney couldn't see his eyes, she had the distinct feeling he was looking right at her.

Maybe it was just the totality of the day, but it was the same feeling she'd had when she'd left the bar, and thought someone was watching her then. She slammed the car door, telling herself that she *was* imagining things. It was a hospital parking lot. No one was watching her.

No one but Mr. Ford Tempo, who apparently wasn't done with them. He put his car in reverse, backed up, flipped them off again, then gunned it out of there to the far side of the lot.

Dixon shook his head. "Can't believe the manners on people these days."

"Sort of like your manners stealing the guy's parking

space?" she said, hefting her briefcase, then pulling her jacket closed against the wind.

"Details," Dixon said, and they walked up to the emergency room doors.

Their victim, a young girl, maybe eighteen, had been moved to a single-bed room. The strawberry-blond hair above her right temple was shaved; the staples that held her scalp shut glittered in the fluorescent light. Her face was a mosaic of black and purple splotches, her cheeks swollen. Tomorrow it would be worse.

Sydney set down her briefcase, while Dixon quietly approached the girl, who didn't open her eyes. "Tara?" he whispered.

Tara took a deep breath, but didn't respond, and Sydney knew she was trying to gather the strength to go on with this, to talk to the cops. It was the part Sydney hated, making them relive the events, but without it, without walking them back through the crime, some of the finer details and memories would be lost.

While Dixon got all the preliminary questions out of the way, Sydney leaned against the wall and shoved her hands in the pockets of her coat, concentrating on the smell of antiseptic wash, trying to forget what day it was tomorrow, trying but failing. All the while, Dixon spoke quietly, urging Tara to talk to them, to cooperate. His voice was soft, soothing, and Sydney glanced out the window into the parking lot below, letting her thoughts drift. She was a million miles away from the dim hospital room, when somewhere in her conscious mind, she realized she saw a man wearing a yellow ball cap walking in the shadows of the parking lot. Though he did nothing that shouted he was a threat, her gut told her something was up, perhaps because he wasn't walking toward the ER, but away from it. Sydney scanned the parking lot, looking for accomplices. She saw none. What she did see was that damned white utility truck, parked illegally near a delivery door. Who the hell made deliveries at two in the morning? The next guess was a logical conclusion, because of that feeling of being watched, that he was making his way to their car. Maybe he hadn't been watching her, just the vehicle, finding a mark that looked like they'd be inside for a while.

She glanced over at Dixon. He was still talking to the victim, trying to get some basic information.

"I hope you don't mind," she said, walking up to him, putting her hand on his shoulder and squeezing hard enough for him to know she was doing anything but what she was telling him. "I really need to get some fresh air."

He looked up at her, his brows raised, but he nodded, and she gave a gentle smile to their victim, something she hoped would alleviate any fears. Tara Brown was supposed to be safe here. Last thing Sydney wanted to do was announce that she was going after a suspicious person in the parking lot, something she was sure would shatter any semblance of peace the girl had left.

She walked out, heard Dixon quietly say, "I'll be right back," and a moment later, he followed.

"What's up?"

"Not sure if you noticed that guy in the white truck. Maybe it's nothing, but my gut tells me he's set his sights on your car."

"That's all we need," he said, glancing back toward the room.

"I'll grab someone before I go out. You stay with her, tell her I went for coffee or something."

"Be careful. And make it quick."

Sydney took the elevator down, walked through the emergency room, and stopped the first cops she saw. They were guarding a drunk who had apparently fallen and needed stitches. She flipped open her credentials, said, "One of you feel like chasing down someone with me in the parking lot?"

The two officers looked at each other, and the taller nodded. "I can go. What'd you have?"

"At the moment, nothing more than a feeling this guy doesn't belong in the parking lot," she said, as they both strode out the ER doors. The SFPD officer introduced himself as Bryan Harper, and they shook hands. "Sydney Fitzpatrick. Nice to meet you." She quickly told him what she saw from her victim's hospital room that overlooked the parking lot. "Maybe it's nothing," she said, as they walked down the ramp, "but it's my boss's car, and he'd like to keep the windows intact."

"You get points for that?"

"I hope so," she said, slowing him when they reached the aisle where Dixon's car was parked. They could see the top of the guy's head, or rather the top of his yellow ball cap just over the row of cars, and then he ducked down; perhaps had seen them come out. That itself told her it was more than nothing.

They moved out of plain sight, sidling along the row of parked vehicles. At one point, the suspect looked up, and she had to duck between two sedans. Harper motioned that he was going to parallel on the next aisle over. When he was in position, he pointed, and they started moving forward.

The suspect skirted to the opposite side of Dixon's car, and they froze. He was facing them, but apparently they weren't his focus, since he cupped both hands to look in the car window.

Harper edged against the retaining wall in front of the cars. Sydney moved closer from her row, could see the guy's breath steam up the window of Dixon's car. Suddenly he ducked, and she wondered if he was trying to jimmy the door open. She shouted, "FBI. Freeze!"

The suspect rose. Saw her. Harper jumped out. The man dove out of sight. Harper and Sydney edged to either side of the car. When they got there, he was gone.

"Damn," she said, looking around. She caught a shadow out of the corner of her eye. Glanced over, saw the suspect running toward the aisle of cars Harper had just left. "There!"

They ran over. Came out in front of a dark-colored Toyota.

"Where the hell'd he go?" Harper said.

She lifted her finger to her lips. Listened. Nothing at first. Then the slightest of splashes from a puddle the next row over. She pointed. He seemed to be moving toward the center of the lot. Harper nodded. He took one side of the Toyota; she took the other. Again, they emerged to nothing.

She happened to look down. Saw a red and white peppermint candy, still wrapped, in the midst of the puddle. As much rain as had fallen, the thing couldn't have been out there that long and not started disintegrating. "You think he tossed that?" she whispered. "Throw us off?"

Harper pulled out his radio. "Either way, time for reinforcements." He called the PD, who simply radioed for a couple of officers to step out of the hospital. Convenient.

While Harper walked toward the building to brief them, Sydney eyed the candy, thinking that something was not quite right. A simple burglary, or something more? One of the officers walked over to Dixon's car, and shouted that it was untouched. She looked from the candy on the ground to where their car was parked against the retaining wall. If the suspect had thrown this, he wanted them to move off in the opposite direction . . . She swung around. Saw Harper walking toward her, saying something into his radio, something she couldn't hear because an engine started up.

"The truck!" she shouted. Before anyone could act, the vehicle sped from the delivery doors. Its headlights blinded her. Its wheels screeched across the wet pavement.

And headed straight for them.

2

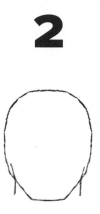

Officer Harper dove between two cars. Sydney jumped up on the hood of the nearest car, felt the cold metal through her clothes, the wet droplets soaking her knees. The truck sped off, its red taillights fading in the distance. She saw no rear plate, wondered if he'd removed it recently, or if it hadn't been there when he'd first pulled into the lot.

"Damn it," she said, sliding from the hood. She checked it for dents, didn't see any, but on the off chance, tucked her business card in the windshield. Two officers jumped in a patrol car and sped off after the vehicle, and she heard them on Harper's radio, calling out they were in pursuit of a newer model Chevy utility truck. A moment later, they were asking Harper on the radio what the suspect was wanted for. Translation: How hard were they going to search for him?

"Stand by," he said, then looked to her for guidance.

She glanced over at Dixon's car, saw a few smears in the raindrops on the driver's window, but no apparent damage. All she really had was some suspicious activity, not enough for SFPD to waste their time. "I wouldn't mind knowing who he is, but unless he's got a pocket full of burglar tools, I've got nothing," she said, quite simply because other than no license plate on his car, maybe speeding at them through the parking lot, she had bigger fish to fry. And rules were rules.

Any crime would've been the SFPD's jurisdiction anyway. As busy as they were tonight, she doubted they were interested, a fact confirmed when Harper nodded, then into the radio said, "FI, only." Field investigation. Which basically meant *if* they caught him, they'd identify him and hope for something more concrete to make an arrest from, like an outstanding warrant.

"Ten-four," the officer radioed back.

"You think he was trying something?" Harper asked her, as they walked back into the ER.

Sydney thought about that feeling of being watched. "Hard to say what he would've done if we hadn't gotten out there."

"What're you here for?" he asked her.

"Rape case we picked up from your office."

"Yeah. Heard about that. Tough case. All the way from Reno. Got any leads on, what'dya call your suspects? UnSubs?" he asked, referring to the FBI term for unidentified subject.

"Not yet. I'm going up to do a sketch of him now."

"Good luck. We'll keep an eye on the parking lot in case this idiot decides to return. Couldn't be real bright. Not like you can't tell that's some sort of cop car once you look inside the thing."

"Thanks. I appreciate it."

She gave him her card with her cell number on it, then returned upstairs.

Dixon was waiting just outside the victim's door. "What happened?" he asked.

"Not much." She glanced into the room. Tara Brown looked like she was asleep. "I saw some guy in a white utility truck, newer model Chevy. Thought he was about to smash your car window, called out, and he took off."

"You crawling around in puddles?" he asked, eyeing her wet knees.

"A few. She talk to you yet?"

"When she wasn't sleeping. The only thing I got from her

was that our UnSub stole a ring she wore, when he left her for dead. Wouldn't say a word after that. I was hoping you could work your magic."

She brushed at her clothes, tried for an appearance of calm as she walked in. Her briefcase was right where she'd left it by the door, and she picked it up and walked over to the bed, shaking off the bit of adrenaline from her chase outside. Tara appeared to be sleeping still, and when Sydney thought she seemed calm enough, she called out her name, pasting on her best soft smile, steeling herself against the mental drain of empathy needed for a drawing, the feeling that every time she completed a sketch, she was leaving a small part of herself on the paper with the victim. Sometimes it surprised her that she had anything left to give after all the drawings she'd done. "Hi, Tara. My name's Sydney. I'm an artist for the FBI, here to do a drawing of the man who hurt you."

Tara made an attempt to shake her head. "I told the other guy that I can't remember what he looks like . . ."

Sydney waited, not wanting to push her just yet, but when it seemed Tara wasn't about to continue, she asked, "Did you see the face of the man who hurt you?"

"Only for a minute. He—I was blindfolded after . . . He pulled my shirt up . . ."

"It's okay," Sydney said. "But you'd be surprised what you really do remember. And I'm here to help you."

"I can't describe him. I don't want to."

"Well, let's start off with something easier. I just want to know what you were doing before you were attacked."

That seemed to relax her. "I was with my boyfriend. We were in a bar—I'm not going to be in trouble for that, am I?"

"No, Tara. You're not in trouble. We're only interested in who hurt you. Tell me what you were doing, maybe an hour before you were attacked."

"We—we were drinking. I, um, had a fake ID," she added quietly, and Sydney knew she was blaming herself for the events. If only she hadn't done this. If only she hadn't done that.

"Go on," Sydney said, trying not to think of her own past.

"The bar was closing, and I had to use the bathroom, and

he was there, hiding inside it, and he grabbed me." She didn't speak for several seconds, and just when Sydney thought she might have given up, she said, "He tried to rape me, and I told him my boyfriend, Eric, was there and would come after me, and he said—he said he hoped he did, because he'd kill him." She looked up at the ceiling, tears streaming down the sides of her face. "I was so scared. Eric was—he was waiting in the bar when all this was happening. And then the man bit me. My breast. He said it was his mark. He had my mouth covered, but I tried not to scream. I didn't want Eric to hear. I—I didn't want him to be killed . . ." And then she started sobbing, and Sydney let her, not wanting to upset the fragile balance of tumultuous emotions.

When her crying subsided, and her breathing became more even, Sydney asked, "Did you see his face? There in the bathroom?"

Tara nodded. "But I can't describe it. I don't ever want to see it again."

"Tara. I know this is hard for you."

"How can you know?"

She blazed right past that question with "Trust me when I say that you have it in your power to help us catch this person and stop him from hurting anyone else. But we can't do it without your help."

"I can't—"

"How old was he?" Sydney cut in, not giving her a chance to think about what she was doing.

"Um, late twenties, early thirties."

"What race?"

"He was white."

"You're doing good, Tara. How tall?"

"A few inches taller than me. I'm five-six."

"Weight?"

"Just regular."

"Was there anything about him that stuck out in your mind? Anything about him that reminded you of someone or something?"

She nodded, and seemed to shiver. "He smelled like fire. Like smoke from a fire." Then, placing her finger along her right cheek, she said, "And there was something on his face. A scar, a wrinkle. I don't want to remember. I want to forget what he looks like. Please . . ."

Sydney stared at her sketch pad, the tiny descriptive notes she'd jotted in the corner, trying to ignore the stirrings of things she never wanted to remember at the mention of this man's scar. And now she didn't want to look at Tara, didn't want to see the pain in her eyes, didn't want to tell her that, though they'd suffered completely different crimes, even after twenty years, there were some things you never forget . . .

She shook it off, took a breath. "We're just going to do a simple sketch. Real basic at first." Sydney took her pencil, held it to the paper. "Now how would you describe the shape of his face?"

"Oval."

And so it began. While Dixon stood by the window, trying to remain unobtrusive and watch for wayward vandals in the parking lot, Sydney drew the shape, showed it to Tara, and Tara nodded. Again and again, Sydney drawing, Tara nodding, or shaking her head no, a back-and-forth dance, meeting of the minds, wider, shorter, higher, less, more. What started out as a simple sketch slowly, feature by feature, began to take shape. Two hours and several short breaks later, the sketch nearly complete—all but the shading of the shadows and planes—she showed it to Tara one more time and asked, "If you could make one change on this, what would it be?"

Tara bit her lip, studied the drawing. "The nose . . . I think it's too pointed. And I don't think the scar was that long . . . if there even was one."

She rounded the nose tip, then stopped, her eraser poised over the scar. She stared at the drawing, the scar on the cheek, her stomach twisting. This wasn't something she was supposed to remember. Not after twenty years . . .

"Syd? You okay?" Dixon moved from the window, walked toward her.

She closed her eyes, took a breath, then shortened the scar, lightened it to where it looked more like a wrinkle or mark—

who knows what it could have been—then held up the drawing, saw her victim's face crumple, tears streaming down her cheeks as she said, "Yes. That's him. That's the man who raped me."

And as it usually did at this point in the process, it struck her, the difference between her father's case and Tara's, the difference in all the cases for all the drawings she'd done over the years.

There was no guarantee that her work would result in an arrest. In her father's case, an arrest had been made almost immediately. It had allowed her to live these past twenty years with the firm belief that justice prevails, and she couldn't imagine the pain of living otherwise, never knowing if the man who had committed that crime was out there still. What if that Good Samaritan hadn't copied that license number, called it in to the police? What if her father's killer had never been caught?

She supposed it was this last thought that made her look twice at the drawing she'd just finished. Perhaps she was being too empathetic. Trying too hard to see the suspect as Tara saw him. She stood, handed the drawing to Dixon, surprised her hands were steady. "I, um, need a minute. Ladies' room."

Sydney walked out, not waiting for a response, her gaze taking in the long gray hallway, looking for a sign indicating the restroom. She found it, stepped in, closed the door, trying to figure out just why this drawing had affected her so, and she eyed her pale face in the mirror, the darkening circles beneath her eyes. Her heart was beating as if she'd been running, her hands were sweaty, her stomach nauseous. She knew the reason, told herself there was no other explanation for such a reaction. That milestone. Twenty years. Here Sydney was, doing a drawing of a rapist, not even the same type of crime. And all this time, she wanted it to be him. The face she must have blocked from her conscious mind for twenty years. The man who'd killed her father.

But it wasn't. That man was sitting in a jail cell and he was never getting out.

3

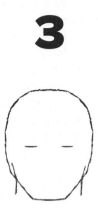

The night air was refreshing, washed clean. A few stars peeked through the breaks in the clouds, and the cars around them glistened with droplets beneath the parking lot lights, as Sydney and Dixon navigated the puddles to his car. They walked around the vehicle, giving it a good look, making sure nothing had happened since they'd chased off the would-be car burglar, and for a short time she actually thought that maybe Dixon hadn't noticed her reaction to that drawing. The moment he unlocked the car, gave her that look, she knew otherwise.

"Something going on that I should know about?"

There was no way Sydney was going to tell him what the anniversary of her father's murder was doing to her head, so she gave a slight shrug. "It's nothing. Really."

His gaze held hers for several seconds before he replied, "Whatever that *nothing* is, make it gone by the time you get back to work."

One could only hope, Sydney thought, giving him a smile of reassurance. Conversation over. He drove her home in silence, and as they neared her street, in the midst of the neighborhood called Inner Sunset, wisps of fog started to thicken.

When Sydney transferred to the San Francisco field office the only thing she remembered about the city was that the traffic sucked. Hence Sydney contacted a real estate agent, put her life in the woman's hands, telling her she'd take anyplace as long as she didn't have to deal with the commute. When the agent came up with a rental in a large house that had been divided into two apartments above the landlord's home "just three miles from the Pacific Ocean," and "very near Golden Gate Park," never mind the clincher, a real garage, Sydney figured it was perfect. What she didn't realize was that the neighborhood suffered from some of the worst weather in the *entire* Bay Area all year round. It could be sunny three blocks over, but not in the Inner Sunset. Some days Sydney never saw the sun. Some nights Sydney wasn't sure the stars were in the sky. She happened to live right smack in the middle of the fog zone.

Damned good thing she liked the fog, she told herself as Dixon pulled onto her street. He stopped the car in front of her driveway, about to say something, no doubt about tonight's incident in the hospital, her odd reaction to the drawing.

She didn't give him a chance. "See you at work," she said, before he decided to question her anew. With a quick wave, she exited the vehicle, then hurried up the stairs to her apartment. She let herself in, closed and locked the door behind her, glad the night was over. Her throat was parched, and she made a beeline for the kitchen, filled a glass of water, then took a long drink. Her answering machine flashed. Four messages, according to the prompt, the first from one of her girlfriends, Kate Gillespie, a San Francisco PD homicide inspector, who wanted to set her up with a friend, an ex-cop or ex-attorney turned bartender—Sydney couldn't really remember which—not that she was in the market. "And do me a favor?" Kate finished. "Call me with your new cell phone number? It'd be nice to get in touch with the real you, not some machine."

Two days ago, her FBI-issued cell phone had suddenly stopped working, and for whatever reason, the powers that be couldn't issue her a new phone with the same number.

Typical government bureaucracy, always making things more difficult than they were.

The next message was from her mother. "I need to know if you can watch Angela overnight next week. Jake's taking me to a bed-and-breakfast up in Bodega. Let me know. If you can't, maybe I can call your neighbor, Rainie. Angela seems to like her."

Nothing about their argument two days ago. Not that she'd expected anything. It was the same each year, had been ever since Sydney brought up the idea of going to San Quentin and facing her father's killer. A little over four years ago, when Sydney had joined the FBI, a psychologist who was teaching one of her academy classes on the psychology of murder had posed the question, asked her if she'd ever thought about facing her father's killer, finding out why he'd done what he'd done, not just from a victim's standpoint, but also from that of a special agent.

At first the thought horrified her, but then, the more she thought about it, the more she realized he might be right. Go to San Quentin, face him, find out his reasons for committing the murder, find out why he continued to deny his guilt when the evidence was overwhelming. Carefully she'd broached the subject with her mother. And while she hadn't expected well-wishes for what she'd suggested, she had hoped for a modicum of understanding. Instead it turned into an emotionally disastrous argument, with her mother insisting that Sydney be examined by a psychiatrist, and even her stepfather, Jake, declaring that her entrance into law enforcement was a mistake.

Perhaps she could have gone, not told her mother, but that somehow seemed dishonest, and so she put it off each year, reminding herself that she wasn't the only victim here. Her mother's feelings should also be taken into account, though Sydney knew that part of those feelings were simply her mother's attempt to protect her in the best way she knew how.

But this year had been different, perhaps because of the impending execution, now just ten days away. Her mother, worried that Sydney was going through with what she called her "insane idea," had enlisted outside help. She'd called an old family friend, Donovan Gnoble, who just happened to be a U.S. senator, and told him what Sydney had planned. That resulted in a call to her office last Friday from his office in Washington, D.C., begging her not to go through with this idea. "For your mother's sake," he'd said. "She deserves some peace after all these years. If nothing else, think of her and how she feels. And if you just let it alone, in a couple weeks he'll be gone."

Exactly my point, she thought, jabbing the button to play the next two messages. Both were from Scotty telling her to call him, that it was urgent.

When they were living together, he was hardly ever home, and it seemed they never had the time to sit down, talk, but the moment she moved to the opposite side of the country, it was like he had her number on speed dial.

They'd met at the academy in Quantico, where he'd been assisting with the firearms training, though they hadn't started dating until after she'd graduated. To say he was ambitious would be an understatement. Scotty had his entire life planned out, knew where he was going, what he wanted to do. And she'd liked that about him, because in many ways it reflected how she preferred to live her own life. Structured, planned, scheduled. Black and white. That was, in essence, how she'd survived since her father's murder. There was no chaos with order.

But neither was there spontaneity, as Scotty had pointed out.

That she didn't like to look at too closely. Their breakup was not entirely her fault. Hard to be spontaneous when the other half is always away from home, working some big political corruption case. So when Dixon was promoted and transferred out West, she took that as a sign, put in for a transfer herself.

Not that Scotty had any intentions of giving up that easily. He seemed to think all Sydney needed was a little time apart, and once she got it, they'd be back together. With a frustrated sigh, she glanced at the clock, figured with the three-hour time difference, he'd be up for work anyway, so she might as well get it over with now. He answered on the second ring.

"Hey, Scotty."

"Syd?" He cleared his voice, "What time is it?"

"Late. Got called out on a sketch. Were you sleeping?"

"Yeah. I'm actually not at home, just having my calls forwarded to my cell."

"Where are you?"

"Hotel. I tried to call. You okay with the anniversary and everything?"

"I'm fine."

"You sure? I heard you're taking the day off today, but when I tried to call—"

"New cell phone," Sydney said, then gave him the number. One of these days, she was going to have to have a talk with whoever was feeding Scotty his information about her and her life—and she had a fair idea just who was doing it. In the meantime, she decided to play the whole thing down, because the information highway in her office was a two-way street, and the last thing she needed was for anyone working with her to think that she couldn't handle the stresses of her personal life. "And I'm taking the day off because . . . I want to paint," she said, eyeing the blank canvas on the easel in her kitchen. "You know how much it relaxes me. In fact, I'm painting right now." She plucked a wide brush from a coffee can filled with brushes sitting on the counter, then, holding the phone close so he could catch the sound effects, she dunked the brush in her water glass, swirling it around at warp speed. "Acrylics."

"Sydney, we need to talk. I'd thought I'd come by."

"What do you mean come by? Where are you?"

"In San Francisco."

"This is not a good idea, Scotty."

For once, however, he wasn't demanding she reconsider her position about their relationship. Quite the opposite. "I know you said you needed space, but this isn't about that. Besides, I was worried about the article."

"What article?"

"The one that came out in yesterday's *Chronicle*. The

fact he's getting new attorneys. You did read the paper yesterday?"

She looked at the newspaper on her coffee table, tossed there when she'd left for her morning run, untouched when she'd gone into the office on her day off yesterday to catch up on paperwork, because she knew she was taking today off. "No," she said, trying to keep the emotion from her voice. Phone to her ear, she walked into her living room, sat on the couch, removed the rubber band from yesterday morning's paper, and flipped through it, finding the article about five pages in.

"You there, Syd?"

She didn't answer. She couldn't. Her gaze was fixed on the photograph of Johnnie Wheeler, the man convicted of killing her father, and what stood out to her was the damned scar on his cheek.

"Syd?"

"Yeah."

"You okay?"

"I'll call you back."

She hit the off button, then tossed the phone on the couch, trying not to look at the photo, feeling as shaky as she had when she'd finished that sketch in the hospital. She tried to take a calming breath, told herself it was just a photograph. It couldn't hurt her. Finally she forced herself to look. It was the same picture she'd seen of him several years ago, when she'd worked up the courage to read the investigation report. Wheeler's photo had been included in that report, and though she did not want to see the eyes of the man who'd killed her father, she'd found her gaze drawn to the photo anyway, was surprised by the scar she'd seen on his cheek. Even now, staring at the news photo, it was the same.

As then, she had no memories of this man, had thought surely, of all things, she'd remember a man's face, his scar, but she'd been told that she'd blocked a number of things from her mind that fateful night. There was much she didn't remember.

The sound of the gunshot.

The blood.

The killer's face.

The human brain is an amazing thing, and hers had neatly compartmentalized just about everything. Or so her childhood psychiatrist had told not only her, but also the officers who had investigated the case at the time.

The sight of his face in the paper shook her more than she'd expected, and finally she grabbed a magazine, dropped it on top so she wouldn't have to see it.

Nor did she want to read the article, and yet she told herself she should read it, see what it said about the man who had killed her father, find out *why*.

There were no answers, though. Not for her. Perhaps because only part of the article detailed Johnnie Wheeler, just ten days shy of being executed. Apparently he was professing his innocence, no surprise there, and there were plenty of people supporting him, assisting him in locating new attorneys.

And as much as that bothered her, that there might be a chance he could get out, what she found even more upsetting was the main thrust of the article, which wasn't really about Wheeler at all. Senator Donovan Gnoble was personally involving himself in the case. Elections were a little more than a month away, and here he was using her father's murder and Wheeler's impending execution for his get-tough-on-crime stance. The timing of his involvement galled her, and she didn't care how close of a family friend he was, or that he'd been her father's friend from way back, or that he lived in the same damned town as her mother.

He didn't need to use this case for his platform, use her father's death for his political gain. Not with his pedigree. Though Donovan Gnoble was affectionately known as "The Colonel," partly due to his kindly face, his white hair, mustache, and trademark goatee, making him look like a true Southern gentleman, he also had the real-life military background to go with the name. A retired lieutenant colonel, he was the frontrunner, the favorite. A Yale graduate who later became a decorated war hero with the scars to prove it, he was one of the few conservative Republicans who held sway with the Democrats when it came to his politics, and there were many who thought he stood a good chance of becoming president if he ever decided to throw his hat in the ring. He was the quintessential politician, who happened to be married to the quintessential politician's wife, because a vote for Gnoble was a vote for Marla Gnoble, a woman who came from a long line of prominent politicians, and yet one who stayed out of the spotlight, all while running her philanthropic charities with the liberal eye for the poor and the gift for getting big corporations to open their checkbooks.

The phone rang. Scotty apparently couldn't wait for her to call him back.

"You okay?" he asked again, as if her state could have changed in the last five minutes.

"How can he do this? Use my father's murder for his campaign? If I'd had an inkling that this was what he'd been planning, I would never have agreed to go to that damned rally of his."

"Maybe you should bow out, Syd. Or, if nothing else, you could take me, and I can be your buffer. I've always wanted to meet him."

"I wonder if my mom saw this?" she said, ignoring his self-invitation.

"If she did, she'd be cheering, especially after that bombshell you dropped two days ago about going through with this harebrained idea to visit that idiot in prison today."

"And you would know, because . . . ?"

"Because I talked to Jake. He asked me if you were seriously considering going to San Quentin, and I told him that you had talked about it before, but in truth, I didn't know."

She glanced at the newspaper, pushed aside the magazine so that she could see Wheeler's face. "Just looking at his picture gives me the creeps," she said, not really directing it to anyone.

"Then don't go."

"What did Jake say about this article with Senator Gnoble?" she asked, closing the paper, shoving it aside.

"He actually called the senator, who told him he was genuinely upset at the article, the way it made him look. You know my feeling. He's a politician. End of story."

She didn't know what to believe. She was tired, couldn't think straight, and she got up, walked into the kitchen, staring at her blank canvas, not really wanting to face any of this right now. "Look, my paints are drying and it's late."

"You're really painting something at this hour?"

"Something blue."

"Maybe I should come over now," he said, as if he knew this whole painting thing was some sort of subterfuge. "Besides, I really do need to talk to you."

"I'm fine. The moment I'm not, I'll call you."

"I love—"

"Good-bye." Sydney disconnected, figuring she'd averted a visit by the narrowest of margins, though how long she could avoid him when he was in town, she wasn't sure. What she needed right then was a good stiff drink, but alcohol wasn't the answer, and she glanced at her blank canvas, thought, what the hell, might as well make the lie real. She squeezed out a generous portion of blue acrylic onto her palette, eyed it, then realized it wasn't dark enough. She changed it to black, added water to it, and brushed the wash on the canvas, covering it completely, eliminating every last bit of white. She had no idea what form the painting might take. That wasn't the point. She painted for relaxation and rejuvenation. She painted because she loved the smell of acrylics and oils, the feel of a brush in her hand, lavishing the paint onto a canvas. The whole process enticed her in a way that no bottle of alcohol ever could, and she stood back to view her work—not that it was much to look at—nothing more than a black wash. So much for inspiration and interpretation. Perhaps it was a reflection of her mood, trying to decide who was worse? Gnoble for using someone else's tragedy for his gain, or Wheeler for refusing to admit the truth, accept his punishment and give them all peace?

She could almost hear her mother telling her to accept the past. Move on. But that was not a possibility tonight, and she put away her paints and went to bed. Finally, in the dim glow of the night light, she stared at the framed photograph of her father on her bedside table. Of all the photos and pictures, this was her favorite, perhaps because it was the last taken of them together. She was sitting next to him on the back of a fishing boat, its name, *Cisco's Kid*, visible beneath her dangling feet. Her father was holding a large bright orange fish, caught off the shore of Baja, and she was grinning, leaning as far away from the fish as she could get.

They'd made that trip the summer before he was killed, went to visit his friend, Bob the Boat Guy. Funny how the name popped up, because her father's friend was the least memorable thing about that trip, one she was sure she'd never forget. There were times just looking at the photo when Sydney could almost hear the water lapping against the boat, smell the salt in the air, feel the heat of the sun on her back, and taste the radishes in the fish tacos she and her father ate for lunch that afternoon.

But not tonight. Though Sydney willed herself to remember the fragrant memory, nothing came, and she reached out, touched the picture, the glass cool beneath her fingertips.

She closed her eyes, but sleep would not come, and her thoughts drifted to the article, the date, the fact that Johnnie Wheeler's case was being looked at by new attorneys. She realized then what bothered her most about the little she'd read in that article. Somewhere it should have read how twenty years today she would have lived without her father in her life. Not once did it mention the family left behind. Not once did it address what this day of days meant to her or her mother.

And suddenly one thought filled her mind: making sure that the man responsible for her father's murder didn't forget what day it was.

How, though?

The very idea of being in the same room as Johnnie Wheeler chilled her to the bone. She hadn't even been able to look at a damned news photo of the guy. How the hell was she going to stand there and force herself to look into his eyes, look into his face, the face of a killer?

4

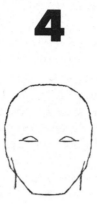

Nicholas Prescott, personal aide to Senator Dono-
van Gnoble, glanced at his watch, saw it was a little after
ten, then looked out the Town Car's backseat window as they
sped southbound on the 101. "You know the senator can't
abide being late. Can't you step it up?"

The driver, Eddie, a burly, dark-haired man with a nose
as crooked as Lombard Street, eyed Prescott in his rearview
mirror. "Next time order a helicopter."

Prescott ignored his sarcasm. Good drivers who were
discreet *and* would take orders from an aide without question, no matter what the request, were hard to come by. With
no choice, Prescott sat back in his seat, waiting, knowing
Senator Gnoble wouldn't be pleased. So be it. Fifteen minutes later, they pulled up to the curb at SFO, where Donovan Gnoble, tall, round-faced, with thick snowy hair and
his trademark goatee, stood by his suitcase, clearly trying
to keep the impatience from his face as he waited for his
car. The man hated airports, and San Francisco's was at the
top of his list. Oakland was only slightly better, and Prescott
had tried to book that flight instead, to no avail. The driver

parked, got out, and walked around to the curb, opening the rear door for the senator.

"Sir."

Gnoble managed a smile before sliding in. The moment the car door closed on him, shielding him behind the dark glass, he looked at Prescott sitting at the opposite window. "What the hell took you so long?"

"Traffic and a few loose ends, now dealt with." He handed Gnoble a printed sheet. "These are your stops this morning. Boys and Girls Club of Oakland, then the Association of—"

"I can read, thank you."

"Bad flight, or something else?" he asked, watching as Gnoble read through the list, then handed back the sheet.

"The flight was fine. It was the call I received the moment I stepped off the plane that disturbed me."

"What call was that?"

"About Wheeler's case. That damned article in the *Chronicle*. Makes me look like the worst sort of politician. Kevin Fitzpatrick was my friend, for God's sake. I might as well be standing over his tombstone, waving a 'Vote for Me' sign."

"Not a bad idea."

"*Not* funny. I can't imagine what his daughter must think. Especially after her mother asked me to intervene on this whole damned prison visit issue. I hope for her sake she isn't really going to go through with this."

"I thought this was par for the course."

"Maybe I can talk to her tonight at the rally, assuming she can even look me in the face," he said, staring out the window, his gaze distant. Several seconds of silence passed, then, "You heard who's picking up Wheeler's case?"

"I heard last night."

"And you didn't think it important enough to call?"

"There was little anyone could do at that late hour, and I figured you had bigger problems." Like the background and security clearance on McKnight. The very thought gave Prescott a headache.

"We should never have suggested McKnight's name for that appointment," Gnoble said, his gaze fixed on something unseen out the window.

"I didn't think you had a choice."

"No. I didn't." The car lurched forward, then came to a sudden stop, and Gnoble eyed the gridlock in front of them. "How far behind are we?"

"Maybe ten-fifteen minutes. Don't worry. I've already called and alerted our next stop," Prescott replied, sorting through the papers on his lap. He pulled out several, handed them to Gnoble, then gave him a pen. "Signature on the bottom of each . . . I heard McKnight left a note before he killed himself?"

"He did. And it's exactly the sort of note I expected you to have anticipated and handled before it came to light."

"Had I been informed about *everything* before you submitted his name, I might have."

"Well, now you know." Gnoble eyed the top document, signed it. "I can only hope no one makes sense out of what he was rambling on about before he did the world a favor. If anyone does figure it out, getting reelected will be the least of my concerns."

"Not to worry, sir." He handed over the next set of documents. "That's what spin doctors are all about."

And the best didn't always use conventional methods.

Two things came to mind when Sydney opened her front door that afternoon to a sky threatening rain, and saw Scotty walking up the driveway toward her stairs. First, that she should've skipped her run and left for San Quentin much, much earlier. Her second thought was that she wished she had a back door, because he hadn't yet seen her. If she could just step back in, not bring any attention to herself—unfortunately he glanced up just then, and she was stuck.

He waved at her as he walked up the driveway, then stopped at the row of three mailboxes. Hers looked like it was bursting at the seams, and he called out, "I'll bring this up to you?"

Before she could utter a word, he grabbed the mail, started up the steps, looking every inch the G-man. Blond hair in a slightly-longer-than-military cut, the requisite dark suit, white shirt, and navy tie; he had it down pat. The shoulder holster tended to accentuate this look, but even without it, he'd be pegged as a cop, at least in her opinion. It was in his walk, and in his sharp blue gaze that seemed to miss nothing. He had presence, and frankly, after her months of abstinence, an acute sense of what she'd left behind hit her.

She missed him.

The thought came out of left field, and she berated herself for even thinking it. He'd never been home when they'd lived together, and she'd missed him then, too. So what was the difference?

"How are you doing?" he said, before kissing her cheek.

"Fine." She held out her hand for the mail. When he hesitated to hand it to her, she took it from him. "What's so important you couldn't tell me over the phone?"

He didn't answer right away, just stood, looked around her small living room, then into the kitchen, his gaze falling on the canvas with its black wash. "I thought you were painting something blue?"

"Changed my mind," she said, flipping through the mail. "Why are you here?"

"Like I said, I just wanted to see how you're doing. And to talk."

"I'm fine." She dumped the bills on the kitchen counter, threw the political fliers in the trash, and was left with one card from her aunt, and a large manila envelope with no return address, just a postmark from Houston, Texas. Her aunt always sent a card this time of year, saying she was thinking of Sydney and her father. Sydney put it aside, eyed the manila envelope, and tried to think who she knew in Texas.

"That doesn't have a return address," Scotty said.

"I see that." She slid a finger beneath the flap.

"You're just going to open it?"

Curious, she stopped, looked at him. "You've been working political corruption a little too long. It's not a letter bomb. Relax." She ripped open the envelope, slid out a few sheets secured with a paper clip. The top sheet was folded binder paper, a bit yellowed from age, and she removed the paper clip, unfolded the sheet. Inside was a deposit slip, the blank sort you filled out when you didn't have a preprinted one of your own. She didn't recognize the bank, Houston Commerce Title and Trust. The note scrawled on the front read simply:

For Cisco's Kid. Send the money to this address.

She stared in incomprehension at the address listed, even as her brain told her she knew who had written that note, where the address belonged. "What the . . ."

"Sydney—"

"This has to be from my father. *Cisco's Kid* is the name of a boat he and his friends owned, and the address written on here belonged to the pizza parlor he owned."

"Can I see it?"

She ignored him, sat on the couch, wondering why someone would send this to her. An envelope had been clipped behind it, and she looked at it, figured it was probably the one the letter had originally been sent in. It was postmarked Santa Arleta, twenty years ago, and addressed to William McKnight in Houston, Texas. He was one of her father's old army friends, which somewhat explained the last item: an old photo of her father standing near several other men.

At first she thought it was from her father's army days, because she recognized a very young-looking Donovan Gnoble, regulation haircut, sharp-pressed uniform, an obscene number of medals on his chest, a senator in the making, waiting only for the brilliant idea to grow a goatee and bring his Southern charm to California politics. Her father stood on one side of Gnoble, McKnight on the other. Two men in the photo she didn't know, the blond man standing next to McKnight, and the black man crouching down in front of her father, flashing what looked like some sort of gang sign.

Judging from the longer hair her father and McKnight wore, it had to have been taken after her father's discharge from the service. As far as she knew, her father and McKnight had both done their four years, then got out. Not that her father had actually left the service completely. He went on to work for the army as a civilian, taking photographs for promotional material, recruitment posters, and the like.

It hit her then. The explanation. Someone sent this as sort of a remembrance of her father, just like her aunt always sent a card on the anniversary. Maybe these men were part of her father's photography crew . . . Or they all went to college together, since they appeared to be wearing college rings, with red stones, each one of them. That had to be it. With the exception of Gnoble, none of the men wore any sort of legitimate uniform other than black fatigues that merely hinted of military wear—not a bit of U.S. Army insignia on anything. Her father and McKnight were holding what appeared to be black plastic helmets, and she had the absurd thought they were about to hit the paintball courts, only she wasn't sure it was even a sport back then.

"I don't understand," she said, flipping the picture over to see if it was marked in any way, a date, something. There was nothing. "Why would someone send this to me and not put a name on it?"

Scotty gave it a quick glance. "I'd just ignore it. Who knows?"

Something about his voice, the way he said to ignore it, made her look up. He couldn't even maintain eye contact, and she recalled how he'd grabbed the mail on his way up, not even hesitating when there were two other mailboxes besides hers. The names were actually on the tops of the boxes, which, when filled with mail, you couldn't even read. Almost as if he knew right where to look, when he'd never been to her apartment before. "Do you know something about this?"

"Not exactly."

"What the hell does that mean?"

"It, uh, might be related to a background that Jeff Hatcher was doing on McKnight. I mean, you're going to hear what happened anyway."

Special Agent Hatcher was Scotty's hero and mentor, primarily because Hatcher worked closely with all the political bigwigs, handling the sensitive backgrounds for security clearance on political appointments, which was where Scotty wanted to be, thinking it would take him straight to the top. The closest he got was working political corruption, something that didn't endear him to any politicians.

"A background for what, exactly?" she asked.

"My understanding is that McKnight's name was submitted as a nominee for political appointment. They wanted us to start the background before the announcement was even made, to avoid months of delays in the appointment. Administrator for Federal Procurement Policy."

She wasn't one to keep up on political appointments or positions, but that one she remembered, because of a fairly recent investigation and arrest of one of the past administrators for lying and obstructing a criminal investigation into a Republican lobbyist who was also arrested due to nefarious dealings with the federal government. And because of that past, anyone appointed by the president to be the czar of spending for the entire federal government's budget was bound to be placed under the microscope. "I take it he failed the background?"

"You know damned well some of this stuff is classified."

"Then tell me what you can talk about."

He seemed to wrestle with the decision to mention anything, then finally, "Nothing gets out of this room, Sydney. Nothing."

"I'm listening."

And still he hesitated.

She stood, pointed to the door. "If you're not going to talk, Scotty, then I'll damned well ask around until I find someone who will."

He ran his fingers through his hair, and she knew he was torn. Duty came first, the world be damned.

"Scotty . . ."

"Okay, okay," he said, glancing at the photo. "Everything was going fine until Hatcher contacted this guy's soon-to-be-ex-wife, Becky Lynn McKnight."

Another name she hadn't heard in years, except the vague recollection of her mother being upset about the woman moving back to the Bay Area after separating from McKnight. Becky Lynn had worked for Sydney's father, up until his death. "Becky Lynn? What does she have to do with this?"

"I take it you remember her?"

What she remembered about her was her mother's comment at her father's funeral on seeing Becky Lynn. Something about seeing who she dug her greedy claws into next. "Barely. I was just a kid . . ."

"Her name was flagged by OC."

"Organized crime?"

"She's a woman living well above her means, beyond even the checks McKnight had been sending her since their separation. I can't go into specifics, but as soon as Hatcher saw that, he knew this wasn't going to be a simple background."

Sydney glanced at the photo, trying to figure out where it all was leading. "What does any of this have to do with why someone would send this to me?"

"Hatcher was told that was being mailed to you. By McKnight."

"Which explains what? Why you are here in town? To intercept it from my mailbox before I got to it?"

"I only wanted to save you the pain, in case . . . Look. There are some holes in Becky Lynn's story about the time she worked for your father and when she hooked up with McKnight. When Hatcher first started digging into it, he went back to McKnight, who at first said Becky Lynn was lying, that he didn't know anything about her past or the money in her accounts when he met her. He said your father introduced them. And then Hatcher finds out McKnight was actually a partner in your father's pizza parlor—"

"I think several of his old army buddies went in on it. They were sort of doing my father a favor, after that explosion blew a couple of his fingers off and he couldn't do his photography anymore."

"Well, that wasn't really the problem. Not at first. It had more to do with Becky Lynn's ties to organized crime and her story about where her money in these offshore accounts came from, not matching up to her ex-husband's, who happened to have records of it all, which he gave to Hatcher by mistake. That, of course, sort of puts the kibosh on his being approved for any political appointment. Becky Lynn tells Hatcher she can clear it right up, calls McKnight on the phone, telling him it was time to come clean. What happened next was—" He stared at the photo before meeting her gaze. "Hatcher talked to McKnight on the phone, Syd. Hatcher said his voice was slurred. He was upset. He kept apologizing."

"Apologizing?"

"For what he did to your father."

"What are you talking about? McKnight was in Texas when my father was killed, wasn't he?"

"I don't think McKnight was talking about the robbery, Syd."

"Then what?"

"Becky Lynn said that someone was blackmailing McKnight about something that happened when he and your father were in the army together. Something to do with a big banking scandal way back when."

"What do you mean someone was blackmailing him? Did Hatcher ask him about it?"

"He couldn't. McKnight killed himself first. Hatcher thought he was drunk when he was talking to him on the phone, mumbling about sending you some letter that explained it all. Next thing he hears a gunshot. Hatcher called a field agent to drive out to McKnight's to check on him, but he was already gone. Police were already there. Apparently a neighbor heard the shot, too, and called."

She tried to think about her father's friends. She had a vague remembrance of a few of them coming over to their house in North Carolina, sitting around, drinking beer . . . and talking about fishing. Her father's big dream was to retire and spend every winter at some fishing villa in Baja California. In fact, that seemed to be a common dream among them, talking about beer and fishing and boats, but for the life of her, she couldn't picture names or faces. And what preteen kid would? She was too busy worrying about more important things like pimples and boys, even after her father was injured, left his job, and they picked up and moved back to California. Her father's military career was something he rarely spoke about. Even when Sydney asked him about his time there, what he did for the army, he always put her off with some response about taking photographs for posters, making the army look good.

But that didn't explain any of this. "I don't understand what this has to do with my father?"

"Hatcher thinks your father was the blackmailer."

Syd stared mutely, then shook herself, tried to think past the hurt, the betrayal she felt at Scotty for imparting such lies about her father. "He's wrong, Scotty."

"I don't think so, Syd."

"My father was a good man."

"Look at what your father sent to McKnight," he said, pointing to the yellowed letter she held.

"This could mean anything. He was *not* blackmailing anyone."

"There are indications that your father might have been involved in more than just that. That he might have been doing the same to—"

"I don't want to hear it." Sydney dumped everything back in the manila envelope, then tossed it onto the coffee table. When he tried to reply, she interrupted with "I have no idea why you felt it necessary to fly across the country to ruin my father's name."

"Sydney."

It was that voice he used when he needed to impart bad news, though in her experience, it had been news such as why he couldn't come home that night.

She hated that voice, but waited for him to finish.

"The stuff McKnight sent you," he said, nodding at the manila envelope. "I need to take that."

"Why?"

"Evidence of a crime."

She picked it up, started to hand it over, but then thought better of it. "No. I don't think so."

"Sydney, listen to me."

"No, Scotty. Unless you tell me exactly what that crime is, it stays with me."

"I told you. It involves McKnight's suicide. The blackmail."

"And he mailed it to me *before* he killed himself. And the statute of limitations ran out on anything my deceased father did a long, long time ago."

"Syd—"

"Get a warrant."

"I'm sorry. I thought you should know. In case anything leaks out."

She said nothing. And he stared at her a moment longer, his expression filled with apology, embarrassment, and something else she couldn't define. Finally he leaned over, kissed her on her cheek, and she jerked back, wanting nothing to do with him.

"I'll be in town for a few days if you need to get in touch with me."

When she didn't answer, he let himself out. Sydney glanced at the envelope, then ran to the door, opening it, as she called out for Scotty to wait.

Midway down the steps, he stopped, looked back at her.

"What do you mean, 'in case anything leaks out'?"

"McKnight left a suicide note before he died. I don't have all the details; I don't even know if it mentions your father. The cops got the note before Hatcher did, and they booked it. But he was being investigated for a political appointment, and you know how those things make it to the press. Especially during election years." He waited on the steps a moment, perhaps looking for some reaction from her.

She closed the door, leaned against it, not willing to believe any of what he told her. She glanced at the envelope, but couldn't even force herself to touch it again. Scotty was wrong, and that was all there was to it. Her father was good, just. He'd been cut down in the prime of his life. If McKnight was the one who mailed this to her, he did it simply as a memory. Nothing else.

And with all that she told herself she should put off going to the prison. The thought of facing her father's killer after Scotty's news was not something she could deal with.

But she knew she'd go, and it made her wonder if her day could get any worse.

Apparently it could.

Calling her mother to inform her that she was on her way to visit the man who killed her father wasn't the best of ideas.

She knew this. Clearly she was delusional when she'd punched in her mother's phone number at precisely 2:32 that afternoon, but she wanted some reassurance she was doing the right thing. Or maybe she just wanted to speak to someone who knew her father was a good and just man, no matter what Scotty had said. The contents of that envelope could have any number of explanations. It proved nothing.

"Hi, Mom," she'd said when her mother answered the phone.

"Sydney. What's wrong?"

"Nothing."

"Don't tell me nothing. I can hear it in your voice."

"Dad was a good man, right?"

"What's going on?"

"Mom, I'm really sorry, but I've done a lot of thinking about going to San Quentin. I heard he has new attorneys working the case. That means he could get out."

"Not again. I can't imagine how you ever came up with such an idiotic idea to go there."

"Mom—"

"Trying and doing are two different things. I don't want you near that man."

At least Sydney was smart enough to have waited until she was pulling up to the prison gates before she'd called. "I need to know why he killed him."

"Jake!" Her mother shrieked her stepfather's name. "Jake! Will you come here and try to talk some sense into Sydney!"

"Mom. I have to go," she said, not wanting to talk to Jake at all. He always took the day off on the anniversary so that her mother wouldn't be alone, which only served to intensify her guilt for driving out to San Quentin on this day of days.

"You promised to be at Uncle Don's campaign rally tonight," her mother said. "What am I supposed to tell him?"

"You don't need to tell him anything. I'll be there."

"Sydney—"

"I'm sorry, Mom. I shouldn't have told you."

"Jake!"

"Sydney?" Her stepfather's voice was calm, quiet. "What's going on?"

If anyone could talk her out of this, Jake could. Her father's best friend after he moved them out to California, Jake had stepped in to help her mother after her father was killed, and almost a year later, they'd married. He'd always been the calm one, taking charge when her mother's emotions got the best of her, which, thanks to him, was less and less as the years went on. But he'd also been a strict disciplinarian, and even now that Sydney was grown, no longer living under his well-ordered roof, she hesitated, not wanting to incur his anger.

"Sydney?"

"I'm sorry. I have to go." She heard her mother crying just before she disconnected, then left the phone on the car seat beside her, wracked with guilt, but knowing she couldn't go through with this and *not* tell her. She'd never lied to her mother. Never. But the truth was that the emotions of all this were overwhelming her, and when it came right down to it, she wanted to know that her mother, even Jake, cared as deeply as she did about her father, that they understood why she could not stand by and allow the man who had killed him to forget what day it was, or to escape justice by conning his misguided attorneys into believing he was innocent. But it was more than that, she realized. So much more. This was the chance her mother had denied her, the chance to face the man who had killed her father.

He had exhausted all his appeals and was supposed to be put to death for the murder, but the wheels of justice turn slowly, too slowly in his case. And though no one else might care, Sydney knew just why she'd made the trip. She wanted, *needed* to know what, if anything, this man had thought about during these past two decades.

She wanted to know if he was sorry.

That thought fled the moment she took her first real look at the entrance of San Quentin. She had never been there before. Had no wish to go. But she was there now, and what came to her mind was the absurd and surreal thought that the prison appeared to be a gothic fortress set on the shores of a windswept coastline. The picturesque effect was ruined, however, by the guard towers and fourteen-foot-high razor-wire fences—and the fact she had to stop just inside the first gate and place her gun in a gun locker before driving through the second gate.

Sydney parked in a lot adjacent to the bay, where the cold wind whipped the water into a froth of whitecaps and the waves pounded the retaining wall, sending white spray over the top and misting the air with salt. She pulled her blazer tightly about her and glanced up at the dark sky, hoping the rain would hold off until after she finished with her interview and was back in her car.

Inside the building, after passing all security checkpoints, she ran her fingers through her windblown hair, in hopes of looking a bit more professional for the prison official who had agreed to help her when she'd called that morning. He was waiting in a conference room that smelled of coffee that had been percolating too long. He stood when she entered, his uniform neatly pressed, his shoes shined to perfection.

"Thomas Sullivan?" she asked. "I'm Special Agent Sydney Fitzpatrick. I appreciate you seeing me through this."

"Not a problem." He nodded at an empty pink bakery box on the table. "You just missed the last of the donuts. Or do Feds eat donuts?"

"This Fed does. But after my late night, what I really need is coffee," she said, anxious to get the interview started, yet willing to stall at all costs.

"That we got plenty of," he replied, and walked over to the counter. He poured coffee into two Styrofoam cups, then brought them to the table, indicating she should sit. "You ever been here before?"

"Other prisons, not this one." Not until today.

"California's oldest prison. I'm thinking if they had a crystal ball when they built the place back in 1852, they might've held out for condos. Think of the money they would've made. Four hundred thirty-two acres of priceless bay-side real estate, right here beneath our feet, not that the prisoners give a rat's ass."

She smiled, then sipped at the sharp coffee, nervous. He must have sensed it, because he asked, "How do you want to do this?"

"I'd like to interview him face-to-face with no partition."

"Anything else?"

"What're the chances of not giving him my name? I'm . . . not here officially."

"Don't see a problem, long as we know who you are and log it. Not like you're interrogating him or anything."

Not in the real sense, she thought, and before she knew it, she was being led into another interview room in a secured part of the prison. Their footsteps echoed down the long hallway, and she thought that if she were smart, she'd turn back, ignore the temptation to ask this man why he'd done what he'd done. What did it matter? It was not going to bring her father back. It was stupid on her part. He wasn't worth the effort, and after what Scotty had dropped in her lap, she didn't need the emotional turmoil. But then they led him in, shackled at his hands and his feet, and her heart started pounding.

Johnnie Wheeler.

This was the man who had changed her life forever.

5

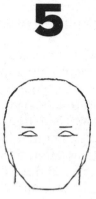

The guards seated Johnnie Wheeler at the table across from Sydney. When they turned to leave, she stood, desperate, wanting them to stop. She'd changed her mind. She did not want to be alone, not with this man, this murderer, and she was about to call out, tell them to wait. But her throat went dry, her voice failed her. Suddenly she was thirteen again, finding her father dead, and his pizza parlor burning down around her.

And now she was locked in the same room as the man who had killed him, and her lungs constricted. She sat, weak-kneed, told herself to breathe normally.

Just breathe.

Slow and steady. Don't give him the satisfaction of knowing his presence affected her.

With considerable effort, she willed herself to calm, then truly looked at him. Even though she had seen his photograph in that newspaper article, she was surprised by the man before her. Dressed in prison blues, he was average height, early forties, thin face, dark skin, one dark eye that seemed to take in everything, the other eye clouded, bluish-white; she wasn't even sure he could see through it. One more thing she didn't recall from the photograph. That and his tightly curled hair, short and peppered with gray. All she had apparently committed to memory from the photo was the scar she'd seen that ran across his right cheek. She'd pictured someone much bigger, but figured it had something to do with being only thirteen at the time the crime occurred.

"You from the Innocence Project?" he asked when the guards left.

She couldn't believe she'd heard correctly. His cloudy eye seemed to focus on her, as though it could see right into her, know that his words struck directly at her heart. *The Innocence Project.* Reading in the newspaper that he was getting new attorneys was one thing. *Nothing* in the article had mentioned the Innocence Project, very selective attorneys and staff who took on cases that were practically sure things . . .

Why the hell had she come here? She was only torturing herself, torturing her mother. But then she saw his hands scarred from the fire that he'd set to cover up the murder. The hands that had held the gun that had killed her father. Anger burned through her. She stood, forced her gaze to his, made sure he was looking right at her, and said, "I'm Sydney Fitzpatrick. The daughter of the man you murdered." And when she knew she had his attention, knew that her name meant something, she continued. "My mother got her chance to speak her mind at your sentencing, but I wasn't allowed to. And now I'm here to make sure you take my words to your grave."

"What the fuck? I'm gonna call the—"

"Shut up!" She crashed her fist onto the metal table. He jerked back, his eyes going wide, his jaw dropping. "It's my turn, and by God, I'm taking it, because you need to know what you *stole* from me, and for what? A few dollars?" She let that sink in, then leaned in closer, to make sure he heard every word. "Two *months* after you killed my father, I was the only girl on my soccer team who went to the father-daughter dinner with her mother. My father taught me how to ride a motorcycle and drive a car, even though I wasn't old enough, but he wasn't there to see me get my license. He didn't get to see me graduate from high school, or accept an athletic scholarship to college. Or watch me graduate with honors and go to the police academy, and then the FBI academy. Because of you, he can't walk me down the aisle if I get married. And now—now my mother and I fight every year because of *you* . . ." She pushed away from the table, but kept her gaze pinned on him. "*You* did that to me. You killed him, and you stole a huge part of my life. My mother's life. We have *never* been the same. And it's not fair that my father's dead, and you're sitting here, and *that's* what I came to tell you."

He stared at her for several seconds, not moving, just watching her, as though he couldn't understand, even now, why she came. And then, so quiet, he said, "I'm sorry. I'm sorry it all happened to you, but you gotta understand. I didn't do it."

This time it was her turn to stare. How could he still deny it? "Don't tell me you're sorry. You contacted the Innocence Project."

"You one crazy bitch, you know that? You give that speech to them? That why they turning me down?"

"They're turning you down?" Elation swept through her. He *wasn't* getting out.

Wheeler made a scoffing sound. "That why you coming 'round here now, when they're about to do me? Go fuck yourself."

She leaned against the door, eyeing him as though it mattered little whether he talked or not. "I *want* the truth."

"The truth ain't never changed. Yeah, I was there that night, but why the fuck I wanna kill the guy when he giving me money? I told 'em it had to be the guy sitting in the car when I got there. That officer did one of those pictures of the driver from my description. They find *that* guy, they got a killer. *He* the one set me up, no doubt in my mind."

A setup. How original. And the picture of the killer he was referring to had been an Identikit picture, plastic overlays, a technique that often produced terrible results. It hadn't been an actual sketch—not that anyone ever *believed* there had been another person there. His story had too many holes in it. "Then how did you get those burns? Those scars on your hands?"

"I didn't touch him," he said, avoiding the question entirely, just as he'd done when he'd been arrested. "How many times I gotta tell everyone that? I liked him."

"You *liked* him?" She slammed her palms on either side of his cuffed, scarred hands, pinning her gaze on him. Her father should have been sitting on his fishing boat down in Baja. That had always been his dream, even before he was forced into early retirement as a civilian contract employee from that stupid accident, building some set for a recruiting poster he was photographing. Part of her wanted to blame someone, *anyone*, for that accident, because if not for that, he'd still be snapping photos, he'd never have opened the pizza parlor, and never been there that night.

She held Wheeler's gaze a moment longer, then straightened, moved back to the door, assumed her couldn't-give-a-shit-persona. "I don't believe you."

"Fuckin' believe what you want. It's the truth."

"Why, then?" she asked, meaning, Why did he kill him if he liked him?

"'Cause he was helping me get a job, go straight," he said, misunderstanding. "My old man, he was in the army, got killed, and Kev, he said he knew what it was like, so he was gonna help me. Clean me up, got my name from his church, you know? Clean eight weeks. I had a kid, a baby. That's the only reason I was there."

She wasn't moved. That had always been his claim, that her father had befriended him, was trying to help him go straight, a claim that the prosecution disputed. Their contention was that Wheeler had made up the phony relationship, the tenuous military connection, to cover for his being in the pizza parlor, and to come up with this "lent me the money" defense that he'd used to explain his print on the cash register.

His defense attorney had never been able to locate the supposed church charity that was allegedly responsible for hooking up Sydney's father with Wheeler. In fact, her father didn't even attend church, and no one ever recalled seeing Wheeler at the pizza parlor before that night. "What time did you get there?"

He shrugged. "Late is all I remember. Place was empty. He was walking out of the back office when I got there."

She tried to reconcile her thoughts to Wheeler's claim that her father had just left the office when Wheeler said he'd walked in. *She'd* been in the office, asleep, which meant her father had just left her. This was it. The last moments . . .

"And then what happened?"

Wheeler shifted. "Told him I came by just like he told me. To get the money."

"He *told* you to come by?" For someone who'd had twenty years to think up a good story, he wasn't coming up with anything innovative.

"Yeah. Said he ain't giving me nothing unless he see my face, wanna make sure I ain't working my game, make sure I ain't high, before he give me the green, you know? Gonna help me out."

"But you robbed him."

"No!" He struck his manacled hands on the table, and she started at the sound of metal hitting metal. The guard peeked in the window, checked on her, but she ignored him, intent on Wheeler's statement.

"*He* told me to take the money."

"From the cash register? That was where your print was found *and identified.*"

He hesitated. "Wasn't enough, just some change was all he had in some little flowered can he kept under the counter. Got 'raided,' he said, joking like, you know? I needed more. Kev told me to get it out of the register."

And suddenly everything she'd believed these past twenty years started to unravel. *Raided* had been one of her father's favorite words pertaining to her and her habit of dipping into that small metal canister for video game money. And on that particular night, she'd nearly emptied the thing. With that thought came another, more frightening question: Would her father still be alive if she hadn't taken the money?

Her parents kept that canister beneath the counter, throwing odd tip money in it. There was usually no more than twenty-five or thirty dollars within, if that, a petty cash fund for whatever might come up. Sometimes that *whatever* was her wanting quarters to play the video games in the back room of the restaurant. Sometimes it was her father's pet projects, anything from handing out money to the Girl Scouts selling cookies, or even a homeless person digging through a Dumpster.

Or, possibly, a drug addict, needing money for a job . . . ?

"Why didn't you mention this canister with the money when you were arrested?"

"They was already saying I stole money. I ain't never touched the can. He did. But *he* sent me to the register, just like I told the cops."

"Why would he send you to the register?"

"'Cause he already put the money in the safe. But he tells me he got a double-saw in the cash register. Says it's always there after he close out. Underneath, you know?"

Sydney told herself that this could all be coincidence, that he was simply a con, good at his game—something he'd had two decades to perfect. Knowing *why* there was a twenty under the till after closing was not something that appeared in the police reports. "You didn't think that important enough to mention?"

"Have your ass dragged to the joint on a life jolt, see what you remember. Me, I been meditating 'bout it twenty years, you know? All they cared about was finding my print on the register, and the moment that happened, I was guilty. So I quit talking."

And she wondered if it would've made a difference. She doubted her mother would've said something, even if she'd had the presence of mind to think clearly at the time, because what cop would think such a trivial detail was important enough to ask about? Leaving a twenty beneath the till was something her father did—at her mother's request. She'd said if the place was ever burglarized, it was better to give them something to steal, to keep them from looking for something else. But if Wheeler was pointing a gun at her father, he could've told him to take the twenty, that there was always one there after closing. That didn't mean a thing. She started pacing again. "A twenty under the till?"

"Yeah. Told me to get it and—and I could pay him back."

"Pay him back, when?" She glanced over.

His gaze narrowed ever so slightly as he seemed to contemplate her question, then as though he were surprised he even remembered, he said, "On Tuesday."

She stopped in her tracks. Several heartbeats passed before she responded. She heard him, but her brain was doing a double take. "Tuesday?" she finally repeated.

"Yeah."

"You're sure that's what he said?"

"Yeah."

Her thoughts raced. *Tuesday* . . . It couldn't be true. Her father could have lent him the money and Wheeler killed him anyway. At least, that's what she told herself.

But the thought came too late.

The damage had been done.

A seed of doubt planted because of a few minute, trivial details that did not appear in any police reports. Details that only someone close to her family would recognize. Anyone might know her father had been in the army. And they certainly knew he helped out people all the time, handed out a few dollars. But Sydney could count on one hand the number of people who knew of the little flowered canister her father kept beneath the counter at the pizza parlor, or that he often chided her for "raiding" it to get video money. Even fewer were those who might have known that he kept a twenty beneath the till after he closed out.

And fewer still were those who knew what it meant if her father requested a loan to be repaid on Tuesday.

Sydney banged on the door to alert the guard, then left without speaking. What could she say?

She needed to know the truth. If this man was going to be executed, then he better damned well be guilty.

And if he wasn't guilty . . .

Her father's killer was out there still.

6

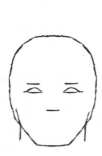

Sydney went through the steps of signing out of the prison, thanking everyone, returning her visitor's pass, then finding herself in the parking lot, standing next to her car, grateful to be outside. She stared out over the bay, the wind rushing in her ears, not sure if it was the first few raindrops that hit her face or the sea spray. She didn't think she'd ever felt so alone as she did in that one moment, and she had nowhere to go, no one to turn to.

It wasn't like she could take this to her mother, not yet. In fact, everyone Sydney knew, her mother, her stepfather Jake, even Scotty, they all believed that Wheeler was guilty without a doubt. Who was going to believe a few trivial, though in her mind critical, details that came from a convicted killer and could only be verified from the traumatized memory of a girl just thirteen at the time?

Her thoughts consumed her for most of the drive. When she approached the Golden Gate Bridge her cell phone rang, and she was relieved when she saw it wasn't her mother's number on the screen.

"Fitz?" It was Lettie, Dixon's secretary. "You are coming in tomorrow, aren't you?"

"I have to. Subpoenaed for court in the morning. Why?"

"That officer from Hill City called again. She's sounding pretty desperate and wanted to know what your schedule was."

Sydney tried to remember what the officer wanted, but her mind refused to cooperate. "Do me a favor, pick a time, have her come in, whatever."

". . . pick a time . . . You okay?"

"Yeah. Just a lot to deal with right now."

She disconnected, tossed the phone on the car seat, then tried to figure out what to do next. By the time she crossed the bridge, the rain was coming down in a steady patter, and she drove around aimlessly, finally ending up at the parking lot at the top of Bernal Hill. The five-hundred-foot undeveloped peak, a rarity in the midst of the city, was mostly used as a dog park, and sometimes on the rare occasion that she varied her running schedule, she borrowed her neighbor's dog just to have a place to walk, enjoy the peace away from the city's dense population. It was one of the area's best-kept secrets, offering unsurpassed panoramic views of the city and the Bay Bridge. During the winter the rains turned the slopes of brown annual grass into a vast sea of green, reminding her of something she might see in Ireland. When it wasn't raining, it was one of the few sunny spots to be found, and after work, she sometimes drove up here just to watch the fog roll in, an amazing sight that often helped calm her thoughts after a particularly stressful day.

But there was no fog rolling in now, and her thoughts were not calming as the wind blasted the rain against the car, and thunder rumbled in the distance. She could just make out the complex of the hospital below, where the sight of Tara Brown's sketch had shaken her, or rather the scar Sydney had drawn, the scar that reminded her of Johnnie Wheeler.

And yet, if he could be believed, he wasn't the man who killed her father.

Then who?

Her thoughts drifted to the envelope left on her coffee table. What was it that Scotty had said about McKnight? That the man kept apologizing for something he did to her father? McKnight was in Texas when her father was killed.

At least that was what she'd always thought . . .

Lights from the city below dotted the landscape as darkness seeped in. For a few moments she took in the view, and a thought hovered just out of her grasp, something she thought she should remember about her father and McKnight. Something important. But a gust of wind shook the car, and when she saw a flash of lightning off to her left, quickly followed by a clap of thunder, she decided that parking on a bare hilltop below a microwave tower in this weather wasn't the best of ideas. And maybe once she got home, whatever that thought about McKnight had been would come back to her.

She trudged up the rain-slicked steps, still unable to think what she was missing. Her front door was adjacent to her neighbor's front door, both accessed via stairs on the side of the house that overlooked the driveway. Their landlord lived below them in the renovated house. With the exception of the teenage boys next door who thought this particular street of mostly single-family homes was their personal drag strip, she liked her neighbors. They were an eclectic group, diverse, much like the city itself. Sydney's immediate neighbor went by the name Arturo, as opposed to the more formal Arthur on his birth certificate, because he thought using Arturo would bring him more commercial advertising jobs. He was single, in his twenties, made quite a bit of money, and rode a motorcycle, which was why Sydney had ended up with the garage. Arturo lived alone with a large white poodle, Topper, not, thankfully, a prissy poodle, but the sort without his fur trimmed, which made him look more like a giant sheep.

Sydney loved that dog. She liked Arturo, too. He had a key to her place and watered her plants when she was out of town on cases. The neighbors below them, Darlene and Rainie, a lesbian couple in their late fifties, owned the house, and told Sydney they thought Arturo was gay, but had yet to come out of the closet. Of course they based this observation on the fact that their across-the-street neighbor had a daughter, single white female, early twenties, and Arturo barely gave her a second glance. The only thing Sydney knew for sure about Arturo was that he was a closet chef, and there were many nights when she came home to find that whatever recipe he had experimented with, she was the willing recipient of his largesse. Of course, there were often strings attached. Dog sitting for one. Sydney didn't mind. The pay was good. Now if she could just convince him to let her take his ultra sleek, ultra fast charcoal-black Ducati motorcycle out for a spin. Unfortunately that was his baby, and *no one* touched that bike. But a girl could dream . . .

Tonight as she stood on her porch stomping her feet dry, then fitting her key into the lock, it was to the scent of simmering garlic and other savory herbs. She hadn't even realized she was hungry until that moment, and just when she was wondering what sort of store-bought entrees she had stashed in the freezer, and could heat up before she left for the rally tonight, Arturo's door opened and out bounded Topper. The dog shoved his nose into her hand, forcing her to pay attention to him. "Hello, sweetheart," she said, scratching him behind his ears. "I was up at your favorite place just a little while ago."

Arturo watched for a moment, then said, "Can you babysit Topper for a couple nights? I have to fly to L.A."

"Shouldn't be a problem." She opened her door and Topper stepped in, circled up on a braided rug in front of the couch as though he already knew the drill.

"Pawn him off on Rainie downstairs if you end up on some callout. Any chance you're up for garlic-encrusted rack of lamb?"

"Hmm, let me think about that."

"Ten, maybe fifteen minutes," he said. "And bring the dog."

He shut the door, leaving Sydney and Topper to themselves. She tossed her keys onto the table by the door, glanced at the envelope containing her father's photo and the letter, and told herself she'd look at it tonight when she got back from the rally. Right now she wanted nothing more than to relax, put everything that happened today, yesterday, all of it out of her mind. She sank into the couch, laying her

hand on Topper's head. "Long day at the office," she said.
Topper said nothing.
She loved that dog.

Senator Gnoble glanced around the festivities held at the
area skating rink, watched the dozen or so kids trying to
do the limbo, of all things. "For God's sake, were there no
amusement parks open? A zoo?"

"In the fall? Too cold. Turnout would be low," Prescott
said, double checking his clipboard, making sure he hadn't
forgotten to call anyone. "And remember, it's all about photo
ops. This way we get a guaranteed crowd with kids in the
picture. And it's in the middle of your home territory *and*
close to your targeted families."

"We could've done better than this, surely."

"Right now your biggest supporters are the local police
unions. Much easier to get them and their kids here in a
show of support. And it was the only thing we could find
at the eleventh hour, never mind that it is several hundred
thousand dollars less to rent this and open it up to the public
than Great America."

"Don't expect me to put on skates."

"Not even for the hokey pokey? Might make the front
page."

"Speaking of the press, who showed?"

"Still waiting on the *Chronicle*. And that one we definitely
want. After the way they painted you in that death-penalty
case article involving Wheeler and your friend Kevin Fitzpatrick, we need a kinder, gentler image. You've already
got the conservative vote. Now I'd like to get the bleeding
liberals in the city to buy in." He nodded toward the lobby.
"Speaking of targeted families . . ."

He saw Gnoble glance at the area that appeared to be used
for birthday parties and the like, where Sydney's mother,
Mary Fitzpatrick-Hughes, sat helping to tie the skates of
Sydney's half sister, Angela Hughes. No sign of Sydney, yet.
Come to think of it, no sign of Gnoble's wife . . .

Gnoble started toward them. Prescott followed, getting in
one last instruction. "Think camera angles."

He was pleased when Gnoble fixed a broad smile on his
face, calling out, "Mary? Tell me that's not the baby, Angela? I didn't even recognize her."

"Mom, can you tell him I'm *not* a baby?"

"Honey . . ."

Angela gave an exaggerated sigh, leaned toward her mother, and in a rather loud whisper, said, "Do I call him *Uncle*
Don or *Senator* Gnoble when we're in public?"

"Angela, please," Mary Fitzpatrick-Hughes said, with an
apologetic look toward Gnoble as she smoothed the child's
blond curls back from her face. Prescott made a mental note
to ensure this child was rounded up for photos. Perfect face.
Angelic.

The child stood, held out her hand. "Thank you very much
for inviting me."

Gnoble shook hands, smiled. "Have a good time." She
skated off, and he turned to Mary with a look of concern.
Prescott tried to maintain a discreet distance, while still being able to hear what Gnoble was saying. "How are you
holding up?"

"Fine, Donovan. It's good to see you."

"You too. And Sydney? Is she coming?"

"She might be delayed. But she said she would."

"And Jake? How is he?"

"Fine. He had to run a couple errands, but he'll be by as
soon as he can get here."

"Good, good. I look forward to seeing him again."

The damned press had finally gotten their act together, a
few of them heading their way with cameras at the ready,
and Prescott gave a discreet cough, alerting him to their arrival. Gnoble clasped Mary on her shoulder, stepping just
close enough to imply concern, and Prescott kept his expression somber as he listened in. "Tell me how you're *really*
doing? Today of all days. Twenty years . . ."

She took a deep breath, tried to smile, and when the flashes
went off, Prescott could've sworn her eyes were glistening
with tears. It was a perfect shot, and truth be told, he was impressed at Gnoble for instigating it. "I try not to think about it.
Some days it's easier than others. Today's not one of them."

"I'm sorry," Gnoble said, before letting go. "I can't imagine what you've gone through these past two decades." A moment of silence, and then he glanced toward the skating floor. "Cute kid. I can't believe how big she's gotten."

"Eleven in a few days. We're going to have cake. You should stop by," she said.

Prescott happened to look toward the lobby just then, saw the arrival of a tall, thin young woman. At last. Sydney Fitzpatrick. She did not, however, look happy to be there. When he chanced to catch Mary's expression on seeing her older daughter, he realized something was up. Even Gnoble saw it, because he asked, "Mary, what's wrong?"

She looked away, and the tears Prescott thought he imagined were definitely there, ready to spill. "It's Sydney. She went to San Quentin."

"What are you talking about?"

"She went to see *him*. Wheeler. You know she's been talking about doing it for years."

"I thought when I'd called her that she'd changed her mind."

"She didn't."

"Oh my God. Mary. I'm sorry."

She tried to smile. "It's fine. I just don't understand why."

"Maybe I should talk to her again."

She nodded, then turned away.

"Prescott, take Mary to have some of that wonderful punch."

"Right this way, Mrs. Fitzpatrick-Hughes."

Gnoble left them, walked toward the lobby, and it was everything Prescott could do to settle Mary in with a paper cup filled with punch, seat her at the tables, then hurry toward the lobby to make sure he was kept apprised of their conversation. Lucky for him the senator was waylaid by several well-wishers, and by the time Prescott arrived, Gnoble was merely greeting her. "Sydney? How's the FBI treating you?"

She held Gnoble's gaze. "I don't appreciate you using my father's murder for your campaign, Senator."

"Senator? What happened to Uncle Don?"

"The Uncle Don I used to know would never have used tragedy for personal gain."

Goddamned *Chronicle*, Prescott thought, as Gnoble said, "That wasn't me, you have to believe it. They're out to sell newspapers, and took everything I said out of context." She said nothing, but her eyes spoke volumes. This was not something Gnoble was going to be able to fix so easily. "I heard you went out to the prison today. Your mother's extremely upset," he said, just as his wife, Marla, walked up to take her place at his side. Tall, thin, her blond hair swept up in a chignon, she gave Sydney a warm but neutral smile, no doubt picking up on the tension.

"I did go," Sydney said.

"I thought we agreed you weren't going to go? What happened?"

She held Gnoble's gaze, her mouth pressed together as though trying to decide if she should even answer. And finally, "No, you agreed I shouldn't go. And it wasn't your decision to make. So I went. And he says he's innocent."

"They all say they're innocent. It's called self-preservation."

She looked away. "I think I believe him."

"Believe him? Why?"

"He knew things. Things that wouldn't make sense to anyone unless they knew my father particularly well."

"What things?"

She glanced to the skating floor when her sister called out her name, then waved as the young girl glided past. "I'm really not comfortable discussing this here."

"That makes two of us," he said, then paused to smile for a photographer. "Sydney. I read that investigation. I spoke with the investigators back when it all happened. He's guilty. That's precisely one of the reasons I've decided to run again. Keeping a man like Wheeler alive for twenty years does nothing but torture him as well as the families of the victims. I'm going to do something about this."

"Something I'm sure your constituents will appreciate."

"Something I was hoping *you'd* appreciate."

"It's not going to bring my father back. And what if that

man is innocent?" she asked, crossing her arms, clearly disturbed by whatever it was she'd found.

Marla Gnoble reached out, placed her well-manicured hand on Sydney's arm. "Then you need to come forth with whatever it is, dear," she said, her voice soothing and low. "They're going to execute him in ten days, and if you have something that will exonerate him, my husband needs to know. This affects too many people. You, your mother . . ."

"I'd rather she didn't know all the details just yet—"

"—and," Gnoble interjected, "not to sound crass, but it affects my campaign."

"For God's sake, Donovan," his wife said. "Pretend you're not a politician for once. Can't you see what this is doing to her head? My God, Sydney. Have you talked to anyone about it? Anyone besides my idiot husband, that is?"

"No." And then, as if coming to some sort of internal decision, Sydney looked Gnoble in the eye, her expression cold, hard. "Do me a favor. Leave my family and especially my father out of your campaigning."

"Sydney." He grasped her arm, and she stopped, looked at him. "You have to believe me. That article was *not* my idea. I've known you since you were born. You know I'm not like that."

"I don't know what to believe right now."

"Then believe me when I say I'll help you in any way I can. If you think he's innocent, I will stand by you. But I have to know what proof you have, and it's got to be something more than his word. There are police reports and physical evidence showing otherwise. I've just come out publicly staking my reputation on his guilt, for God's sake," he said, trying to keep his voice low.

"This isn't politics. It's my father's life."

"You're right. I'm sorry. I can call someone, the best investigator, have him look into it. Come talk to me. At my office, away from the cameras."

"I'll think about it." She walked off.

Prescott thought Gnoble looked as though he'd go after her, but then his shoulders sagged, and he turned away, stared out to the kids skating round and round. His wife gave him an exasperated look. "For such a smart man, sometimes you're an absolute idiot," she said.

Prescott cleared his throat. "Sir?"

Gnoble ignored him, but his wife said, "Prescott, a few moments, please . . ."

"Of course. I have a couple calls to make anyway." Prescott took out his cell phone, stepped away where he wouldn't be overheard, hit the speed dial. "It's Prescott," he said, when the man on the other end answered. "What have you heard on the Wheeler case?"

"The Innocence Project is turning him down, and the governor's a Republican, so I'd say he's toast."

"They're turning him down?"

"That's what I heard."

"It's confirmed. Sydney Fitzpatrick went out to the prison. She's pretty upset, and I don't—"

Prescott glanced up, realized he was being watched. By Sydney Fitzpatrick's young half sister.

He laughed into the phone as though whatever they were talking about was some big joke. "Hold on," he said to his caller, keeping his tone jovial. He wondered how much the kid had overheard, and looked right at her, gave his best disarming smile. "Shouldn't you be skating, young lady?"

"Aren't you supposed to be out there making sure the senator's shaking hands?"

He decided she was too young to figure things out. "You're absolutely right. And I'm going to start now."

"Is my sister upset with your boss?"

"No. Of course not. It's just this thing with her father. The time of year. She's worried."

The girl glanced back at her sister, before pinning her shrewd and annoying gaze on him. "I think she's upset about that article in the paper, so if you don't mind, I don't think I want to take any pictures with you guys."

"Your mother really wants you all to pose for a get-together photo. It'll make her happy. And think what it'll do for your future, to be seen with a senator."

"You *do* realize that by the time I'm old enough to

vote, Senator Gnoble *so* won't even be a blip on my radar screen?"

"Prescott?" his caller said.

"One second." He looked at the girl again, tried to think of what he should tell her, but in the end, figured it was best just to let it be. "Smile for the camera, eh?" The kid rolled her eyes, skated off, and he returned his attention to the phone, making sure his expression read friendly and fun, as he lifted his hand to cover his mouth on the off chance someone there could read lips. "I need the senator reelected. If he's not, then not only do I lose my job, you lose yours and something much, much bigger than that measly salary he pays us. We don't have much time to make this go away. The sooner, the better."

"Here's the thing. I can't do something unless you tell me what it is you want done."

Prescott hated depending on other people. His glance strayed across the rink to where Sydney Fitzpatrick stood off to the side, avoiding her mother, avoiding pretty much everyone. "I'll get back to you on that. Shortly."

7

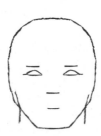

Any chance Sydney had of sneaking out of the skat-ing rink was thwarted when her half sister, Angie, insisted she skate a few rounds with her. It was hard to resist anything Angie requested. She'd been a surprise midlife baby, born eight years into her mother and Jake's marriage. And while neither had expected or wanted any children when they were married the year after Sydney's father had been killed, no one would guess it now. They were devoted parents. As for how Sydney felt about Angie, her heart had belonged to her baby sister the very moment she grasped Sydney's finger in her tiny little fist. Sydney knew right then and there that she'd give her life to protect her sister's. Not that she needed to worry about Angie. Jake was easily the most overprotective father on the face of the earth, though at the moment conspicuously absent, which surprised her.

At the skate desk, Sydney checked out a pair, then carried them well away from the senator and his groupies. She sat, removed her shoes, wondering about Donovan's interest in learning anything that might exonerate Wheeler. Because he was truly concerned? Or because of his real agenda, doing what he thought was right to keep his numbers up in the polls? He certainly didn't need help in that regard, but she supposed it was the nature of the beast, none of which had anything to do with why she didn't come out and tell him exactly what she'd learned from talking to Wheeler. Out of context it would sound completely ridiculous, she told herself as she tied her skates, then sought out Angie in the rink, somehow managing to skate without falling on her face. She tried to remember the last time she'd even worn skates. Probably when she was Angie's age, she realized, eyeing her sister.

Sydney had always thought Angie resembled Jake much more than their mother, with Angie's blond hair, dimples, a dusting of freckles across her nose, a smile that lit up the room, and a sharp eye that missed nothing. As in now.

"Are you upset with Uncle Don?" Angie asked.

"Not just him. Politicians in general."

"I'd rather be a cop than a politician." She grasped Sydney's hand, helping her to get her balance.

"A very wise decision. The not being a politician part." Sydney lurched, wobbled, but remained upright with considerable effort. "Didn't think I could skate, did you?"

"Is that what you call that?" They'd made it all the way around, then twice more, before she added, "Why's Mom staring at you every time we pass her?"

"Is she?" Sydney didn't doubt it, was purposefully avoiding her mother's gaze.

"Yeah. Is she mad at you?"

"Just worried."

"What is that? The grown-up way of saying mind your own business?" Angie craned her head to see as they skated past. "That is *so* not a worried look." Then, "Oh my God. Do you have any of your cards?"

Angie came to a stop, and Sydney nearly fell in the process. She pulled her hand from Angie's, grabbed the wall. "For what?"

"Nick Santos just skated on. He thinks he's all that, because his dad is a deputy sheriff. You *have* to show him your card." And then, before Sydney knew it, Nick Santos, the boy in question, skated alongside them, and Angie gave him her sweetest smile. "Hi, Nick."

"Angie."

"This is my sister. She's an FBI agent."

"I know," he said, giving Sydney only a fleeting glance as though he'd heard this line before. "My dad's a deputy. He's on SWAT."

"Yeah," she said. "But Sydney draws dead people."

Nick eyed her with renewed interest. "Really?"

"Yeah," Angie said, crossing her arms with a burst of confidence. "You have to see her card. It says *Forensic Artist* on it."

Nick gave Sydney a skeptical look, and, to defend her sister's honor, she pulled out the soft card case from her blazer pocket and removed a business card, handing it to Angie, who then gave it to Nick.

"Dead people? That is so cool," he said, tracing his finger over the embossed letters that spelled out *Forensic Artist*. He glanced at Angie, his gaze more respectful, as he shoved his hands into his jeans pockets, keeping the card. "You want to skate around with me?"

Her eyes lit up, until she looked at Sydney, no doubt recalling that she had promised to skate with her.

"I really need to take a break," Sydney said.

Angie gave her a grateful smile, then skated off with the boy who was "all that," leaving Sydney no choice but to face their mother.

She navigated off the floor, feeling her mother's gaze on her the entire time.

"Hi, Mom," she said when she reached the table, where her mother sat monitoring the shoes and kids' belongings strewn about the several tables claimed for the occasion.

Mary said nothing at first, while Sydney sat, deciding to remove the skates before she broke her neck. Mary watched her for several very long silent seconds, then, "Why?"

"I told you, it was something I had to do."

"You've said that every year for the last, what? Four, now? And you've never done it." Sydney had no idea what she should say, what made it different, except that with the impending execution, she knew this was her last chance.

Mary Fitzpatrick-Hughes fixed her gaze on Angie as she

skated round and round with the boy, Nick. "Did you get my message about babysitting Angela?"

"Yes. I'm sure it'll be fine, Mom."

"It'll just be overnight, and she doesn't have school the next day, but I can call Rainie if you'd rather not."

"Mom. I want to do it."

An uncomfortable silence stretched between them, and finally her mother said, "So what happened?"

Sydney wanted to let her know, quite simply because she longed for nothing more in that moment than to have her mother wrap her arms around her and tell her that everything was okay, that there was some mistake, and the killer wasn't out there still. But Sydney couldn't. It wasn't for her to burden her mother with anything more than what she'd already been saddled with in her time, and Sydney ignored the thought that she'd done that very thing, just by telling her mother of her visit. "Nothing, Mom."

"Nothing? He just sat there and stared at you? I thought you went there to ask him why?"

"That was only part of the reason I went. And I don't want to talk about it right now. I can't."

Her mother's lips pressed together in a thin line. She sat there for a moment, still watching Angie. Finally, "I can't believe you went. How could you do that?" And then, with one last stab of maternal guilt to bestow, she added, "On today, of all days."

"I'm here, aren't I?"

Her mother's gaze remained steadfastly on Angie, and Sydney slipped her feet from the skates, and into her shoes.

She walked over, kissed her mother on the forehead. "Good-bye, Mom. I love you."

Mary stared at her clasped hands, and reluctantly Sydney turned away. And then, in a barely audible voice, her mother said, "There are things you don't know about your father. He's not the saint you thought he was."

Sydney stopped in her tracks, thinking of what Scotty had told her. "What do you mean by that? What did he do?"

"Nothing you need to worry about. But you put him on a pedestal he should never have been on. And I was willing to let you live with that belief. He's your father. He loved you."

"You can't just tell me that and not say what he did."

"Yes, I can. Like you, I don't want to talk about it. He's gone, and you have to get on with your life."

Her mantra. Sydney had gotten on with her life just fine, and wanted to tell her mother exactly what she thought of it right then, but she heard Angie laughing and realized this was not the time or the place. "I should go."

Mary said nothing, not even demanding that she stay and get her photo taken for the senator's campaign, and so Sydney kissed her once more, then left, stopping only long enough to tell Angie that she had to leave.

"Why?"

"Work," Sydney said, waving her cell phone at her, and earning a look of awe from Nick.

An easy lie, and at least Angie was smiling when she left.

But things did not get better, because Sydney ran into her stepfather, Jake Hughes, in the parking lot. He was tall, fit for a man in his fifties, and like Angie, he had blond hair and dimpled cheeks, though you couldn't see the dimples. He was not smiling when he saw her. "I can't believe you entertained such an idiotic idea."

And then Sydney wondered if telling her mother of her visit to San Quentin was selfish, that maybe, had she really stopped to think things through, she would have realized this. "I shouldn't have told her. I just thought—"

"Thought? You weren't thinking. You should have left well enough alone, without putting your mother through that sort of misery."

"Her misery? What about mine? You have no idea what it was like for me. He was *my* father."

"And it's been twenty years, for God's sake. Twenty years today. You can't go on like this forever, letting your father's death define your entire life."

"That's not true. And I resent your saying so."

"Resent it, then. But think about why it is you chose a profession that lets you carry a gun twenty-four/seven. Your father's killer has been caught, he is not coming after you or your mother. She has moved on with her life. You should do the same, and not drag her back into the pain it took her so long to get past. Nothing is going to happen to you if you vary from your schedule, or you break a rule, Sydney. Nothing."

She crossed her arms, staring down at the ground, feeling his hard gaze on her, not daring to tell him she thought Wheeler might be innocent. She wasn't sure that was the best move right now. In his mind she had crossed the line. He had been her father's friend, was there for her mother in her time of need, had helped to raise Sydney, and voiced his objections when she chose to go in law enforcement.

He was right in some respects. Her father's death *had* given her purpose, *had* defined her. "Just tell Mom I'm sorry."

He gave an exasperated sigh, took a couple of steps toward the door, then paused. "Was it worth it? Did he tell you something that made a difference?"

She hesitated. She wanted to tell him, wanted someone on her side. But she couldn't. Not without proof. "Nothing that would make a difference."

He stared at her for several long seconds, and then he shook his head, pulled open the glass door, and walked inside. Sydney stood there for a bit, alone in the parking lot, feeling the rain start up again, wondering what she should do, what she could do. She wanted things to be right with her mother and with Jake. She wanted things to be like they were yesterday, before she'd opened her mouth about going to San Quentin. Maybe if she apologized to her mother, found the right words to say . . . But as Sydney opened the glass doors, looked inside, it was just as Angie discovered her father's arrival, and she skated off the floor to give him an excited hug. He embraced her, lifted her from the ground to give her a kiss, and Sydney glanced over at her mother, who was watching her husband and young daughter with a smile, her disappointment in her older daughter momentarily forgotten.

Sydney backed out, unseen, feeling a bit of envy, thinking that it all seemed so . . . normal, that if she went back in right now, the daughter of a murdered man that her mother had tried to forget, it would change things. Everyone would somehow discover that the world her mother had built around herself, her young daughter—and her older—was only a facade.

The rain let up by the time she got home, but her mood was still dark, especially when she had to double-park, knock on the next-door neighbor's house, asking the sullen teen who answered the door to have his friend move his car from her driveway, so she could pull into her garage. She waited by her car, while the lanky friend exited the house next door, sauntered to his car, got in, revved the engine. He rolled down his window, flipped her off, then sped away, doing his best to lay some rubber on the wet pavement.

"Slow down!"

Like that helped. His car fishtailed around the corner, tires squealing. She pulled into her driveway, parked in the garage, wanting to forget this day had ever occurred. She trudged upstairs, unlocked her door, and Topper was there to greet her, not caring that she'd gone to some prison, or might have upset anyone else. And just in case Topper's presence wasn't enough to remind her that she was watching him for a day or two, there was now a very large bag of dog kibble set inside her door. The big red bow stuck to the top of the kibble bag was a nice touch, but not as nice as the note taped to it, telling her to look inside the fridge. Not one but two dishes therein. One was cheesecake, with a note taped to the plastic wrap, and she pulled it off to read: *Cheesecake does not count as one of the four essential food groups. Look in the casserole dish. Love you, Arturo. P.S., don't give any to Topper.*

As if, she thought, lifting the lid on the casserole dish, and discovering enough lasagna to last her the week. A girl could get used to this.

Topper, however, wasn't about to let her sit down and relax. He nudged his snout against her thigh, then turned and walked toward the door, waiting with baleful eyes. A very orderly canine. She liked that in him.

"You ready for a walk?"

He wagged his tail, then pranced by the door. When she picked up the leash, she caught sight of the envelope

McKnight had sent. She knew she should look at it, try to figure out what it meant, but Topper whined. She'd get to the damned thing later. First things first.

"Sit."

Topper sat as well as his wiggling tail would allow. She clipped on the leash, then off they went. The pair circled the block in companionable silence, Sydney lost in her own thoughts until they turned the corner that led back up the hill to the house, and Topper stopped at his favorite fire hydrant just a few doors down. Suddenly he started growling. Sydney gripped the leash tighter, figuring Topper was defending the neighborhood from whatever cat was straying nearby. She glanced up, saw a sedan cruising down the hill, slowing in the vicinity of her house, its headlights keeping her from seeing who was driving.

"With my luck, it's probably Scotty."

Topper gave a sharp bark, then resumed his growling.

"Where were you when I met the guy? Hmm?" She gave a tug on the leash. "Let's go see what he wants."

They started up the hill, but as they neared, the car's engine revved, its high beams came on, blinding her. The screech of tires on the wet pavement echoed off the houses.

And the car headed straight toward them.

8

Sydney's heart slammed in her chest as she yanked
Topper's leash, forcing him from the curb and away from
danger. She fell back, knocking over a garbage can, and
Topper barked as the car sped past them down the hill, then
turned the corner, tires screaming across the wet pavement.
A car started up at the bottom of the hill, took off, but she
paid it little attention.

The cold air smelled of rain and wet wood, and she sat
there a moment before assessing the damage, nothing more
than scraped hands and a soaked bottom from the puddle
she'd landed in. Topper came up, shoved his wet nose into
her face, and she stood. "You okay?"

He wagged his tail.

She glanced down the hill, her senses on high alert as she
tried to figure out what had just happened. Clearly it wasn't
Scotty, which begged the question, who was it? And were
they really trying to run her down, or was it her imagination
that she was being targeted at all? Shaken, she brushed the
dirt from her hands, then noticed one of the juvenile delinquent next-door neighbors standing in front of his house,
his face lit by the glow of a cigarette as he inhaled. The ex-

planation for it all hit her. No doubt one of his drag-racing buddies showing off, maybe even the one she'd had to evict from her driveway earlier. She marched up the hill to confront the kid.

He eyed her, apparently unconcerned.

"That one of your friends who just left?"

"I don't keep time cards on my friends, see who's leaving when."

"You didn't see the car that just sped down the hill?"

"Like I just walked out here," he said, then tossed the cigarette into the wet gutter. It landed with a hiss, and Topper lunged toward it to investigate.

Sydney pulled the dog back, then looked at the boy, noted his glassy eyes, the heavy lids. "Tell your friends to slow down, would you?"

"Yeah, whatever." She walked away. Just as she started up the steps, she heard him call out, "Why don't you check one of those satellites you guys use to spy on people, see who it was?"

"Because they don't work nearly as well as the devices we implant in your brains."

"Yeah . . ." He gave a hesitant laugh, turned around, went back into the house.

Sydney waited until she heard the door close behind him, then looked up and down the street. The neighborhood was blissfully quiet, though, and finally she and Topper trudged up the steps. Once inside, the door locked behind them, she sat, tried to relax, and finally opened the envelope, looked again at the contents, the letter in her father's writing. Except for the reference to her father's boat, it still meant nothing. And what of the photo? She could almost understand if it showed the men doing something, but they were merely standing there in front of some nondescript army building, and there was nothing in the background that told her anything. She shoved the photo back into the envelope, and it occurred to her that what she really needed after a day like this was a good stiff drink. Several of them. But even if she had something decent in the house, drinking wasn't an option, since she needed to be in court in the morning. There was, however, one thing she could do that would calm her, and her gaze fell on the easel in her kitchen, on the jet black canvas.

She stared into depths of the black background, then picked out her paints. Normally this helped soothe her soul, but as she painted the colors onto the canvas in long sharp strokes, colors of burnt sienna, bright orange, yellow ocher, all on that sea of black, she was anything but comforted. Taking a step back, she eyed the sharp points of color, trying to figure out what they were.

As usual, she painted by instinct, letting the brush do the work, trying not to think, telling herself that nothing mattered, not Wheeler, not Gnoble, not Scotty's accusations about her father's character or her mother's vague comments regarding the same. None of it mattered. But the more she stared at the black background, the more she was struck by the thought that there was something missing from the canvas. What that might be, she had no idea, and when it became apparent that she'd lost all sense of creativity, she cleaned her brushes, put away her paints, and readied herself for bed. Just as she crossed from the bathroom to her bedroom, she glanced down the hall to the front of her apartment. Her gaze caught on the painting, lit by the porch light shining in from the kitchen window. It reminded her of something, and bothered her greatly. Teeth, she figured—long, sharp, pointed teeth—and she thought of the rape victim Tara and the bite mark she'd reported. But then Tara had been stabbed, and Sydney wondered if she'd been painting long sword blades or knife blades.

But she knew it was neither of these things. It was something more disturbing, something she didn't want to face, couldn't face, and though it would've been far easier to simply close her bedroom door so that she couldn't see down the hall, she walked all the way into the kitchen and turned the easel so that she couldn't see the painting.

Even that didn't ease her thoughts. Topper curled on the floor beside the bed, and she was tempted to invite the dog to sleep on the mattress next to her, unsure if it was because in the back of her mind, she knew a simple painting shouldn't evoke such emotions. Or perhaps it was a separate thought swirling in the forefront of her mind. One that told her that the car speeding down her street looked nothing like those driven by her juvenile delinquent neighbors.

9

Shortly after ten the next morning, fueled by more cups of coffee than Sydney cared to count, she was present in court, glad for the distraction of testifying, because for a few short minutes she might be able to forget that she'd ever spoken to Scotty about her father, or visited San Quentin yesterday.

What little enthusiasm she had for the court case waned along with her caffeine level, and soon she was wishing she'd had time to run an extra mile this morning to eliminate the fog in her brain. Since this was a bank robbery, the case was being tried in the federal court by an assistant U.S. attorney. Although AUSAs were simply the federal version of the deputy district attorneys she'd worked with as a cop, things tended to be handled more formally in the federal courts, and Sydney needed to mind her Ps and Qs.

She sat as directed, facing the AUSA, who asked her to identify herself and her occupation for the record.

"Sydney Fitzpatrick. Special agent, FBI."

"Special Agent Fitzpatrick, how long have you worked for the FBI?"

"Four years."

"And do you have prior law enforcement experience?"

"I was a police officer for eight years in Sacramento."

"Thank you. And on the day of February first, were you assigned to any special duties?"

"Yes, sir. I was part of a detail assigned to covertly follow Mr. Gerard Hagley."

"Is he in the courtroom today?"

"At the defendant's table."

The judge, a gray-haired woman, said, "Let the record show that the witness has identified Mr. Hagley."

The prosecutor stood and walked toward her, buttoning his gray suit coat. "Can you tell us, Agent Fitzpatrick, how it came that you were following Mr. Hagley?"

"Several weeks before, I had done a composite sketch from a witness description of the man who robbed the First Security Bank. We received an anonymous tip after the sketch appeared in the *Chronicle*, that our suspect was a Gerard Hagley, and that he was planning on robbing another bank near Union Square the following day. We staked out the banks in the area and waited until he showed up."

"Is this the sketch?" he asked, holding up Sydney's pencil drawing of a white male adult, short, curly brown hair and narrow, dark eyes. A damned good likeness to the defendant, Sydney thought, glancing over at the man who was trying his best to give her an intimidating glare.

"Yes."

"What happened that afternoon?"

"I saw him walking into the Bay Trust Mutual. Our task force moved in, but he made us and took off running. Which is when I saw him drop something in the planter as he took off. He was arrested about a block away."

"And where were you when this occurred?"

"In front of a store across the street."

"What was it he dropped?"

"I recovered a note that read: *Give me all the money. Now.*"

"Thank you. No further questions."

The defense attorney stood, a middle-aged man with a receding hairline, a crisp white shirt and red power tie beneath his navy suit coat, and a look that told Sydney she was pond scum. "Special Agent Fitzpatrick," he said, checking his notes. "You say that you saw my client from across the street?"

"Yes, sir."

"And approximately how far is that?"

"Fifty, seventy yards. I'm not sure."

"Do you wear glasses?"

"Sometimes." She had slight astigmatism, and really only wore the things if she was trying to do fine artwork, which lately in her abstract painting kick was a rarity.

"Were you wearing them that day?"

"No."

She could swear he started salivating. He got up, walked toward the jury box, rubbing his chin as if in deep thought as he paced in front of the empty seats. Suddenly he stopped. "And yet . . ." He looked right at her, pausing for emphasis, before saying in a firm voice, "You say you *saw* my client from seventy yards away?"

"Yes."

"And you *saw* a small scrap of paper being dropped. From *seventy yards away?*" He stressed each word as he eyed her. "That's two hundred and ten feet."

"I didn't measure the exact distance."

He started his pacing act again. "Just how far can you see without your glasses?"

"I don't know."

"You *don't* know?"

"I can see the moon. How far is that?"

He stopped in his tracks. Opened his mouth, shut it again, then walked to the defendant's table and sat. "Er, no further questions."

She gained a smile from some sandy-haired man in a blue suit sitting behind the defense attorney—probably a cop, fairly good-looking one, too, but that seemed to be the extent of her cheering section. Judging from the expression on the AUSA's face, Sydney scored zero points for her wit. Definitely not like her, but chalk it up to lack of sleep. She left the stand, then sat next to the fingerprint expert who was about to testify that the found note had not only the defendant's prints on it, but also the prints of a teller from the last bank he'd robbed—a hazard of recycling his tools of the trade, or being too lazy to make up a new note. Either way, things weren't looking good for Hagley, especially considering that when court was recessed for a break, his attorney was suggesting he change his plea before it was too late.

Not that it mattered. What did were the fifteen other cases sitting on her desk, and the coffee she fully intended on getting when she walked out of the courtroom, dismissed for the day. She did not get far. About midway through the rather crowded federal courtroom lobby, she heard a woman calling her name.

"Agent Fitzpatrick!" The woman hurried in her direction. Apparently she'd followed her from the courtroom. She was young, maybe early twenties, with long auburn hair pulled back in a ponytail, and she wore a tan blazer and matching slacks. Sydney figured DA fresh out of law school until she said, "I'm Officer Glynnis. Kim Glynnis. Hill City PD."

She held out her hand and Sydney shook it, feeling slightly guilty for not returning her call. "What can I do for you?"

"You're a forensic artist."

"Among other things."

"I'm sorry to bother you," she said, having to step aside to allow a number of people still filing out of a nearby courtroom to walk past. "Your supervisor, Agent Dixon, said you were here, and I have a case I was hoping you could help with. An unidentified murder victim. We've tried dental, checking the missing persons database, prints. Nothing's come up. I was hoping you could do a forensic sketch for ID purposes."

"Are you the detective on the case?"

She reddened. "No."

Sydney's curiosity was piqued at her response. "You want to tell me what's going on?"

Officer Glynnis took a deep breath, as though bracing herself against Sydney's reaction. "I should probably tell you that I'm just a patrol officer and I'm going over the detective's head. But it was necessary, or I wouldn't be here," she said in a rush. "I also heard about the case SFPD picked up the other night. I thought mine might be related, but the detective wouldn't call you. He thinks she's just a prostitute, and it happened here, not in Reno." Her smile was hopeful. "I thought if I drove up here, presented you with what I think, that you might be able to help. I know you've done some drawings for other agencies, so I figured it couldn't hurt to ask."

"How are you involved?"

"I was the officer who found her."

Sydney noticed the dark circles beneath her eyes, which reminded her that the poor woman worked midnights. "Coffee?"

"Love some."

"We have a café in the building. Nothing fancy."

"Doesn't matter to me, as long as it's strong."

"The café, then," and they weaved their way through the crowd, to the elevator banks. There were four, each designated to a certain block of floors. One had a sign indicating the Midway Café, so named because out of twenty floors, it was situated on the tenth. Sydney jabbed the down button, then stood back, which was when she noticed the guy who had smiled at her joke in the courtroom standing behind them, holding a newspaper in one hand, then glancing at his watch. More than likely a cop, definitely cute, she thought before stepping onto the elevator with Officer Glynnis. Cute Guy got on as well, asked her what floor, pressed the requested button, and the door slid shut.

Other than that, the ride up to the café was uneventful. And disappointing when Sydney noticed that even though Cute Guy was also going to the café, he wore a wedding ring. She really needed to get a life, she thought, as she bought two coffees, then directed Kim Glynnis to a table by the window, not that there was much of a view. The state building across the street blocked most of it, unless you leaned out and looked to the left to catch a sliver of the bay. They sat in the corner, and Sydney listened to her story. Apparently Kim Glynnis was not only one of the first female officers at her department, and a rookie to boot, all of one and a half years on, but she also suffered from the typical if-it-comes-out-of-a-female's-mouth-it-must-be-bullshit syndrome prevalent in some agencies where the good ol' boys still ruled the roost. Unfortunately for her, many of these same agencies took a dim view of the Feds walking in and getting involved in their cases.

Even so, Sydney listened to her explain how, on patrol, she'd found the victim dumped in a marsh adjacent to a park in the outskirts of town. After several days in the water, the victim had lost most of her hair, and what was left of her prints hadn't yielded a hit. She'd been stabbed several times, and a number of apparent defensive wounds marked her arms and hands. Though it was believed she was the victim of sexual assault, no seminal fluid had been found.

"What makes your detective believe she was a prostitute?" Sydney asked.

"She had a tattoo, and a pocket full of condoms."

"And what do you think?"

"Me? I think she was somebody's daughter. Isn't that what counts?"

The officer's words surprised her. Touched her. "Yes," she said quietly. "It is." Then, putting her own thoughts aside, Sydney asked how she intended on getting the FBI involved if the case investigator objected.

She gave a sheepish smile. "I was sort of hoping you could help me with that part. I mean, I don't know if it is related to the case San Francisco picked up the other night. Even if it isn't, we need to get her identified."

"Do you have a card?" Glynnis gave Sydney her business card, and she set it on the tabletop. "I have no idea when I might be able to get down there, but I'll try. That's all I can promise."

"Thank you," Glynnis said, then, after shaking Sydney's hand once more, she stood, picked up her paper coffee cup, and left.

Sydney didn't follow, just sat there, sipping her coffee, thinking about Officer Glynnis and her persistence and determination to do the right thing, even if it meant going against the tide. And she thought about how a rookie's perspective should serve to remind the rest of them why they'd gotten into law enforcement.

She knew why, would never forget. But there were others, more seasoned than she, who did forget, their interest in anything but high-profile cases quickly waning. And finishing her coffee, she wondered how many cases fell victim to such apathy.

That was not something she liked to think about. To believe that others out there didn't care as Glynnis cared. Or others cared like Donovan Gnoble cared, for all the wrong reasons. They forgot that a victim could be someone's daughter, or mother.

Or father.

She picked up the business card, ran her fingertip along the edge, knowing she should go to Hill City, help out, but right now what occupied her mind was that damned envelope sitting at her house. How could she think about a case when her father's reputation was at stake? And how was it that her father's reputation suddenly became an issue so close to the execution date of the man convicted of killing him? A man whose guilt bore shades of doubt?

That was a coincidence she wasn't willing to overlook. What she needed was answers, and it occurred to her that there was one man who might have them. One man, who happened to have an office in this very building.

Senator Donovan Gnoble.

10

Richard Blackwell waited a good five minutes after
Special Agent Fitzpatrick left the café and was seen stepping onto the elevator before he dumped his coffee and the
newspaper, and left. Not until he was standing outside the
federal building did he call Prescott, only to have Gnoble's
damned secretary put him on hold. He didn't like waiting.
Had it been anyone else he wouldn't have.

"You learn anything?" Prescott asked when he finally
came on.

"I followed her into court. She was a bit of a smart-ass on
the stand. I thought you said she was straitlaced and by-the-
book?"

"According to the senator she is."

"More importantly, it might be hard to get close. She
seems to pay attention to her surroundings."

"Yeah. Found that out last night."

"What's that supposed to mean?"

"Nothing," Prescott said quickly. "For God's sake, you get
anything we can use?"

"Maybe," he said, then waited as two women walked past.
The moment they were out of earshot, he said, "She might

be assisting an outside agency with a sketch. The officer who requested it thinks it might be tied to a case the Bureau picked up the other night."

"And what the hell good is that going to do? Following her into court? Finding out what she's working?"

"Because you never know what gems might turn up."

"Oh shit." Prescott lowered his voice to a whisper. "Guess who's walking into the senator's office as we speak. Find out everything you can on the cases. Get back to me. More importantly, get back to me with something we can use."

"Will do."

Blackwell dropped the phone into his pocket, then glanced over to the long row of cars parked in front of the building, most with placards in the window identifying them as Bureau cars. Agent Fitzpatrick's car was the fifth from the corner, a dark blue Crown Vic, one of many dark blue Crown Vics. The Bureau wasn't too imaginative when it came to doling out the wheels. He glanced back into the building just to be certain he wasn't being followed. Prescott had gone to great lengths to get him an ID to get in and out. A start. But Blackwell definitely made a mistake in following her to court, then laughing at something she said. He didn't normally slip up like that, but her comment had been unexpected.

Unfortunately, she'd looked at him. Made a connection to his face.

That was something he couldn't afford.

11

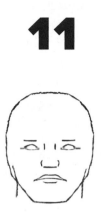

Sydney had worked in the federal building for six months now and never once visited Senator Gnoble's office when he was here, or one of his other offices, and not in D.C. Of course, he lived in the same town as her mother, and she'd never visited him there, either, but it really had more to do with the fact that he was her mother's friend, a generational thing. That might be why he appeared genuinely surprised when his secretary showed her in.

"Come in, sit down," he said, waving her toward one of the thick-cushioned leather chairs. "Can I get you something to drink?"

"No, thank you." She sat in the almost silken leather, a bit beyond the government-issued chairs she was used to in the Bureau offices. Senator Gnoble smiled at her, waiting, and she wondered just what she really expected of him. He'd always told her that no matter where he was, what he was doing, his door was always open to her, because her father would've done the same if something had happened to him and he'd had children. When Sydney had graduated high school, her mother had said he'd even offered to pay her way through college, though she hadn't needed it, because of her scholarship. But sitting here in the senator's office, it was hard to think of him as her mother's friend, the man she'd grown up calling Uncle Don. "I was hoping you might have a few minutes."

"If it's about that article, Sydney—"

"It's about McKnight's suicide."

His gaze flicked to the open door. He got up, closed it, then came and took the seat opposite her. "How on earth did you hear about that?"

"The background the FBI was doing on him."

"Of course. I forgot. For the confirmation."

"He left a note. I want to see what was in it."

"Sydney—"

"Do you know what it said?"

"I only heard there was a note . . ." His gaze drifted to the window, and he started turning a ring around and around on his finger. It looked like a class ring of some sort, red stone, antiqued gold, and brought to mind the rings all the men in the photo wore. When he noticed her watching him, he stopped, took a deep breath. "I, uh, think it was something about what was found in his background that would've precluded him from being appointed to the position."

"Was it something to do with my father?"

"Why would it have anything to do with him? McKnight wanted one thing only, to hurt those of us he thought got in his way."

"One of the agents who spoke to McKnight said he apologized about something he did to my father."

He frowned. "That doesn't make sense."

"They were in the army together. You all were. That's where you met. Isn't that why you all wore the same rings?"

He looked down at his hand. "Yes. I'd forgotten. But we met in basic training. After that, we all ended up in separate units, and I'm the only one who stayed in the service. But unless you count the time we got caught sneaking into boot camp drunk, there wasn't a lot that happened between us."

"What about after, when my father was a civilian employee? Was there something my father did that was wrong? Something McKnight did that he'd apologize for?"

Gnoble took a deep breath. "Your father was a good man, Sydney."

"That doesn't answer my question."

"A stellar military career for the short time that he was in. And then the contract work he did, the photography, the artwork . . . Had he not retired because of that tragic accident, who knows? Maybe we'd be viewing his work at some gallery."

"Why would McKnight be apologizing?"

"I have no idea. Your father overextended himself, made a few mistakes when he opened up the pizza parlor. I think McKnight might have lent him money, money that didn't come from the most reliable source, which is what was—I think that's what was found in the background check. I don't have all the details."

That could possibly explain the note telling McKnight to send the money to her father's pizza place, but not the reference about why it would be for the boat, *Cisco's Kid*. Nor did it explain Scotty's remark about her father's manager, McKnight's wife. "And Becky Lynn's involvement?"

"Sydney. Don't ask me about this."

"I need to know."

He hesitated, looked away for a moment, before saying, "I think your father and Becky Lynn were having an affair . . ."

The first thing she thought of was her mother telling her that her father wasn't a saint. Then she thought about Becky Lynn's connection to organized crime.

Sydney stood, walked toward the window, then paused at a photo of Gnoble shaking hands with the president. "Did McKnight have something to do with my father's death?"

Silence reigned. She turned, faced Gnoble, who still sat, giving her a look of sympathy. Finally, he stood. "We know who killed your father. He's in prison."

"And he says he didn't do it."

"He has the burns on his hands."

"Which I can't explain. But he knew things."

"What things?"

Suddenly she felt foolish for even bringing it up, but she

was in it this far, and she wanted answers. She told him. And when she finished, his look once again held nothing but sympathy.

"You're tearing yourself up for a few little things, coincidences, if that. I saw the evidence, Sydney. I read the investigation. He's guilty."

"But what if he isn't?"

"A twenty under the till? A can under the counter? Even if it was true, there isn't a court that would reverse it based on that."

"No, but you could contact the governor and tell him there are doubts that need to be looked into."

"I've publicly come out in support of his death sentence, and now you want me to approach the governor for clemency? Never mind that they'll rip me apart on every campaign ad between now and the election, the man killed your father."

"And if he's guilty, he pays. But what if he isn't? What if this has something to do with why McKnight killed himself? You might be the one man who can do something about this."

"All right. I'll look into it. But I want some sort of promise from you in return."

She waited.

"You tell no one of this conversation. Not your mother, not your stepfather. No one. If this gets out before I have some proof, my opponents will ream me."

"Agreed."

"And I don't want McKnight's name brought up publicly. It's already bad enough that he's linked to me through the nomination process, then ends up killing himself."

"I'd like to see this letter for myself—" She stopped when Gnoble's secretary knocked on the door.

"Sorry to disturb you, but that call you were waiting for came through."

"Yes. I'll pick it up." He turned back to Sydney. "Call me the moment you discover anything that . . . might help with your case. I'm here for you. You know that."

"Thank you, Senator," she said, then walked out the door.

As she left, she heard Gnoble say, "You can put the call through," and she couldn't help but wonder if he would really do as he said, look into the matter, or was it just another politician's promise?

12

Sydney took the elevator to the thirteenth floor, thinking about Donovan Gnoble and his answers, his nonanswers to her questions. In her mind most politicians that high up in the political spectrum got there or stayed there by means less than altruistic. Gnoble, however, had always seemed on the up-and-up. Surely her mother would never have remained friends with him otherwise? She was about to add that her father would never have remained friends with him, but she wasn't quite sure what to make of her father after the last two days.

She waved at the receptionist who buzzed her into the Bureau offices. Just down the hall to the left, she stopped at a wall-mounted counter, pulled her time card from the slot above it, and signed in. Hard not to see the blank space from yesterday, a day that was supposed to be spent in quiet introspection, remembering her father as he was supposed to be remembered.

She didn't necessarily trust Gnoble to do what needed to be done. Not because he wasn't a good politician, but precisely *because* he was a good politician. He'd always put his political interests first. That was the name of the game. And what of McKnight? she wondered, as she shoved her time card back in the slot. Could she trust that Gnoble would look into that, tell her what he found, even if it conflicted or cast doubt on his political ideals? After all, McKnight committed suicide while being looked at for a political appointment, and his name was connected to Gnoble's.

And wasn't that the point? Damned good one at that. She took out her cell phone, called Scotty as she walked to her desk.

"What are the chances you can get a copy of McKnight's suicide note from Houston PD?" she asked.

"Hello to you, too."

"Can you?"

"Figuring you'd want to see it, I've already tried. It's not going to be easy. Hatcher's already back in D.C., and Rick Reynolds, the agent who was looking into it after Hatcher left, says he's not touching it with a ten-foot pole. There's some political voodoo on the case, according to him, and he's this close to being transferred to an outhouse in the wilds of some state with a population less than a thousand."

"What do you mean political voodoo?"

"The note's off-limits, which, I suppose, is good news, because if there is anything about your father in it, it's not coming out in the papers. Gotta go. Another call coming in."

"Scotty—" He disconnected, and before she could try calling him back, Lettie walked by, saw her, and said, "Dixon told me the moment you get back from court, he wants to see you."

The first thing anyone noticed upon walking into Dixon's office was the brochure for Tahiti on the wall, and below that a calendar marking off how many days until his retirement, which Dixon could cite not only to the day, but to the minute, maybe even the second. The calendar's placement, as well as the Tahiti brochure, were there as a not-so-subtle reminder that if his subordinate agents knew what was good for them, they had better not do anything to screw up and keep him from the long-anticipated trip he intended to take once he reached the magic age of fifty. According to the calendar, he'd hit that in about four years.

Those in the know used that calendar as a gauge for his moods. If he was staring at it, be careful. At the moment Sydney walked in, he was buried in paperwork, a good sign, or so she thought, and she knocked on the open door.

Being a supervisor, he had his own agenda, because the first thing he said was "Thought you might like to discuss what happened the other night with the drawing."

"Actually, I wouldn't."

"*Pretend* you would."

"I had my mind on something else at the time?"

"Like what?"

The million-dollar question, and she sure as hell wasn't going to throw it out there now. "The usual, wondering if SFPD had any leads, was Reno PD doing the follow-up?"

"No, they haven't. And Reno PD doesn't have anything, either."

"Which means whoever you assign is going to have a lot to do on the case," she said, trying to deflect his attention.

"It's not like you to feed me bullshit, Fitzpatrick. What the hell is going on?"

If a lie would get her out of this, and she was any good at it, she would have concocted one on the spot. And the truth sure as hell wasn't going to work. Then again, maybe part of the truth . . . "Don't suppose you caught the article in the *Chronicle*. The one on the death penalty?"

"I scanned it briefly. Why?"

"One of the cases they detailed is the guy convicted of killing my father." Dixon put down his pen, gave her his full attention. "He's due to be executed, but claims he's innocent. It was twenty years yesterday, so it got to me. The anniversary."

"I'm sorry," he said. "That's why you asked for leave."

That and the hangover she'd been anticipating. "In a nutshell."

"You going to be okay? Or you need more time off?"

His more-time-off question was double-edged, something

Sydney knew from experience, and she decided right then and there that she wasn't about to reveal her visit to San Quentin and definitely not Scotty's news, either. Not yet. Dixon didn't want to hear that any agent working for him was having issues, was emotionally involved in anything that would take time from real work. Bottom line, he had to make reports to HQ in Washington, and her caseload was part of his stats. She gave a casual shrug. "I'll be fine."

He stared at her for several seconds, perhaps to ensure that she really would be okay, then, finally, "You talk to that officer from Hill City who drove up here about a sketch?"

"Case is a couple weeks old. Partly decomposed body, no available ID, though the officer thought it might be related to our case we picked up last night."

"I agree with her."

"Since it's cold—"

"I don't like coincidences. I'd like you to go down today, see what can be done."

"Today?"

"You have something else that's more important?"

"The Harrington report." That particular report was due on his desk last week, and his expression told her she'd just given the wrong answer. She quickly added, "But it's almost done."

"Get to the point where the 'almost' part is eliminated from the 'done' part when you come back tomorrow. I'd like that guy sitting in a jail cell."

"First thing in the morning," Sydney said, hightailing it out of there. She wanted the time to contact Houston PD, find out about that suicide. But between the sketch and the Harrington report, she wondered when she'd have the time. The Harrington report was left over from her last assignment working white-collar crimes, an insurance fraud operation that was about to result in the arrest of more than ten individuals, including a prominent doctor, George Harrington, who had masterminded the ring that had netted his medical practice several million dollars.

Unfortunately for George Harrington, he was caught when his office billed an insurance company for a procedure his patient didn't need. An appendectomy. The insurance company brought it to the Bureau's attention, pointing out that said patient had already had his appendix removed several years before.

If Sydney wanted any peace in looking into the matters involving her father, she'd need to get on that sketch and get the Harrington report turned in. Lucky for her, the case *was* virtually done, which meant she could devote her full attention to turning in a sketch on the Hill City victim. Well, devote as much attention as her swirling thoughts would allow.

Hill City, located just north of San Mateo, was a quaint town of middle-class homes that were probably worth a small fortune, thanks to their proximity to San Francisco. The police department was located in an antiquated building in the center of town, where a large sign posted out front depicted the new building forthcoming once a bond was passed.

Sydney walked up to the glass double doors, pushed one open, then stepped into a small lobby. To the left was a door that led to the police department, where Sydney was greeted by a woman at the front counter.

Credentials in hand, Sydney said, "I'm Special Agent Fitzpatrick. Is the detective who is handling the Jane Doe working here?"

"Jane Doe?"

"Body found out in a marsh."

"Oh. That'd be Detective Rodale. I'll call him for you. Just have a seat."

She directed Sydney to a very small waiting room consisting of four chairs just off the records section. Sydney sat, waited. About five minutes later, the detective walked in. He was wearing tan slacks and cowboy boots, and a navy sport coat that did little to hide the belly that protruded over his large silver belt buckle, the sort given out as trophies for a rodeo.

"You're with the FBI?" he asked, his tone implying he was anything but impressed.

"Yes. I understand you have a Jane Doe that needs to be identified."

"How'd you come about that info?"

Call it intuition, call it her previous eight years on the force before becoming a special agent—it was clear he wasn't thrilled about her presence. There were two strikes against her. One, she was a woman. Two, she was a federal agent. Thank God not all officers were of similar mind. That same intuition told her, however, that if he knew Officer Glynnis had tipped her, Glynnis would bear the brunt of his anger. "National database. That's why we have y'all entering every tiny detail from your reports." She gave him her sweetest smile.

He seemed to buy it. "Yeah. Okay. Right this way." And so Sydney followed him back to the detective bureau, which consisted of about six desks in a large room. He sat at his desk, didn't offer her a seat, then hefted a thick black binder from a shelf behind him. "Everything's in here."

Sydney pulled up a chair from beside the desk, sat, opened the binder. "What's your take on it?"

"Probably a hooker got mixed up with someone who didn't like what she was charging. Or you Feds got a better scenario? I'm assuming that's why you're here? To take over the case?"

She flipped through the pages, trying to see if it might be related to the case they picked up the other night. The injuries were so much more severe, she couldn't judge on that factor. "I'm here only to do a forensic drawing to assist you. For identification purposes."

"Wouldn't it be easier to post her picture?" He crossed his arms. "Maybe one of her *clients* will recognize her."

She examined the close-up photo of the victim. "If you think someone can get past the caved-in skull, filmy eyes, and the fact there are only a few strands of hair left on her head because of decomposition. And did you plan to show the neck stab wounds with it?"

He didn't respond, which made her wonder if he was truly contemplating such a thing. For the public to view a photo of a victim in that manner was incomprehensible, and Sydney glanced at him to see if he was serious.

She decided he was, and figured she'd move on. "Dental?"

"Negative."

"Prints?"

"Only partials left. Submerged too long. Nothing came back. Not one lead panned out, so you can say this is one cold case. Which doesn't change the fact that we don't want or need you here."

"Lucky for you my presence here isn't required," Sydney said, thumbing through the autopsy report. "At least not to do my job." She stood, handed him the binder. "I'll need a complete copy of your report and the autopsy. As soon as I get that, I'll head on over to the morgue and you can play with the case all you want."

"And if I don't?"

"Then maybe your superior officer will explain the finer details of federal jurisdiction to you."

He picked up the phone, punched in a number, and after a moment said, "Lisa, it's Rodale. I'm sending someone up to get a copy of our marsh homicide. Give it to her." He dropped the phone in the cradle, stood so that his tall frame towered over Sydney and his rodeo belt buckle was about her eye level. She shoved her chair back and stood, still having to look up at him as he narrowed his gaze at her and said, "Don't think that just because you're with the FBI that you're better than us. I've got more Code Seven time under my belt than you have time out on the streets."

Code Seven was the cop term for lunch hour, and she gave a pointed look to his large belly. "I see you do," she said, nodding. "But don't worry. A little diet and exercise, no one will ever know how you spend your day." And with that, she walked out the door.

The morgue was typical county fare, pale green tiles lining the walls, the floors slick concrete, the usual stainless steel wall of refrigerated compartments for body storage. Unlike Detective Rodale, the on-duty clerk assistant to the pathologist did not have an attitude. He was in his late fifties, balding, but his blue eyes twinkled with humor when he saw the name on the report. "That guy's a piece of work, isn't he?" the assistant commented.

"To say the least."

"Got our Jane Doe here," he said, opening one of the small square doors, and sliding the body out. "I've never had someone come in for a drawing before, but then, I haven't been here that long. You going to work in here?"

"Actually if she's not in terrible shape, I might be able to work from photos." Something she preferred to do, primarily because looking at photos was easier on the mind and the nose, and far easier than standing in the morgue, staring at the actual corpse for hours on end.

"I'll put her out on a table for you."

She opened her briefcase containing her camera gear, while he readied the body for viewing. She figured she'd snap some digital, and some film. But before Sydney did that, she'd need to check the body to determine if she could work from photos. If decomposition was too far along, the next step would be boiling the skull to remove all flesh, then working with a forensic anthropologist to determine what the measurements and thickness of facial flesh would be for the particular race and sex of the victim—the standard process used, for instance, when the subject is a found skull that can't be identified through dental records.

She put on some latex gloves, then turned to the gurney that held the Jane Doe. A post-autopsied body is not a pleasant thing to look at. Long tracks of sutures attempt to hold the victim together, though never enough to keep from exposing the inner pinkish-yellow flesh that always seems to escape the stitches. In this case, the chilly weather had slowed the decomposition of the victim, and as a result, the smell was tolerable, mostly masked by the heavy antiseptic scent that permeated the morgue.

If Sydney had to guess her age just from sight, she'd put her in her late teens to late twenties, but that was a job best left for the medical examiner. Even so, her victim's face was devoid of any wrinkles, but it was also devoid of most of her hair, including eyelashes, eyebrows and scalp. This would be the greatest challenge, trying to reconstruct the proper hairstyle, which could drastically change someone's appearance and hinder an identification if she guessed wrong. There

were just a few strands in various places on her scalp. All
appeared to be straight, light brown, and as Sydney carefully
held them out, measured them, jotted the information down,
she was pleased.

The assistant, curious, walked up. "You can tell something
by the hair?"

"Possibly the hairstyle," she said. "Here, these three
strands remaining in the front are short. Tells me she probably wore bangs." Sydney measured the few strands left on
the side of her head at the top and back, then said, "See here
how it's longer in back? Two separate lengths?" He nodded.
"Indicative of a layered style."

That done, Sydney gently probed her face, determining
that the flesh was still fairly firm against the skull, that the
gases from decomposition had not overly disfigured it, giving it a swollen appearance. It was a lesson she'd learned
from her first drawing, thinking the floater's face was swollen. As a result she'd narrowed the jawline. Turned out the
victim had a round face. Sydney no longer guessed.

The assistant watched, clearly fascinated. "What happens
if the body's in bad shape?" he asked. "You do one of those
clay things?"

"I only work sketches," Sydney said. "The clay models
have their place, but I think the sketch is easier to ID from."

"That right?"

"You ever see a clay model?"

"On TV."

"Remind you of anything?"

He laughed. "Yeah. A clay head. A Neanderthal clay head
with a wig."

She smiled. "Though I've seen some excellent examples,
very few artists are skilled enough to pull off a sculpture.
Sketches, in my humble opinion, tend to be more forgiving,"
she said, stripping off the gloves, then taking the Polaroid
camera and snapping a few shots of the woman's face. "The
eye tends to see right past the softer lines from a pencil, filling in the blanks and forgiving tiny errors." Sydney replaced
the Polaroid, took out the digital camera, took photos from
all angles, having to stand on a stepladder to get her over-

head shots. Next she stepped down and lowered the sheet that had covered the length of her, wanting to get a shot of the tattoo.

That's when Sydney saw the bite mark on her left breast. And when she realized that this had just elevated from a cold case into a priority.

13

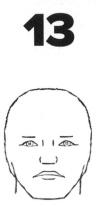

Sydney had no idea if the bite wound appeared in the medical examiner's report, since she hadn't had a chance to read it completely. One thing she did know, however, was that it did not appear in the police report that she had viewed, and she pointed to the victim's left breast, asking the assistant, "Do you know if this is documented in the autopsy?"

He looked over, nodded. "I'm the one who typed it up after the pathologist dictated it. Bite wound, left breast. His words exactly."

She took out a measurement card with a color chart on one edge, laid it against the wound, and snapped several photos with the digital and then the film camera. The fact this was not mentioned in the police report was significant. Sydney wondered if it might be a simple oversight, or if Mr. Big Belt Buckle didn't think it was important. Unfortunately, not noting it meant that it wouldn't appear in the information normally entered into the national database, a database used to link crimes that might be connected.

Crimes like the rape and attempted murder of Tara Brown, who also happened to have reported a bite mark on her breast.

And two things occurred to Sydney in that moment. One, it seemed highly probable that they might have a serial rapist and murderer in their area. The true test would be when they had both bite marks examined by a forensic dental expert, especially if no DNA was found. Two, if the suspect was one and the same, she now had a sketch of him in her office, thanks to Tara Brown.

Sydney called Dixon to let him know what she'd found, called Rainie to check up on Topper, finished up at the morgue, then drove back to the city to get started on the forensic drawing of her Jane Doe. Staring at a corpse, or even photos of a corpse, often riddled with stab wounds, bullet holes, or any number of untold injuries, was not easily forgotten. Each time she found herself in this position, she wondered why she'd chosen a profession that forced her to look at death and destruction, especially when she found herself working with victims—like the one she was sketching now, victims of crimes so horrific that death must have seemed a relief. Doubt always crept in at times like these. What made her think she was good enough or even qualified? What if she failed in her attempt at an accurate drawing? What if no one was able to identify the woman? Who would speak for her if no one knew her?

She knew the answer. Quite simply because her father's death *had* defined her. Just not in the way her stepfather had thought. True, she'd been unable to help her father, couldn't stop fate from taking his life, but there were others out there she could help. An advocate for the dead. That was why she had chosen this path all along, honed her artistic skills, willed herself to look at victims so mutilated that the public was not allowed to view them. In a perfect world she'd be painting landscapes. In her world she drew dead people, and so she sketched away, losing track of time until Scotty called.

"I thought you might be home by now."

"I'm working a priority case. Picked up a sketch that might be related to the rape the other night."

"About your father . . ."

She leaned back in her chair, closed her eyes. "Scotty . . ."

"If you can't talk to me, who can you talk to?"

"Can you get me a copy of McKnight's suicide note?"

"I already told you."

"Do that. Then we'll talk."

"I thought I could stop by—"

"Get me that note, Scotty."

She hung up, glanced down at her sketch, thinking that sometimes dealing with the dead was much easier. She put Scotty and her father from her mind for a few short minutes, finished up the hair, figured she had a good likeness of her Jane Doe, then put away her things. Copies of the sketch in hand, she dropped everything off with Dixon, who was working late, and wanted it for release to the press.

That done, she drove home, desperate to clear her mind as she took Topper for a walk. She started at the sound of every car that drove past, though Topper seemed unfazed. When they were safely home, she tried dabbing a bit of paint on her unfinished canvas, but soon found that her favorite pastime did little to ease her thoughts, and her gaze kept straying to the envelope McKnight had mailed to her. She doubted she'd find anything different; there wasn't that much in there to see. What was it Scotty used to tell her? Have a beer. Loosen up. Maybe she needed to finally take a piece of advice from her ex, especially when it came to delving into one's father's alleged illegal doings. "Hey, Top," she said to the dog. "Doesn't your daddy keep a shitload of high-end beer in his fridge?"

Topper wagged his tail.

"That's what I thought. Desperate times call for desperate measures." She raided Arturo's refrigerator, walking out with a six-pack of Sierra Nevada, while Topper raided a basket of dog toys, walking out with something that squeaked. Back at her place, she popped the first beer open, didn't even look at the envelope until she'd finished her second. Finally she dumped out the contents of the envelope, stared at the writing, knowing in her heart it belonged to her father. *For Cisco's Kid. Send the money to this address.* But what that meant was anyone's guess. The note might hint at blackmail, was cryptic at best, and the two men who could explain it were both dead.

Of course, that left the matter of McKnight's suicide, and why—if her father was blackmailing him—would McKnight be apologizing for something he did to her father? She needed to know what the hell was in that suicide note, and it bothered her that Scotty, the king of the greased wheels, couldn't get it for her. A lot of other things bothered her, like the fact she was sitting here, drinking alone. And if that wasn't reason to open another beer, she didn't know what was. About two sips in, Topper ran to the door and started growling. "Were you that fuzzy-looking a half hour ago?" she said, getting up. She lost her balance, fell back onto the couch. "Damn, I'm a lightweight." She got up, peeked out the window, saw the empty stairs, the still driveway below. "There's no one there, Toppie."

Topper growled again, and this time she heard a car door slamming shut. The dog seemed to have an innate sense about what cars didn't belong in this neighborhood, and she'd had too many beers to override his good sense.

Her Glock sat on the counter next to her purse, and she walked over, slid it from its holster, then shut off the light. "Topper," she whispered. "Quiet." She returned to the door, tried to listen past her quickening pulse. The sound of someone talking, an accent she couldn't decipher, saying, "Be careful. Don't kill—" Another car door closing. Topper pressed his nose to the threshold, his growl low, vibrating. She told herself it was nothing, just a couple of guys. She tightened her grip on her Glock, looked out the peephole.

And saw the silhouette of a man walking toward the steps.

14

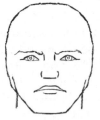

Topper's sharp bark scared the crap out of her. Her heart raced. It was a good second or two before she realized that Topper started whining to get out. And a second or two after that before the mysterious figure walking up her steps materialized into her neighbor Arturo.

She flicked on the porch light, opened the door, and Topper bounded out.

"Hey, baby!" Arturo lowered his suitcase onto the porch to greet his dog.

Sydney slid her pistol behind her, shoved it between her waistband and the small of her back, then stepped from behind the door, smiling as best she could under the circumstances. "Have a good trip?"

He looked up at her. "Yeah . . . Oh my God. You've been drinking."

"Why is it no one thinks I drink?"

"Because you don't. What's wrong?"

"Nothing. Just didn't expect you back this late."

"Change of plans. Hope the great white ghost wasn't too much trouble?"

"Never," she said, as a taxicab took off. Score one for Topper. It *was* a strange car, it didn't belong, and the accent she heard was probably the driver's. "Guess I didn't expect you in a cab."

"Suitcases are hell on a motorcycle. They're hell in a taxi when you nearly whack your hand off trying to get it out of the trunk."

"Well, dump it, come over and join me for a beer. It's yours, and I can use the company."

He dropped his suitcase inside his door, then walked in. Sydney brought him a beer from the fridge, saw he'd picked up the old photo of her father. "Your dad, right?"

"Yeah," she said, grateful he didn't seem interested in the other two papers left on the tabletop. Not that they'd mean anything to him. Hell, they didn't mean anything to her, yet.

She handed him his beer; he took it, nodded at the photo. "You never mentioned he was a D-boy."

"A *what* boy?"

"Delta Force. The dark soldiers," he added at her look of incomprehension. "Come on, Syd. You had to have known. Long hair, hockey helmets, the guy in front flashing the letter D . . ."

"Those are hockey helmets?"

"You never saw *Black Hawk Down*? God, my little brother dragged me to see that at least fifteen times. His big dream. These guys are the best of the best. They went in to do things no one else could."

Sydney laughed at the thought. "Not my dad. He enlisted for a couple years, but after, he was like a contract employee or something. He took *photos*. That's it."

He opened his beer, tapped the picture with his finger. "Your dad and these other guys are special ops. Well, except maybe the guy in uniform," he said, pointing to Gnoble's picture. "The D-boys, they didn't wear uniforms. You should find out what he did. Might be interesting. God knows my little brother would be all over it." He dropped the photo on the table, drank his beer, talked a bit about his trip to L.A., while Sydney pretended interest. Even so, her gaze kept straying to the photo, trying to determine if what Arturo said could be true. After several minutes, he glanced at his watch, took one final swig of beer, then said, "Hope you don't mind, I gotta get up for work in the morning."

"Yeah, me too," she said. "And thanks for the lasagna and cheesecake."

"Anytime." Arturo and Topper left, and Sydney sat there, staring at the photo, wondering what else about her father she didn't know.

Prescott hated black coffee, but he'd been up all night reading poll reports, trying to see where the senator needed to beef up his campaign, and the only thing that was bound to keep him awake at six in the morning was the thickest, darkest coffee that Starbucks sold. Of course, that's what they made cream for, and he dumped a ton in, replaced the top on his cup, then stepped from the store into the chilly October morning, still dark. He turned the corner, walked about a half block, when someone pushed him into a darkened doorway. His coffee went flying. He landed against an iron grid covering the windows of a closed business. Before he could move, right himself, a hand came up, shoved his head against the cold metal of the grid. He could feel it cutting into his cheek, and he couldn't breathe, couldn't move.

"You goddamned son of a bitch," came the harsh whisper in his ear. Richard Blackwell. Prescott recognized the voice.

"Let go of me."

"The fuck I will. I should kill you right here, you bastard." Blackwell pulled up on Prescott's arm. Pain shot through him, lifted him to his toes.

"If you don't let go of me, I'll have you arrested. Here. Now."

"For what?" Blackwell whipped him around, slammed him into the grating, his hand at Prescott's throat. "I'll break your windpipe so fast, you won't get the first word out."

"What do you want?"

"I want to know what the fuck you were thinking the other night. Or did you think I wouldn't find out you tried to run over the senator's favorite FBI agent with your car?"

"It just happened."

"Happened? How the fuck? You're lucky you missed. You know what sort of evidence is left when a body hits a car? Evidence that can be traced back to *your* car."

Blackwell loosened his hold slightly and Prescott sucked in air, tried to remain calm, but his heart thumped in his chest. "It was a mistake. I admit it."

"A big mistake. Which means I'm outta here."

"No!"

"And what? *You're* gonna stop me?"

"I'll double the offer."

Blackwell narrowed his gaze, as though contemplating. Prescott had hired Blackwell because he came highly rec-ommended, with a history of working black ops for the mili-tary, a clean record, and a checkered past. He was perfect for the job.

"Here's the thing, dickhead," Blackwell said. "The mo-ment I find out someone else is horning in on my mark, that person becomes a liability to me. Even if it's the person who hired me. You do *not* want to become a liability to me. Clear?" he said, tightening his hand around Prescott's throat once more.

"Abundantly."

"Good. Unfortunately for your stupidity, you've removed one course of action. Using a vehicle as a means of death. She's bound to have said something about nearly being run over. That makes it suspicious if she's killed by a car down the line. Which is why I've come up with this idea." He stepped back, pulled out a folded newspaper from his over-coat pocket, then pointed to an article.

Prescott took a deep breath, tried to look calm as he eyed the newsprint, read something about identifying a Jane Doe. "A drawing of a dead girl?"

"Not just *any* dead girl. It fits close with the case the Bu-reau picked up from San Francisco PD, the girl who's in the hospital. I'd say they're working with a serial killer who missed his mark by one. But they're not even connecting the cases publicly."

"A serial killer?"

"Yeah. We could do something with it, but it'd be complicated."

"Why can't we just do a simple hit? No muss, no fuss?"

"Because, dumbfuck. The FBI isn't likely to sit back and ignore a hit on one of their agents. Nor would they ignore a hit-and-run on one, either."

"What about a suicide?"

"FBI, remember? They suspect everything. This is the best way."

"We—I don't want her to suffer."

Blackwell eyed him, his gaze fixed with a look of disbelief. "And what? Being slammed with a car was gonna ease her pain?"

"She's a friend of the senator's, for God's sake."

Blackwell stepped closer, put his face right up to Prescott's. "This is a no-brainer. One agent stands in the way of the objective. Remove the agent, obtain the objective."

"As long as you don't forget the idiot who left a suicide note, which several people have read. We remove them, too?"

"Whatever it takes. I've got a friend at Houston PD. We were partners in the service. He's looking into the note to see if the situation is salvageable . . ."

Prescott pushed Blackwell away from him, trying to regain some control, make sure the man knew he wasn't afraid and was the one really in charge. "Tell me why you think this Jane Doe case works in our favor?"

"My sources tell me that there's absolutely no DNA found on that Hill City Jane Doe. They've got no way to tell if she's the victim of the guy who did the girl in the hospital. And top it off, the investigating detective's an idiot."

"What's your plan?"

"Your little agent's been in contact with the girl in the hospital, *and* her sketch of the Jane Doe conveniently appeared in every Bay Area paper this morning. So why not set up your agent as the next victim?"

"You think you know enough about their cases to do that?"

Blackwell smiled. "Like I said, it's a no-brainer."

* * *

Richard Blackwell watched as Prescott walked off, before heading in the opposite direction. He took out his cell phone, hit the speed dial.

"We're on," he said, to the man who answered. "With double the salary."

"Nice job. You know what to do."

Perhaps Sydney shouldn't have finished the remaining two beers in the fridge last night. That thought magnified when, head pounding, she pulled on her gray sweats for her normal morning run. She'd made it as far as the bottom of the stairs, then turned around and went back inside. Running was definitely out. Not that she'd gotten dead drunk, more that she wasn't used to drinking that much. Instead she spent the time allowing the hot shower to erase some of the night's stresses. It did little but give her time to think, which, looking back, made the run seem so much easier in comparison, headache and all.

What she couldn't figure out was how could her father be in some sort of special ops and never mention it? How could her mother never have mentioned it? And what the hell did her father do in the service if his job wasn't simply to take the damned photos and drawings he'd always said was his responsibility? She thought of Gnoble, his political aspirations, and it occurred to her that if they were doing something glorious, he, of all people, would have announced it to the world. Instead, McKnight committed suicide when he was being investigated for a high-powered political appointment, after mentioning something about her father. Something worth blackmailing for.

By the time she dressed, grabbed the envelope with the photo, then left for work, her mood was downright ugly, and she attributed it directly to stepping outside her routine. She cussed out two drivers who'd gotten in her way, and left the McDonald's empty-handed when the poor clerk couldn't figure out how to ring up a sausage sandwich without egg, something Sydney thought was a perfectly reasonable order. Somewhere in the recesses of her mind she realized that her temper was flaring at a pace that had all the earmarks of

post-traumatic stress disorder. Probably nothing to do with
the drinking or missing her run, and everything to do with re-
visiting her father's murder case and the man who had been
convicted of killing him. Not that she could forget Scotty's
bombshell and that damned photo McKnight had mailed
to her. At least that's what she told herself, when Lettie informed her that Dixon wanted her in his office for a briefing
on the Jane Doe from Hill City.

She shoved the manila envelope in her top drawer, schooled
her features, trying to appear calm, not let on that she was
having any issues unconnected to the current cases. A moment later, Michael "Doc" Schermer walked in. Tall, slim,
with white hair and dark eyes, he'd been given the nickname
because he looked more like a doctor than an FBI agent.
Rumor had it that he'd originally wanted to be an eye doctor, but somewhere along the way ended up at the FBI. And
the Bureau took full advantage of that "look," using him in
any undercover operations that involved the medical field,
including the Harrington insurance fraud case that Dixon
was so anxious for her to finish.

"Morning, Fitz," Schermer said, with a polite nod.

"Morning, Doc." She liked him for two reasons. He was
nice *and* he'd never been friends with Scotty. That not only
earned him bonus points in her book, it also meant that she
could trust him not to feed info back to Scotty—which was
a lot more than she could say about Scotty's old roommate
from the academy, Tony Carillo, who walked in a moment
later. Carillo was just a few years older than she, late thirties,
stood maybe an inch shorter than Schermer's six-three.

Carillo was *not* an easy man to ignore, and for more reasons than his warped sense of humor and quick Italian temper. He had dark eyes and olive skin, with a perpetual five
o'clock shadow, even at eight in the morning, which always
gave her the feeling that he'd just climbed out of bed—
leaving a very satisfied woman behind. She wasn't sure he
would've been amused at such a thought. Word had it that
he'd recently taken up celibacy after discovering his wife
was sleeping with another man.

That was not, however, the reason she'd done her best to

avoid Carillo ever since she came to San Francisco. It was more to do with the fact she was a by-the-book agent. If Carillo followed any rules, they were of his own making, and sometimes she wondered how it was he and Scotty, polar opposites, ever became friends in the first place.

Carillo and Schermer flanked the doorway to Dixon's office, and Schermer said, "Heard you think we have a serial killer working the area."

She handed Dixon her notes on the case. "So it appears."

"Yeah?" Carillo said, crossing his arms, eyeing her. "How'd you get it, when you weren't even here the past couple days?"

Dixon replied, "The case isn't hers. She was on a sketch down in Hill City. Found a Jane Doe with injuries similar to our kidnap victim, Tara Brown. Possible sexual assault, head wound, stab wounds, and a bite mark on her breast, which, I might add, wasn't noted by the investigator, but was found in the autopsy."

"They *missed* it?" Carillo asked. "How the hell do they miss something like that?"

"Could be an oversight," Sydney replied. "Small department. Possibly the detective wasn't advised at the autopsy." Or possibly he was an idiot, but that thought she kept to herself. She briefed Carillo and Schermer on what she'd found. "If there's nothing else," she said, after finishing, "I have another case I need to finish up."

"What?" Carillo said. "You're not going to try to get assigned?"

"I've got cases of my own to work," she replied.

"Thanks," Dixon said. She left, glad to be out of Carillo's company, and she overheard Dixon tell the two, "I agree with Fitzpatrick. Good possibility we've got a serial rapist-murderer on our hands. I want the two of you to head down to Hill City, see if they missed anything else of significance."

She thought about warning Carillo and Schermer about the detective down there. Maybe she would after she got something to eat, then dug up a contact for Houston PD to see if she couldn't get a copy of that suicide note. She took the elevator to the deli, realized she'd forgotten to get money, and managed to dig up enough change from the bottom of her purse to cover a bag of cookies. Some breakfast. She couldn't even get the damned bag open. By the time she returned to the office, cookie bag still intact, Carillo and Schermer were back at their desks, talking with a few other guys. They were laughing about something, but shut up the moment they saw her, their expressions suddenly turning far too innocent.

She had bigger things to worry about, like breakfast, and the cop-proof bag it was contained in. The guys mumbled their faux greetings as though nothing were amiss, and their laughter gained momentum after she passed by.

She ignored them, reached her cubicle, gave one last tug on the bag, and cookies went flying, one of them rolling four cubicles down, landing at Schermer's feet. "Crap!"

A burst of laughter followed, and Sydney could see them over the top of the divider. They were looking right at her, no doubt having seen the cookie debacle. Schermer leaned down, picked up the cookie, and tossed it back at her. Carillo was on the phone, trying to appear serious, and he turned his back on them and her, waving for everyone to be quiet—just as her phone rang.

On cue, they all shut up. Well, two could play this game, and Sydney picked up her phone and said in her cheeriest voice, "Special Agent Fitzpatrick."

"Are you the agent who did the drawing? The one in the newspaper?" The voice was low, not a whisper, but definitely sounding as though the caller was trying to disguise his identity.

She brushed the cookies and crumbs into a pile on her blotter, then picked a broken one, eyed the men. "Which paper?"

"The *Chronicle*."

"Yes." Surely these guys could come up with something original?

"I *like* your drawing."

"Do you have some information regarding the case?" Sydney asked in her best official voice. The guys were leaning over Schermer's desk, and Carillo was still shushing them to be quiet.

"Yes," came the voice. She looked at the cookie, couldn't believe the thought that just crossed her mind, because it was totally out of character . . . *Do it*, a voice seemed to say, and for once, she listened. Threw the cookie. And was horrified when it hit Carillo on his back. Schermer nearly died laughing. That was when she realized she couldn't hear the laughter on her phone, as the caller continued with, "I'm going to look for another one. And bite her, too. Just like the others. Just like the girl in the drawing. Maybe I'll bite *you*. I *really* like your drawing."

"*Who* is this?"

A click, and then dial tone. And the cookie came flying back at her, bounced against her shoulder and onto the floor, just as Dixon stepped out of his office. "What's going on?"

"I have no idea," Carillo said, covering the phone receiver with one hand as everyone hightailed it back to their cubicles. Schermer wasn't so lucky and tried to blend into the background.

Dixon's gaze swung past them, down the hall, at the clerical staff who apparently had left their work to watch. "You three, my office, now."

"The guys were just having a little fun. Me, I'm innocent," Carillo replied. "For once."

"*Now.*"

Carillo said into the phone, "Look, I have to go. We'll continue this conversation later."

The three of them marched in, and before Sydney could get a word in edgewise, Schermer said, "Hey, it was just a sketch, a parody." He opened a manila folder, showing a piece of paper inside. "HAVE YOU SEEN THIS SUSPECT?" was scrawled on the top just above a stick figure with a smiley face. He'd signed it: *Michael Jacob Schermer, substitute artist.*

Carillo eyed the drawing. "Pretty good likeness, don't you think?"

Sydney barely glanced at the drawing. "Please tell me *you* were the one who called my desk?"

"Not unless *you're* the one asking me for alimony."

"Did you?" Sydney asked Schermer.

"No one did."

She knew what she was hearing, but didn't want to believe it. She had to believe it. There was no other explanation. "Son of a bitch . . ."

Dixon looked at each of them in turn. "Someone want to tell me what I'm missing here, besides the fact we've mistaken our office for a high school cafeteria food fight?"

The room felt suddenly chilly, and Sydney crossed her arms as she tried to comprehend the full impact of what this meant. "The phone call," she said, trying to think of all the possibilities, one being that someone was playing a cruel, sick joke. Sydney looked at Carillo. "We haven't released info on our victims being bitten. So either someone with enough knowledge about the case just called, or the UnSub did. And if it was him . . ." Sydney thought about the words she'd heard. "He's about to kidnap another woman."

15

Sydney repeated the phone conversation as she remembered it. Dixon, Carillo, and Schermer listened, and when Sydney finished, Carillo said, "Well, now we know he's following his victims in the paper."

"Okay," Dixon said. "This case moves up on the priority list."

Carillo cleared his throat, and Schermer said, "Uh, yeah. One problem. I just got a page that I'm due in court in a half hour."

Before Sydney could decipher the subtleties of that by-play, Dixon said to her, "You're going to have to assist Carillo for the day."

"But the Harrington report—"

"Moves down on the list. You have any other cases that need immediate attention, give them to Schermer here." He nodded to the stick figure drawing. "Seems to me if he has this much free time, he needs the work. Now see if you and Carillo can't get along for the short time it takes to get this investigation under way."

Though Sydney wasn't happy about being paired with Mr. Pipeline-to-Her-Ex Carillo, in the grand scheme of things, she had much bigger issues, and she returned to her desk, expecting that Carillo might follow, at least to get her notes on the case, go over what she'd found at Hill City and in her interview with Tara Brown. Typical Carillo, he didn't follow, left her sitting there twiddling her thumbs while God only knew what the hell he was doing.

First thing, she thought as she got up to look for him, was that they needed to set some ground rules, number one being that Scotty needed to be left out of the loop.

Carillo wasn't at his desk, and after wandering the halls, she found him in a different office on the phone. Judging from the conversation, his wife was on the other end. "No," he said. "I am *not* selling the condo. You're living in a goddamned mansion, with a guy who makes ten times what I make. You think you could see fit to allow me a goddamned place to live?" He listened to whatever it was she had to say, then finished with "Whoever wrote the line 'for better or worse' sure as hell never had to live with the worse." He slammed the phone in the cradle, and seemed to stare at it for several seconds, then looked up, saw Sydney, and in a surprisingly calm voice said, "Give me a minute and I'll meet you at your desk."

By the time he arrived, he was all business, and she picked up her case file and handed it to him. "This is everything I have on the Jane Doe." Then she handed him a manila folder, which he opened. "That's the suspect sketch from our victim the other night, the woman we think may have been abducted and raped by the same suspect."

He sat in a chair, dropped the binder on his lap, then opened the folder with the drawing. He took a good look, handed it back to her, then opened the case file. "And you think these two are related because of the bite marks?" he asked. "Because the way I see it, your Jane Doe has way, way more wounds."

"But when you look closer, there are some similarities besides the bite marks. Body dumped near an isolated area at a park and in water for one."

"Not a lot to go on."

"You're right. Until Dr. Armand compares the bite wounds, and either confirms or denies—"

"Or states it's inconclusive."

"Or states it's inconclusive," she agreed, "we won't know. But either way, you have two crimes that are clearly savage and in need of solving. One's ours, the other Hill City's. And I can tell you they won't be pleased by your presence."

He flipped through the report, perused each page, not commenting. After several minutes of silence, part of which she was sure was meant to let her know that he was the one running the show, he said, without looking up from the reports, "Give me about ten minutes to make another set of copies. I'd like to get down there as soon as possible." And with that, he stood, took the reports.

"Hey, Carillo." He stopped, eyed her. "How is it I suddenly got assigned to this?"

"Don't know what you're talking about."

"Schermer doesn't have a subpoena for court, does he?"

"He's, uh, got some personal business he needs to take care of. Off the radar, if you know what I mean."

"No, I don't. Care to explain?"

"Let's just say I figured you'd be chomping at the bit for a case like this."

She patted her hand on the stack of manila folders piled atop her desk. "Got enough of my own."

"A few days ago, you'd have been all over it, wanting to work it."

"And you'd have been convincing Dixon why you needed Doc Schermer or one of the other guys to work with you, because you don't like me. What happened?"

"Guess I'm slipping. Meet me at the car in about ten."

Scotty, she thought. That son of a bitch got Carillo to get her assigned to this damned case to keep her busy and away from McKnight's suicide. That was the only explanation. Hell with that, she thought, pulling out her directory of FBI office numbers, searching for the Houston, Texas, field office. She punched in the number, identified herself, and asked to speak to Rick Reynolds, the agent Scotty had said he'd contacted about the note.

A long stretch of silence greeted her when she identified herself to Reynolds. Finally he said, "Look, I can't talk right now. Give me your number. I'll get back to you in about ten-twenty minutes."

She'd be stuck in the car with Mr. Pipeline himself if she waited that long. "Any way we can make it sooner?"

"Take it or leave it."

She gave him her cell phone. Ten minutes later, she and Carillo were en route to Hill City.

Carillo hated owing favors. And Scotty's last-minute request, making sure Fitzpatrick somehow got assigned to this case with no explanation other than "you owe me one" was a prime example of why. Wasn't that he didn't like Fitzpatrick, he told himself as he signaled for a lane change on the southbound 101 heading toward Hill City. She was as good an agent as any working in the office at the moment, just not the type he liked to work with. Guys like Schermer, though. Now there was a partner. They knew each other's ins and outs. And they knew when to look the other way.

Which was something he couldn't say about Scotty. His obsession with Fitzpatrick was starting to wear thin. The guy really needed to get a life. Or a new girl. None of which explained why Scotty needed her assigned to this case, because God only knew the guy had no trouble picking up the phone to find out what the hell she was working on at any given day and time. Bad enough Carillo had to deal with his own wife and her daily diatribes about alimony, lawyers, and anything else she could torment him with.

They were nearly to the Hill City turnoff when Fitzpatrick's cell phone rang. She answered with a brisk "Fitzpatrick," listened for a moment, then, "What do you mean there is no note? I was specifically told one existed, that it was booked into evidence . . . That's bullshit, and you know it." She flipped the phone closed, looked out the side window, her body rigid. "Idiots."

"Something wrong?"

"I don't want to talk about it."

And sure as shit, she didn't say one word for the rest of the trip. Just the way he liked it. Unfortunately he had to break the silence when they got to Hill City, because one thing he hated was surprises, and he wanted to know what the hell to expect. When she informed him, he figured she was exaggerating a bit by saying Detective Rodale hadn't made much progress on the case because the victim was a woman, Rodale didn't like women, and especially didn't like FBI women. As they walked into the station, what went through his mind was that she was laying it on a little thick.

"Un-fucking-believable," Carillo said, when they walked out fifteen minutes later, undeveloped photos in hand.

"Didn't believe me, did you?"

"Someone needs to take that idiot's big fat rodeo belt buckle and shove it down his throat."

"You volunteering?"

"Wouldn't waste my time." He handed her the film, then unlocked the car. "Two weeks. He's been sitting on this for two fucking weeks, and never once pulled it out to develop it."

They got in the car, drove to the downtown area, looking for a one-hour photo developer, and found one on the main strip, El Camino Real.

Back in their vehicle, Fitzpatrick thumbed through the pictures while he drove to the crime scene. The park was a grassy area with a few oak trees and a covered picnic area adjacent to a marsh that gave way to the bay. A steady wind swept off the gray choppy water, bending the reeds in the marsh. Nice place for a summer barbecue beneath the covered picnic area, but in the winter probably unused by any but school kids looking for a quiet place, out of view of the cops, maybe drink a few beers in their cars. Too damned cold, otherwise, with the constant wind.

Of course the cold was to their advantage. It kept the people out, which meant there might be something left at the crime scene. Then again, the rain that came down the other night undoubtedly washed out any tire tracks and other trace evidence that might have remained, assuming the PD didn't run over everything in their haste to get to the body.

Carillo parked at the far end of the lot, away from where the parking spaces butted up against the picnic area. They'd walk the lot first, a grid pattern, hoping to find something.

First, though, they sat in the car, viewing the photos, trying to determine where the body was found—about ten feet into the marsh past where the grass ended. There was a shot taken from the parking lot, showing a female uniform standing out in the reeds, pointing down to the body.

"She's the officer who found the victim," Fitzpatrick told him as she handed that photo over. "Said that Detective Rodale wasn't going for a forensic artist, because the victim was just a hooker. She went around his back to get me to do the drawing."

He held up the photograph so that he could view it against the backdrop of the bay. "Looks like we need to be about thirty yards past the covered picnic area," he said, then tucked the photo in his pocket. "Guess we're going to get muddy."

"*You're* going to get muddy," she said, handing him the next photo. "*I* brought waders in my gear bag."

"Good partner would've warned me there was mud."

"Ah, but we're not partners. You don't even like me."

"Got a lot on my mind. Divorce, heavy caseload." He stared out the window, tried to shrug it off like it was no big deal.

She handed him the next photo, asking, "Why?"

"Why what?"

"Why don't you like me?"

He was going to kill Scotty for this. "Look, it's nothing personal. There's a lot of people in the office I don't like to work with."

A few seconds of silence, and he thought, *Thank God that's over.* Then, "But *specifically* why don't you like to work with me?"

"Jesus, Fitzpatrick. You turning this into one of those Kumbaya things?"

She shoved a photo at him, clearly perturbed. "I just want to know. I've been here six months, and no one stands around my desk and jokes."

He studied her to see if she was really serious. Apparently she was. "Okay, I'll bite. You're like the fucking Eagle Scout of FBI agents. Pollyanna with a gun, a rule book, and no sense of humor."

"I have a sense of humor."

He noted she didn't dispute the other two claims, and wondered if maybe he'd been a bit too hard on her, when she seemed to be staring at the next photo a little too long. And just when he was about to apologize, tell her it wasn't all that bad, she started humming the tune to "Kumbaya, My Lord." He laughed. "Touché, Pollyanna. E for effort and T for truce?"

She looked over at him, said nothing for a second or two, seemed to consider it, then, "Fine. Truce."

"Just don't expect perfection right away."

"*No* worries there," she said, handing him the last photo, a close-up of the victim lying in the marsh, her filmy pale eyes staring up at nothing. She was wearing a once-white shirt, now stained with blood, mud, and dirt.

They got out, and Carillo popped open the trunk, while Fitzpatrick scraped her hair back into a ponytail, fighting against the salt-tinged wind. They each had a bag of gear in the trunk, and he handed hers out to her.

She put on her waders, then stood there for a moment, looked out over the marsh toward the area where the body had been found. If anything, she seemed preoccupied, more than she should have been, even after their strange talk, and he wondered if that phone call she'd received was part of it. He moved beside her, stared toward the water, heard nothing but the wind drumming in his ears. "Let's get started," he said.

They traversed the parking lot, looking for anything that might have been missed, before making a sweep of the grass, seeing several muddy-water-filled scars left in the turf, indistinguishable for any purposes of tire identification. The wet grass quickly soaked through his shoe leather as he walked the distance to the covered picnic area. It was there that he looked over and noticed some muddy tire tracks on the cement, as though a vehicle had pulled up beneath the shelter.

His gaze followed the smeared, now dried mud, wondering if it was from a police vehicle, perhaps a CSI pulling in to get out of the rain, he thought, noticing the tracks went right up to a table.

Fitzpatrick stopped at the edge of the cement, bent down to get a closer look, perhaps to see if there was a distinguishable pattern that could be photographed. He followed the tracks to the table, scarred with graffiti. Something dark appeared to have been spilled across the surface of the table, and had seeped into several deep and seemingly fresh gouges in the wood before it had dried.

His stomach turned as he realized what he was looking at.

"Fitz."

She looked up from the edge of the cement area. Saw what he saw.

This was where their victim, their Jane Doe, had probably spent her last moment alive.

16

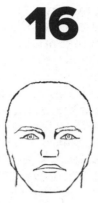

Undoubtedly, Sydney thought, as she stood there surveying the picnic area, Mr. Big Belt Buckle had failed to locate this as part of his crime scene.

Carillo called Dixon to let him know what they found, and to request the Evidence Response Team to come process the scene. "And tell the ERT to bring a panel truck, something large enough to haul off an entire picnic table. Looks like the asshole stabbed her so hard, the knife went right through to the wood."

He disconnected. Eventually they moved into the car to get out of the constant wind, and Sydney knew she needed to act like her head was in the game, and not miles and years away on her father's case. She took the time to write up her notes on the scene, draw a sketch of the picnic area and what they'd found and where. It wasn't until they were driving back to the city that Carillo looked over at her, asked, "You okay?"

"Yeah. You know, thinking about the case. What we found out there."

He shook his head, no doubt recalling the grisly scene at the picnic table.

Back at their office, they booked their evidence, wrote up their reports for Dixon. Sydney intended on staying to finish the overdue Harrington case. Carillo was giving his report one last read-through before printing it off, when his phone rang. "Hey, Scotty . . . Yeah, working late. Picked up a Jane Doe from Hill City."

She listened with one ear as he told Scotty about the case and what they'd found at the crime scene. In the empty office, with Carillo's desk only four cubicles down from hers, she couldn't help but hear his side of the conversation. What she couldn't hear was Scotty's side of things, and for a while there, it seemed Scotty was doing all the talking, as Carillo merely said, "That right?" or "No kidding." She did not hear her name once, she thought, and for that she was grateful. A few minutes later, Carillo was walking past her desk to turn in his reports. "I'm going to grab a bite to eat across the street. You want anything?"

"I'll get something later," she said. "See you in the morning."

"We should hit Golden Gate Park pretty early to go over the Tara Brown crime scene, see if we can't dig up any more evidence." He rapped his knuckles on her desk. "By the way, thanks for your help today. You did good." He continued on to Dixon's office, turned in his reports, then retraced his steps, stopping long enough to pick up his overcoat, his keys. He stood there a moment, eyeing her. "You've been pretty quiet. Even for you. Something up? Something you want to talk about?"

She hesitated, not used to Carillo showing empathy. Maybe she should have tried to talk to him weeks ago when she first realized he didn't like working cases with her. "Just the work. Wondering how I'm going to get it all done."

He held her gaze a moment, nodded. "Know that feeling. See you around."

Maybe it was the quiet of the office, or even the thought that she didn't want to go home just yet, be alone. Just as he reached the door, she called out, "Carillo?"

He stopped, looked at her.

She thought of every reason why she shouldn't say a thing,

the fact he was friends with Scotty being foremost in her mind. "I think I'll go get that sandwich with you, after all."

"So there is something you want to talk about?"

"Yes—no. I mean, I want to, I'm just not sure I can." She sounded like an idiot, she knew that. But when it came to her father and his murder, she was an emotional mess. "It's . . . sort of personal."

"Is this another one of those things where I'm gonna have to be nice and pretend I'm interested and all that?"

"You need alcohol for that?"

"Copious amounts."

"I'll buy."

17

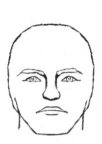

Sydney grabbed the manila envelope from her top
desk drawer, and she and Carillo walked to the Chili's across
the street, took a corner table by the kitchen, because they
could both sit with their backs to the wall, and the waitress
who worked that section knew Carillo. Without asking, she
brought them a pitcher of beer and two glasses, and said the
appetizer was en route.

"So what's on your mind?" Carillo asked as he poured the
beer and handed one to her.

"No small talk first?"

"Guess that depends on how much of it you want me to
remember," he said, lifting up his glass. "So feel free to pro-
ceed at will."

"Ground rules, first. This stays between us, without being
pipelined to Scotty."

"Scout's honor."

"My father's murder," she said, figuring it best to just
come out with it.

"He was killed in a robbery, right?"

"So it was reported. I went to San Quentin and spoke with
the man who allegedly killed him. He's due to be executed

within a week, I don't think he did it, and there's this stuff
about my father's military background that isn't making
sense, and only came to light after the suicide of a nominee
for the administrator for the Office of Federal Procurement
Policy."

"Okay . . . Nothing complicated there. But just to keep this
simple, remember, I'm drinking here, so start with your old
man's murder."

She gave him a rundown on her father's case as she recalled it, ending with Wheeler's arrest, and then her recent
interview of him. She stared down into her beer glass, shaking her head, again feeling as though what Wheeler had told
her sounded so inadequate, inconsequential. "I can't help
asking myself what if he didn't do it?"

"Do what? The murder? Are you nuts?"

"No," she said, taking a sip of her beer. "I am not nuts.
And I am definitely having doubts."

"I'll admit I'm not completely familiar with the case, other than what Scotty told me," he said, refilling his glass. "But
even so, you can't be serious that a ten-minute conversation
with the convicted killer could change your mind."

"Just added a new perspective. Especially in light of everything else that's come about recently."

"Perspective?" He held the pitcher over her glass, but
she waved him off. "Then clue me in, because frankly I'm
lost."

"The prosecution said he'd lied about being friends with
my father, that he'd made it all up to cover for the robbery.
That this church who gave Wheeler's name to my father never existed. They based their case on that. But what he said in
there, he could only have known if my father *had* befriended
him. They were private things."

"Like what?"

"Like the canister under the counter." And she told him
about what she'd done as a kid, taking the money to play
video games.

"You're feeling guilty, is all. You took some money,
blamed yourself, and now you're trying to justify that guilt
so that you don't have to—"

"Trust me. When it comes to psychoanalyzing something, I've got the market cornered. It's more than that. He knew about the twenty under the till, and why my father kept one there after he closed out each night."

"Not enough."

"And my father told him to pay him back on Tuesday. That meant it was a gift."

"Okay. That one I definitely don't get."

"Popeye?" she said. "Wimpy?"

"Your point?"

"Wimpy was my father's favorite character, always begging for money, offering to gladly pay on Tuesday for a hamburger today? If my father told someone they could pay him back on Tuesday, it meant he didn't expect the money back."

"Hate to tell you this, but you're not giving me anything earthshaking."

"He only told that to people he cared about. They didn't even have to know what it meant. But we knew. My mother and I."

"News flash. Empathy with cartoon characters does not make for good court cases."

"It tells me there's more to this than meets the eye."

Carillo said nothing for quite some time, just sat there, drinking his beer. Finally, "I know I'm going to regret this . . . Let me look at the case."

That was the last thing she expected. "You're going to help me?"

"No. I'm going to look at the case. I want to see if he fits the profile. Give it to me when we go back."

Better than nothing, she figured. "And if he doesn't fit the profile?"

"It'd be interesting to find out why, because it doesn't make sense. Santa Arleta PD is a good department. Too small to facilitate a cover-up of that magnitude. The suspect has the burns on his hands, from the fire being set to cover for the crime. Beyond that, I'd have to ask, who had motive to kill your father? He owned a pizza parlor, for God's sake."

"Maybe there was something else going on there. His old manager had ties to organized crime."

"Like what? Money laundering?"

"Or something. And, like I said, I think he lied about his military background. This only came to light after Will McKnight's suicide the other day."

"Who is Will McKnight?"

"He was a friend of my father's and Senator Gnoble's. They were all in the army together."

He lowered his beer to the table. "What does this have to do with Gnoble?"

"I'm not sure, unless Gnoble was somehow involved in getting McKnight's name in front of the president for consideration as the U.S. procurement czar."

"Wouldn't that sort of make the big news? Some guy about to be appointed to oversee the entire federal government's purchasing budget offs himself and it doesn't even make the *Chronicle* headlines, much less every network on TV?"

"His nomination wasn't made public yet. They wanted to do the background first to avoid delays in the appointment."

"So either the government is finally becoming efficient, or someone knew he might not pass muster? I'm assuming the Bureau did the background?"

"Special Agent Hatcher."

"He's sure it's suicide?"

"As far as I know. More importantly, McKnight left a suicide note, which I want to see, if only for the timing of it all."

"You think it's going to tell you something?"

"I won't know until I see it, which is probably why Scotty made sure I was assigned to the Jane Doe case."

Carillo, mid-sip, nearly spit his beer from his mouth. "What makes you think Scotty was involved?"

"You tell me he wasn't, and I'll believe it."

He held her gaze, took a breath. "All right, he did ask. But knowing Scotty it's got everything to do with scoring points with you later, if you do good on the case, get assigned to violent crimes, then hear who got you assigned. Grateful you hops in bed with helpful him, isn't that how it works? I mean, why wouldn't he want you to figure out what's going on with your father's case?"

"Some misguided sense of shielding me from the hurt and painful memories of it all? At least I'm hoping that's what it is, because this was delivered in the mail, sent anonymously." She held up the envelope, then slid out the contents, handed them to Carillo.

"And what does any of this have to do with Scotty?"

"It was something he didn't want me to see. Why else would he show up in town the day before it arrives, then appear at my house and pluck it out of the mail, like maybe he was expecting to find it."

"And was he?"

"He said McKnight mentioned mailing it just before he died. Hearsay via Hatcher's interview of him over the phone. Regardless, McKnight kept apologizing for something he did to my father in the army. So if that's why he sent the photo, it's not making sense to me. Not only that, but McKnight left a suicide note that no one can seem to get me a copy of. I think they found something in that note that sent them scrambling, and I want to see it."

Carillo stared at the photograph a good long time, asked her who she could identify. She pointed out her father, Gnoble, and McKnight, and he asked, "Special ops?"

"That's what my neighbor said when he saw the picture. I was always under the belief my father was a contract civilian. A photographer."

"That's a standard cover, saying they do something innocuous for the government. It'd be nice to know who these other two are. Maybe that'll tell you something. Scotty didn't say anything about this?"

"Other than he thought it pointed to my father being involved in some blackmail scheme against McKnight, right before he tried to take it from me? No."

"You want me to ask him about it?"

"If he went to this much trouble to keep me from looking into it, I don't want him to know I think there's more to it. He has too many connections, and I can picture him getting me transferred to some file room back at HQ just so he can keep tabs on me."

"You saying you want me to lie to the guy? I'm not sure you're ready for a big step like that, Pollyanna. That'd be going from black and white to downright murky," he said, as the waitress arrived with a heaping plate of nachos, covered with sour cream, guacamole, chicken, and cheese. She gave them each a small plate, set out a fresh bowl of salsa, and took away the old. Carillo refilled his beer glass, eyed the foam, watched it settle, dissipate, before pinning his gaze on her. "You want this, you're going to need to take that rule book of yours and stash it. You know how many cases wouldn't get solved if everything was done by the book?"

"You're not suggesting anything illegal, are you?"

Carillo gave a heavy sigh, the sort that told her he wished he hadn't opened his mouth at all. "First thing, Pollyanna, there are rules. And then there are *rules*. Bend a little, break a little. You do what needs to be done without killing the case. The question is, how bad do you want this?"

She hesitated. But not for long. "So what you're saying is that they're sort of like principles or guidelines?"

"Exactly."

"How is that going to get me to Houston PD to get a copy of McKnight's alleged suicide note when it's not even one of my cases?"

"It is *now*. Scotty's got to be all hot and heavy over it for some reason, which means some crime going on somewhere. What you're doing is following a hunch. Taking the initiative. So, first thing I'd do, when we get back to the office, you make copies of the photo and the letter McKnight sent you, tuck them away, then call Scotty and tell him you thought better of it, now that you've had time to calm down. You give them back to him. Next up, you give me your father's murder investigation, so I can read up on that tonight, figure out where it all ties in. Lastly, we look for a case that'll get you to Houston."

"I'm not good at this whole lying thing. I don't think I can take some case, try to pretend it's related to something I'm working on."

"Proficiency comes with experience," he said, lifting his glass in a toast. "And my experience tells me you might want to thank Scotty for getting you assigned to the Jane Doe case after all."

"Why is that?"

"There's a lot of land in Texas. There's gotta be a crime somewhere near there with an MO we can fit into the parameters of our Jane Doe case. And once we find one, someone's gotta fly out, check into it. Wouldn't be right if we didn't investigate every lead."

"And who better than me?"

"You catch on quick, Pollyanna."

18

"Webster, Texas?" Dixon's gaze swung from Sydney to Carillo, then back. "You think our UnSub might have committed a murder *there*?"

"I think we need to rule it out," Sydney said, before Carillo could react on her last-second switch. That was not the case they'd agreed on, and Carillo was no doubt wondering what the hell had happened to it. "The victim was a hooker, last seen in a bar before she was found stabbed to death."

Dixon eyed the stats on the report that the agency in Webster had faxed to her that morning. "We're not even talking the same MO. She was burned in a trailer fire."

"But she *was* stabbed," Carillo pointed out.

"Find something closer to home and our MO." He held up the report, his expression dubious, and Sydney realized if she didn't think of something fast, he was not going to approve her flight.

"The smoke," she said, and both Dixon and Carillo looked at her, waited. "When I was doing the drawing at the hospital, Tara Brown said something about our UnSub smelling like smoke from a fire."

"Yeah . . ." Carillo nodded, like he'd known this all along.

"So of course we were looking for similars that might contain that element, the, uh, smoke. Timing's good. Just a few days before Tara was kidnapped from Reno. Like maybe he committed the one, hightailed it out of state wearing the same clothes, stops off in Reno, grabs Tara, and he's off again. We're thinking maybe that's what he does. Drives from state to state. At least based on our short history we have of him. Figured Fitz could fly there, check it out."

"Have we gotten anything back from profiling yet?"

"The report should be coming in today. But Fitz ran the case by Doc Schermer, since he did a short stint in profiling. He says it looks good."

"Seems a little far out there."

"Unless," Sydney said, "you take into consideration that there's lots of places to stop between there and Reno. And we've got a couple other rape-murders that somewhat fit the MO on a direct route from there to here." She dropped several reports on Dixon's desk as well. Reports that had little or no connection other than they were unsolved.

Dixon held her gaze, as though he suspected something, but couldn't come up with whatever that might be. He gave a pointed glance at his retirement calendar on the wall, signed the order, and laid it across the reports she had offered up as proof. "Make it a quick trip," he said, without looking at either of them.

Carillo grabbed the reports and they left. Once out of hearing, he said, "Webster? Trailer fire? You didn't tell me you were using *that* report."

"They were a little short of dead hookers in the time frame we needed."

"What happened to the one we decided on last night?"

She flipped open the manila folder they'd carried the other reports in. "I swear I didn't catch it until we were walking into his office." She pointed to the name of the victim, Dana Edwards, then the box next to it, stating the sex of the victim, where a big letter M was written.

"Dana's a male?"

"Apparently he was into cross-dressing, which is probably

what got him stabbed in the first place. My guess is whoever did the data entry made the same mistake, which is why we didn't see it when we pulled it up on the computer."

They stopped at Lettie's desk, and she looked up from her computer screen, her fingers poised over the keyboard. "Well?"

"He approved it," Sydney said.

Lettie smiled, hit a key, and a few seconds later, her printer spit out a copy, which she handed over. "Your only option going in is the redeye tonight, arriving in Houston at 6:06 A.M., but that'll give you several more hours tomorrow to investigate . . . well, whatever it is you're investigating. Your return flight is set for 3:30 P.M., arriving back here at 5:58 P.M. tomorrow night. Nonstop, so it'll give you a little over four hours to catch a nap."

"You're a jewel."

"I know. Remember it on your trip back. I like dark chocolate. In the meantime, ERT's setting up at Golden Gate. They're about to start dragging Stow Lake, for evidence in your Tara Brown case, and they want to know what your arrival is."

Carillo glanced at his watch. "We're on our way."

Forty-five minutes later, Carillo and Sydney were standing in Golden Gate Park, at Stow Lake, the location where Tara Brown had been dumped and left for dead. The actual park was vast, more than a thousand acres. Stow Lake itself was a body of water that surrounded a small island called Strawberry Hill, accessed by a bridge for day hikes on trails that meandered through the trees and foliage. From the moment Tara was found, there had been road blockades to the entrances of Stow Lake Drive, the street that circled the water. They intended to keep this area of the park closed off to the public until the Evidence Response Team gave the thumbs-up. How long that might be was anyone's guess. During the day the lake was a popular boating, fishing, and picnic area near the De Young Museum and the Japanese Tea Garden. During the night, with the visitors gone, it was entirely possible to dump a body at the water's edge and not be seen.

Their hope was to find a piece of evidence that had somehow been overlooked, and Sydney and Carillo intended to expand the area being searched for just that purpose.

The main crime scene was located on the west side of Stow Lake, but Carillo and Sydney walked over the bridge to Strawberry Hill. Sydney took one half of the small island, while Carillo took the other.

After about an hour, finding nothing, they took a short break, returned to the parking lot, leaning against the car, eyeing the lake. Devoid of the usual day crowd, it was peaceful and postcard-perfect with the stone bridge reflecting in the calm water, turtles climbing onto rocks, even an egret standing among the graceful reeds. Nothing here gave testimony that a horrific crime had touched Stow Lake's tranquil shores, until one caught sight of the crime scene tape and the ERT crew setting up shop in the small parking lot so they could drag the lake.

Carillo was drinking from a bottle of water he'd just opened. Sydney was sipping from a travel mug filled with now lukewarm coffee, thinking about her upcoming trip to Houston, and what could possibly be in that suicide note, when it struck her. "I can't go."

"What'dya mean you can't go?"

"In five days, they're executing Johnnie Wheeler, and what am I doing? Running off on what could be a wild-goose chase, because I don't like it that my father has been accused of being involved in some . . . whatever the hell Scotty says he's involved in. What if this suicide note is nothing? What if it makes absolutely no difference to my father's reputation?"

"Then it makes no difference. You tried. And when you think about it, you sure as hell don't know that looking into Johnnie Wheeler's case will make a difference. Seems to me it's a crapshoot either way. You just gotta pick which one means the most to you."

"But it makes a difference to the guy sitting on death row. He's only got five days until they execute him, and I might be his last hope. I need to deal with that first."

"He also might be guilty. And you might not get another opportunity to get to Houston this easily."

"But Johnnie Wheeler won't get another opportunity at life."

"Tell you what." Carillo twisted the cap back on his water bottle, then tossed it into his car. "While you go to Houston, I'll start the digging on Wheeler's case. I read some of it after you gave it to me last night. I'll finish it up tonight, see if I can't locate some of the witnesses and enlist Schermer to help. He's a whiz on the computers, digging up old data. Who knows? Maybe he'll find something the investigators missed the first time around."

She hesitated.

"Think of it this way," Carillo said as they walked the circumference of Stow Lake. "With Doc Schermer and me both working on it, that's two investigators, which is better than one. *And* we've both got a helluva lot more experience in violent crimes than you. So unless you can come up with something better than that, I'd say you'd be turning down a golden opportunity to find out what's in that suicide note."

And that was what she wanted, wasn't it? But before she had a chance to think about it, she noticed some tire track depressions where the grass had been torn up, the ground showing through, still muddy from the previous rains. She took a closer look. "What are the chances this is from our suspect vehicle? It would fit this guy's MO, driving close to a body of water to dump his victim."

From the sidewalk, Carillo bent down, examined the track left in the grass. "Sort of far from where the body was dumped, when you think about it."

She glanced over at the curb, saw a smear of black from where tires had obviously run up and over the pavement and onto the grass. "Unless he was looking for a good spot? Someplace not likely to be seen from the main road? Pulled up here, but changed his mind for some reason. Too many benches, too many rocks?"

"Possible," Carillo said. "But why pick another spot and not this? Just as close to the water here. Maybe even closer. And there's a perfectly serviceable bench he could use to lay out his victim. Not quite a picnic table, but a close second."

"Maybe just a bit too visible from the street? A car drives past, he sees the headlights . . ."

The two stood there, looking around, trying to piece together what significance, if any, the tire tracks had. They were located on the narrow strip of grass between the street and the path that circled the water. There was a driveway, probably to allow lawn equipment up to care for the grass. At first glance it might seem a logical spot to drive up, get closer to the water, but the way was blocked by the row of green benches where people could sit and view the lake and the pagoda. Then again, as Carillo mentioned, maybe the benches so close to the water were what drew him there to begin with.

As Carillo placed a marker to direct the ERT there for photos and trace evidence collection, and with luck a cast of the tire marks, Sydney pulled out her cell phone to call Dixon. She wanted to know how likely it was that their Un-Sub had pulled onto the grass here. "Need a favor," Sydney said, when Dixon answered the phone.

"As long as it doesn't cost me manpower."

"Not if you go yourself. I need someone at the hospital to ask Tara a couple things."

"Such as?"

"We're hoping she might remember something about the terrain she was driven through. Bumps, noises, that sort of thing. We're trying to recreate his route through the park." And then Sydney told him about the tire track gouges in the lawn.

"I'll check and get back to you."

Carillo nodded his approval as Sydney hit end and clipped the cell phone on her belt. "Not bad, Fitzpatrick. Didn't know you had it in you to be proactive."

"Just when I start thinking you're a nice guy. You must have had a deprived childhood."

"Think how boring I'd be if I hadn't."

They spent the next hour watching ERT dredge the lake around the area where Tara was found, because according to SFPD, Tara thought he threw something heavy in the water just before he dumped her, something that made a loud splash. She didn't think it came from the back of the vehicle, nor did she have an idea of what it might have been. She didn't dare open her eyes to see, not wanting him to know she was still alive. And so Sydney and Carillo stood there, watching, wondering what they might recover. So far they'd pulled up a child's sneaker, a few empty beer bottles, a crushed metal trash can painted the same green as the benches, a woman's purse, a bicycle that looked as though it had been run over, and an ice chest filled with rocks, no doubt to make it sink. No weapons, nothing that stood out.

The ice chest was what the techs were concentrating on, thinking that the suspect might have tossed that in, purposefully sinking it, because he'd used it in his crimes. They were in the process of photographing it when Dixon called.

"I'm at the hospital now. The only thing she remembers about the drive that night was the guy started swearing when he hit something."

"Like a curb?" Sydney thought of the black mark near the mud-filled tire tracks.

"Like a car."

"A car?"

"Or something solid was what she told me."

"When?"

"Just before he dumped her at the park. Sort of woke her up, the loud noise at the back end of the vehicle."

"You mean he hit a car *in* the park?"

"Yeah. Backed into it, then took off, swearing, panicked from the way he was driving. She said it was only a couple minutes after that he threw something in the water, came back, dumped her in the water, then fled. Prior to that, he'd been very meticulous, took his time, like it was planned, laid out. That's all I got, though. She'll have the nurse call if she remembers anything else."

"Thanks," Sydney said, then related the info to Carillo.

"Damn," Carillo said, looking around the park with renewed interest. "What the hell did he back into?"

"Parked car? Telephone pole? Whatever it was, it was in a couple minute drive from the dump site."

"We should check everything from about a two-minute to four-minute radius."

She looked around the park, beginning to wonder if there might be a different explanation. "What if you struck something while you were backing up, hit the gas a bit too hard? Drive around for a minute, maybe two until you were sure no one heard? The street makes a circle."

Carillo eyed the tire tracks. "Panic that might be increased from hearing tires ripping up grass and wet soil? Nothing like getting stuck in the park with a body in the back."

"Exactly," Sydney said. "But what would he have hit?"

And that was when they both turned and looked out at the water where they were still dredging the lake, and then on shore where ERT had deposited all the detritus and junk they'd found on the bottom.

"The trash can?" Sydney said. "That could sound like a car if you hit it."

"Sure as hell make a splash if you got pissed and tossed it in the water. If you're right, lunch is on me."

"Lunch. You're on."

They walked toward the garbage can, which was resting on its side, dent down, and Sydney signaled for someone from ERT to come over.

"Any way you can tell if this thing's been involved in a recent vehicle collision?" Sydney asked.

The agent, Maggie Winters, pulled some latex gloves from her pocket. "Well, something definitely smashed it," she said, putting the gloves on, then righting the can so that she could walk around it. It wasn't but a few seconds later that she said, "Not sure that it was a vehicle collision, but it definitely made contact with something." She pointed, and they had to move closer. "See this? Fresh gouges in the green paint, where it scraped against whatever hit it. Metal's clean right there. Shiny. No oxidation."

"Could that have been made by the dredging equipment?" Sydney asked.

"No. Whatever hit it, hit it pretty hard. Hard enough to rip the metal." She stopped, looked around, spied another green trash can, and pointed. "That one's held to the post by a chain. Makes sense," she said, returning her attention to their trash can. "It looks like it was jammed between something vertical, like a post. The chain probably held it in place, which no doubt caused more damage than if it had just been loose." She circled the trash can, stopping on the other side. "And whatever hit it on this side was also narrow, which means if it was a vehicle collision, the vehicle hit it at an angle, not straight on. See this here? Little bit of white paint transfer. What color was the UnSub's vehicle?"

"We don't have a color from the witness. She didn't see it."

"It'd be nice if this was it," Carillo said to Maggie, eyeing the paint transfer. "We can use a break."

"If this *is* it," Maggie said, "your color is probably white. Going on the theory this is from a vehicle collision, then most of the damage occurred from whatever was *behind* the trash can when the vehicle hit it. Had to have been something solid, not giving, otherwise we wouldn't see damage on both sides. And if someone was driving fast enough to do some damage to this, tear it from the chain and grommet, that means there was probably damage to the car."

"If he was backing in?"

"If I'm correct and he hit it at an angle, look for pieces of taillight or brake light. If he was pulling in, broken headlight or signal lamp. Those are usually what'll give before the metal does. And if you find out where this trash can was located, you might find some green paint transfer on whatever was positioned next to the can. You also might find some green paint transfer on the vehicle."

"Do me a favor, Maggie," Carillo said. "Assume our UnSub did hit it and take all the necessary precautions."

"Will do."

They thanked Maggie and walked back to the gouged-up grass.

Carillo kicked at another trash can nearby. "Maybe we could get the guy who empties the things every day. See where one might be missing."

"Or," Sydney said, eyeing the tracks, and noting they came in at an angle from the sidewalk to the benches just as Maggie had conjectured, "we assume the collision was where the tire marks ended and start our search there."

"Don't try to work this into more than one free lunch."

"Not sure if I can handle more than one meal with you," she replied, moving forward, stopping where the tracks ended, right at the backside of one of the benches. "Fresh scratch marks on the back of the bench frame . . . And if that isn't a dead giveaway, then maybe the chain hanging from this grommet is?"

"Unfortunately it's green, just like the garbage can."

"But taillights aren't," she said, spying a piece of broken red plastic at the base of the bench, something she'd missed on the first go-around.

"One thing about our evidence collection team. They know their stuff."

Maggie definitely knew her stuff, Sydney thought, as she dropped to her knees and started digging. Sometimes brake lights had part numbers on them, numbers that could be traced back to specific car models, something to help narrow down their search, especially if he decided to fix his van and purchase the part at a car repair shop that kept records of customers.

Carillo merely stood there, watching.

"You could always get down here and help."

"When you're doing so good?" He leaned against the bench, enjoying himself a bit too much at her expense, especially when her cell phone rang. "You might want to answer that," he said, crossing his arms.

"Funny," Sydney said, standing, assuming it was Dixon. There was nowhere to clean her hands, unless she wanted to walk over to the lake and dunk them. "See if it's Dixon and answer it, would you?" Sydney stood and cocked her hip so he could grab the phone.

He took it, looked at the number, then flipped it open, while Sydney got back to squishing through the mud. "Carillo here," he said, listening, then, "Her partner. She's kind of . . . indisposed at the moment. Digging through the mud."

"Who is it?" Sydney asked, suspicious because she was pretty certain that Carillo didn't consider her his partner by any stretch. Her suspicion doubled when he gave a catlike smile. "Give me that phone."

"Your hands are muddy," he whispered.

"Then put it up to my ear."

"Yeah," he said, into the phone. "I'll tell her. What time?"

She stood, reached one muddy hand toward him. "Phone. Now."

"Seven. We'll be there." He flipped it shut, then clipped it back onto her belt.

"What the hell do you think you're doing?"

"Accepting a date for you."

"You said 'we' as in both of us."

"She invited me, too."

"Who?"

"Your sister. She said you forgot to call her this morning to wish her happy birthday, and she wanted to make sure you were coming over tonight for cake."

She sank back against the bench, her hands held out so she wouldn't get any mud on her clothes. "Damn it. I forgot. I've got that redeye tonight."

"Make a quick run up there, say happy birthday, then off to the airport. Plenty of time. So, when do you want me to pick you up?"

"You don't have to go."

"I like birthday cake."

"Let me put it this way. I'm not sure you want to go— never mind I *don't* want you to."

"Problems on the home front?"

"My mother and I are having . . . issues, and me not calling my sister this morning is just going to be one more nail in my coffin."

"Oh, good. Entertainment while we eat."

19

Carillo called Dixon while Sydney found one more
piece of taillight stuck in the mud, this one with a bit of
marking on it, which meant it was possible to identify the
type of vehicle it might have come from. That done, she gave
the pieces to Maggie Winters, who bagged and tagged them,
then Sydney walked to the restroom to wash her hands in
water so cold it felt like pins and needles spouting from the
faucet. There were no paper towels, and her fingers were
numb by the time she walked back to their car, where Carillo was waiting, holding up a sack from McDonald's. She
looked around, saw several McDonald's bags in the back of
the ERT van. "Don't even think about claiming this is my
free lunch."

"I can pay Johnson for you, and it could be."

"No way. I'm going to stick it to you for something better
than fast food."

"You know . . ." Carillo grabbed several french fries from
his bag, pointed them at her. "You should think about taking
that photo of yours to your mom's tonight. See if she recog-
nizes the two guys." He ate the fries, nodding as though he
was supremely pleased he'd come up with that idea himself.

"I told you we have issues. She's pissed I went to visit Wheeler in prison, and if I drag that thing out there, start asking her about it, Jake's going to lay on the guilt trip."

"Jake?"

"My stepfather. Don't get me wrong. He's a nice guy, but he's taken it as his personal quest to shield my mother from the past."

"You worried about your mother's feelings, or finding out what the hell is going on?"

"Fine. I'll bring it."

"You going to eat your fries?"

She handed over the bag.

By the time they left the park, it was close to five, and she was hoping that Carillo would have changed his mind about coming with her to her mother's house. He did not, saying he'd pick her up at her place. When Sydney met him out front, a brightly wrapped package in her hand, the photo safely tucked in her purse, she was surprised to see him holding up a child-sized white tee with "San Francisco FBI" emblazoned across the front. "Your sister doesn't have one of these, does she?"

She had several, but Sydney wasn't about to mention it. "Trust me, she'll love it. But you didn't have to get her anything."

"She invited me over for birthday cake."

"Because she's polite and you hijacked my phone."

"You asked me to answer it. Her name's Angela, right?"

"She goes by Angie." To everyone except her mother.

Carillo scrawled the name across a large manila envelope, slid the T-shirt in, handed it to Sydney, then shifted to drive and took off.

Traffic was still pretty heavy heading out of the city, especially crossing the Golden Gate, and what should have been a twenty-minute drive up to Santa Arleta took an hour.

Her mother lived at the very north end of town, on a hillside accessed by a narrow winding street. Sydney directed Carillo to take the exit just past Santa Arleta—not because it was quicker, but because Sydney tried to avoid the city itself, the neighborhood where she grew up, and the restaurant where her father had died. If Carillo guessed why they took the longer route, he said nothing, and for that she was grateful.

"Nice area," Carillo said, slowing as he rounded the curve just before her mother's house. Typical for the locale, the property lines were narrow but long, extending up into the hill, the houses and yards separated by oaks and eucalyptus and ivy vines with twisted, gnarled trunks as thick as a tree's. An old-growth hedge, as well as the ivy, hid the front of her mother's house, so that if you were standing in the street, you'd have to know it was there or you'd miss it. The illusion of privacy was one of the things her mother loved about the place, one of the reasons she stayed in Santa Arleta.

When they pulled up in the driveway, Angie came running out, throwing her arms around her older sister with her usual exuberance. "Guess what?" she shouted. "I got a puppy! I got a puppy! You'll *never* guess what I named it. Sarge! My own police dog!" She stopped long enough to cock her head at Carillo. "Are you Sydney's new partner?"

"Tony Carillo, at your service. So, where's this canine-in-training?"

"In the kitchen," she said, pulling on Sydney's hand, trying to get her to walk faster.

Angie opened the side door, letting them into the kitchen, then paused and in a quiet voice said, "Whatever you do, *don't* mention that I'm going to make Sarge a police dog in front of Daddy."

"Not a word," Sydney said, ignoring the amused look in Carillo's eye, as Angie led them straight to a cardboard box tucked in the corner, waving for them to move quicker. Inside, curled up on a towel was the cutest little . . . mongrel. *Maybe* a cross between a beagle and a wire-haired terrier, and judging from the short little legs, a breed as far from a police dog as Jake could get, probably part dachshund.

"Isn't Sarge cute?" she asked.

"Adorable," Sydney said. She set her purse on the floor by the box, then knelt down beside her sister.

Angie reached in, lifted the puppy out. "Did you have a good nap, Sarge?" she asked in a singsong voice.

Carillo eyed the little dog's belly and kicking feet, then grinned. "You, uh, realize Sarge is a girl?"

"Yeah," she said, nuzzling her face against the puppy's. "But girls can be sergeants, and everyone knows you *can't* name a police dog some sissy name."

"I see what you mean," he said. "Of course, if you're going to have a proper police dog, you have to train her with sign language."

"Really? Do you know any?"

"The three most important ones. Stop," he said, holding his hand palm out, just like a crossing guard. "Down," he said, lowering his palm so it was parallel to the floor, then making a downward motion. "And sit." For this he turned his palm so it faced the ceiling, then jerked it upward. "You do this every time you train your puppy, she'll know what to do even if she can't hear you."

"Really?"

"Just like the real police dogs do," he said, as Jake and her mom walked into the kitchen.

Angie dutifully made the introductions. Jake shook Carillo's hand. Sydney's mom smiled at him, but gave Sydney a reserved "Glad you could make it, or will you be getting called out to work before the night's over?"

Sydney was saved from responding when her sister peered out the kitchen window and shouted, "Aunt Eileen and Uncle Leland are here!" She raced out the door to show off her puppy, and, Sydney, feeling uncomfortable in her mother's presence, followed Angie out to say hello, and was surprised to see Donovan Gnoble stepping from a black Cadillac parked in the driveway behind her aunt's car. Angie waited on the sidewalk, holding tight to Sarge as she looked up at Sydney and whispered, "I did *not* invite him. Mom did."

"Moms are like that," Sydney whispered back.

"I'll bet if my birthday was *after* the election, he wouldn't come."

Sydney laughed, gave her sister a hug, before turning her attention back to her aunt and uncle, who shook hands with the senator, then walked up to the house with him.

Aunt Eileen was Sydney's father's sister, Uncle Leland

her husband, both of whom made the extra effort to remain closely entwined in their lives after her father's death. Sydney had spent nearly every summer on their farm, starting at about age five. She'd learned to ride motorcycles around manure piles, and race speedboats in the Delta. Character building, her father had called it. Her mother had agreed, and, apparently, after Angie was born, so had Jake, because Aunt Eileen asked if they'd allow the same with her, and they did so gladly—though Jake put the nix on the motorcycle and speedboat lessons. Not that Angie had any interest in that or the horses or the cows or the chickens, the things that Sydney loved. What captivated Angie's attention, much to Jake's chagrin, was that Uncle Leland was a retired cop, and had no shortage of exciting war stories to tell her.

Angie allowed Aunt Eileen and Uncle Leland to hug her, and when Donovan seemed ready to step in for the same, she held out her puppy to him and said, "Isn't she *cute*?"

Donovan gave the dog a tentative pat on the head. "Very."

Sydney stifled a grin, putting her arm around her sister's shoulder. "Let's all go inside. It's chilly out here."

"Oh, Leland," her aunt said, stopping them. "Run to the car and get that box of photos for Sydney."

Her uncle returned to the car, and Aunt Eileen linked her arm through Sydney's, saying, "I found the most wonderful photos of your father for you. I thought you might like to have them, maybe start a scrapbook."

"Thank you," she said, as they walked to the front door.

"I'm sure your mother must have some stored away. You should ask her for them."

"Ask me for what?" her mother said, kissing Eileen's cheek as she stepped in.

"Photos of Kevin. I think Sydney should start a scrapbook."

Her mother smiled that vacant smile of hers. "I'll put the kettle on for your tea, Eileen."

Eileen followed her mother into the kitchen, then helped set the table. Uncle Leland and Donovan were discussing the election process, and Jake and Carillo raided the fridge for beer, while Angie attempted to teach her puppy sign language, saying, "Sit," and pushing Sarge's little rump down as she made the sign, bringing her palm upward. Eventually she put Sarge in her box, then came out to stand by Sydney in the living room. She looked back at Carillo, who was busy talking about fishing with Jake, and she whispered, "You two guys aren't going out, are you?"

"No," Sydney said. "He's here for the free food."

"That's good. Because I helped make the cake. It's sort of lopsided. If you were going out, I'd at least want to give him one from a bakery, or something."

"He won't mind," Sydney said, as the doorbell rang.

Jake walked over, opened the front door. "Hey, Scotty. Didn't expect—"

"—me to miss Angie's birthday. I know. Just had to drop by, since I was in town."

Sydney glanced over at Carillo, who gave her a didn't-know-he-was-coming shrug. Or something close to that, she supposed.

Scotty walked over to where she and Angie stood. "Happy birthday, squirt," he said, handing her a business envelope, preprinted from the FBI.

"An official ID card?" she asked.

"Last I checked, your dad wanted you to be a ballerina."

"A doctor," she said, rolling her eyes. "I want to be in the FBI. Now if this were an application . . . ?"

He laughed. "Sorry. Just a little money to buy that new pup of yours a real dog bed."

"Thank you! How'd you know I have a new dog?"

"Your mom told me."

She smiled, reached up, gave him a hug. "I didn't even know you were here. I thought—"

"I wanted to surprise you."

"You did!" She ran off to show her mom what Scotty had given her, and then Carillo got into the act, saying he, too, had a gift.

The moment she was out of earshot, Sydney asked Scotty, "What are you really doing here?"

"Can't I come by to give Angie a gift?"

Someone had let Sarge out of her box, because the puppy

came scurrying out of the kitchen, sliding on the hardwood floor. Scotty glanced past her when Donovan Gnoble, her aunt, and her mother laughed at the puppy's antics, and it hit her why he'd suddenly shown up. Scotty, Mr. Fast Track to the Top, had always been inordinately fascinated by her family's connection to the senator. He'd just never been able to arrange a meeting until now, apparently. And sure enough, he made a beeline to her mother, who introduced him.

If anyone could make something out of that connection, Scotty could, she thought, then chanced to glance over at Sarge, who looked ready to squat on the floor. "No!"

Sydney scooped her up, rushed her into the kitchen and out the side door. She lowered the puppy to the ground, then stood there, while Sarge waddled about, sniffing at the grass, and then the pansies.

A moment later, her mother walked out, gave an exaggerated sigh. "I think she's too young to take care of a dog."

"She'll be fine, Mom."

"But apparently you won't? Why else would you need to run off to some prison?"

It seemed her mother was not going to let them get past this issue. "I'm sorry. I shouldn't have told you I was going to the prison. I didn't realize it would hurt you this much."

"Hurt me?" Her mother crossed her arms, looked away. "My God, Sydney, I can't even understand what *possessed* you to do such a thing."

Part of her wanted to shout out that her mother had another husband, a new family, but her father would be lost to her forever. She bit her tongue. Her mother had married Jake, and he'd always been there for her. For both of them. And there was Angie, full of life and love, the sister Sydney couldn't imagine living without . . . "I can't explain it, Mom. And I don't expect you to understand it. Going to San Quentin was just something I felt I had to do."

Angie bounced out the door, wearing her new FBI tee. "Where's San Quentin? What did you have to do?"

"Nothing, sweetheart," her mother said, then threw a look at Sydney that seemed to shout: *See the problems you're causing?*

Angie narrowed her gaze, but before she could ask any further questions, Carillo called out from the dining room, "Hey, Angie. Come show me that shirt," and off she went.

"Mom, please . . . I said I was sorry. But he was my father. His history is mine. I know absolutely nothing about what he did before he opened that pizza parlor."

Her mother looked away, and in a strained whisper said, "Some things are best left buried."

Sydney bent down, picked up Sarge to bring her back inside. But then her mother offered a wan smile and, surprising her, gave her a hug, then took Sarge from her arms as they walked inside. "I know I'm being silly, just wanting to protect you from bad memories," she said, setting Sarge inside her box. "Of course you want to know about your father. And I'm sure all this talk about photos and your aunt's scrapbooking makes you want to do something yourself."

"Well, yes," Sydney said, grabbing on to that idea for all it was worth. "I even have an old photo I was hoping you could look at, see who was in it. For the scrapbook."

When her mother didn't balk outright, Sydney walked over to her purse, still on the floor next to Sarge's box. She glanced into the dining room, watched as Angie pirouetted about in her new shirt, while the men talked about the old Chris-Craft boat Jake was refurbishing in the garage. Figuring they'd be occupied for a few minutes on that topic alone, she slid the photo from the envelope. "I don't suppose you know anyone from this, do you?"

Her mother had just opened up the dishwasher to put away the clean dishes, then looked over. "Of all the pictures for your album, do you really want that one?"

"Why? What is it?"

"With the exception of your father and Uncle Don, a bunch of jerks, from what I remember. They thought they were God's gift to the military. What did they call themselves . . ." She slid a glass into the cupboard, but her gaze was fixed out the window, then, with a sound of disgust, said, "The Posse. That was it. You want my advice," she said, reaching into the dishwasher for another glass, "leave that photo out."

"But who are they?"

"They worked with your father taking photos for those
recruiting posters. He loved that job . . . They were always
flying off to some exciting locale to get the best shot of
someone jumping out of a helicopter, or blowing up something to make it look real. That's how your father lost his
fingers, you know. Those idiots he worked with set real
charges instead of the fake ones for the photo. Thank God
he was smart enough to get out and start his own business.
As for their names, I have no idea."

"Did anyone ever mention that Dad was in Delta Force?"

Her mother stilled. "What on earth are you talking about?
He took photographs." With a glance toward the dining
room, she resumed putting glasses away.

"Was Dad doing some special ops thing for the army?"

"Special photographs, maybe. Why are you asking this?
Where did you get that photo?"

Sydney would have preferred a direct answer, not a stall-
ing technique. Then again, her mother was always trying to
prolong a simple conversation into a bonding talk, and perhaps it was nothing more than that. "Just trying to put names
to faces," she said as the men walked in, apparently on their
way to the garage to look at the boat.

Sydney's mother seemed to pale, and it occurred to Sydney that she'd known all along about the special ops thing.
"That's why you said he wasn't a saint?"

But before her mother could answer, Angie skipped over to
take the dog from her box, then looked at the photo. "Wow!
Army guys! Dad! It's like when you were in the army."

Jake looked over, saw the photo, his gaze narrowing. Be-
fore he said a word, Donovan Gnoble walked up, saw it.
"Where'd you get that old thing?" he asked, taking it from
Sydney.

Carillo gave a subtle nod toward Scotty. She looked, saw
him standing there, leaning against the doorway as though
nothing were amiss—if one didn't know him. His gaze held
hers, his blue eyes cold, hard. He wasn't here for the lofty
climb up the ladder after all, she realized, and she looked
away, smiled at the senator. "You know, it's the funni-
est thing. I just found it in some old album I had bouncing

around my closet. I probably dumped it in there years ago, forgot all about it." The room grew silent, the undercurrents palpable. "So . . . that was back when my dad used to take photos for those posters?"

"That's what he did." Donovan Gnoble stared at the picture. "Talk about your blast from the past. This thing's so old, I barely recognize myself, especially without my goatee."

She was in it this far, so she said, "Someone told me these guys look like they're in Delta Force."

He shook his head, laughed. "I think I'd know if that was the case."

"Then who are those guys?"

"Other than your father . . . oh, and William, of course," he said, pointing to McKnight. "Who knows about the other two . . . But if you'd like, I can take it, ask around next time I meet up with some of the guys at the VA."

"That's okay," Sydney said, holding out her hand for the photo.

Donovan handed it over, almost reluctantly she thought, and then he smiled, looked at his watch. "I've really got to get going. I have a cocktail party back in the city I promised I'd attend."

Sydney's mother said, "It was so nice of you to stop by, Donovan."

"Wouldn't have missed it for the world." He looked around for Angela, but she'd disappeared into the den to give Sarge another lesson on sign language, and so he shook hands with Carillo, and then Scotty. "Nice to meet both of you. If you ever need anything, just give me a call."

And Scotty smiled broadly. "It was a real pleasure. Thanks."

"Angie, honey," Jake said. "Come say good-bye to Uncle Don."

"Good-bye, Uncle Don!" she called out, not bothering to emerge for his departure. "Sit. Sarge! No!"

Donovan didn't wait around to learn what dire emergency Sarge had created, but whatever it was, Angie resolved it by the time the cake was served. And yet no one but Angie seemed to be talking, as though the photo was some dreaded talisman that everyone knew existed, and no one could speak of. Sydney wanted to ask what the hell was up with it, but Scotty's look quelled her to silence, and for once, she decided it might be best to follow his lead. A little after nine, Jake glanced up at the clock. "Time for bed, Angie."

"But I need to finish training Sarge."

"Sarge needs her rest," he said, despite that Sarge was busy trying to get out of her box, and whining pitifully. "Say good night to our guests."

"Dad . . ."

And Sydney, realizing she had a plane to catch in a couple of hours, said, "We have to get going anyway."

"That's right," Carillo said, standing. "Big day tomorrow. Gotta go out and catch bad guys."

Angie's eyes lit up. "I am *so* gonna be one of you guys when I grow up."

"You are *so* not," Jake said. "Now kiss your sister and get in the bath." Sarge gave a little yelp, and when Angie hesitated, her father crossed his arms. "Bath. I'll get the dog."

Angie gave Sydney a hug and a kiss. She moved to Scotty next, held out her hand and said, "Thank you for the money. I hope you can come over again."

Scotty shook her hand. "I hope so, too. It's always great to see you."

And then, as she let go, she beamed a smile at Carillo. "I *love* my FBI shirt. I hope you can come over again, too."

Carillo smiled back, ruffled her hair, and said, "Me too. Good night, Angie."

Sydney gave her mother and Jake a hug, then followed the others out.

Scotty stopped at the curb, patting his pocket. "Left my keys inside. I'll be right back."

When he started toward the house, she grabbed his arm. "I hope you plan on explaining what you're doing here."

"Actually, that's why I came over tonight. I just didn't realize you, uh, weren't going to be alone." He glanced at Carillo.

"It was an unexpected invitation," Carillo said. "From her sister."

"Get to the point, Scotty."

"Maybe I can give you a ride home? Tell you on the way?"

"Sure. Go get your keys." Scotty returned to the house, and she faced Carillo. "I'm assuming you can find your way home from here?"

"Somehow I'll manage." Carillo opened up his car and took out something from the center console, a white envelope, which he handed to her. "In case I don't see you again tonight. This is the contact information for a friend of mine who works in the Houston field office, Dr. Vincent Pettigrew."

Sydney took the envelope, eyed it as though she had serious doubts. "I'd rather keep the number of people who know about this to a minimum."

"This way you don't have to rent a car. Less of a paper trail, and he's just what you want. Like me, he doesn't give a rat's ass about being promoted. More importantly, unlike me, Vince is getting ready to retire any day. I told him to expect your call as soon as you touch down in Houston."

"How much did you tell him?"

"The basics. Enough to know why you're making the quick stop to the little town of Webster. You can trust him."

"Okay."

"Do me a favor, though? Make it look good in Webster, because if there's one thing I hate, it's sitting in front of someone from OPR, trying to explain things that, in their eyes, don't have shit to do with what we're supposed to be doing."

The agents who worked OPR, Office of Professional Responsibility, were the internal affairs watchdogs of the Bureau, doing their best to make sure no one stepped out of line, and ready to quash them if they did. "I'll make it look good. Promise. And thanks. I owe you."

"No mush. I should've stated that up front." He stood there, looked at her over the top of his car. "And don't worry. Soon as I get home, I'm cracking open your father's case. If you want to talk later . . ."

She gave a sigh, looked back at the house, saw Scotty speaking to Jake inside. "I'll try to call you. Let you know what's going on."

"Yeah, sure," he said, then got into the car, starting it up.

She shoved the envelope into her purse. A moment later, Scotty walked out, tossing his keys in his hand. He waved as Carillo drove off.

"So what'd you want to tell me?" she asked.

"How about we talk when we get to your place?"

"How about we talk now."

"Syd, you have to trust me on this."

Right. She got in his car. When they were well away from her mother's house, she said, "You're working a case on Senator Gnoble, aren't you?"

"I really think we should talk about it when we get to your place."

"You showed up to my little sister's birthday working a case? My God, Scotty. How low can you sink?"

"A lot lower than that."

"What's that supposed to mean?"

"It means I made a bad decision." He glanced into his rearview mirror, then looked over at her. "I thought it was the right thing to do at the time, but—"

"But what?"

". . . I was wrong."

If Scotty was anything, he was meticulous. He planned out every move. Not only did he not like to make a mistake, he hated to admit it. And that had her worried. "About what?"

He said nothing, just kept eyeing the rear and side view mirrors.

"Just tell me, for God's sake. Before I get out and walk home." An empty threat, since they were now hurtling down the freeway.

He took a breath, both hands gripping the steering wheel. And then, in a voice so quiet she had to lean toward him to hear, he said, "We have reason to believe someone is trying to place a hit on you."

20

Sydney stared for several seconds, certain she'd heard wrong. He looked over at her, then back to the road. "A hit? As in someone's trying to kill me?"

"We're taking all precautions."

"Well, let me breathe a big sigh of relief." Bastard. It took several seconds to cool off enough to even think clearly. Scotty's sudden appearance at her mailbox, the way he seemed to caution her about how she came into possession of that photo, his surprise visit to her sister's party . . . Her first instinct, a right hook to his chin, was not a good idea while he was driving. That could wait until *after* they'd parked. "How long have you known about this?"

"We got wind of it right after we learned that McKnight mailed you the photo."

"So the photo started it."

"That's what we think."

"The photo you let me walk into my sister's house with."

"I did try to take it from you. And if you were smart, you'd hand it over, before you do any more damage."

She now had a copy of it and the letter, but didn't want him to think she was capitulating so easily. "I have to think about it. Had you mentioned everything surrounding it, I might have turned it over sooner." He didn't respond. "Which means that Donovan Gnoble is behind this?"

"That part we don't know."

"How can you not know? You knew enough to show up to my house and try to steal it out of my mailbox, for God's sake. And if it's so goddamned important, how is it you didn't come back to get it? At least warn me?"

"It's . . . complicated. I have a source who can trace the threat to someone on his staff, but that's it."

"So you don't know if Donovan's behind it?"

"Not yet."

"Not yet?"

"We're investigating."

"And at what point were you going to tell me?"

"I wanted to, but the timing was never right."

"What the *hell* were you waiting for? The moment someone started taking potshots at me with my family standing nearby? My little sister as she's blowing out her candles? Or me when I'm walking my neighbor's dog, and some car tries to run me over?"

"We weren't sure if that was related. We were watching your house, and they thought it was one of the neighborhood teens."

"I'm being *watched*?"

"You don't think we'd just let you walk around without protection?"

"No. What I think is that you'd fucking *tell* me that someone wants me dead so I don't stupidly put myself or anyone else in danger."

"Damn it, Sydney." He slammed one hand on the steering wheel. "We had to make a decision. We thought we were going to get it taken care of before anything happened. We thought—"

"You thought wrong." She turned, stared out the side window, trying to stay composed enough to piece everything together, but some idiot pulled in behind them, his headlights out of whack. One shone slightly higher than the other, making direct contact into the passenger side mirror, blinding

her. She turned away, shifted in her seat, decided she needed
to keep her eye on Scotty, the better to figure out what the
hell was going on. "Fine. You can have the photo and the
other stuff when we get back to my place."

"Thank you."

"And *who* exactly are the *we* you speak of?"

"I can't discuss it."

"It's my life you're screwing with here."

"There are a couple other agencies involved, because of
some national security issues."

"National security issues? What does that have to do with
me?"

"Not you. Your father."

"So he was Delta Force?"

"Not exactly. From what I understand, his specialty was
clandestine ops. Black ops."

"Black ops?"

"The kind of things that don't end up in any official records. Not sanctioned by any known government officials."

Up ahead, the Golden Gate Bridge lit the night sky, but
she barely registered it. "How do you know this?" she finally
asked. "How do you know any of it's true?"

"From the background on McKnight. Apparently that's
what your father had over his head, why he was demanding money from McKnight. Your father, McKnight, and the
other guys in the photo worked together, possibly for or with
Gnoble. We're still trying to piece it together. Your father
wasn't a photographer. That was his cover, up until the explosion that blew off his fingers, which we think occurred
on whatever their last operation was. The one your father
was allegedly blackmailing McKnight about . . . The reason
McKnight killed himself."

"Okay, let's say all this is true. Then what the hell does it
have to do with me?"

"McKnight sent you that photo and that letter. For some
reason, he thought you should know. And for some reason,
it upset someone in Gnoble's office, because that's when we
heard about the threat to your life. Apparently whatever it
was they were working on twentysomething years ago, it's

something someone feels will haunt Gnoble, and no doubt cost him the election."

"Something to do with that big banking scandal?" When he didn't answer, she took that as a confirmation. "But you don't know if it *is* Gnoble?"

"No. It could just be someone in or connected to his office who wants to ensure his position there." Scotty slowed as they neared the tollbooth, the line blissfully short at this hour. "But that's one of the reasons we decided not to tell you right away. We knew you'd be meeting up with him when he came out here for that rally. We wanted to make sure you didn't act any different around him. In case he or whoever it is on his staff was watching you. There was so much press around, and so many undercover agents, we knew you'd be safe."

"How comforting." Her thoughts raced, tried to fit the pieces, determine what was so important about this photo of a handful of men just standing there. Even the accompanying *alleged* blackmail letter didn't make sense. And then it struck her. The missing element. "The suicide note," she said aloud.

Scotty said nothing.

"There was something in that note that ties all this together." When he didn't respond, she said, "Did you get the copy that I asked about?"

"I told you, I can't get it. I wasn't lying about that."

"Do you even know what it says?"

No answer.

She wanted to scream at him, but he pulled up to the tollbooth to pay for the bridge crossing. She glanced at the clock on the dash, its neon green digits showing half past nine. Her redeye to Houston took off in a little more than three hours from then, and it didn't take a secret agent to figure out that if she were to mention her little trip to Scotty, he would find a way to stop her. The government wanted whatever this was kept under wraps, and for the good of the government, Scotty had done and would do what he was ordered.

"So, just how close am I being watched . . . ?"

He looked over at her, no doubt trying to read something behind her question, and she figured it was time to act as though she trusted him and the government to do what was right. "What I mean is, how am I supposed to know that the person following me is a good guy or a bad guy? How many people are watching my house, tailing my car?"

"Two cars are sitting on your house, and two others are designated to you and wherever you go."

She crossed her arms, then uncrossed them. The need for protection was clear, something she could appreciate, but right now she needed the freedom to move around, fly off to Houston without interference from Scotty and whatever government entities he was involved with. If her situation weren't so dire, she could almost laugh. One week ago, if someone had told her she'd be skirting rules right and left, creating fake cases to investigate a crime of blackmail long past the statute of limitations, she would have told him he was nuts.

Apparently she was the one verging on the brink of insanity.

Past the bridge, Scotty turned off, took a different route to her place. She looked over at him, then started watching the side view mirror, seeing the same car with the headlight needing adjustment. "How long has that car been following us?"

"From the time we left your mother's."

"Tell me it's one of yours."

"It's one of ours."

Since he didn't take evasive action, she believed him. Which meant the unusual route was probably another precautionary measure. She focused, tried to plan how she was going to get to the airport without him finding out. Last thing she needed was for him to make a couple of calls to Houston PD, get her banned from the building, or worse yet, stopped at the airport before she even got there.

When he finally pulled up in front of her house, he radioed whoever was watching her place, got the "all clear." If they were watching her this close, was it possible they were monitoring more than just her physical presence and her home? Her phone calls, perhaps—not that she was about to ask him. "I'd say thanks for the ride," she said, opening the door, "but I'm not sure I'm grateful."

"I'm only the messenger. Maybe I should come up. Check out your apartment."

"Whatever." Okay, so she was being short with him, forgivable under the circumstances, she figured. Even so, she had an agenda, something she couldn't afford to forget, and countdown to takeoff was now only two and one-half hours. She tried to smile, said, "Sorry. It's just a lot to absorb right now."

"I know. And if I could make this all go away, I would," he said, sounding so apologetic, she almost sympathized with his position. Almost.

"Who knows about this? Who am I allowed to tell?" she asked as they walked up the stairs. She saw Arturo through his kitchen window, drying a dish, and wondered what delights he'd cooked up tonight.

"No one in your office knows. We'll be informing the SAC, once we get clearance."

And she could well imagine what Dixon would do the moment the Special Agent in Charge, Dixon's boss, walked into his office, notified him of what was going on. Dixon was going to know in a hot second that her trip to Houston had nothing to do with their serial killer case, something she'd have to deal with later. Right now, she needed that suicide note.

She unlocked her door, and to make it seem as though she were buying into Scotty's presence and all he'd told her, she asked, "You want to check out the place, make sure it's okay?" There was really only one way in or out, and that was via the front door, or, if desperate, through the kitchen window, accessed via the balcony. The only other windows, her bedroom and the front window, were fairly secure, being on the second story with no access unless one used a ladder, something that might be noticeable, since they'd have to prop it up in the front or side of the house, both visible from the street.

Just as she thought, he walked in, checked out the place, then walked out. "I can stay, if you like."

She handed him the originals of what McKnight had mailed to her. "Actually I might have to go to the office tonight. Finish up a couple reports with Carillo from our search at the park."

He hesitated, before saying, "Do you know how long you'll be?"

"Couple hours at the most. Would've done it earlier, but I wasn't about to miss Angie's party." And then, just to get a bit more info on how close they were watching her, she asked, "Do you need me to call when I get to the Bureau?"

"Don't worry about it. We'll know."

"What if they lose me?"

"They won't. But if you're worried, don't drive too fast." His laugh sounded forced. "Actually it might not be a bad idea if you do let us know what you're doing. Eliminate the surprise factor. More importantly, Syd, eliminate your routine factor. Go running earlier. Or later. Better yet, don't run until we get this cleared up. And if you can't reach me, call this number." He took out a pen, jotted a number on the back of one of his business cards. "Jared Dunning. He's in charge of your surveillance, and if he's not on, he'll have this number forwarded to who is."

She took the card, noted it wasn't one of the local FBI prefixes, and wondered what agency this Jared Dunning worked for. Something else to check out, she figured, dropping the card into her purse.

He leaned forward, kissed her cheek. "This will all work out. Trust me."

In a heartbeat, she thought, as she closed and locked the door. When she heard his engine turning over, she took out her cell phone to call Carillo. Somehow they were going to have to figure out how to get to the airport and shake this surveillance. Her thumb poised over the send button, she eyed the brand-new phone, issued just a few days ago.

Because hers had stopped working.

Suddenly stopped.

Her glance strayed out the window, to Scotty's departing

car, wondering if they would go that far, jam her signal so she'd have to be issued a new phone. A phone they could listen in on, or at the very least track her movements with GPS . . .

A disturbing thought. The little bit Scotty had told her did nothing to help. She was still upset he'd kept this from her, which made her wonder who had issued the orders keeping her in the dark, and just how far they were going to keep tabs on her.

Don't drive too fast.

She looked over at the number Scotty had left her, this Jared Dunning, and what bothered her was Scotty's mentioning that other agencies were involved. So, other than the FBI, who?

She started pacing. Her father had worked black ops for the army . . . That scenario didn't fit with the FBI, a domestic law enforcement agency. Army, covert operations . . .

Son of a bitch. She stopped, upset she hadn't thought of this earlier. Then again how could she, since they'd purposefully kept her in the dark? How the hell had she not seen this?

Calm down. Maybe she was wrong.

Calm down, my ass. She grabbed the recycle container from beneath the sink, and then her keys, and marched downstairs, pushed in the code for the garage in the keypad, waited. When it opened, she walked past Arturo's motorcycle and headed straight for the recycle bin, throwing the top open and dumping her container into it, promptly dropping several cans on the ground. They bounced and clattered, one rolling beneath the car.

Right where she wanted it.

She bent down, made a show of looking for the can, then walked to the front of the car where she wouldn't be seen from the street. She knelt, shone her tiny blue light from her key ring on the undercarriage.

And saw it. The GPS tracking device attached near the wheel well. That meant she was right about her phone. They had no doubt jammed her signal, making her think something was wrong with it, so she'd be forced to get a new one, which they conveniently had waiting for her. If she had to put money on which organizations Scotty was working with, she'd bet NSA or CIA.

Didn't matter which one. Both played by their own rules. Only one problem. No one knew what they were.

21

Jared Dunning sat up when he saw Sydney Fitz-
patrick disappear from sight in the garage. He'd been sitting
on her house all night. Just like the night before. And the
night before that. One would think seniority would have ad-
vantages. Like maybe he could take the day shift part of this
babysitting operation. He glanced over at his partner, saw
him snoozing in the passenger seat, and whacked his arm to
wake him. "Hey. She's moving around in there."

"Huh?" Mel focused on the apartment. Or tried to.

"She's in the garage. Dumped some stuff, then ducked
down in front of the car."

"Shit. She's not trying to take off on us, is she?"

Jared watched, saw her get up, toss a can into the bin, then
brush her hands off. "Guess not. Looks like she dropped
something. Picked it up." And a moment later, she walked
upstairs, but instead of going home, she knocked on the
neighbor's door.

Several minutes later, she emerged, disappeared back into
her own apartment. "We shoulda bugged his phones, too,"
Jared said.

"What for? You ever see him home for longer than a few hours the whole time we been sitting on this place?" About five minutes later, as if proving Mel's point, the neighbor came out, dressed in full-on motorcycle gear. Black pants, boots, black leather coat, a backpack with reflective strips slung over his shoulder. In one hand he carried a jet-black helmet. And in the other, somewhat ruining the whole ninja biker look, the leashed giant white poodle, which he was apparently leaving behind. Again. Seemed that's all their target did was watch the neighbor's damned dog for him, Jared thought as she opened her door, petted the dog, then stepped aside to let them both in.

"What the hell's he doing in there?" Mel said, when after a couple of minutes the guy didn't come out.

"Kissing his dog good-bye. Not like he has any women over."

"Think he's gay?"

"He's wearing all black."

"So he's a masculine gay guy."

The door opened a few minutes later, and they saw him standing in the doorway, adjusting his helmet strap around his neck, then pulling on his backpack as he exited. He turned and gave the dog a rough pat, then walked down the steps and into the garage, where he got on his motorcycle, started it, revving the engine.

Mel perked up at the sound. "Damn, that is one cool bike. You ever ridden a Ducati?"

"No." Jared focused on the apartment, just as the neighbor took off on the charcoal-black Ducati, zipping down the street, the red taillight disappearing around the corner.

"Wouldn't mind taking that bike out on the road," Mel said. "See what it could do."

Jared shook his head. "It's just a bike."

"You are so wrong. It's a Ducati." He leaned back in his seat, closed his eyes. "Wake me when she takes off for the office. *If* she ever decides to go."

"Maybe she'll stay home, now she knows what's up."

"One can only hope."

Ten minutes later, her front door opened, the dog pranced out on the porch. Jared reached over, whacked Mel in the arm. "Okay. She's moving . . . Shit! Shit, *shit!*"

"What?"

"It's him. The neighbor."

"*What?*"

Mel looked over. Saw the neighbor closing Sydney's door, carefully locking it, then taking his dog and entering his own apartment. "Goddamn it!"

Jared picked up the radio, keyed it. "Any of you guys get the plate on the neighbor's motorcycle? The one that took off?"

Curtis, parked at the opposite end of the street, radioed back, "Didn't think we needed to watch him. Why?"

"Our target just left on it. About ten minutes ago."

"Okay. Don't panic. We can track her on her cell phone . . ."

Jared started his car, ready to take off as soon as the location was given.

"Okay," Curtis radioed. "You can panic now. It's still showing at her apartment."

"Goddamn it!" Jared hit the gas, took off in the last direction he saw her, keying the radio. "Two of you stay on the house. Somebody get me that plate number, and get a BOLO on it. *Now.*"

Sydney was grateful for two things in that moment, dry pavement and light traffic, because Arturo would kill her if anything happened to his bike. Of course, he'd have to wait his turn. There seemed to be no shortage of people willing to do her in for one reason or another.

She checked her rearview mirrors, saw no signs she was being followed, and relaxed slightly. If she were ever in the market for a motorcycle, this one would be on the top of her list, she thought, stopping at the signal, one foot to the ground, waiting to make a left turn onto the 101. A police car pulled up next to her, the cop glancing over, checking out the bike, looking at her. Several heartbeats passed, and she wondered if Scotty's team would've called in the bike's plate by now, have her stopped. *Turn green. Turn green . . .*

The signal changed; she accelerated at a steady pace. Tried not to bring any more attention to her. If she was lucky, they didn't have Arturo's plate, and if they did have it, maybe they hadn't called it in yet. The moment she was on the freeway, she looked behind her. No cop car. Though tempted to open it up, see what this baby could do, she drove the speed limit, kept a close eye on the cars around her.

She'd done it. Now all she needed to do was get to the airport. Park. Get on that plane. She drove to one of the offsite lots that required the keys be left behind, one with indoor parking. She handed the keys and the helmet over, explained to the attendant that the bike's owner would be by to pick it up in the morning, and registered it under Arturo's name, but paid for it under hers. The shuttle pulled up in short order, and a few minutes later, she was walking into the airport a good half hour before boarding.

Not bad for a night's work, she thought, heading into the ladies' room to see what the helmet had done to her hair. A little flat, and she fluffed it up with her fingers and some water, eyed her leather coat and black jeans in the mirror. Not quite the outfit she would've chosen for visiting another agency on a case, but one had to make do, and she slung Arturo's reflective backpack over her shoulder. It contained her Bureau ID, shield, and gun, along with her ticket, paperwork, and a few other essentials, including a toothbrush and Arturo's cell phone.

She checked in at the desk, then with security, so they could examine the reams of paperwork and ID necessary to get the gun on board. That done, she walked to her gate, sat, waited, nearly jumped when Arturo's cell phone rang.

"Restricted" showed on the caller ID, and she was tempted to ignore it, knew it had to be Scotty. But then she wondered if she'd somehow gotten Arturo in trouble. She answered it with, "Arturo knows absolutely nothing about this, so leave him out of it."

"I'm not interested in your neighbor. It's your safety. Where are you?"

"A little late to be worrying about my safety, don't you think?"

"I'm ordering you in."

"You're not my boss. And since you saw fit to keep me in the dark about all this, I'm not even sure I should be listening to you right now."

"Then I'll have your boss order you in."

"You haven't informed him yet?"

"No."

Of course she knew why he hadn't called Dixon yet. Because Dixon would have to call the Special Agent in Charge, and Scotty would have to face them and explain why he'd lost an agent he was supposed to be protecting. An agent they didn't even know was in danger. An agent he'd failed to warn. "Mind if I ask you a question, Scotty? Does *your* boss even know?"

"Of course he does."

"Let me rephrase that. Does he know that you didn't tell me?"

A long stretch of silence told her that answer.

She smiled, got up, walked away from the other passengers seated near the boarding gate, and prayed no one would make any airline security announcements over the loudspeakers. "The shit is going to hit the fan come morning. Isn't it?"

"This isn't funny. Where are you?"

She rather liked having one over on him. That aside, she had some quick thinking to do, or she'd find herself on some sort of administrative lockdown the moment Scotty made the necessary calls to save his career. "I have a deal for you."

"What sort of deal?"

"Don't tell them."

"I can't do that."

"Yes, you can. Just like you didn't tell me. At the very least, wait. Your bosses know what this is all about, right? What you're investigating?"

"Of course they do."

"They just don't know that I wasn't told."

"Correct."

"Well, now I do know. And I choose to be an active part of this. Which should cover your ass quite nicely."

"Meaning what?"

"Meaning now that I am aware of what the inherent danger is, I choose to go about my business, my investigations as normal, so as not to tip off anyone. And that, Scotty, will allow you and . . . whoever it is you're working with to conduct your own investigation."

"You need to be off the streets."

"If I'm removed from my investigations and tucked away, they're going to know we know. I work in the same damned building as his office for God's sake. But if I go about investigating my serial killer case as normal, everything's fine."

"I don't like it."

"You really don't have a choice. Because the moment I'm pulled off my cases, I'm going to put in a formal complaint about how your incompetence put me and my family and my very young and innocent sister in the most extreme danger."

"Damn it, Sydney! Where are you?"

"Working a follow-up on my serial killer case. Oh, and you might want to inform Carillo. I think he has a right to know that for the past few days, he was an unwitting target. That way he can make an informed decision on whether or not he wants to be sitting in the same car as me. Gotta go," she said, just as the gate attendant picked up a microphone to announce the boarding of her flight.

"Syd—"

She shut down the phone, then dropped it in the backpack.

22

Special Agent Vincent Pettigrew of the Houston
field office was a tall, gray-haired man with a lined face that
spoke of a love for the outdoors and the sun, and an expen-
sive navy suit that spoke of a love for the finer things in
life. If he thought anything of Sydney's unusual biker garb,
he didn't mention it, nor did she offer an explanation. He
picked her up from Intercontinental airport, drove her to
Webster, where they did a quick check on the murder case
that, who would've guessed, turned out not to be related to
her case at all, and then started on their drive to Houston,
where she queried him about how he got started in the Bureau. Apparently he owed his title of doctor to the Ph.D. he'd
acquired before being lured to the FBI twenty-three years
ago. They'd asked him for assistance in a stolen art case, and
he'd discovered it was a lot more exciting than his first-year
teaching job at the university in Virginia. "It was the guns,"
he told Sydney after they'd stopped for much needed coffee. He checked his rearview mirror, changed lanes, merging
onto the freeway. "I was fascinated by all these smart guys
running around like 007. I got to hold an actual Renoir in my
hands. Figured it was going to be all artwork, all the time,

some sort of specialized art task force, so when one of the
operatives on the case told me I should think about joining
up, I jumped."

"And how many art cases did you get to investigate?"

He glanced over at her, his brown eyes sparkling with
amusement. "In the twenty-three years I've been with the
Bureau? Quite a few, but only two that made me salivate
over what was stolen. Consulted on several more. In the
end, I'll get the best of both worlds. I'll be retiring in a few
weeks, and I've just accepted a university teaching position
in art history that could lead to tenure in Virginia, so all in
all, can't complain."

"Not bad."

"How about you? Why'd you go into law enforcement?"

"Same as you. Fascinated by the guns." She left it at that,
too tired to do much talking herself. And as they drove, she
couldn't help but remember her stepfather, Jake, telling her
that she'd let her father's murder define her. Maybe it wasn't
the fascination of the gun as much as the knowledge that
if she carried one, she'd have some power to protect those
she loved. But how could she protect them against something she had no knowledge about? She'd called Carillo as
soon as she'd landed, told him what Scotty had told her last
night, asked him to look up anything and everything on the
banking scandal Scotty had mentioned. And now she had
to content herself with waiting, because what she was asking was no small feat. How much of her father's murder,
McKnight's suicide, the hit on her life, was tied up in that
old case?

"Except for the skyline, it's not exactly the most inspiring
of scenery," Vince said several minutes later, looking over at
her, perhaps seeing her eyes drift shut. "Most people think it
should be wide open land with longhorns grazing."

She smiled, tried to act interested, and only then noticed
there was nothing to look at but strip malls and car deal-
erships that lined the freeway. The downtown skyline was
impressive from this distance, though, as several high-rises
actually reflected the blue sky and the puffy white clouds
that graced it. "It's a pretty city."

"Clean, too. But somehow I don't think you're here for the travelogue . . ."

She laughed, appreciating his attempt to make her at ease. "So, what can you tell me about this matter?"

"Nothing, except it's one hot potato. Someone came in, sanitized the entire case."

"Why?"

"Right-wing Republicans taking the brunt of yet another scandal? Then again, maybe something bigger."

"And if it is something bigger?"

"Whichever agency did the whitewashing, they're higher up the food chain than us. You can't just march into a police department the size of Houston and make a suicide note disappear."

"It's gone?"

"That's the rumor. Every photocopy and mention of it. The report was computer generated, so if it was mentioned in the original, and we've got no reason to think otherwise, you couldn't tell. And Hatcher, the agent who was first looking into the case because of that background he was doing? Well, he pretty much spooked Reynolds, the guy you first called, with his talk of national security Patriot Act stuff."

"You think it really is a national security issue?"

"Knowing the way the gazillion branches of our government all fail to communicate with each other, who the hell knows? Me, I like the scandal theory, because it fits in with my all-top-government-officials-are-dirty theme."

They arrived in downtown Houston, and just as Vince said, it was indeed a very clean city. The PD was in the heart of the city, located in a white and tan, twenty-six-story building on Travis Street. Vince pulled into a monitored parking garage, filled with undercover cars, numerous white marked police vehicles, and a few older-model sky-blue police cars, probably being phased out of the fleet.

Vince called from his cell phone, letting his contact know they'd arrived. "Alexander's waiting for us at his office," he said. Inside were two banks of elevators, and Vince hit the up button on one that covered floors one through sixteen, then held the door for Sydney to step in.

"What floor?" she asked.

"Six. Homicide."

She hit the button and the door slid shut. Investigator Alexander Hilleary was waiting in the doorway of the homicide office when they got out, a manila folder tucked beneath one arm. He was about the same height as Sydney, five-nine, with brown hair and brown eyes, maybe in his thirties, wearing a gray suit and a burgundy tie. He walked up to them, shook hands with Vince and then Sydney, before leading them to his desk, and its collection of Yu-Gi-Oh!, Pokémon, and ninja figures that seemed out of place next to the odd assortment of books on homicide and forensics. The file cabinet next to it was filled with family photos, a number of them showing a young boy playing soccer.

Hilleary opened the file drawer, deposited his folder, then asked them, "You two want coffee or something?"

Sydney nodded. "That would be great."

Vince declined, and Hilleary poured two Styrofoam cups, handed Sydney one. She sucked hers down, while Vince asked Hilleary, "So, what the hell's going on in this place?"

"How about we go sit in one of the interview rooms. Get a little privacy." He led them down the hall, showed them into what was commonly called a "soft" interview room, one with a couch and armchair, usually reserved for witness interviews as opposed to suspect interrogations.

Sydney asked, "You were on the McKnight suicide?"

"That's right. We really didn't do much, other than go in, look around, confirm that, yeah, it's a suicide. Then get back to the real work."

"You're sure it's a suicide?" she queried.

"Definitely. Got a neighbor who was trimming the hedge that's between their properties. She just climbed up the ladder to get to the top, looked over, witnessed him drinking at his kitchen table, writing notes, talking on the phone with a gun right there beside him. Don't ask me why she didn't think that unusual enough to call in until she heard the gunshot, but there you have it."

"Other than that, anything?"

"Nothing," Hilleary said. "That's what doesn't make

sense. I mean, until Vince here called me, asked me to take a look at that note, I wouldn't have given it a second thought, even after the Feds came in, wanting the whole thing kept hush-hush, and removing the note from evidence. That part I figured had to do with the Senate confirmation stuff. No big, you know? Especially since it wasn't murder."

Vince asked, "You recall what the note said?"

"It's like this. That guy had quite a few notes scattered around his kitchen table, apologies saying he wished it didn't have to end this way, crumpled up like he was trying to get it just right. I lost track. Glanced at most of them, but didn't really take notice, at least not until one of your guys called me up right after, asking about the guy. Even then it didn't seem out of the ordinary."

"Who from our office called you?" Vince asked.

"Some agent named Hatcher. Said he was doing a background on the guy for something. Wanted to know if I thought it was a legit suicide and if he left a note. I told him, yeah, that he left several notes, all booked into evidence. He wanted us to release the notes to him. They were booked by that time, so it was too late. He had to satisfy himself with the photocopies that were in the evidence file. I figured if it was a big deal, he'd pull the proper strings, get the originals. You know, if the Bureau was taking over the case, or something."

"The photocopies," Sydney said. "Can I see them?"

"Copies of the copies." He opened the manila folder and handed them to her. The top sheet was a copy of the property record, showing, among other things, six suicide notes, along with a variety of other stuff found at the scene.

She read each note contained in the file, seeing nothing but the same words. "I'm sorry it had to end this way." One was actually addressed to his ex-wife, Becky Lynn, and he'd signed it. The shadows and creases that appeared on each told her these had been the crumpled notes that were no doubt straightened by the CSI for copying. "This is it?" she asked.

"That's all I saw, but like I said, I wasn't really looking." He ran his finger on the edge of the manila folder, eyeing it before turning his gaze on her. "Here's the thing. We run a

tight ship here, and it made some of the guys nervous, what
with the Feds coming down on us saying no one discusses
the case, because it's a matter of national security. A bit
overkill for a suicide, you ask me, but in this day and age,
who are we to question it? Especially considering there isn't
shit here in the notes, or even in the investigation. I could see
if there was, say, some big government conspiracy, kill him,
make it look like a suicide, but like I said, his neighbor saw
it. Of course, you want the real scoop about what was out
there, I'd ask the crime scene investigator, Sandra Sechrest.
If there was something there, something more than the nothing you got in those photocopies, she'll be able to tell you.
That woman's got a memory for detail."

"She here today?"

"Yeah. I can take you up to her office. She works in CSU
on the twenty-fourth floor."

It took two separate elevators to get up to the Crime Scene
Unit's level from the sixth floor. The first elevator took them
to the sixteenth floor. "Chief's office," Hilleary said, indicating why the carpet seemed a bit nicer on that level. From
there, they moved to the second elevator bank, rode up to
the twenty-fourth floor. The firearms lab was on one side,
the CSU offices on the other, accessed by a rather humble-
looking wooden door.

Hilleary knocked and waited. "No one gets in or out, without being escorted," he said. "Evidence."

A few moments later, the door was opened by a young
man wearing navy combat fatigues and a shoulder holster.
"Hilleary. What're you doing way up here?"

"Hey, George. Sandra in?"

"At her desk." He stepped aside, revealing a large office
of cubicles. Posters and Halloween decorations covered the
walls, photos and knickknacks littered the desks where the
investigators worked. Sydney scanned the room, saw the top
of a snowy white head just on the other side of a cubicle;
other than that, the office was empty. George escorted the
three to the woman's cluttered desk. A nameplate reading
"Sandra Sechrest" sat atop a stack of reports, finding more
use as a paperweight than a desk marker.

Officer Sechrest held a phone tucked beneath one ear, talking to someone as she rifled through a file cabinet, searching for something among the masses of hanging folders. She was a small woman, her white hair cut short, blue eyes that lit up when she saw Hilleary standing there with them. Sydney put the woman in her sixties, probably close to retiring sometime soon.

"Gotta go," George said, waving at Sandra.

She nodded, and he walked out. "I'm telling you they're wrong," she said into the phone. "It's in here somewhere, Evan. Copied it myself right before I went into court . . . Wait, wait. Got it!" She pulled out a file folder, opened it, and removed a printed document. "*Five* latent print cards from the trunk portion of the victim's car. I lifted those myself, so if they're trying to tell you anything different, they're full of— Yeah, yeah. I'll have it here for you when you get in."

She hung up, swiveled in her chair, and eyed the three of them waiting in front of her desk. "This looks a tad official . . ."

"Trust me," Alexander Hilleary said. "It's *un*official business."

Sydney leaned across the desk, shook the officer's hand. "Special Agent Fitzpatrick. Not really here."

"Special Agent Pettigrew," Vince said. "Not here, either."

"Sandy Sechrest. Nice not to meet you." Officer Sechrest leaned back in her chair, smiled. "So what can I do for you?"

Hilleary leaned forward, whispered, "The McKnight suicide. Now that you know that much, I gotta get back to work. But help 'em out, would ya?"

Sechrest raised her brows as he left. "Yeah. Sure . . ." The moment the door closed behind him, she said, "You do realize we were ordered not to discuss the case?"

"So Investigator Hilleary never mentioned," Sydney replied. "Which is why we're not really here . . ."

"Not sure what I can do for you. There wasn't much there. Seemed pretty cut-and-dried."

"In particular the suicide notes he left behind. What they said."

"Mostly he was sorry it had to end that way. Every single one of them. Pretty much the same."

"One in particular. One that might be missing from the files."

"What do you mean missing?"

Vince glanced around the otherwise empty office, while Sydney replied, "We have reason to believe that . . . another government agency removed the original suicide note from the files, perhaps due to political reasons."

Officer Sechrest shook her head, her smile bemused. "Removed them? This is that guy who was being looked into for some political appointment, right? I don't know about anyone removing the notes, but I do remember the FBI agent I gave copies to. He said it was a matter of security. No discussing the case with anyone, no releasing copies to anyone. Heaven forbid something nasty makes it to the press in an election year."

Sydney recalled Scotty mentioning his concern over things leaking to the press during elections. Somehow there had to be more to this than political scandals and swaying the voters. "So you think that maybe the notes are still there, that maybe they just didn't want them somehow leaked to the press?"

"Sure they are. More than likely they removed the copies from records so some clerk wouldn't accidentally set it in front of a reporter."

"Can you check in evidence? See if their copies still exist?" Sydney asked.

Officer Sechrest seemed to consider it, then shrugged. "You're the FBI, no reason I can't discuss the case with you." She picked up the phone, talked to someone, waited a couple of minutes, then said, "Thanks. I appreciate it. Hey, what about the photographs I took? The film . . . ?" Her gaze narrowed as she listened to whatever the evidence clerk told her, then hung up. "It's not there, and she checked with the film lab. The film was developed, and all photos of that note, including the negatives, are gone . . ."

Vince asked, "Any chance you recall what the notes said?"

"Not much. I mean, it really didn't make much sense,

but— Wait! The ME's office. They get copies, SOP, for the autopsy. How did I not think of them?"

Officer Sechrest called the medical examiner's office, her fingers tapping a cadence on her desk as she waited for them to check their files. Sydney knew what the result was by the way she'd hung up the phone. "Okay. This is really, really strange. The copy of that particular note is missing from their office as well . . ." And just when Sydney was beginning to despair that she'd ever find out what was in that note, Officer Sandy Sechrest smiled, grinned actually. "Ya know, I almost forgot we were dealing with a suicide here. That's a whole different game."

"Why is that?"

"The guy that just walked out when you got here, George? He studies suicide notes. Collects them in an unofficial capacity, much like your unofficial visit. A bit unusual as far as collections go, but you'd be surprised what you can learn from these things. Highly educational. And if we're lucky, he snagged a copy for his file."

23

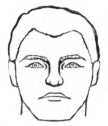

She sat in the airport, bone-tired, read the note for the fiftieth time, while she waited for Carillo to get back to her, because he wanted to do some research of his own. But as she examined it again, she wasn't sure what he could do, because nothing in it seemed to be the sort of thing you could check on.

Dear Sydney,

I'm sorry it had to end this way. I should have sent the money to your father. He only wanted it for Cisco's Kid, but Iggy said no. They could tie it to BICTT and it would ruin us all. I tried to call Boston. I always thought he'd be sick of fish and beer after twenty years. He was the only smart one. We should have all gone down there. What was I supposed to do? God, I'm so sorry. Sorry about your father. I'll make it right. Screw Iggy. BICTT is going to take him down, because they're still operating. The bastard gets what he deserves for

*what they did to you. Your father was right all along.
I know it now.*

Will

The note made very little sense. The evidence log showed it had been found under the table. That it was addressed to her might somewhat explain why Scotty had been waiting at her mailbox. They must have figured it was a draft, that another copy had been mailed, perhaps. But according to Scotty, McKnight had also been drinking, and if this thing had been found under the table, chances were that it never made it into the mail.

About twenty minutes later, Carillo finally got back to her. "I've got a couple things. One of them big," he said.

"Scotty was right," she said, not letting him finish. She'd had plenty of time to think about the note, decipher it while she was waiting for his call. "It had to have been about blackmail. *Cisco's Kid* was my father's boat. I have a picture on my nightstand of him sitting on it . . . If he was demanding money from McKnight, money for *Cisco's Kid*, I have to assume he was talking about the boat. The name *Cisco's Kid* was on the note that McKnight sent to me, the, um, one that Scotty said showed he was blackmailing McKnight. That's what you found, isn't it?"

There was a long stretch of silence on the other end. "Maybe it was money owed, and had nothing to do with boats and blackmail. It's the BICTT reference that must have spooked the CIA enough to come in and sanitize the files in Houston. Look at it from McKnight's point of view. Whatever made him eat his gun has to be a lot bigger than a little blackmail to finance the purchase of some fishing boat, especially after being singled out by the president to oversee a gazillion dollars of the federal budget. The fact McKnight even wrote the initials B-I-C-T-T just before he killed himself is pretty telling in my book."

"BICTT?" she repeated, pronouncing it as he did the first time, as one word, like *bikt*.

"You said Scotty mentioned some big banking scandal

when he showed up at your door? BICTT is one of the biggest banking scandals in U.S. history for what it encompassed, and for how it was whitewashed after the fact. They had a key witness who could pinpoint top government officials and major CEOs, who not only were bribed, but also had knowledge that the international bank was corrupt before it opened its doors on U.S. soil, all with their blessings."

"So what happened to the witness?"

"Speculation has it that he took off with some inside help, and hasn't been seen in the U.S. since. The blowout twenty-something years ago was huge."

"Huge enough to make someone kill himself, even today, long after the statute of limitations has run its course?"

"This isn't about statute of limitations. We're talking reputations of entire countries, including their CEOs and politicians and religious institutions, fortunes lost, careers ruined, wars financed kind of thing. After 9/11, *no one* wants their name associated with *anything* remotely related to terrorists, and that includes the CIA. And this banking operation hosted some of the biggest terrorists in the world, all while numerous OGAs in the U.S. turned a blind eye," he said. OGA was a common military term for other government agencies, and could encompass anything from the FBI to the NSA. "Hell, CIA was in on the ground floor when this bank opened a branch on U.S. soil, so they could run their own operations." She could hear the clicking of a keyboard as he typed. "Here it is. Bank of International Commerce Trade and Trust. BICTT."

"And we're sure this is the one?"

"As soon as I mentioned banking scandal to Schermer, this is the one he pointed me to. Schermer's source says it was known in the CIA as the Bank of International Crooks, Terrorists, and Thieves, and when it was busted open, helped cement the acronym of CIA as Caught In the Act. It was the ultimate banking institution if you were looking to evade taxes, handle illegal transfers of money, off-the-record deposits, or any other nefarious conduit for drug and crime money."

"So how was it exposed?"

"The bank got caught laundering money for the CIA, something to do with selling arms to one of the Agency's pet projects in South America or something. Word got out, and there was a big hearing. McKnight and his business partner, Robert Orozco, were supposed to testify before the subcommittee, but the Department of Justice kept interfering, blocking their depositions. And when Orozco disappeared off the radar, the whole thing ended up being whitewashed. The Senate turned out their subcommittee report, a few lawsuits were filed, and everyone went about their business as if nothing happened. Par for the course in government. If someone starts to notice something, they wag the dog and deflect attention elsewhere."

"McKnight testified?" she asked, moving out of the way of a woman wheeling a suitcase in one hand, and trying to keep hold of a toddler in the other.

"Not sure, yet. I haven't finished reading all the particulars. The congressional subcommittee report's about as long as *War and Peace*. But the Freedom of Information Act combined with the Internet is a beautiful thing. If you type McKnight's name into the Internet with the initials BICTT, it brings up the congressional subcommittee report. His name shows up under the chapter heading 'CIA and Arms Sales.' Same with Orozco. Since McKnight's sort of dead, I think you need to find this Orozco dude."

"Brilliant deduction. Any chance you've found out *where* to locate this Orozco dude?"

"Unfortunately, no. Doc Schermer checked every government file he could get into. Like I said, the guy dropped off the face of the earth about twenty-two years ago."

Twenty-two years ago was when her father was injured, and when he uprooted them to move to the Bay Area. The timing wasn't lost on her, but how it might help her was. Another dead end, or something more to be checked out? And thinking of things that needed checking . . . "Please tell me you and Doc Schermer found something on Wheeler's case? As of tomorrow he's at four days and counting."

"We did. The news isn't good. Not a lot to go on, I'm afraid. The original investigator died of a heart attack a

couple years ago, and out of the three witnesses that testified on Wheeler's behalf, only one is still alive. Wheeler's
girlfriend, the mother of his baby, overdosed on heroin about
a year after he was incarcerated, leaving their baby in the
care of Wheeler's maternal aunt, one Jazmine Wheeler. Had
a hard time tracking her down, because she's listed under
the report by her married name, *and* her first name was in-
correctly spelled in the report with an S, instead of a Z. You
know what a bear it is if the first name's not right. Apparently she went back to her maiden name, Wheeler, shortly after
the trial, when her husband, witness number three, walked
out, leaving her to raise Wheeler's baby on her own. Her ex
was killed in a car crash about five years back, so she's it."

"Any luck contacting her?"

"Not yet. She's a nurse at a methadone clinic in the city,
but she's out of town for a couple days."

"A *couple* days . . . ?" What chance did Wheeler have?

"Sorry, kid. Our best chance of talking to her is at the clinic, Sunday afternoon, or maybe at her house before. I hate to
break it to you, but between her and the photos, there's nothing left you can do. And the way I see it, the photos might be
Wheeler's last hope, or his ticket to the big house in the sky."
He was referring to a surveillance camera from a neighbor-
ing business that had caught stills of someone climbing into
the pizza parlor's rear window.

"But I thought those photos were unusable. That they
couldn't identify anyone."

"And that may still be the case. But there's been a lot of
progress with image enhancement techniques since the trial.
Back then they didn't have the digital tools they have now
with all the bells and whistles."

"That's good, then?"

"That's real good. The photographs are still logged into
evidence. I've got a contact out at DOJ who can enhance the
images, print up some photos that might just tell us who was
climbing in that back window. If it turns out it's someone
other than Wheeler, we've got our case."

An immense wave of relief swept through her, but a short-
lived one, when she realized that with only four days left,

there wasn't a lot of time. "How soon can we get those pictures?"

"My contact is putting a rush on it, Sydney. Thinks he can get it back to us in one, maybe two days, working on his off hours. Schermer's driving out to pick up the photos as we speak."

"Tell him I owe him."

"He knows. And really, there's nothing else we can do for the guy if this doesn't pan out . . ."

In other words, Wheeler's last hope was probably in those photos. "Call me if you find out anything more on either of the cases. I've got about an hour before my plane boards."

"Will do."

She disconnected, then started down the terminal toward her gate, walking past a gift shop decorated like some tiki hut. At least there was some progress on Wheeler's case, even if it did seem to come at a snail's pace in comparison to how much time he had left. That was more than she could say on this other matter. Who the hell was this Robert Orozco? The name meant nothing to her, but she felt as though it should. Just as the whole BICTT scandal meant nothing to her. No doubt it was covered in some course at the National Academy, but not to any great extent that would make an impression over any other scandal funding terrorists, she thought, reaching her gate. She chose a seat that backed up to a support column, giving her something to lean her head against, because she was wiped out from the redeye. Sinking into her seat, she propped her backpack behind her head and closed her eyes, feeling herself drift off, and wondering if she'd hear the boarding announcement if she did.

Bob.

The name popped into her head and she jerked awake, sat up.

Robert Orozco . . . Bob the Boat Guy. She dug the letter from her backpack, read through it again: *I tried to call Boston. I always thought he'd be sick of fish and beer after twenty years. He was the only smart one. We should have all gone down there.*

She called Carillo back. "I know who he is."

"Who?"

"Robert Orozco. He has to be Bob, the guy my dad fished with every year in Mexico. They were going to open up a fishing business in Baja when they retired. That was my father's big dream."

"Baja's sort of a big place."

"That boat I told you about, *Cisco's Kid*? There's a picture on my nightstand of me and my dad on that boat, and I need a copy of it."

"How am I going to do that?"

"My landlord, Rainie. She's always home. She can get it for you. I also need a contact number from my desk for Pedro Venegas of the AFI." AFI was Mexico's version of the FBI. Sydney had done some work for Venegas, and now it was time to call in a favor.

"Okay, so what's the purpose of going to Baja?"

"Because Bob, the boat guy, told me that was the first boat in their fleet. If he's the same guy, he's eating fish and drinking beer just south of Tijuana, and that boat is docked down there with him. He's got to be 'Boston' in the letter. It seems McKnight was using nicknames."

"Hold up, there, Pollyanna. Swinging over to Texas is one thing. How're you going to justify a trip to Tijuana?"

"What any good agent would do when they want to look in on something on their own time. Claim I have serious jet-lag and call in sick."

24

The temperate offshore wind gusted, then died, and Sydney brushed her hair from her face and her eyes as she stepped out of the Rosarito hotel where she'd spent the night, and taken a blessed shower. A light marine layer covered the sky, made her glad for her leather coat, though no doubt she'd be stuffing it into her backpack as the haze burned off later in the day. Her AFI contact, Pedro Venegas, was waiting for her out front.

"Senorita Fitzpatrick. It is good to see you again," he said, his English perfect, with only the slightest of accents. He wore a dark suit, a crisp white dress shirt, but no tie.

"Senor Venegas," she said, shaking his hand. They did not greet each other officially, primarily because she wanted no attention drawn to her. "Thank you so much for agreeing to meet me."

"I regret I can't offer you more, but perhaps what little I found will be of help. I hope you don't mind. I took the liberty of bringing you some good Mexican coffee." He waved his hand toward a black sedan parked nearby. On the hood was a cardboard carrier with two insulated coffee cups sitting within. They walked over, and he gave her one, took the other for himself. "This is from the best coffeehouse in all of Rosarito. Off the beaten path."

The scent of cinnamon and chocolate mixed with coffee swirled up from the cup as she lifted it to her mouth.

Venegas wasted no time, however, as he'd made it clear the night before when she'd called him that he could stay but a few minutes. "I worry about your presence here, looking for this Robert Orozco," he said.

"Why is that?"

"His name is, how do you say it . . . flagged? in our system. More importantly, there was an automatic audit, in that I couldn't run him without including which agency was requesting the info. I fear it may present a problem, but your name and mine are now linked to the internal audit. I did, however, say it was via phone call. How am I to say you were actually in our country when you called?" He eyed her as she sipped the fragrant brew, savored the cinnamon and chocolate warming her tongue. "Unfortunately there is much that worries me about this, and if you want some advice from me, I would go back to your country, the sooner the better."

"What do you mean?"

"Aside from the initial want of money laundering and being armed and dangerous? He remains as elusive now as he did twenty years ago when your government first started looking for him." Agent Venegas glanced at his watch before turning his somber dark gaze on her once more. "Your statute of limitations has long since run its course on Orozco. It makes no sense that my government still has his name flagged. What, then, is your government's real interest in him?"

"Precisely one of the reasons I want to talk to him. That and what he might know about my father's murder." She showed him the faxed photo of *Cisco's Kid*, but he had no suggestions on where she might find it.

She thanked him for his help and the coffee, and after they shook hands, he held her gaze a moment longer. "Be careful, Senorita Fitzpatrick. I am uncomfortable with this flag on Orozco's name. Computers are fast, and Baja so easily accessible."

"I'll be careful."

He turned, got into his car, and drove away, leaving her standing there, contemplating his words. That there was still a computer link to Orozco down here meant someone had a fair idea he'd been in Mexico all this time, and was just waiting until someone stumbled across him. No doubt the flag was of the sort that would send notification to whomever was looking for Orozco, but that was a detail she had little control over. What she needed to do was find him first, get the information she needed, then get the hell out of there. She'd spent a few hours the night before in Tijuana, asking around about the boat and Robert Orozco before she'd hired a car to drive her down to Rosarito when it soon became obvious that she wasn't far enough south.

On the one hand, she was disappointed she couldn't find him so easily, on the other, it confirmed in her mind that her memory had served her correctly, that her father had taken her to someplace south of Tijuana. And Rosarito Beach, one of the fastest growing cities for tourists and locals, fit that description. What didn't fit, however, were her memories. Hers had been of a much smaller, sleepier town. Now there were high-rise condos built between the pink and turquoise motels everywhere she turned, and multitudes of houses built into the once desolate chaparral-covered hills that looked out over the Pacific Ocean. Urban vacation sprawl, Americans snapping up dirt-cheap villas and condos that if purchased and built north of the border would cost millions for a slice of ocean views and rugged coastlines.

She walked through the town, trying to get a feel for it, see if there was anything she remembered. A giant arch with "Bienvenidos a Rosarito" painted across it welcomed tourists to the town. It was still early, but the shopkeepers beneath tiled roofs were sweeping the storefronts and setting out their pottery and knickknacks in preparation for the day, giving the area an old world feel as they spoke in Spanish too rapid for Sydney to understand. She wandered about, asking about fishing charters, and Robert and *Cisco's Kid*, but no one could offer her anything further.

Several times that morning, she felt as though she were

being followed, watched, but when she turned around, looked, she saw nothing that stood out. Nothing but workers, tourists, a few locals smoking on the street corner. Perhaps it was Venegas's warning about the flag on Orozco's name, or simply a feeling of guilt for all the rules she'd broken in the last few days, the least of them being that she was carrying concealed. Mexico was not the place to get caught carrying unauthorized weapons, and she, not being there officially, was completely unauthorized on many counts. A week ago, she would never have even imagined breaking such a rule. But she was no longer that same person. The day before, she'd deplaned in San Diego, dropped by the FBI field office, picked up the copy Carillo had faxed of her and her father on *Cisco's Kid*, before crossing the border on foot, armed not only with her Glock, but also with lots of cash.

The almighty dollar went a lot further down here, and she'd had no trouble hiring a car to drive her down to Rosarito from the border, but as she walked the shops and then the beaches, showing the copy of her father's photo, asking if anyone knew Robert and *Cisco's Kid*, she began to wonder if she'd remembered wrong. She'd spent the hours before sunrise surfing the Internet on the hotel's computer, trying to look up fishing expedition companies. Most, she'd discovered, were owned and operated in San Diego, even though their boats were docked down here. Those she immediately discounted. Robert Orozco wouldn't chance any U.S. ties, she was certain. But neither would he chance having a company in his own name, which made it a lot more difficult.

She took a taxi to the marina south of the hotel, had the driver wait, then walked around, and knew without a doubt this was not the right place. Too modern. The marina couldn't have been more than a few years old, nor were the condos built behind it on the hill. Frustrated, she returned to the taxi. "Are there other marinas around here?"

"Do you want to fish? Or go boating?"

"Neither. I'm looking for a boat and a man who owns it." She showed him the picture.

He nodded, traced his fingers across the background.

"Different now. But maybe near Ensenada. You want me to drive you?"
"How far?"
"Maybe fifteen minutes?"

Robert Orozco's two-year-old granddaughter, Rosa, picked up a small rock and tossed it into the surf. She laughed, toddled ahead, searched for another rock, not venturing too far from Robert's watchful gaze as he and Tomás walked behind her, talking.

"I'm getting worried," Tomás said. Tomás was the brother of Robert's common law wife, Juana, and the only one who knew his true background.

"We knew this day might come."

"It was not supposed to turn out this way."

"Who's to say how it should have turned out?"

They walked in silence for a while longer, while little Rosa chased a seagull, falling into the soft sand on her hands and knees, and Robert thought that all in all, he'd had a good life these past couple of decades. They didn't live in a palace, but it was still a good life, and one he would sorely miss. Perhaps if he was careful—

Rosa screamed, ran back to him. An odd wave rolled up, catching her chubby little legs. She jumped into his arms, laughing as he lifted her. He kissed her, set her back down, and she was off once more, and he sighed. "A good life, no?"

"What will you do?"

"Just what we planned. I have no choice. What did she look like?"

"An American woman dressed all in black. Wearing a black leather coat. She stayed at a hotel in Rosarito."

"You have all my account numbers."

"Yes."

"My will."

"In the safe."

"You know what to do if anything happens. Make sure my boat is ready."

"Maybe there's another way?"

"You know that's not possible. We knew this as soon as we heard the news . . ." He wondered how much time he'd have to say good-bye, how to say it. "Let's finish this walk." His last with Rosa, he thought, but couldn't say the words as he watched his granddaughter race across the sand, her tiny footsteps disappearing as the foamy water swept across the beach, erasing them as though they'd never been there at all . . .

Sydney realized all too soon that she'd started at the wrong end of the marina in Ensenada, walking the slips filled with yachts and pleasure boats, wading through passengers disembarking from a cruise ship. When she finally made it to the sports fishing piers, the air heavy with the scent of fish and bait, the gulls thick on the docks, it occurred to her that she was far too late if she was looking for fishing boats. The place was filled with empty slips, the sports fishermen having left at the crack of dawn if not earlier. Nor did she think she needed to talk to anyone in the large commercial ventures. What she needed was the older establishments, the ones who could point out to her the mom-and-pop operations, the sort you found out via word of mouth, assuming Orozco was even still in business.

Or had he ever started it up? Was it simply wishful thinking on her part that she could come down here after twenty-some-odd years and hope to find a man who clearly never wanted to be found?

She looked around, tried to figure out where to go next. Early in the morning the place had been filled with fishermen. Now the area was filling with boaters who had no interest in catching fish, unless it came already cooked and served on a platter. The tourists were starting to come out en masse, and for a moment she had no difficulty understanding why they were drawn here, and she took a moment, soaked in the sound of the gulls, the gentle breeze, the salt in the air and the sun on her face.

A brown pelican swooped down, landed in the water beside the dock where several other pelicans floated, perhaps waiting for the boats to come in, or resting after having fed all morning. A sea lion poked its head up, eyed a floating dock that already bore the weight of three other sea lions.

The water glistened, and white sails dotted the horizon. The sun had long since burned through the marine layer, warming the day to a balmy seventy according to the thermometer hanging outside the office of Tomasita's Fishing Charters, a small building no bigger than a couple of outhouses, paint flaking, hinges rusting at the edges. A sign out front advertised the cheapest rates in all of Ensenada. They probably were, since it was about the last place left to charter a boat. She reached for the door, but found it locked, and when she peeked into the dusty window, discovered it was empty.

"Great." She turned, looked around. A dark-haired man standing a few slips away stood coiling a rope, speaking heavily accented English to someone onboard a nearby boat. She walked over to him. "You know when they might be back?" She pointed to the office.

"Only early morning when the boats go out."

She took out the copy of *Cisco's Kid,* and showed it to him. "Any idea where this might have been taken?"

"Hmm." He squinted against the bright sun. "Puerto Nuevo, perhaps?"

"Puerto Nuevo?"

"*Sí*, a fishing village." He pointed up the coast to the north. "Famous for lobster. But you might ask at the fish market. Ernesto. He used to live in Puerto Nuevo."

"How will I find him?"

"Just ask anyone in there. They all know him."

"Thanks."

Which meant she was back to square one, because one guy who used to live in a town didn't mean she was any closer. She didn't have a clue where this boat was. What was it Carillo had said? Baja was a big place. It would be like walking up and down the coast of California searching, assuming the boat was still in existence. Hell, as far as she knew it could be in San Diego, and she'd remembered it wrong all these years. On that cheery thought, she left the pier. Just before she turned into the fish market, she looked back, saw the man on the boat who had pointed her this way talking to two men, one wearing jeans and a white golf shirt, the other in a pale Hawaiian shirt. Tourists or would-be fishermen, she thought, walking to the fish market that overlooked the waterfront.

Families lined the concrete bulwark, some eating tacos, others eating churros. Kids tossed bites to the gulls, laughing as the birds snapped at the pieces and each other. Pelicans waddled through the trash, poking their bills at it, searching for food that had been dropped. The scent of cinnamon and deep fried dough drifted from one of the many stalls, although most advertised tacos, the vendors shouting out, "Tacos *pescado*," as she walked by. The brightly painted signs advertised fresh fish tacos, apparently the specialty. Just beyond that stood a large building with "Mercado de Mariscos" painted at the top. In smaller print was the story of how the marketplace came to be. Sydney stepped into the cool interior, the smell of fresh fish over ice apparent and growing stronger as she wove her way through the various stands inside, asking for Ernesto, always being pointed farther in. She'd been to plenty of fish markets in the States, but there was nothing like the variety here. Everything from octopus and squid, to fresh or smoked tuna, not to mention the jumbo shrimp, albacore, lobster, clams, and many others she couldn't name.

But as she worked her way through, finally found Ernesto hawking rock cod, and tried to understand his heavy accent as he was directing her through a side door, she had that feeling again that she was being watched, a feeling that went beyond the simple knowledge that anyone holding out a picture, asking questions, would garner attention. She ignored the side door Ernesto wanted her to exit. No one inside was able to help her, most shaking their heads, or saying, "*No habla ingles.*"

She left, bought a couple of tacos at one of the stands out front, was certain she'd never tasted anything so good, the battered fish flaky, the tortilla fresh off the grill, the spicy

taste of radish bringing with it the instant memory of eating
fresh fish tacos with her father. And she might have gone for
that second taco, had a young boy of maybe ten or twelve
not walked up to her, his eyes jet-black, with a bit of sunlight
glinting from their depths. "Senorita? You are looking for
the boat *Cisco's Kid?*"

His question surprised her enough that it took a moment
for her to gather her senses. "Yes."

"This way, *sí*?" He beckoned for her to follow.

She crumpled her napkin, tossed it and the remaining taco
into the trash, then hurried after him as he raced from the
market, then on across the street. "You know this boat?" she
called out as she tried to keep up with him. "*Cisco's Kid?*"

"I know it," he said, darting around several women admir-
ing something in a shop window.

Before she could query him further he was a good twenty
yards away. She looked back toward the market, the water,
then to the boy, running away from the docks. Away from
the boats.

He stopped, waved at her. "Hurry, senorita. There isn't
much time."

This *was* what she came for, right? The moment he saw
her start in his direction, he was off again, running, zipping
around pedestrians, light posts, and trash cans. He made a
right, then a left, disappeared down a narrow cobbled street.
There were no shops here. It seemed to be mostly residen-
tial, older homes. In the back of her mind was the strong
sense that she was being set up, but she'd come too far to
pass up even the slightest lead. And just when she was about
to give up, figured he was definitely setting her up, probably
for a robbery, she saw it, a boat, high and dry and filled with
flowers as colorful as the painted, tile-roofed house it sat in
front of.

Out of breath, she stood there, stared, looked around for
the boy. She thought she heard him calling out, "Senorita."

"Hello?" she said in reply, starting down the narrow street
toward the boat, just as a car drove up, parked in front of it.

A slight rustling sent her senses on high alert. Before

she could turn, someone stepped from a shadowed alcove. Reached out, grabbed her from behind. With one swift move, he slid her gun from her waist, then clamped his other hand over her mouth. He pulled her against his chest, whispered in her ear. She barely heard him over the pounding of her blood. "Do not move, senorita, and no one will be hurt."

25

Sydney's heart slammed into her throat. She caught a glimpse of the boy at the end of the alley near the boat. Tried to silently plead with him to run for help—an absurd thought since he was the instrument used to lure her here. The man pulled her against him, held her arm behind her back. His hot breath hit her ear as he said, "Senorita. Slowly we walk to that car. Nod if you understand."

She struggled against him, and he gave a slight tug on her arm. Pain shot through her. She forced herself to still, waited a moment, knew who had the advantage. It wasn't she. He could snap her neck in one quick move. Attempting to nod her acquiescence, she felt him loosen his grip around her mouth, slightly, perhaps to test her cooperation.

"Quietly to that car. Do you understand?"

She nodded, figuring any forward movement was good. A chance to get away. Get someone's attention. But if he thought she was getting in that car, he was dead wrong. Bad enough she'd allowed her desire to find a boat she wasn't sure still existed get in the way of all rational thought. "I have money," she said. "Several hundred dollars."

"Move, senorita," he said, holding her tight, while he

walked her down the narrow street to the waiting car. She could see the boat just beyond it, taunting her, the long tendrils of some hanging plants, rosemary she thought, growing down the sides of the boat, while large pots of flowers filled the middle. And as they neared the car, she eyed her surroundings, saw the boy was gone. There was a man behind the wheel on the opposite side; no one else seemed to be there and the doors were closed. She knew that would be her chance, when he'd be at his most vulnerable. Because he was going to have to let go with one arm to open the door. And she could use the strength in her legs to brace herself, fight back. If nothing else it would cause a scene; maybe someone would report it.

And then they were at the car. He reached out, opened the door, and she put her foot on the floorboard, ready to push off and back, take him down.

Except the wind gusted in that one moment.

Rustled the plants hanging down the sides of the boat. In that split second, her foot poised, her body braced, she read two words: *Cisco's Kid.*

And she thought of the picture in her pocket.

And allowed the man to place her in the car.

"Who are you?" the driver asked. "And did you come alone?"

Hispanic man, maybe late forties, he eyed Sydney from the rearview mirror, waited for her to answer, and she thought he looked vaguely familiar, at least the two square inches of him she could see in the mirror. She glanced at the man seated beside her, didn't recognize him at all, thirties, also Hispanic, busily searching through her backpack. He opened her wallet, bypassed her money, and pulled out her license, reading her name, then replaced it. So this wasn't robbery. "Sydney Fitzpatrick, and yes, I'm alone."

"And what are you doing in Ensenada, Senorita Fitzpatrick?" the man beside her asked, as he eyed the suicide note, then shoved it into the backpack, before he took out Arturo's phone, pulled it apart, examined it. He dropped it back into the pack, not bothering to put it together.

"Searching for that boat," she said, nodding out the window, thinking about the picture of it that was in her coat pocket, something her captor didn't appear too interested in at the moment. "You don't happen to know the owner, do you?"

No one answered her. Instead the driver shifted into gear, took off. She watched for street signs, tried to remember the direction, in case she was able to call for help. Several minutes later, as he wound his way in and out of the narrow streets, around corners, it was clear he was trying to keep her from recognizing a location, or keep someone from finding them. Or both.

"Where are we going?" she asked.

As if in answer, he slowed, checked his mirrors, then made a quick left turn into an arched drive that led into the courtyard of a salmon-colored villa. A tall blond man stood in the center of the brick-paved courtyard, holding what looked like an old leather bank pouch. His bearded face was deeply lined, darkly tanned, his collar-length hair bleached from the sun. She put him in his mid-fifties. The car slowed just long enough for him to get into the front seat, and the moment he did, they exited.

"Were you followed, Tomás?" he asked the driver as they pulled out.

"I think we lost them. She says she came alone."

The blond man turned in his seat, looked right at Sydney, his gaze searching her face. "You look like him. Your father."

She eyed him for a moment, decided that the sun had aged him more than she'd expected, but he was probably the man in the photo. "You're Robert Orozco?"

"I am."

"Boston?"

He smiled. "Not a name I've heard in a while. So, little Sydney, why is it you are here, asking about *Cisco's Kid*, a boat that I sold twenty years ago, after your father was killed?"

"I remembered it from a photo of my father's, a trip we took." She removed the scanned photo from her pocket, showed it to him. "You disappeared the year before he was killed. I think you have answers."

"That will only lead to more questions, I'm afraid."

"And I'm willing to take the time."

"Which we don't have. You think that no one knows you are here? You came to my charter boat office. Do you not recognize my driver, Tomás?"

She glanced over, and this time the driver turned, looked right at her. The man from the pier who had thought the boat looked like something from Puerto Nuevo.

"You were being followed even then, which is why he sent you into the fish market. The men approached him, asking about you, what you wanted. Tomás sent them on a wild-goose chase in the opposite direction that he sent you. They are, we hope, checking out a boat to the south in Punta Banda, no doubt wanting to get to it before you. We hope they don't figure it out too soon, since we did not expect you to stop for tacos." His eyes sparkled, despite the concern that laced his voice.

"Do you know who these men are?" she asked. "Who they work for?"

"I can only surmise."

She had so many questions for him that she wasn't sure where to start. "You heard about McKnight?"

"Yes."

"He mailed me a photo of all of you. And he left a suicide note." She took that from her backpack, gave it to him.

Orozco looked at it, handed it back, and she saw a glint of red from the ring on his right hand, one like her father used to wear. "So that's what started it. Twenty years of peace gone because some guy wants to clear his fucking conscience. Iggy and company have got to be sweating bullets right about now."

"Iggy?"

"Iggy Ignoble. Your senator."

"About what?"

"I assumed you knew." He held up the pouch. "Why else did you come down if not for this?" he asked as Tomás whipped the car around a corner, then accelerated. "Everything you wanted to know about just how dirty your government really is."

"And just how dirty are they?"

"You've heard of companies like TriAmeriCon?

"Aren't they into construction?"

"Multibillion-dollar worldwide construction and shipping firm, based in the good old U.S. of A. They're the superman of global companies, able to leap U.S.–imposed sanctions and embargos with one simple phrase to the country they need to enter: Look the other way and we'll make it worth your while."

"BICTT? Part of the scandal twenty years ago?"

"It wasn't a scandal, it was the tip of an iceberg so large, they didn't dare let the American public know the truth. With companies like TriAmeriCon, Blienett Subsidiaries, KeenAnex Oil, to name a few, it was in their best interest to whitewash the entire affair. This pouch has key information that would literally cripple corporate America if the public knew what these companies were really involved in, and end treaties between a number of countries. It's like the little black book of corrupt governments and corporations. If there's a country that needs to be rebuilding due to war, or a war that needs starting to drive economy, or drugs traded for arms, arms traded for oil, or money paid to revolutionists to protect foreign enterprise, you name it. One of these companies has their hand in it, all with the blessings of the government, sometimes even the manpower of black ops teams, and the public has no idea."

"So if they closed down the bank, exposed those involved in the Senate hearings twenty years ago, made laws that prohibited dealing with terrorists and the like, why the interest now?"

"Because BICTT was only one small part of this, like I said, the tip of the iceberg. BICTT's Black Network is still operating today, still has ties to governments around the world. In here is a peek at what's below the surface. What's *still* going on."

She looked at the pouch. "In there?"

"*If* you can break the code. The government prefers to whitewash it all to keep the economy stable. Just like they did the first time. Because in the end it's all about money.

And don't expect a miracle if you get this information back home. They'll pick some schmuck of a corporation, force it to pay a hefty fine once it's discovered they were playing with countries in the evil axis, invite the press to watch, and that'll be the last you hear of it until some other idiot blows his brains out, leaving incriminating letters behind."

Tomás said, "I think we're being tailed. They either have more than one team, or they didn't buy my story."

Robert looked back, eyed the cars behind them. "What are our options, Tomás?"

"The boat is still the best option. It's fueled and ready."

"Get us there," he said, then pulled a Beretta from beneath the seat. "Return her weapon, Jose. She'll need it."

Jose withdrew her weapon from his waist, handed it to her. She checked to see it was still loaded, then glanced behind her. A black Mercedes was gaining, then had to back off as another car changed lanes. "This is going to sound like a dumb question, but who are these guys?"

"My first guess? The Black Network. If not them, maybe a team from the CIA, trying to get this info. Either way, they're men who can follow orders and not ask questions. That was part of the problem for Frank and your father, too. Didn't like going into anything blind. If your father hadn't been killed in that robbery, chances are he would've ended up dead anyway, because he balked at keeping it quiet. He got emotionally involved after the explosion, then insisted it was no accident. Didn't help that he blamed McKnight for his sleepless nights and missing digits."

"Was my father blackmailing him?"

Robert scoffed. "Your old man was guilty of a lot of things. Nature of the job. But blackmail? I don't think he saw it that way. His problem was that he started a family. Changed his way of thinking. Same with Frank, though his old lady was smart and never married him to begin with."

This was the second time he'd mentioned that name. "Frank?"

"Frank White. Kind of a misnomer. Half Puerto Rican, half black. Our fifth team member," he said, and she made a mental note on the name. "Having a family didn't do him or your father much good in the end. Too many ties. Too much to lose. Which is why I set up a safety system that would set things in action if they came after me," he said, holding up the bank pouch. "Insurance, if you will. And I made sure everyone knew my connections to the press, and just what would happen to this info on my demise. Bought me twenty years . . ." He seemed to give himself a mental shake. "Now that McKnight's dead, it's a hell of a lot easier for them to send in a black ops team, take me out and get rid of this pouch. That's the problem when your only contact in the States is playing both sides, and the remaining guy you had planned on as part of your insurance plugs a bullet into his own head."

"Who was your contact?"

"Becky Lynn McKnight. She's great when it comes to getting passports and fake IDs, but after that, wouldn't trust her for a second." He gripped his gun, shifting in his seat to face the back. "I'd suggest the two of you duck way down in the back. They want what's in here real bad, and they're playing for keeps."

Tomás stepped on the gas, made a quick succession of turns, staying out of the crowded areas of the city. She gripped the doorframe, leaned into a turn. "So what's in that pouch besides bank info on BICTT?"

"Account numbers and identifiers from all the major players. This bank financed some of our major ops, and a lot of terrorist stuff all over the world. Stuff our government knew about, stuff our government wanted done. We knew this when it first tried to take over a savings and loan in Texas. They needed legitimate businessmen to facilitate the opening, get past the governmental red tape. That's where McKnight and I stepped in. To lend our business names, well, his. Mine was more of the security side of things. The computers. One of my specialties back when your dad and I worked together. Breaking into places, hacking computers. Which is how I ended up with the info in this pouch, and how I know their Black Network is still operating. Proof's in here."

Tires screeched as they skidded around a corner. "Hold

on," Tomás said, slamming on the brakes. The antilock kicked in, the brakes thumping as they took hold. The scent of burning rubber filled the car as he waited until a truck passed, then gunned it, squeezing into traffic.

"When the shit hit the fan," Robert continued, "I had a feeling that we were going down hard to save some political ass. Didn't want to end up on the bottom of that dog pile, because it was either prison or a coffin. Either way, I didn't like the odds."

The car jerked as Tomás switched lanes. Sydney glanced behind her in time to see the black Mercedes speeding up after them. "Might want to sit even lower," Robert said, shifting in his seat, to keep an eye on that back windshield.

Tomás gunned it, turned again, and now they were on the open road, heading north up the coast. "Why now?" she asked.

"Because Willy McKnight couldn't let sleeping dogs lie. No one cared as long as it remained buried. When he wrote that note before he killed himself, he stirred up more shit than he could fit on the end of his stick." Robert ejected the magazine from his Beretta, checked to see if it was full, then slapped it back in. "Ripple effect."

"Why didn't you just testify back then?"

He looked over at her. "Like I said, BICTT had their Black Network, and they tried to kill me. That's when I took off. Haven't been back since."

The rear windshield shattered. "Stay down!" Robert yelled.

Sydney and the man beside her ducked. Robert aimed, returned fire. The shot deafened her. Tomás drove as fast as the winding coastal road allowed. "About two minutes," he yelled to Robert.

Robert fired a second round. "We're going to turn into a dirt lot," he shouted back to her, over the roar of the wind that rushed in. "Tomás is going to slide the car in, and we're going to use the dust as a cover. So hold your breath, grab onto Jose's hand, and trust him like you've never trusted anyone in your life. Got it?"

Like she had a choice?

Tomás made a sharp left onto a dirt road, and she caught

a glimpse of a cliff and the ocean below. *"Now!"* Tomás said, whipping the car around. Dirt sprayed out behind the wheels; a cloud of dust mushroomed up.

"Go!" Robert yelled.

Jose threw the door open, grabbed Sydney's hand. She had enough sense to grab her backpack as they slid out. Her throat constricted on the dust. She glanced back, caught a glimpse of the Mercedes through the dust cloud, and Tomás hit the gas, racing straight for it, kicking up more dirt, completely obscuring her vision.

Her eyes stung; she couldn't breathe. Jose pulled her straight toward the cliffs. "Hurry," he shouted. And the next thing she knew, he dragged her over the side. She felt nothing for a moment, a freefall, then her feet hit solid dirt, her back end slammed into the cliff's side. Down, down, she slid. Her heart thumped and she could hear the ocean pounding below them. Her eyes watered from the dust and the wind, and she tried to see through the blur. Wondered if she'd stop before she plunged straight into the jutting rocks below.

26

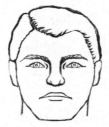

"There's a path down here," Robert Orozco called out to Sydney as she slid down the side of the steep hill. "My boat is at the bottom in the cove." And sure enough, two seconds later, her feet found solid purchase. She slung her backpack over one shoulder, gripped her gun tightly in her right hand. The path was carved into the dirt and stone of the cliff, narrow and treacherous. Jose was in front, Sydney behind him, and Robert took up the rear. A sharp crack rang out, echoed on the cliffs. Robert fired back. Another crack. Dirt sprayed up in front of them.

Ten more feet to a large rock outcropping. She turned. Fired two rounds, then raced for the rock. Robert fired off several rounds, then stumbled after them. Blood soaked his pants leg. "They shot my fucking knee."

Several sharp cracks followed. Jose said, "We can carry you to the boat."

"We'll be Swiss cheese before you get me down there."

"I can't leave you, *Tio*."

Robert looked at Sydney. Dust streaked his face, covered his once blond hair. "You drive a boat?"

"Not in a while." She'd grown up in boats, first with her father, then with Uncle Leland.

"Hasn't changed that much. Just a lot faster." He took the leather bank pouch, handed it to Sydney. "This is what they want. Take it. Go!"

"I can't leave you here."

"The hell you can't." He stopped, listened. The faint sound of a siren could be heard over the top of the cliffs. "I think Tomás made it. Help is on the way. Even if it isn't, they'll think it is. You do this, maybe I get another twenty-year re-prieve."

Still, she hesitated.

"Jose and I will hold them off. Take that thing out of here. Make sure you wave it around so they see it." He grinned. "They'll start shooting at you, instead of me."

Two sharp cracks echoed from the cliff tops. It was all the convincing she needed, and she shrugged her backpack securely over both shoulders, grabbed the pouch, ran down the path, only to hear him shouting, "Watch out for chop-pers," before he and Jose fired off several shots, buying her a few seconds.

She hugged the cliff side, trying not to expose herself. Gunshots cracked and echoed around her. At the bottom was a small strip of white sand and smooth pebbles, then tide pools and rocks. No boat.

She looked up, saw the two men on the cliff top, saw Rob-ert and Jose firing at them, diverting their attention, Robert leaning heavily on his nephew. Her ears rang with each shot fired, the waves roared, crashed beside her, sending a spray of water across her face.

Cove. He'd said something about a cove, and she raced across the thin stretch of sand, eyeing the cliff, the rocks to her right. And there it was, a sleek Cigarette Gladiator rac-ing boat, custom painted in shades of black and gray, which meant one thing in her mind: speed and control under the cover of darkness. Pirates. Robert Orozco probably had no intention of leaving here in broad daylight. Not until she'd led his enemies right to his doorstep. And now here, bobbing in a small cave, protected from the waves that crashed just the other side of the rocks, moored to a piece of jutting rock out of sight from the men shooting above, was a boat worth as much as the finest villa on the rocky shores above her. Knowing Robert's background, she pictured this as some sort of smuggler's cave, wondered how far it went back beneath the cliff. Was she supposed to drive inward, find some secret exit?

But no, he would have said something. Unless he was distracted. Being shot will do that to a person, and she eyed the cavern, before turning her attention to the narrow mouth. If . the only way out was via the front, the question was, how to get it out of there and not be smashed into the rocks? It wasn't until she waded to the boat, gun high up in one hand, the pouch in the other to keep them dry, that she saw the channel between the rocks, only visible between waves, as she tossed in the two mooring ropes. She had to assume that if someone drove the boat in there, it could be driven out. Whether *she* could drive the thing remained to be seen. It was far more boat than she was used to. Hell, the cockpit looked like it belonged in a jet. The basics were there, clearly some extras. Throttle, bilge pump, blowers, oil and temperature gauges, and the tachometer. The keys were hanging from the ignition, and she hit the switch, turned on the bilge blowers, and gave it as long as she dared to clear fumes from the motor compartment, using the time to secure Robert's bank pouch inside her backpack, then sliding it onto her shoulders. Whatever was in there was too important to chance losing it, she thought, pulling in the docking bumpers, then running through the check of the instruments, putting the throttle in idle, gearshift neutral. She tried to listen, couldn't hear any shots, shouts, sirens, or any other noises down here, and hoped it was the same, that no one up there could hear her. Maybe she'd have a chance after all.

But not if she didn't get the hell out of there. She turned the ignition key and released the starter switch as the engine rumbled to life. Switching off the blowers, she listened to the slow, steady roar that filled the cavern, vibrated the boat, and she let it idle. Watched the water. If she didn't time it right, she'd be shark bait and the boat would be tinder crashing on the rocks. Definitely in the timing. She waited a few seconds, tried to get the feel of the water, the timing of the waves. The boat bobbed gently, up, down as each wave came in. And just when she thought she had the timing, a sleeper crashed, filling the channel with deadly white water.

But she knew time wasn't on her side. Her best chance was at the crash of the white water. Start forward as it came up, hope the water was receding as she sped through.

She tucked the gun into her waist, held her hand on the throttle, pushed it forward the moment the next wave crashed.

White water sprayed her face; wind whipped her hair. Before she could breathe, she was through, open water in front of her, the rocks receding behind her. She glanced back and up. Saw the men at the top change their stance when they saw her. And then Robert bracing himself as Jose jumped out, fired at the men. She pushed the throttle. The boat screamed forward, bounced across the surf, jarring her. She steered to the north, zigzagged, hoping for some cover from the rocks, before moving out into the open water, where a bullet could ricochet across the surface like a skipping stone, then bounce up and take her out. It was rare, but she wasn't about to take a chance. Only when she was far enough out did she dare a second look back, and she thought she saw the black Mercedes speeding north on the highway. Just south, where she thought Robert and Jose were holed up, it looked as if the cliff top was filled with flashing red lights of patrol cars.

Perhaps Robert was okay, she thought, turning back, watching the water. The police had come. She only hoped this evidence he'd given her, whatever it was, was enough to cover her ass, because she was bound to be in trouble by the time she got back, especially if Scotty happened to mention her midnight foray to the airport via Arturo's motorcycle and someone found out about her unauthorized trip south of the border. Not that anyone *had* to find out. If she was lucky, she'd slip into port in San Diego, casually leave the boat behind, catch a cab to the field office, then a plane to the city, with no one the wiser, her good-girl reputation intact.

Of course she had to get north of the border first, and now

that the threat of being shot at was gone, she pulled back on the throttle, and the boat settled into a much smoother cruising speed. If she ignored everything that had happened to her, it would almost be enjoyable in the bright sun, passing the sailboats that scudded across the surface. To her right was a small town, she guessed Puerto Nuevo, the place to go for lobster, if she recalled correctly. Several minutes beyond that she could see the brightly colored hotels that lined Rosarito Beach. About fifteen minutes from there until Tijuana del Playa. Every now and then, she glanced behind her and to the shore, searching for a boat that seemed to be coming after her. So far nothing but pleasure boats and sailing vessels, no one paying her the slightest heed, though a few waved as she zipped past.

She couldn't wait to get to shore, out of the bright sun. Her head was beginning to pound as the shores of Tijuana grew closer, and just beyond that, San Ysidro and San Diego. All she could think about was ibuprofen, a dark room, and quiet. No roar of the engine, no thudding in her head . . .

Something made her look up and back toward shore, and she realized it wasn't her pulse thumping, but the beating of a helicopter. Tijuana was right there, and she thought perhaps a tourist attraction. Hoped it was a tourist attraction. But Robert had warned her. And the chopper wasn't flying like some gentle tourist ride, hoping to sight a few dolphins. It was heading straight for her.

She pushed on the throttle, felt the boat bounce across the surface. They could shoot her out here, drop down, retrieve the bag, then leave, no one the wiser until her body washed up on some beach.

If it washed up.

Sydney eyed the shore, wondered if she should make a break for Tijuana, hope the crowds would deter them, or keep heading north. But that was the direction the copter was coming from. And while this boat might be the Ferrari of the sea, in comparison to the chopper, she might as well be driving a Volkswagen van. Time to open it up. The boat shot forward, and she gripped the steering wheel feeling as out of control as a being caught on a runaway horse as each bump sent her flying. The copter grew closer, and she almost imagined she could hear the beating of the rotors over the roar of the wind and engines.

She thought of Arturo's phone, wished she'd had the sense to put the battery back in it. Who the hell knew if it worked this far south of the border?

A radio. She glanced over, saw a marine radio, the microphone hanging. Channel 16. Her father, her uncle, and then Jake had pounded it into her head. Emergency channel 16. She flicked it on, then gripped the steering wheel again. One glance back, and she saw the chopper closing in.

Shit. Let it work, she thought, picking up the mike and keying it. "Mayday, mayday, mayday," she called, then released the button, hearing nothing but static. What was it Jake used to tell her? If you didn't hear them, it didn't mean they couldn't hear you. They could call someone else for help.

She had no idea what the name of the boat was, and so she used the brand, along with her FBI radio call sign. "This is FBI Gladiator thirty-six, mayday. I'm northbound off Tijuana. Being chased. Helicopter. Armed and dangerous."

Again, nothing but static. And then what she thought was the faint report of a weapon.

Crap. The helicopter could go at least hundred miles an hour faster than she could. She thought about returning fire, but figured she couldn't drive and shoot at the same time. She glanced back, saw a man leaning out. Robert thought they were some sort of black ops.

If so, what chance did she have?

But the copter didn't look like some military craft, so maybe she had a chance after all, because one thing these boats could do was move across water. And a moving target was damned hard to hit. She started a zigzag pattern, kept it up, wondered if the small bursts of white water were rounds hitting.

A group of sailboats glided ahead, their skippers oblivious to the threat. With no choice, she had to zip between them. The helicopter suddenly backed off. Apparently taking out a civilian wasn't acceptable; someone would have to answer.

Just as Robert said, *she* was the target. This pouch she carried guaranteed that.

There were more sailboats, but she wasn't about to take the chance she was wrong. And as she passed them, the helicopter veered closer, banked in. And her radio squawked to life. "FBI Gladiator thirty-six. This is the coast guard. Identify your position."

She didn't have time to pick up the radio. Not if she wanted to stay alive. She continued her pattern, trying to outmaneuver the chopper. Its shadow crossed her hull as it banked, coming in from the front. It hovered, its beaters churning the water around her. A man leaned out.

She reached for her gun, figuring this was it.

"FBI Gladiator thirty-six," came a booming loudspeaker. "This is the coast guard. We have you in sight."

Just beyond the copter, she saw the welcome sight of a gray coast guard cutter, speeding south toward her. And then a hail of gunfire, as the man in the chopper opened on her.

27

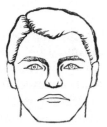

Somehow Sydney made it through, unlike Robert's
boat, which had more holes in it than she cared to count.
Lucky for her the cutter made decent time and the helicopter
pulled up and out of there, before the coast guard trained its
two .50 caliber machine guns at it.

From there it took her twenty minutes to convince them
she needed to get to the San Diego field office at warp speed,
when what they wanted to do was question her for hours
about what she was doing in Mexican waters driving a
world-class speedboat, being chased by a helicopter bearing
men with guns.

Sydney, having no clue as to what Robert really did for
a living these days, claimed she was merely in Mexico on
a pleasure trip, when she was set upon by smugglers, who
grabbed her in Puerto Nuevo, and she managed to escape on
a boat that just happened to have the keys inside.

When they wouldn't let her off their cutter, she had them
make a quick call to the last person she wanted to talk to,
Scotty. After a brief explanation, with as many holes in it as
the boat she'd left behind, Scotty told her he'd take care of

it, his last words being for her to get on the first plane back
to the city.

Five minutes later, the commander of the boat received a
call, listened to whatever was being told to him, then said
two words, "Yes, sir." He looked at Sydney, said, "We'll be
transporting you to the San Diego field office."

What was it that Vince Pettigrew had said about dealing
with someone very high up the food chain? No doubt who
Scotty was dealing with, because that was one quick turn-
around, and all interrogations about her ordeal had instantly
stopped, further proof that Scotty was investigating something she could only imagine the depths of.

When she reached the Bureau office, she was able to fend
off any questions with a simple "Had a boating accident.
Coast guard rescued me." It worked since everyone there
had assumed she was merely there for a bit of sightseeing,
and her scraped hands, and the tear in the leg of her jeans,
somewhat stiff from the dried seawater, seemed to verify
her story. At least the seawater had washed off most of the
dust. Her leather coat was marred from the rocky cliff, but
had probably saved her a number of cuts and scrapes, and if
nothing else, it added character.

She called Carillo the moment she was at the airport, gave
him a quick rundown, and he said, "Well, that explains why
the shit's hitting the fan here. And I thought it was bad yesterday, after Scotty told them about the you-know-what on
you that I'm not supposed to know about."

"So he did tell Dixon?"

"I'm guessing so, since Dixon's been holed up with him in
the ASAC's office all morning."

"Any word on what they plan on doing?"

"Like find you a nice safe room where you can't get into
trouble? No idea. But they called me in, and asked if I knew
where you took off to the other night."

"What'd you tell them?"

"What do you think? To ask Scotty. He's the one who took
you home, maybe he knew."

"And Scotty said what?"

"What could he say? The big nothing, since he's the one who lost you."

"And Dixon didn't mention my flight to Texas?"

"He was too busy popping Tums. Lettie mentioned that you'd, uh, called in sick this morning. I'm sure he probably thought something's up by now, but frankly, I've been keeping myself scarce and busy. Easy enough to do since Operation Barfly's starting up tonight."

"Barfly?"

"Doc Schermer came up with the name. Our multijurisdictional stakeout of the area bars, looking for Jane Doe's killer. We got a tentative ID on her and a tip that she was last seen at one of our bars with a guy who, at least from the description given, matches your sketch of the suspect that attacked Tara Brown. I've got you assigned to barhop with me, but who knows how that'll go over. Especially after today."

"Any word on Wheeler's photos yet?"

"Sorry. Not yet. But you know the moment we hear something . . ."

And all she could think was Johnnie Wheeler had three days from tomorrow.

Her phone beeped with a low battery warning. "Gonna have to go, before I lose you."

"By the way, whose phone are you using, if you left yours behind?"

"My neighbor's. The one who lent me his bike."

"Nice neighbor."

"Yeah. I should probably get him a Christmas present."

"Before you start shopping, you might want to get your ass back here, see if you still have a job."

"I'm boarding the plane as we speak."

Sydney took a taxi home, stopped there long enough to shower, throw on some clean jeans, on the off chance that they might let her go out, then grabbed the same leather coat, as well as Arturo's backpack, not having time to search out something better, because according to Lettie, her bosses were on the warpath, and Sydney was the star victim.

The office buzzed with activity when she walked in, agents who normally would've been winding down, getting ready to leave for the day, were now just coming in, checking weapons, cuffs, and radios for the upcoming task force operation. Lettie cornered Sydney the moment she saw her. "Dixon wants you in his office right away."

"I'll be right there." She passed Carillo, who gave her a once-over at the sight of her sunburned face and scraped hands, then grinned.

"This the new Baja look?"

"You know me. Cutting-edge style."

"Never seen you dressed casual before." He leaned back in his chair, propped his feet up on the desk. "Want a bit of advice before you go in? Off the record, since Scotty informed me I know nothing."

"Go for it."

"Deny, deny, deny."

"Gee, aren't you the helpful one."

"I'm here for you." As she started toward her desk, he called out, "You look hot in black leather, but the whole reflective backpack? Gotta go."

She walked back toward him, dumped her backpack on his desk, then leaned down so only he could hear. "Which reminds me. Inside is a bank pouch. That's what they were shooting at me for, and maybe what Scotty and his crew are searching for."

He eyed it with new interest. "That right?"

"Don't ask me what the hell it is, but maybe you'll have better luck. Just don't go waving it around unless you're wearing body armor."

She left it with him, walked to Dixon's office, ignoring the stares of her coworkers, who all seemed to know that something was up. She tried to look calmer than she felt, then knocked on the door.

Dixon gave a terse "Come in."

She opened it, stepped in, saw him glance up at his Tahiti brochure next to his retirement calendar, as he popped a couple of Tums in his mouth, no doubt wishing for something stronger.

The ASAC had his back to her, talking, or rather listening to someone on the phone, and Scotty stood to one side, his arms crossed, a vein pulsing in his temple as he pinned his gaze on her. She tried not to look at him. "You wanted to see me?" she asked, then immediately regretted it. Of course he wanted to see her. Everyone in here knew it, and apparently everyone in the outer office knew it as well.

Dixon held up one finger, indicating she needed to wait until the ASAC was off the phone. She'd be lucky if he didn't have her transferred to some safe house in Alaska, then ship her fifty boxes of data entry, just to keep her busy while they finished up their investigation.

Finally the ASAC hung up the phone. He stood maybe two inches taller than Sydney, salt and pepper hair, blue eyes, and pale skin. His wide mouth was set in a stern line as he turned toward her, clearly upset. "Special Agent Fitzpatrick," he said, eyeing her clothes before meeting her gaze. "You are, of course, acquainted with Special Agent Scott Ryan."

As acquainted as sleeping with the guy for six months could make her, she supposed. "Yes, sir."

"I have just spent the past several hours with Special Agent Ryan, discussing an ongoing investigation into one or more persons on the staff of Senator Gnoble, whom I believe you're also acquainted with . . ."

She waited, knew what was coming next, not sure what she could say that wouldn't get her in more trouble than she was already in.

"Damn it!" He slammed his fist on Dixon's desk, and she jumped slightly. Even Dixon and Scotty moved back an inch as he looked at her. "No one, and I mean no one threatens one of my agents and gets away with it."

She stared in incomprehension. "Sir?"

"I don't know how to tell you this. Someone in the senator's office has made a threat to your life."

She glanced at Scotty, his face impassive, before looking back at the ASAC, and saying, "A threat?"

"It may be worse. Special Agent Ryan, please inform her what you told me yesterday morning. And what you are asking of her."

Scotty eyed her, nodded toward the chair, said, "Perhaps you should sit."

"I'm fine, thank you."

"We have reason to believe that someone in the senator's office has hired someone to . . . kill you."

"*Kill* me?" No one answered. She walked over to the window, looked out to the street below, doing her best to act surprised, shocked, realizing this was how Scotty intended to cover himself, inform her *and* let her bosses know—and not a word about Mexico. Finally she turned, faced them. "Do you know who?"

"We think so. We don't know if he is the only one involved, or if . . ." Scotty took a breath, held her gaze, as though he weren't sure how she'd take this. Not bad, she thought. "Or if there is anyone else higher up who is in on this."

"You mean the *senator*?"

"Yes."

"I find that hard to believe. He's a family friend."

"We know that."

"Why would *anyone* in his office want me dead?" she asked, trying her best to look mortified, and hoping one of them might slip up, tell her something Scotty hadn't mentioned.

"We're not sure," Scotty replied. "But we think it may have something to do with what your father did for the government quite some time ago when he worked with Gnoble. And that material is classified."

"Which means you can't tell me?"

"Correct."

She crossed her arms, having no trouble acting angry over that statement. It still galled her. "But of course you're going to go out and *arrest* this person? Take care of it?"

Scotty's gaze flicked to the ASAC's, then back to her. "We could. But our case isn't . . . where we'd like it."

She thought of the pouch in her backpack, wondered if that had anything to do with any of this. "I don't understand."

And the ASAC said, "Apparently this is a joint investigation, the details of which I can't go into right now. But they're asking for your help."

"*My* help?"

"They're worried that if we suddenly pull you from your duties, it might tip off someone to their investigation. I, however, don't care what they're investigating. My concern is for your safety."

She looked at Scotty, his face still unreadable. So he'd done it after all. Kept his promise to keep her on the street. Now it was her turn to make sure she didn't blow her chance. "What kind of help?"

And Scotty said, "Nothing more than you going about your day-to-day job as though nothing were amiss."

She looked out the window long enough to appear as though she were thinking about this, before she turned her attention to the ASAC. "I'll do it. If someone's trying to kill me, I want to make damned sure there's enough evidence to put whoever's behind this away."

"You're sure?" the ASAC said.

"Damned sure."

He turned to Scotty. "And you and your team can provide the security necessary to ensure she's not in danger?"

"We're equipped to provide all necessary security, assuming she can follow *orders*, understand that I'll be her handling agent, and that *if* necessary, *if* we determine it's too dangerous," he said, his gaze holding hers, "we call off the whole thing."

Okay, so he got in his last dig. At least she was assured of some freedom. But was it enough to do what she needed?

Dixon, however, looked unconvinced about the entire affair, his gaze moving from her to Scotty and back again. But it was the ASAC who said, "If anything happens to her, Special Agent Ryan, I'll have your job."

"Yes, sir."

There was a knock at the door. Dixon got up, answered it. Carillo stood there, handed him the op plan to approve. "We're, uh, ready to start the briefing," he said, then looked at Sydney. "We *definitely* need copies of that report, and uh, your sketch."

Sydney said, "Any chance you can burn them for me?"

Carillo nodded, left, and Dixon looked over the plans.

"You're partnered with Carillo on this," he said. "You can bow out tonight if you like. I'll get Ren Pham-Peck to take your place."

"No," she said, standing. "I think it's best to keep things normal. Don't you, Special Agent Ryan?" she asked, looking right at Scotty. "Make sure no one else knows what's going on?"

Scotty's smile didn't reach his eyes.

The ASAC said, "Well, looks like we have everything taken care of." He looked right at Sydney. "I'm glad you're taking this so well. You're an asset to the Bureau."

"Thank you, sir," she said, and almost felt guilty.

He gave Dixon a pat on his shoulder, his public show of confidence. "I'll leave you to handle this, Dave."

After he left, Dixon told Scotty, "Before I get started on the task force meeting, I'd like to speak to Fitzpatrick. Alone."

Scotty pulled a cell phone from his pocket, handed it to her. "You left your phone behind. For safety reasons, we need you to keep it with you."

"Well, *this* would've come in handy." She smiled at him, took the phone, and, if truth be told, was amused at his ire as he strode from the office.

Dixon, however, wasn't amused at anything. He picked up a felt-tip pen from a container on his desk, then stood. "Normally," he said, making a show of marking off a day on his retirement calendar, "I wait until I'm leaving for the day to do this. The way things are going around here, I'm not sure I'll get the opportunity."

She knew better than to speak.

"Your trip to Texas . . ." He snapped the cap on the pen with enough force to break the thing. "How was it?"

"Just as you thought, cases weren't related. Probably a big waste of time."

He eyed his calendar, then dropped the pen back into the container, before turning his gaze on her, and then her scraped hands, his expression unreadable. "Let's hope it wasn't. I'd hate to think you went to all that trouble for nothing."

28

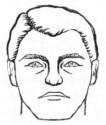

Scotty cornered Sydney the moment she cleared Dixon's office, then dragged her into a vacant one. "I want to know what the hell happened down there," he said.

"Your bosses breathing down your neck?"

"You mean the neck I just stuck out for you so you could remain on the street and run off to Baja, with little regard for your safety and everyone else's in this operation?"

"Maybe if you'd told me what was going on from the moment you came spying around my house, trying to steal my mail, I might not have had to resort to such measures."

"It was for your own safety."

"No it wasn't. Someone's trying to cover some ass. What is it? CYA for the CIA or whatever other government agency has convinced you that whatever the hell this is, it happens to be a matter of national security?"

"That's precisely what it is. Once McKnight left that note, we had to be sure it didn't get out, because it made reference to a matter that we believe is still in operation today. That means government secrets, intelligence and nuclear technology are still being traded and sold. So you can see why it's imperative to find out who and where and not let them know we know."

"It's my father's life. He was involved in this, he was killed because of it, and I have the right to know what happened."

"First of all," he said, closing the distance between them, "your father was not killed because of this."

"You don't know that. You only know what they've told you."

"Two years ago I sat down with you and read your father's murder investigation, because you were worried then, when there were rumblings that some attorney was looking into Wheeler's case to see if he could get out. Back then you wanted him kept in. Now, because some suicidal drunken idiot sends you an old photo that has nothing to do with anything, you suddenly think this guy is innocent?"

"No, what I think is that this drunken suicidal idiot has a lot of very important people running around, scared that they're going to be implicated in a twenty-year-old scandal that they barely escaped from the first time."

"Look, I don't know how to make this any clearer. Some of these matters are of national security. They might look bad on the surface, but could undermine *years* of work involving antiterrorist matters."

"Like the BICTT banking scandal?"

He froze.

"So that *is* what this is all about?" When Scotty didn't answer, she said, "Then why else send someone down to Baja to find the missing records Orozco absconded with on the BICTT matter, then try to kill *me* because I happened to be the sucker who ended up carrying them out of there?"

"You did *what?*" he asked, his face turning ashen. "You didn't say you were carrying anything back."

"You didn't ask."

"Jesus Christ, Syd. Do you realize how dangerous that was?"

"Gee. You'd think I would've thought of that while they were trying to blow my goddamned brains out. Of course I thought of it. But what was I supposed to do, Scotty? Toss it into the water? If someone's going to the trouble to kill an FBI agent for that stuff, then I have to guess it's got someone worried. The question is which OGA would go to the trouble of sending some black ops guys after little old me?"

"What was it you brought back?"

"I have no idea, a sheet full of numbers I didn't understand, some code maybe. It's in a bank pouch. Robert said it had to do with the BICTT records, that part of the original faction is still in operation, something called a Black Network, and that's all I know."

Scotty ran his hands through his hair in frustration. "Jesus. Where is it?"

"My desk."

He stormed from the room.

"This is a secure facility. Who's going to take it in here?" she called out.

He didn't answer, and she hurried after him, wondering if Carillo had returned it yet. When she got there, there was nothing on her desktop, and Scotty was pulling open the drawers. No pouch. "It's not here," he said, looking panicked, not an emotion she usually associated with him.

Her backpack was slung over her chair, and she looked inside. The pouch was there, and she handed it over to him. "Here."

He unzipped it, eyed the contents, then zipped it back up. "Who knows about this?" he asked, keeping his voice low.

"You and me . . ." And Carillo. And possibly Schermer, since Carillo told him about everything.

"This is classified. Do *not* discuss this with anyone."

"Does any of this have anything to do with Senator Gnoble?"

Scotty looked around the room to make sure they couldn't be overheard, little chance, since it was now deserted, everyone having moved on to the briefing room for Operation Barfly. "Look. The guys sent down to Baja? If they *were* black ops, this Black Network, or any other government agency forces, then I don't think Gnoble was behind it."

"What makes you say that?"

"Because we know someone from his office hired someone to kill you. And if whoever that someone is did have access to any black ops, chances are you would've been dead before we found out."

She wasn't sure if that was good news or not. "But won't these guys come after me, because they think I still have that bank bag?"

"First thing I intend to do is make sure they *know* you don't have it. From that point on, the objective changes, and it's all about damage control."

He walked off toward the briefing room, leaving her wondering two things. One, how the hell did he know so much about it, and two, exactly what was the "objective" before they'd realized they'd lost the bank bag.

Come to think of it, the whole "damage control" bit was disconcerting when she really stopped to think about it.

She did not, however, get much time to ponder matters, as Carillo poked his head down the hall. "You want to grab those sketches and meet us? We're getting ready to start."

The briefing for Operation Barfly took place in the SAC's conference room just off the front lobby. Dixon called everyone to order to give a brief outline of the discovery and connections between the crimes—just to make sure everyone was on the same page.

Sydney was standing at the back when Carillo walked up, handed her a copy of the op plan. "Just got done talking with your former sweetheart," he said, nodding toward the front of the room, where Scotty stood just behind Doc Schermer, no doubt to keep his eye on her. "Not sure how you pulled this off, but you're back in the game. At least tonight you're stuck with me for a while."

"Disappointed?"

He gave her a once-over, then shrugged. "Schermer doesn't look near as cute in all black. You should wear it more often. And the stuff I copied? I have no friggin' idea what it means, but the way I see it, if they were trying to kill you over it, it's gotta be priceless."

She glanced at Carillo, but his gaze was fixed on the front of the room, where Dixon started the briefing on their initial call out in the Reno case, Sydney's sketch, the suspect phone call after her Jane Doe sketch appeared in the paper, recounting what the suspect told Sydney about his next victim, along with the remark about biting her.

Dixon continued with "We have a profiler assigned to the case, and so far we believe that our UnSub is what we term an organized murderer." He then gave a partial laundry list of the organized killer, higher than average IQ, but maybe working below his intelligence level, socially competent, usually living with a partner, mobility, decent car. "This individual probably has a continued fantasy," Dixon said. "The fact he contacted our office and Fitzpatrick after the sketch appeared tells us he's following his crimes in the newspaper. Craves the attention."

"What if he really is after Fitz?" one of the agents standing at the opposite end of the room called out.

Great. Like she needed any more negative attention, and she couldn't help but glance at Scotty, thinking, if anything, he'd be using that as an excuse to get her pulled from the case. Dixon, however, continued on, unfazed. "The organized offender displays certain traits. He will often target the same type of victim—so it's highly unlikely he is after Special Agent Fitzpatrick. I'd say it's more likely that he has noted her name and called her simply to draw more attention to himself. In our case, he's kidnapped two women, both from bars. One in Reno, the other here in the city. Although the Reno victim wasn't a prostitute, she was frequenting a bar that is known for prostitution. Our Hill City victim appears to have been a prostitute, and there may be others we haven't connected to him yet, and others we have, such as the series of Sunday rapes SFPD is investigating. Since fantasy and ritual usually dominate the organized offender, we look at the similarities in the known cases. Both victims were frequenting the same sort of bars, both dumped in shallow bodies of water, easily accessed by the public, yet in locations not likely to be frequented at late hours. He may have a fascination with water, or more likely thinks the water will help eliminate forensic evidence. He's taken jewelry from the Reno victim, a souvenir. I expect, once we get the Hill City victim fully identified, we'll learn he did the same with her. Both victims were bitten, and"—he looked at Carillo—"you mentioned we got a call from the forensic odontologist?"

Carillo nodded. "Received the fax this morning." He pulled open his pocket notebook. "The report reads that our UnSub's number eleven, maxillary left cuspid has a fractured mesial-incisal edge. For those of us who didn't graduate from dental school, that translates to a chipped upper left canine, specifically the front corner. Oh, almost forgot," he said, looking up. "Dr. Armand made a positive match to both victims."

"There you have it," Dixon said. "Once we have him identified, despite the lack of DNA, we've got some pretty damning evidence, including a suspect sketch, which, up until now, hasn't been released to the local press, but has been sent to the surrounding agencies. Special Agent Fitzpatrick will be passing out copies with updated info."

Sydney walked to the front of the room, opened the folder containing photocopies of the sketch and kept one, then handed the remaining stack to the agents at the front to pass back. "I've included the physical characteristics on the bottom," she said. "We have this scanned, so if anyone needs a digital copy for some reason, let me know."

Michael Schermer eyed the sketch. "Is there a reason for the delay in releasing this to the press?"

"Yes," Dixon said. "We weren't sure the cases were related. Reno PD released it in their area the moment we sent it to them, since the kidnapping occurred there. But now we believe our UnSub may also be from this area or have connections here, and we intend to hold a press conference. For now, we're holding it back, until after tonight's operation. We'll reevaluate tomorrow. Any more questions before we get started on Operation Barfly?"

"Yeah," Schermer said, eyeing the sketch. "Carillo was telling me that they found some bits of taillight out at Golden Gate Park and white paint transfer, and that you and Fitzpatrick saw a white utility truck out at the hospital. Any chance the two are related, being that both vehicles are white? Maybe the guy Fitz saw driving the truck is this guy?" He held up the sketch.

Dixon said, "I didn't actually see the truck. Fitzpatrick did. But Maggie took the pieces of taillight from Stow Lake to the lab to get a parts identification . . . Maggie?"

She was seated at the table, and stood so everyone could hear her. "According to SFPD's incident report of the suspicious person at the hospital, an Officer Harper described the vehicle as a newer model Chevy utility truck. That doesn't match the bits of taillight found at the Stow Lake crime scene, which belong to a 1970s style of Dodge van. So, other than both are white, we are talking about two unrelated vehicles."

Sydney stilled at the mention of the utility truck, not because of the possibility that the vehicles might have been related. It was more the feeling she recalled, of being watched that night, first at the bar she'd left, then later that night in the hospital parking lot as the truck drove by her . . . "That guy raced out of there so fast, we had to dive out of the way," she whispered to Carillo.

"Which fits with a burglar, trying to get the hell out of there."

And she realized that was entirely possible, that he could've just been trying to get out. A burglar fleeing the scene?

Or something else altogether . . .

Her gaze flew to Scotty's, and she found it curious he wouldn't even look at her. How long had he and his team been watching her? Since she'd left the bar that night? She'd definitely thought she was being followed then. One of Scotty's team?

She thought about the truck in the parking lot, the guy getting out, moving specifically to Dixon's car after they'd gone into the hospital . . . They'd placed a GPS device on her car to keep track of her, so why not Dixon's? What should have been a simple piece of surveillance work failed because they hadn't realized she'd be watching from the window.

Unfortunately, before she could walk over and ask Scotty, Dixon called for everyone to open up his op plan, which contained all contact info, personnel, cars assigned, cell phone numbers, and hospital locations, in essence, operation plans for everything they'd need should the shit hit the fan. "As you can see," he said, "we're expecting this to be low-key. Schermer has an update on our UnSub that just came in. Michael?"

"I went out this afternoon, talked to the bartender who called us to say he overheard a couple talking about Fitz-patrick's drawing. Turns out the bartender's *not* the one who heard it, like we thought when we got the call. He *heard* someone talking about someone who heard it."

"Great," Carillo said. "Won't be any hearsay issues there."

"The good news," Schermer continued, "is that he thinks he can put you and Fitz in touch with someone who may know who it was that did the talking."

"Getting murkier by the second," Carillo whispered.

"Who's supposed to meet up with us?" Sydney asked Schermer.

"Someone named Candy. That's all we know. You'll meet up with her at the Gold Ox, since that's where our informant said she last saw the Jane Doe, who apparently went there, thinking higher-class place, more money from clients."

She looked at Carillo and said, "If that's high-class, won-der where it was she'd been working before."

Dixon cut in with "Okay. That should cover everything. You two meet up with her, determine if she knows who it is you need to talk to. Get a name, see if it was our Jane Doe, hit the other area bars that our Jane Doe was seen in, pop open a beer in each, move to the next bar."

"Do we get to drink the beer?" Carillo asked.

Dixon ignored his comment and said, "Also note that SFPD sent out a warning that a purse snatcher is still work-ing the area, and if we catch him, they'd appreciate it. Just don't blow *this* operation on a purse snatcher. Any questions from the support agents?"

No one had any, and Dixon told them to hit the streets.

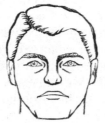

29

Sydney made a beeline for Scotty, who was head-ing out the door and walking toward the elevator. "Scotty!"

He stopped, and when she caught up to him, he said, "This is not a good time."

"Sounds like it's never going to be a good time."

Carillo walked up, just as the elevators opened. "You two lovebirds want to step in, or you flying down?"

Scotty shot him a look of disapproval, but said nothing, and the three of them stepped away from the elevator, and the presence of several other agents who walked up, waiting for the next car. When the other agents stepped on and the door closed, she asked Scotty, "Was that one of your men at the hospital that night?"

Carillo's brows lifted, but he remained silent, as Scotty held her gaze, took a resigned sigh, and said, "Yes."

"Was he placing a GPS device on Dixon's car, too?"

"He did. It has since been removed, once he determined just whose car it was."

"This is rich," Carillo said, laughing. "Dixon's car, too?"

Sydney turned to him. "You might want to ask if there's one on yours."

"Better not be."

"There isn't. But we did consider it."

"Good thing you *re*considered." Carillo glanced at his watch. "Look, we need to get the hell out there, so if I can make a suggestion? Go out, arrest this asshole who made the death threat, and let Fitz and the rest of us get on with our lives?"

"Super plan," Scotty said. "You know who to arrest? Because frankly, I'd like to find the right guy, in case he's fucking serious, and decides to take her out when we arrest the wrong goddamned person." The elevator opened, and Scotty stepped on. "You two want a ride out there?"

Carillo held up the op plan. "Erickson's giving us a lift. But thanks for the offer," he said, in a voice that didn't sound grateful. Scotty disappeared into the elevator. After the door closed, Carillo said, "Okay, he's rattled."

"I gave him the bank bag."

"And you think that's what shook him up?"

"Big time. So, could you decipher what was in it any better?"

"Account numbers, names. I'm guessing in code, at least some of them. Come on back. I'll show you while we're waiting for Erickson."

"I gathered from Robert Orozco that whatever it contained, it would point to all the major players."

"I'd let Doc Schermer have a peek."

"I don't know . . . They're shooting people over this stuff."

"He used to work all that bank fraud. He was even around back when BICTT was making its splash at HQ. Besides, you don't think Scotty's gonna clue you in, do you?"

"Good point."

"I made two copies before I put the original back in the pouch, so you can decide what you want to do with it." He glanced at his watch as they walked through the hallway back to their office. "We need to be out front in five minutes."

"Any more thoughts on that suicide note and how it ties in?"

"Nothing to figure out, with the magic acronym, BICTT, mentioned not once, but twice in it. CIA's been through so much shit, last thing they want to do is open up an old can of worms. Come to think of it, they were probably scrambling to find out just who all McKnight mentioned. Maybe they're the ones who followed you down to Baja, deciding if they couldn't figure out who everyone was, maybe you could?"

"You mean tying them to the bank scandal?"

"Bingo."

"We know McKnight wrote the note. Orozco was Boston, and he told me that Iggy was short for Ignoble."

"If that's Donovan Gnoble's nickname, I'd have to say these men knew something more about him than he portrays to his constituents."

"Especially when you consider that according to the note, Iggy was worried that they could tie everything to BICTT and ruin him."

"But what's the significance of this boat, *Cisco's Kid*, especially now that it's being used as a giant planter for flowers?"

Sydney didn't like to think about that part, that her father was socking away blackmail money, even if it was for something as simple as a fleet of fishing boats. "Since my father ended up dead, I'm guessing the money never made it down there."

"Hence the boat being used as a planter?" He unlocked his desk drawer, pulled out several sheets of paper containing what appeared to be long strings of numbers and letters. "As you can see, this doesn't mean a lot. To me, at least."

"Which literally gets us nowhere."

"I think we need to get that last guy identified."

She looked over at him. "But he *is* identified. I almost forgot. Orozco mentioned the name of Frank White. Said the guy was half black, half Puerto Rican."

"The guy from your photo?"

"Maybe. Not like I have a better theory."

"Let's run his name." He shoved the photocopies back into his desk, locked it, then hit a key on his keyboard to wake his sleeping computer. The screen came to life, and he brought up the name search, typed in "Frank White," put in an approximate age, and hit enter. A few moments later, they stared at the screen. "Well, that was a waste of time," he said, looking at the notation that came up, stating there were too many entries to search the database without further information. Carillo deleted the information, and they retraced their steps to the elevator, while he called Erickson to say that they were just leaving the building and would meet them out front.

Sydney knew it had been too good to be true, that they might be able to plug in the guy's name, come up with something that would tell them anything at all.

"So what's your plan?" he asked as they exited the elevator and walked through the lobby.

"Plan?" They heard the other agents calling in their positions. She looked over at Carillo as she pushed open the glass door and exited the building. "I don't think I've sat still long enough to think of one. Every time I get an answer, I have fifteen more questions." She held the door for him, then let it fall shut. "Something else Orozco told me when I was down in Baja. That if my father hadn't been killed in that robbery, they would've killed him anyway."

"Telling."

"Definitely. Between the guy on death row who says he didn't do it, and an old team member who says my father was marked, I've got to think that Johnnie Wheeler might very well be as innocent as he claims."

"The way I see it, he might be on death row, but he's a lot safer than you are right now. Even before you came home with a bank pouch full of cryptic numbers, someone was trying to kill you."

"It's got to be the photo," she said, just as Erickson pulled up out front with the car, waiting to drive them to the Mission District. "That's what started it. Why else would someone try to kill me when it suddenly arrives in my mailbox?"

"Okay, let's say it is? What now?"

"An age progression on the remaining man who needs to be identified. Might be a helluva lot easier trying to figure out who he is by what he might look like today."

"Not a bad idea," he said, before Erickson rolled down his window, and they had to turn their attention to present matters: serial killers preying on young women.

30

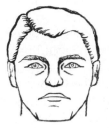

The Mission District had its share of problems, and no wonder. It was a strange and sometimes uneasy mix of culturally diverse businesses and residences, everything from dive bars to coffeehouses, thrift stores to art galleries. Commissioned murals on some walls and annoying graffiti on others coexisted in neighborhoods filled with working-class families and gentrified newcomers. Chic restaurants were popping up in empty lots, and if the food prices were too high, there were still plenty of mom-and-pop joints to round out the menu for those looking for a place to eat after visiting the avant-garde theaters or upscale nightclubs—assuming one could find parking. That wasn't their concern. Nor did they delude themselves about where they'd be looking for their witnesses. Their focus would be on the areas that most cops drove through in pairs, because sometimes the gang factions, whether bikers, Hispanics, Asians, or whoever, had issues. They didn't play well together.

Carillo suggested they hit another area bar first, just to make it look good, so after Erickson and Ren Pham-Peck dropped them off, they walked the half block to the Dusty Rose. Sydney figured no one was making her for an FBI

agent, not in her biker gear, and any stares coming their way
had more to do with Carillo, whose dark Italian just-got-out-
of-bed look was only enhanced by the stubble that graced
his square jaw.

After several minutes, when it became clear that the sort
of clientele that frequented this bar was probably not the sort
they were interested in, they left and walked the couple of
doors down to the Gold Ox, which definitely fit in with their
idea of the sort of bar their UnSub might frequent to pick up
a hooker. The place was dark, smoky, its floors sticky with
spilled beer, never mind a rougher crowd to match.

Once again, Carillo became the focus of the few women
present, as did the men they were with, probably sizing up
the competition. To be honest, Sydney thought, there was
none, even if all Carillo needed was the tool belt to go with
his faded blue jeans, red Pendleton, and white tee. He was the
kind of guy who could dress up or down and still look good.
And although he was trying to look less like a cop, and more
like someone who just wanted to get a drink after a long hard
day at work, Sydney felt that several women were tempted to
tuck some greenbacks into his waistband. Although Sydney
wasn't one of them, she was supposed to act like she was,
and so she kept her hand on his shoulder while he ordered
two beers from the bar—Budweiser for their working-class
persona. They took the bottles, moving away from the bar
to get a better view of the room. Sydney, on the lookout for
not only their hooker informant, but anyone else who looked
like he could be a danger, sidled up to Carillo as they leaned
against the wall, watching a couple of guys play pool.

They weren't there but a few minutes when a woman
dressed in blue jeans and a hot-pink, low-cut, seen-better-
days cashmere sweater walked up and struck a pose, arms
crossed, hips cocked. She eyed Carillo as if he were her next
meal. "Damn," she finally said. "They're making cops better-
looking all the time." He merely looked at her as she moved
even closer, so that her face was mere inches from his, then
whispered, "Don't get me wrong. I like what I see. But next
time, do something a little more. Look the part."

Their gazes held for a couple seconds, and Sydney admitted to being fascinated with the byplay. She'd never seen Carillo in action. Not like this. Apparently she hadn't seen anything yet, because he caressed the woman's cheek with the side of his beer bottle and said, "And if you were me, what would you do to . . . look the part?"

To the observer who wasn't privy to their conversation, it would seem like a typical seduction. A damned good seduction, Sydney thought, even with her standing next to him. In truth, it even put the woman off balance, because it took her a moment to answer. "You're both too squeaky clean. Like you were supposed to be dropped off in Union Square, and took a wrong turn."

"That right?"

"Yeah. Like you want to blend in? Come back with a hooker on your arm, then you'll look like the kind of guy who dropped off his girlfriend in Union Square and is here for a reason."

"What's your name?" he asked.

"Candy."

"Like cotton candy," he said, touching her shoulder, the pink sweater, with his Budweiser.

"Yeah."

"You working for someone?"

"Not a chance. My turn now. A friend said I should come by. Have a chat. *Why?*"

He leaned forward and whispered in her ear. "Looking for someone. Heard you could help."

"Like I told the cops yesterday, if you're looking for that purse snatcher, I have *no* idea who he is. Unless the price is right. No doubt he's the one you're looking for. Psycho."

"We're looking for someone who killed a hooker."

She smiled, reached up, took his beer bottle from him, then took a long sip, before handing it back. "Tell you what. First bit of advice is on the house." She cocked her head toward Sydney. "Biker clothes aren't doing it for her. She needs to be less . . . virginal."

He grinned, holding his beer up in a mock toast. "Not sure that's possible, Miss Candy. But thanks. I'll keep that in mind."

"And you," she said, apparently not quite finished doling out her counsel, "look like you're trying out for the Village People Revival. Even so, I'll help you. For a hundred
bucks."

Sydney tried to keep a straight face, and really tried not to
take advantage of the situation. But before she knew it, she
started humming the "Y.M.C.A." song.

"I think I liked you better when you didn't have a sense
of humor," he said, giving her a dark look. It turned darker
when Sydney started laughing. He handed his bottle to the
hooker. "Have a beer, Candy. Me and Pollyanna gotta go
take care of some business."

Carillo took Sydney's beer, set it on a ledge, as they started to walk out.

"Okay, fine," Candy called out, loud enough for several
nearby patrons to hear. "Sixty."

Carillo kept walking.

"Twenty?"

He stopped, turned, eyed her, then, with a shrug, said,
"Yeah. Sure."

Candy didn't waste any time coming after them, nor did
she waste any of the beer in the bottle, taking several long
sips on her way out the door. The bottle was nearly empty
when she set it down, followed them out.

On the sidewalk out front, Carillo let go of Sydney, turning to face his newfound informant. "You're going to help
for twenty bucks?"

"Easy money," she said, looking up and down the street,
then at him. "Don't even have to—"

"Why?" he asked, cutting her off before she could detail
what it was she didn't have to do for the money.

"Because it's not like anyone takes roll call around here to
see who shows up to work each night, you know? One of my
friends might be missing and no one even knows it."

"What do you think, Pollyanna? Should we pay her?"

As far as Sydney was concerned, the woman had earned
her money by not giving them up. Anyone in there who witnessed that exchange would think that Candy and Carillo
had just agreed on a price for her services—whether for him

or for Sydney, or the both of them, would probably depend on the imagination of whoever was listening. "Why not?"

"You're in, Candy."

The woman held out her hand for payment.

"You haven't done anything," Carillo said.

"COD, or no deal."

"You got any money in that backpack, Pollyanna?"

Sydney dug out a twenty and gave it to him.

He waved it in front of Candy, and she tried to grab it. "Ah-ah. Info first," he said.

"Fine," she said. "Follow me."

Carillo glanced at Sydney and shrugged. So there they were, on a highly detailed FBI op, following a hooker. Not exactly textbook, but then if she'd learned nothing else these past few days, it was that being creative sometimes produced better results. They hadn't gone more than fifteen feet when a brown, older model Cadillac pulled up to the curb, the driver yelling out, "Hey."

It was Doc Schermer. The car was borrowed from DEA. A nice touch, since the typical government ride would be noticed from ten blocks away in this part of town, and Drug Enforcement Agency usually had a nice fleet of cars that were better suited.

Sydney walked up to the car door, leaving Carillo and Candy on the sidewalk.

"That a working girl or your contact?" he asked.

"Both." Sydney told him what happened.

When he finished laughing, he said, "She's right. You two do look too clean. Give me a few. I'll run out to the drugstore and pick you up some stuff to get all dolled up. Didn't you ever play hooker back at your old department?"

"Yeah, except at the time I was supposed to be a hooker. For this operation, I thought I was supposed to be a *date*."

"In this part of town, I think they're one and the same. I'll go pick up your stuff. Don't go into any more bars until I get back."

"What about lover boy?" Sydney asked, nodding to where Carillo and Candy were huddled together in a doorway of a closed shop, looking for all the world as though they were involved in some verbal foreplay, as he stuffed a twenty into her cleavage.

"Poor guy," Schermer said. "They are *never* gonna let him live this down."

She couldn't help but smile at the notion. Schermer drove off, humming the "Y.M.C.A." song, and Sydney rejoined Carillo. "You got a moment?"

"Wait right here," he told Candy, then stepped out of the doorway.

"Don't you think you're getting a bit too much into your role?"

"Jealous?

"You can't imagine. Please tell me you're getting something for my money."

"I showed Candy the photo. Didn't know our Jane Doe's name, but remembers her, because she was complaining about some guy in a white van driving past, giving her the creeps."

"White van?"

"Bingo. And Candy knows someone who knows every working girl down here, so we just might get that positive ID on our Jane Doe."

"And we know our victim was a working girl?"

"Safe bet if she was hanging in the bar we just left. Apparently it's the new hot spot for the working class to find them."

"Tell her to go for it."

"She's gonna want more money."

"And what, you forgot your wallet?"

"It's the beer money. Need to keep that separate from the informant money."

"Don't forget where it came from," Sydney said, digging out another twenty.

About ten minutes later, Schermer was back with the makeup, and Sydney sat in his car, applying black eyeliner, dark red lipstick, and heavy orange-red blush—definitely not her color, and definitely didn't go with her sunburn. But then, this wasn't about her.

"Looks good," Schermer said. "Now run some of this

through your hair." He opened a small jar of styling gel. "It'll give you that haven't-washed-your-hair-all-week look that's so prevalent with hookers."

"It's scaring me that you're so up on this," Sydney said, putting some gel on her hands, then rubbing them together before running it through her hair.

He didn't comment, just nodded out the window. "Isn't that Carillo's hooker? She's looking a bit frantic."

Sydney glanced up to see Candy and another woman on the street corner, yelling and pointing, she thought, at a tall, thin man wearing a gray hood. The man hurried forward, looked back over his shoulder, then took off running, just as Carillo's voice came on the radio. "That's him!" he shouted. "The guy who was with our Jane Doe."

31

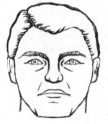

Doc Schermer pulled out, following their suspect's direction of flight, but it was slow progress as cars whipped out of parking spaces, or stopped to claim a coveted spot. Sydney kept her eye on the suspect, darting between pedestrians on the heavily crowded sidewalk. The street was filled with cafés and bars, and a few shops that were open for business.

"We're going to lose him," she said, as Schermer had to stop once again, this time for an SUV that was trying to fit in a space barely big enough for a compact. "I'm getting out."

Schermer picked up the radio. "We still have visual. Fitz is getting out on foot."

"Ten-four," Carillo said, his voice sounding like it was coming from a shaker as he ran. "Call . . . PD . . . get . . . assistance."

Carillo was about a half block back, while the suspect was about a block beyond her in the other direction. Sydney grabbed the portable radio from her backpack, then took off running toward the suspect, paralleling him on the opposite side of the street. He looked back once, saw Carillo chasing him still, and continued on. Sydney was fairly certain he didn't realize she was there, but only because he didn't look her way. Plenty of people on her side of the street did, however, some swearing at her as she raced past them toward the intersection. He was maybe fifty yards ahead of her, when several people exited some nightclub directly in her path, and she nearly bowled a man over.

"Hey!" the man yelled, grabbing her.

"FBI," she said, holding up her radio as if that were proof. He let go and she ran past. Scanned the crowd across the street. A few pedestrians crossed the intersection farther up, but their suspect wasn't one of them. Sydney didn't think he'd made it that far, which meant he must have ducked into one of the businesses. She gathered that Carillo had come to the same conclusion, because he also stopped on the opposite side of the street from her, looking around both directions.

He spoke into his radio, his voice stilted, out of breath. "See which way?"

"No," she keyed back. "Don't think he made it to the next intersection."

Doc Schermer drove up, came to a stop, and held up his hands, ignoring the nitwit in the car behind him, honking.

"Circle the block, see if he made it past here," Sydney radioed. "Carillo and I will check the businesses."

Doc waved his hand, signaling for her to pass, since he was conveniently stopping the traffic. She did, then darted across the opposing lane when that car stopped as well. Carillo, waiting for her on the other side, nodded at a blackboard listing the pasta specials for a café. "That's where I last saw him. In front of that restaurant."

"Then let's start there."

They walked in the entrance, and the woman working the front seemed to stare at Sydney's hooker face a few seconds too long. "Two?" she asked.

Sydney pulled out her credentials, so there was no mistaking their intent. "FBI. We're looking for someone. Where are your restrooms?"

She pointed toward the kitchen in the back.

"You see a white male wearing a gray hooded sweatshirt come in here?"

"No," she said, and they walked past her, eyeing the patrons, who seemed to be eyeing Sydney. Maybe she'd been a bit *too* successful with that makeup. Not that she cared at the moment, and they checked the bathrooms, then into the kitchen. No one saw anything. They left that restaurant and checked the bar next door, with the same results. Two cop cars were cruising past when they stepped out, which meant Schermer had succeeded in getting help at least, and they stepped into a used music store with no customers.

The cashier, a dark-haired twentysomething with a bad haircut and piercings in both eyebrows and his top lip, looked up from his issue of *Rolling Stone* when they walked in, his bloodshot eyes barely registering a reaction when he saw their badges. "Yeah. You must be looking for that guy who ran through here. What'd he do, like rob a bank? Oh, wait. Like they're closed." He started to laugh.

"Which way?" Sydney asked.

"That way," he said, pointing. "Ran through the back. Heard the door slam shut."

Carillo glanced at her as they walked toward the rear of the store. "High?"

"That would mean he had brain cells to begin with."

They checked the few aisles, and the too-small restroom just off the storage room, then stopped at the back door. Sydney put one hand on the push bar, drew her gun with the other, then eyed Carillo. He drew his weapon as well as a Stinger flashlight, gave her a nod, and she pushed open the door.

They came face-to-face with a brick wall. To the left was a padlocked iron gate that belonged to the adjoining restaurant, blocking any access to the catwalk, which meant he had to go right. They started in that direction, but then stopped when they came to a second catwalk separating the music store from the adjoining business, a cleaners that was closed. The well-lit catwalk led back to the street.

"Which way?" Sydney asked.

"You go right, I'll go left. We'll meet up on the corner."

They split up. Sydney continued to the right, holstering her weapon when she got back to the sidewalk at the front of the store. She looked both directions, didn't see their suspect, then started toward the corner, where she'd said she'd meet up with Carillo, shaking the doors of the closed dry cleaner's. Locked tight. She walked to the next business, an avant-garde theater called the Purple Moon, known for its popular drag queen reviews. A show was just breaking, it seemed, when she had to stop to allow a number of patrons to exit. She glanced in the doorway, saw a burly doorman, and decided it couldn't hurt to ask if he'd seen anyone.

"Actually, I did see a guy with a gray sweatshirt," he said. "Kept looking over his shoulder. But we've just had a bunch of people leaving, so he might not even still be here."

She peered inside at the crowd. It was too big a building to search alone. "Thanks. I'll get my partner, and we'll come in and check the place, if that's okay."

"Feel free. We're between shows anyway, so I can turn on all the lights."

"Any chance he could've gone out a back way?" she asked, stepping aside for several more people who were exiting.

"Not without sounding the alarm."

"I'll be right back."

She weaved her way through cross-dressers, transvestites, and just plain old heterosexuals out for an entertaining evening. Some milled about, lighting up cigarettes, others walked to the street corner. Carillo called her on the radio. "Think I . . . a gray hood . . . the corner, where . . . those . . . are . . . your way."

She could only copy about half of what he was saying and moved to the corner to get a better view.

Carillo's voice crackled with static. "Right—"

She looked up. Could just make out the top of Carillo's head as he raced down the sidewalk. And then she caught a glimpse of a gray hood as a man barreled through the crowd, shouldering pedestrians right and left. Before she could move, he shoved her in the street. Knocked the air from her lungs. She heard the squealing of brakes. Her head hit something solid. And the world turned into a mosaic of black and white specks.

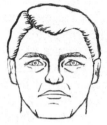

Richard Blackwell shoved his hands into his coat pockets, tucked his head down low, and walked toward the corner, trying not to be seen by the multitude of people gravitating through the area after the fiasco on the corner. He wasn't sure what he'd just witnessed, but either that idiot Prescott had jumped the gun—again—or the serial killer he'd promised to set up as the patsy had unwittingly slammed right into Sydney Fitzpatrick.

And wouldn't that just be rich.

Jobs like this weren't supposed to be rocket science. They were supposed to be neat. Clean. He'd set the whole damned thing up so it couldn't fail, and yet every time he turned around, *something* was going wrong.

Maybe what he needed to do was put a bullet through Prescott's head. Make all their lives easier.

That happy vision faded at the sight of the charcoal-gray Crown Victoria that pulled up on the street corner, then sped off in the direction the attacker fled. A moment later, some transvestite was helping Sydney Fitzpatrick up from the ground. Before he had a chance to clear the area, it was flooded with cops and agents, and he stepped into the doorway of a restaurant, pretended to read the menu posted in the window as he pulled out his cell phone and hit send.

"We have a problem," he said when the call was answered. "It might be bigger than we think."

When Sydney was able to focus, she became aware that there were at least a dozen sets of eyes looking at her, mostly men, and the absurd thought that, clearly, the majority seemed more skilled at applying makeup than she had ever been, swept its way into her consciousness. And she was conscious. A good thing. She could now breathe. Also a good thing. Apparently the car whose hood she had landed on had thankfully been slowing to turn the corner. Sydney tried to stand, felt her knees give way, and was grateful when someone grabbed her and helped her back to the sidewalk.

The driver got out, frantic. "What happened? Why'd you jump in front of my car?"

Jump? Hardly, she thought as Carillo came running up.

"You okay?"

"Fine," Sydney said. "Lost my radio."

Carillo took over for the well-manicured transvestite who had been assisting, putting his arm around her until she was certain she could stand. "You need an ambulance?"

Sydney took stock of her body parts, figured the weakness in her knees was more from the rush of adrenaline than from any injuries. There was a slight lump on her temple, but other than that, she felt okay. "No."

"What happened?"

"Someone pushed me."

"Sweatshirt guy?"

"If I had to guess. You said you saw him here?"

"Pretty sure that's who I was chasing. I was halfway up the block . . ." Carillo assisted her to the curb, eyeing the crowd who'd gathered. "Anyone see what happened?"

There was a lot of looking around, shoulder shrugging, comments that ranged from "She jumped out" to "She tripped and fell."

"I didn't trip, I didn't jump," Sydney said, between gritted teeth.

Carillo drew her away from the others. "Just checking. Don't get so testy."

Like he wouldn't be if someone had pushed him into the street. But Sydney didn't respond, because the burly-armed bouncer from the Purple Moon walked up. "You still looking for that guy? Gray hood?"

"Yeah," Sydney said.

"He ran that way," he said, pointing in the direction they'd come from originally. "Least I think it was him. Saw him take off from about here right after I heard the screech of brakes."

"You're sure it was the guy in the gray sweatshirt?"

"Pretty sure. Ripped his sweatshirt off as he ran. Tucked it under one arm, which is what makes me think it was the same guy. Then again, it ain't like gray sweatshirts are all that unusual."

Unfortunately he was right. Sydney counted three in their general area, though their physical description was off from the first person they saw—a man whose face they didn't see clearly enough to ID.

Across the street a man stood staring, and when she looked at him, he turned, strode off in the opposite direction.

Recognition hit her. "He's the guy from the elevator. The . . . guy."

"What guy?" Carillo asked, looking where she was pointing.

Too late, he was gone. Lost in the crowd, and her head throbbed as she tried to remember, tried to determine what was so odd about his presence. "He was watching me in court during my robbery case, and followed me up to the café."

"In the federal building?"

"Yeah."

"You're sure?"

"Definitely. Cute Guy from the elevator."

"I don't care if he's Ugly Guy from the basement. What's he doing here, watching you, then? Because the way I see it, if he was a cop, he'd be hauling his ass this way, find out what's up, not hightailing it the opposite way. You see him around again, you call for help."

She reached up, touched the tender spot on her temple, trying to ignore the increasing headache. If a guy like that wasn't a cop, and he had access to the federal building . . . She didn't even want to think about it. "I need to find my radio."

"Wait here with the bouncer," Carillo said. "I'll find it."

Carillo left her beneath the awning at the Purple Moon's entrance, then walked to the street corner. A black-and-white had pulled up and was taking the driver's information, but then the officer rushed to his vehicle, saying something to Carillo just before he got in and raced off. Suddenly they were there by themselves, as though SFPD had abandoned them.

"Shots fired," Carillo called out to her, pulling a three-by-five card from his back pocket to start copying witnesses' names. "Takes precedence over lowly agents being pushed into traffic."

The bouncer shook his head. "I gotta get a new job. Shooting here last night, too. Some woman shot her boyfriend."

Carillo went back to interviewing the witnesses, and Sydney asked the bouncer, "Did you see the guy walk out of here?"

"Guy with the sweatshirt?" He crossed his massive arms. "Sorry. He coulda come in here, left with the crowd, but I was busy making sure they weren't walking out with drinks. Didn't notice him until I heard the car skid, and then the cop car sped after him."

"Black-and-white?" Sydney asked, wondering if SFPD had a patrol in the area by that time.

"Nah. One of those undercover rigs. Dark Crown Victoria."

"Could you ID him?"

"The cop?"

"The guy in the gray sweatshirt."

"Didn't get that close a look. Only noticed the sweatshirt, 'cause you asked about it. Figured he probably took it off, you know, to disguise himself or something."

Carillo returned a few minutes later. "Got everyone's name who's willing to give one." He handed Sydney her radio, the hard plastic casing dented and scratched at the bottom from being dropped in the gutter.

She keyed it, heard the feedback on Carillo's radio, and figured it was none the worse for wear. "Great," she said, thinking that the entire operation was ruined for the night. "Now what?"

"Now you go home and we keep looking."

"I'm fine."

"You have a lump on your head, never mind that Elevator Guy is wandering around down here. Either that or you were hit harder than you think. You're going home."

A man pulled up in a dark gray Crown Victoria about two minutes later, and the bouncer said, "That's the cop that took off after the guy."

Sydney looked over to see who it was. She didn't recognize him, figured he was an undercover SFPD. "And you are . . . ?"

"Jared Dunning. One of your shadows." He nodded to the man in the passenger seat. "Mel. One of your other shadows. We're, uh, working with Scotty, and are under orders *not* to lose you this time."

"You find our UnSub?" she asked. He seemed surprised by her query, and she said, "The bouncer said you took off after the guy."

"So it was the same guy. I was looking for you, but saw him running. Thought he matched the description. Unfortunately I lost him a couple blocks from here. Medium height, carrying a gray sweatshirt. At least I think it was the guy. He didn't stop to identify himself."

"Go figure. Apparently in his haste to flee, he pushed me into traffic." Sydney lifted her hair on her left temple and showed him the lump.

"Ouch. You okay?"

"Just a bump." She looked down the street, then said, "There's some other guy I saw here. I also saw him in the federal building." She gave them the man's description. "Any chance you saw him out and about while you've been following me?"

He narrowed his gaze at her head, as though he, too,

thought she'd been bumped too hard. "No, but we'll keep an eye out. Maybe you should have that looked at. We could give you a ride."

Sydney glanced back at Carillo, who walked up to the car to see who she was talking to. "My babysitters," she explained.

And then Carillo nodded to something in the back of Dunning's vehicle. "Tell me you weren't wearing that gray sweatshirt and racing around the Mission District trying to drag hookers from their hidey-holes?"

Dunning looked in the back, then laughed. "Uh, no. Getting too old and fat to go chasing after hookers," he said, though Sydney didn't see an ounce of spare flesh on the guy. "I was wearing it out on the range this afternoon." He reached back and lifted it, pulled a couple of brass casings from it, then tossed it back. "You want," Dunning said to Sydney, "I could drop you off wherever it is you need to go. Doctor? Home? At least if you're in my car, I know where you are."

Before Sydney could answer, Carillo gave the car door a slap. "Thanks, but we've got a ton of paperwork to fill out from the car accident." An SFPD radio car pulled up, the officer who'd raced off at the shots-fired call. Carillo called out to him. "Didn't find your guy?"

"No. Maybe it was just someone popping off a couple shots. Who knows."

"Big city," Dunning said, putting the car into gear.

Carillo pushed away from the door, put his arm around Sydney's shoulder. "See you guys. Don't work too hard."

"How hard can you work, parked in one place? We'll be in that little alley about a half block up. We're monitoring your radio, so call if you need us." They drove off, and Carillo punched in a number on his cell phone. "Dixon?" she heard him saying, and knew without a doubt that her night of working was at an end. "Yeah, it's Carillo. Fitz was in an accident . . . No, the shots-fired call wasn't ours. Not involved . . ." A moment later, Carillo was handing her his phone. "Dixon wants to talk to you."

She took the phone, held it to her ear. "Hey."

"You're going to the hospital."

"I'm fine. I don't think—"

"Call me when you're there. Don't even *think* about coming back to work before you get a release for duty."

She handed the phone to Carillo just as Scotty drove up, and she wondered if her evening could get any worse.

Apparently it could, since he insisted on transporting Sydney to the hospital, because Schermer and the others were going to stay on, help SFPD and their other agents see if they couldn't locate Sweatshirt Guy. She still needed to give a full statement to SFPD, but by the time the officer got to her, started writing it down, SFPD's dispatch reported finding a body slumped in an alley about two blocks away, and the officer taking their report was off again.

Just as well. The lump on her head was no longer numb, but now pulsing with a knifelike pain, enough to where she didn't care who took her to the hospital, and Scotty ushered her into the front seat of his car. He looked over at Carillo, said, "Sorry about the backseat. Office on wheels, you know."

Sydney glanced back, saw a file box, maybe a week's worth of newspapers, and several empty bags of fast food, as though he'd spent the last several days working out of his car—probably parked just up the street from her house, come to think of it. The thought irked her, but not enough to overlook the significance of those files. Scotty was in California to work one case, and she had a strong suspicion some of it was sitting in that file box. Unfortunately, any chances of her getting into it without being seen were slim to none. She thought about texting a message to Carillo, telling him instead of using the damned box for an armrest, he should be looking inside of it. She decided by the time she figured out how to text a damned message, they'd be at the hospital. Had Angie been here, she'd have it entered in and sent before Sydney even brought up the proper screen. Not that it mattered. A few minutes later, they were pulling up in front of the ER. Scotty wanted to swing by the ambulance entrance, drop her off, but she insisted on parking and walking. "I'm not an invalid, I have a goddamned bump on my head," she said, and that settled it.

He parked, the three of them got out, walked into the emergency room, and she had to admit that the nice thing about hospitals was that unless there were some major emergencies going on, the ER staff usually ushered the law enforcement types in pretty quickly. Unfortunately, Scotty hovered over her so closely that she didn't have a moment to get Carillo alone, tell him what she saw. She was poked and prodded, had her eyes checked, and told they'd need to do a CAT scan before they even thought about releasing her. The nurse said it might be a few minutes, and Sydney decided it was now or never. She looked right at Scotty. "Is my phone in my jacket pocket? I should call my mom. Let her know what happened."

Scotty reached into his pocket and handed her his phone. Figured.

"If I call her on that at this hour, she'll freak when she sees the number come up on caller ID. Tony," she said to Carillo. "Check my pocket, see if my phone is there."

Carillo walked over to where her clothes were hanging from a hook on the wall, patted the pockets. "Not here."

"I hope I left it in the car, and didn't lose it out on the street. All my numbers are filed in there. I need that phone."

Carillo said, "You want me to check in the car, see if it's there?"

"If it's not, you'll need to call Schermer, have him check out on that street corner. Oh God, Scotty, my head hurts."

And sure enough, Scotty was at her bedside, taking her hand in his. "You want me to call the nurse, get something for the pain?"

"You know what I'd really like, Scotty? A Coke. You wouldn't mind getting me one, would you?"

"Sure."

"Actually," Carillo said. "I'll do it, soon as I check the car for your phone. I need to make a call anyway. Check in with Dixon. Besides, you send this guy out there," he said, nodding at Scotty, "he's likely to break his neck in a hurry to get back to you." He started out the door, then stopped, patting at his pockets. "Funny thing is, I didn't drive. Keys?"

Scotty reached into his pocket, dug out his keys, and

tossed them to Carillo, his attention fixed on Sydney. There was going to be hell to pay after this, trying to ignore the look in Scotty's eyes, his hope that there might be something left between them after all. "You haven't seen some guy following me, have you?" she asked Scotty after Carillo left.

"What guy?"

She gave him the description, even as a stab of guilt hit her, because she did care about Scotty, and didn't like that she was keeping him occupied while Carillo searched his car. She must have winced at the thought, because Scotty asked, "Maybe I should call that nurse."

"No, I'm fine." As fine as one could be in this situation, and, as Scotty stroked her hand, she sent up a fervent wish that Carillo had no trouble determining that she left her phone behind just so he could look at those files, because she didn't want to think she was messing with Scotty's head for nothing. She sighed, closed her eyes, figuring it was going to be a long, long night.

33

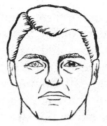

"Three days!" Sydney stared at the release-to-duty
form before turning her accusing glare on Scotty, wondering
if he had something to do with this. "I'm perfectly fine. I do
not need three days to recuperate."

The doctor, unfazed by her outburst, handed her a scrip
for a mega dose of Motrin. "You were hit pretty hard. Get
some rest. See your own doctor in a few days, maybe he'll
reevaluate."

Carillo wandered in right about then, handing her a can of
soda. "Oh good. You're done."

"Oh good. Warm soda."

"The call took longer than I thought. I see the bump didn't
change your lovely personality any."

She held out the orders. "Three days until released for
duty."

Carillo glanced at Scotty. "Guess that should make it easier on everyone all the way around, eh?"

"I know Sydney's not happy about it, but I am," Scotty
said. "Get her off the street with no one thinking twice."

"I am *so* seeing my own doctor tomorrow. I am not going to be pulled from the street."

Scotty took the scrip from Sydney's hand, saying, "Where do you want to get this filled?"

"I don't need it filled. It's Motrin. I have a bottle full of it at home."

"But it's eight hundred milligrams."

"Which equals four little pills. Somehow I think I'll manage."

A nurse came in with a wheelchair, and when Scotty left to get the car, Carillo said, "You're a little upset."

She looked away. "Upset? I am so pissed right now, I could scream."

"Well, don't do it, or you'll end up in the psych ward, and probably for longer than three days. By the way, I found your phone. On the front seat of Scotty's car."

"Is that it?"

"That is what you wanted me to go out there and get, right?"

"You didn't see the file box you had to climb over to get into his car?"

He grinned, and she realized he was playing her. "I was trying to figure out a way to get back in there myself. You beat me to it. Copied a couple notes while I was there. Let me look into it tomorrow, see if it pans out. And I can bring you your sketch stuff for that age progression."

And though she was dying to know what he'd dug up, Scotty walked in, and she had to content herself with the knowledge that Carillo was going to look into things himself. It was not, however, enough to lessen her anxiety over being removed from active duty for three days, and the more she thought about that, the angrier she got.

Scotty drove to her place. As he rounded the corner, his radio crackled with static, no doubt his team keying their mikes, letting him know they had seen him drive up. He pulled into the driveway, turned to Carillo in the backseat. "You want to take her up, get her settled? I need to call the guys, let them know what's going on."

"Sure."

She wanted to snap that she could get herself upstairs on her own just fine. Instead she exited the car, slammed the door shut.

Carillo followed her. About midway up the steps, he said, "I figured after the good news, you'd be calmed down by now."

She stopped, turned, looked him right in the eye. "Calmed down? Scotty's gotta be high-fiving his guys right now. I'm out of commission."

"With very good reason," he said, glancing back at the car, where Scotty was talking on the phone. Carillo ushered her up the stairs. "You work on the age progression on your unknown in that photo, and I'll work on the names I dug up in his files. Orozco was in there. Scotty's gotta be working the BICTT thing. Which means that whatever is going on in Gnoble's office, getting someone all antsy to take you out, it has to do with McKnight sending you that photo, or something close to the timing of it. You didn't receive anything else in the mail right then, did you?"

"Yeah. The card from my aunt commemorating the death of my father. And unless she's hidden a code in it, something I highly doubt, I'd have to say she's not involved."

"Regardless, between the two of us, we might be able to put something together. So in the meantime, play nice with Scotty so you don't get yanked into some protective custody situation."

"Fine. I'll be nice." She unlocked the door. The moment she opened it, Topper's large white head emerged. "Hello, Toppie!"

"Didn't know you had a sheep," Carillo said.

"Topper is not a sheep. He's a poodle."

"A poodle, huh? That's why they give them the foo-foo haircuts? So you can tell they're dogs and not livestock?"

"He's named after a very lovable character in the movie of the same name. He belongs to my neighbor."

"What's he doing at your place?"

"I sort of forgot I agreed to watch him tonight. In exchange for Arturo lending me his motorcycle." He petted Topper while Sydney opened a cupboard to get him a snack.

When Carillo walked into her kitchen, he stopped before the painting on her easel. "What is *that*?"

"I have no idea. Sometimes I just paint and see where it takes me."

He cocked his head, trying to look at it from a different angle. "Don't think you want to go where this one's taking you."

"Why not?"

"Flames in hell."

She gave Topper his dog biscuit, then walked to the easel to look at the painting, thinking it did look like flames. "I started it right after my visit with Wheeler."

"Maybe you subconsciously wanted him to burn in hell for what he did."

The thought she had painted flames bothered her, especially considering that a fire had been set to cover her father's murder. She moved away from it, shook out another biscuit for Topper.

Carillo looked at a few of her other paintings stacked against the wall in her kitchen. "Abstracts?"

"A kick I'm on."

He nodded, then glanced around the kitchen, at the brushes, the cans of turpentine, and other art supplies. "Hope you don't cook in here. This place would go up in a hot second."

"That's why God made microwaves and neighbors who can cook."

"You definitely need to get that neighbor something for Christmas. What's his name?"

"Arturo."

He walked to the door, looked out the window. "So you think these guys bugged your apartment, too?"

"Better not have."

"But you don't know."

"No." Topper finished his biscuit, then sat by the door. "Oh, sorry, Top. You want to go out." She didn't have the energy, but picked up his leash anyway.

"You want me to take him around the block? I gotta wait anyway, until Schermer can swing by, pick me up."

"Would you?"

"Or will he walk me?"

"Topper's good on a leash."

Carillo clapped his hands. "C'mere, boy." Topper clambered over. "You want to go for a walk?" His words sent Topper into a spin before he sat, waited for the leash. Carillo walked him out, no problem, and Sydney locked the door, then dropped onto the couch, deciding she wasn't getting up for anything. Even to let him back in. Well, maybe to let him back in. But that was it.

Her stomach had other plans, and when it started rumbling, she tried to remember when it was she last ate. Cheesecake. There was definitely some of Arturo's cheesecake still in the fridge, and she got up, cut herself a generous slice, and started eating, not even bothering to sit. She glanced over at her painting, thinking about what Carillo said, and it struck her that here she was, eating a slice of heaven, looking at a painting of hell. The irony of it all, she thought, wondering if it had truly been flames her subconscious had painted. Logical, certainly, considering she'd started it after her visit with Wheeler, the man convicted of her father's murder and the arson of the pizza parlor.

She *had* seen flames that night.

A painting of hell . . .

She stared at the canvas and for some reason was compelled to add some paint, and she set down her plate, squeezed some red onto the palette. Deep dark red. Not all over, just a spot near the top left. But something was off, and she took a darker color, dabbed a small diagonal line through the red spot of paint.

The moment she finished it, stepped back, looked at it, she was disturbed. More than disturbed. Her gaze caught between the flames and the black depths she'd painted. And then it was drawn to that red spot, the last thing she saw in her mind. Like a devil's eye, she thought. Staring at *her*.

She ignored the beating of her heart, and felt she should recognize what it was she'd painted. Really, it was nothing more than being stressed from the accident. The blow to her head, never mind the whole shooting in Baja.

And of course she was tired. Who wouldn't be after the

past couple of days? She had no idea what she was looking at, or even if it meant anything. No doubt some psychiatrist could put a name on it, transference of something or other, especially after Carillo had mentioned that she'd painted hell.

She was entitled to be upset, she thought, and decided she'd had enough of painting for the night.

She put the brush in some cleaner, set her empty plate in the sink.

Topper barked outside, and she looked out the window, saw Schermer pull up to the front of the house. Carillo stood in the driveway with the dog, talking to Scotty. He waved at Schermer, then followed Scotty up the steps. She unlocked the door, let them in, and Scotty said, "Should you be up?"

"No. But how else were you going to get in?"

He walked into the kitchen, looked over at her painting, shook his head, and said, "You should take some Motrin and go to bed."

"And what were you planning on doing?"

"I get to relieve one of the guys parked up the street for a few hours. But when I'm done, maybe I could sleep on your couch instead of driving back to my hotel?"

"You need a key to get in, or did your spooks already pick my lock and make a copy?"

"A key would be nice."

"Yeah," Carillo said, handing her Topper's leash. "That way he can make a copy and get it back to you."

"Don't you have to go out and look for serial killers?" she asked, the night taking its toll on her patience.

"As a matter of fact, my ride's out front now. Call you tomorrow."

"Thanks for pulling me out of the gutter." She smiled, hoped he understood her short temper. "See you."

He left, and Scotty looked over at her. "I'll be back in a few hours. Until then, I'll be right up the road if you need me."

"Thanks. I'm sure I'll be fine." She gave him her key, and when he took it, his hand touched hers, sending a slight shock through her.

He took one step toward her, reached up, brushing the hair away from her temple. "You're sure you're okay?"

All she could do was nod, because he looked right at her, and he was standing so close, and she wanted him to move closer. And when he held her gaze, she thought he might say something. But then he tucked her hair behind her ear, allowed his finger to linger a moment, then with one last look, turned away. And all she could do was watch him walk down the steps, feeling the warmth of his touch on her skin long after she locked the door behind him.

When she turned around, saw her empty apartment, she reminded herself of the many lonely nights she'd spent without him, waiting for him to come home.

Apparently she was still waiting, and she wondered if she'd ever stop.

Get over him. There was no hope for the future. None.

The truth was, she actually felt better knowing he was there, outside, watching her. And in a few hours, he'd be sleeping on her couch. She was safe for the night. Her throbbing temple reminded her of the investigation that she'd just left, her run-in with the possible rapist. Maybe in a way that was a good thing. Had she not been injured, she'd be working side by side with Carillo on it, with no time to look into her father's case, determine the guilt or innocence of Johnnie Wheeler, or what McKnight's photo and suicide note meant.

Maybe she was looking at this injury leave all wrong. Stop seeing it as three days unable to work, until she had the doctor's medical release.

Because that pertained only to *on*-duty activity. And looking into her father's case was *off*-duty fare. Under-the-table, not-sanctioned-by-the-FBI fare.

She'd already broken a number of rules just looking into it as far as she had, and she wondered just how many more rules she might break in the next three days.

And if she'd still have a job when she was done.

"What do you think, Topper? So they fire me. What's the worst that can happen? Move back in with my mom?"

He cocked his head, his tail wagging.

"You're right. *Definitely* not a good idea. Let's go to bed. Sleep on it."

He followed her, waited in the middle of the hallway while she undressed, then brushed her teeth. When she came out to double check the lock on the door, she couldn't help but look at the canvas. She quickly turned away, walked to the bathroom, flicked the light on, and wondered just how many other adults slept with night lights in hopes of avoiding past memories that sometimes swirled through their dreams. Sydney suspected there were a few of them who, like her, didn't admit to such a weakness, and she was grateful that Topper was with her that night. So grateful that when he was about to curl up on the floor, Sydney patted the bed. He jumped up, plopped down next to her, and within moments, she could feel the heat of his furry solid form through the covers. "Good night, Topper."

His tail thumped on the bed, and she couldn't help but smile.

34

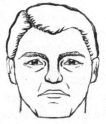

Prescott loved the campaign offices at this hour, be-fore the sun rose. Quiet. No keyboards clacking, no copy machines humming, no poll takers citing their litany. And best of all, no phones ringing. The very sound startled him lately. His nerves were frayed over this entire affair. Perhaps he should have ended it, but the very thought left him cold. He knew things. Knew things about Donovan Gnoble that no one else knew. *Mr. Clean* wasn't near as squeaky as everyone believed, and it was his, Prescott's, job to make sure Gnoble's reputation wasn't tarnished—if for no other reason than to ensure that Prescott's future was secured.

Don't kill the Golden Goose.

Don't get killed trying to protect it, either.

Sort of the golden rule in this business, and why he came armed to this meeting. Richard Blackwell was becoming a liability, a loose cannon. Blackwell wanted things done his way, or no way, even if opportunity reared its head. In hindsight, Prescott never should've hired him, but he came highly recommended. Though, now that he thought about it, it wasn't as if he could go around and check the guy's references with the others who'd used him: *I hear you used Blackwell to assassinate the political thorn in your side. Any issues?*

He heard the office door open, a cold draft sweeping into the room as Blackwell let himself in from the street. Prescott glanced up, saw it was 6:10, twenty minutes before Blackwell had said he'd be there.

Half the time Prescott never even knew he was around. He just appeared.

But he knew this time, because Prescott had made sure he was here early.

No surprises, no getting caught as he walked the empty streets, leaving him vulnerable, he thought, reaching into his coat pocket, making sure the small-caliber semiauto was there. Just in case.

Blackwell strode into the room, his gaze dark, empty, the gaze of a killer. He looked around, took in the deserted offices, always searching. The man trusted no one. Not even Prescott, who deposited the money into his account. Blackwell's services did not come cheap. And that didn't even count what he'd be paid *after* the hit. The perfect crime was not quick. Apparently it was costly. Costly, but necessary.

"What happened?" Prescott asked. "I thought this was all going down last night."

"I take it you didn't hear?"

Prescott paused. Seemed lately like something always came up. He was beginning to wonder if the man wasn't stringing him along on purpose, just to raise his fees. "Hear what?"

"Someone pushed her in the street, and she was hit by a car."

"You?"

"No, you idiot. Not me." He slapped a newspaper on the desk, and Prescott read a short and noninformative article that an off-duty FBI agent was struck by a car, injured, treated, and released. The matter was still under investigation, and no further details were known. "Tell me it wasn't *you*, Prescott."

"No." Prescott stared at the article, thinking of the possibilities. If only . . . "Too bad you weren't closer."

"A reprieve for your sorry ass. Can you imagine the investigation if she had been killed? Trust me. The lousy attempt you made would've been the first thing they looked at. They might even be looking that direction now, unless they connect it to something else."

"It was dark," Prescott said, annoyed that his hands started sweating. Blackwell was right of course. If she mentioned it to one person, what kind of car it was, they'd be checking out every lead. "She couldn't have seen anything that night."

"You hope."

"Which doesn't explain why you haven't done what I've paid you to do."

"I'm doing exactly what you're paying me for. I watch, I wait. When the time is right, I do it."

"I want it done now. We have a timeline."

"And I'm well within it."

"I'm not so sure that's wise, waiting. Things could come out between now and then."

"*In two days?* What sort of things?"

"Nothing you need to worry about. But if you do it sooner, I'll—I'll triple your salary."

Blackwell's eyes narrowed as a small smile played across his mouth. "As much as I like the money, and I'm not saying I will turn it down, you need to understand something. No matter how I kill her, there'll be an investigation. If it's done right, that investigation is minimal, and they close the books without looking too deep."

"And you're telling me this, because . . . ?"

"History is filled with poor souls who are key to all sorts of nasty surprises. Souls who have met their demises due to faulty aircraft, an unforeseen suicide, a sudden heart attack. Someone might cry foul, but nothing comes of it, if—"

"If what?"

"*If* it is done right. *My* job is to pick the best method that raises the least questions. *Your* job is to pay me." Blackwell stepped forward, leaned so close, Prescott could smell the coffee on his breath. "One more thing. That better be your dick you're playing with in your pocket. I'd hate to think you're stupid enough to think you can get a gun out, and shoot me before I kill you."

"I *could* shoot you."

They stood there, faced each other for several seconds, all the while with Prescott's heart thump-thumping in his chest. And then Blackwell flashed that evil smile of his. "And you might even get off a lucky shot. But are you sure you could clean up the mess before the first eager volunteer gets here at the crack of dawn?"

Blackwell didn't move. Prescott wanted nothing more than to pull the trigger. He fingered the gun, but knew he didn't have the guts to try, and before he had time to think about it, Marla Gnoble walked in the front door. "I think you should go," he said to Blackwell.

Marla watched Blackwell leave, then turned to Prescott. "What was he doing here?"

"Nothing," he said, tossing the paper onto the desk. "What are you doing here so early?"

"With less than a month before the election, why wouldn't I be?" She glanced back at the door as she shrugged out of her winter-white overcoat. "You look a bit shaken. Is there something going on? Something I should know about?"

"Nothing. Nothing at all."

"Good. I've got a migraine, and I'm not sure I could put up with any bad news this morning." She paused in front of her office door, her hand on the knob. "I don't suppose there's any coffee made?"

"I'll start it," he said, and she closed herself in her office, leaving him in blessed silence. Prescott sucked in a deep breath, leaned against the desk, his knees going weak. It took a good five minutes before he was calm enough to start thinking. Thinking about the liability issues of having a loose cannon like Blackwell on his staff. But then his gaze caught on the article about the accident . . .

He picked up the paper, read it again. And realized he might not need Blackwell after all. Perhaps fate had provided the perfect opportunity. He could salvage this entire affair, take care of the matter himself, and save the exorbitant fee he'd foolishly promised to pay the man.

At nine the next morning, Scotty was still sacked out on Sydney's couch when Carillo came by with her briefcase from work containing her forensic art tools, and, she assumed, the photo, probably tucked inside. Sydney was barely awake herself when she answered the door, her body still trying to recoup the lost sleep from the last few nights.

Carillo handed the briefcase to Sydney, as well as a cardboard tray with two hot coffees, then eyed the dog. "You walk the sheep yet?"

Sydney looked over at Topper, who wagged his tail, as though he knew just who the topic of conversation was. "No. I just got up myself."

"Where's your leash, dog?" Carillo spied it on the coffee table, picked it up, and Topper raced to the door, circled twice, then sat.

"Thanks," Sydney said.

Scotty managed to sit up. "What time is it?"

"Little after nine," Carillo said. He stood there a moment, looking at Sydney. "Think you're gonna have a shiner. Might be cute with that sunburn."

"Great."

"Drink your coffee. I want to see some beautiful artwork from you in your convalescence. Got one for you, too, sport," he said to Scotty. "Figured you've got a lot of investigating to do."

Carillo walked out the door, and she handed one of the coffees to Scotty.

"Thanks," Scotty said. "How are you feeling this morning?"

"Fine. I thought I'd work on my art since I have nothing to do."

"Great idea."

"I can only paint and draw for so long. How long are we looking at before you arrest someone?"

"I hope not much longer. We're trying to wrap this up. Get the evidence we need."

"Do you have any idea what this is like for me?"

He shook his head. "I swear, Sydney, if I'd had any idea . . ."

After the tender moment at the door, she was fairly certain that wasn't the answer she was looking for. "Time for me to hit the shower."

She left him sitting there, drinking his coffee. In the bathroom, she examined her face. Carillo was right. She had a nice bruise forming on the lump on her forehead, and the first traces of a black eye coming up. Maybe two. The lump was nicely hidden by her bangs. Cover-up should help conceal the rest. Not that she had anywhere to go, she thought, starting the hot water. By the time she got out, Carillo was there and Scotty had left. Topper was curled up on the rug, keeping one eye on her as she opened up the briefcase, took out the photo, her sketch pad, and a pencil.

"How long will it take?" Carillo asked.

"Maybe an hour."

He looked at his watch. "That'll give me time to get back to the office, look up a few things. I'll stop by at lunch, see how it's going?"

"That'd be great."

He left. She reheated her coffee in the microwave, then dug through her file cabinet that doubled as an end table next to the couch, looking for her guidelines on age progression. Not everyone aged at the same rate. Some showed the years quicker, or looked older for a variety of reasons—drug use, time in the sun, smoking, to name a few. Others held on to their youthful looks, or even looked younger than they were, whether due to genetics, environment, health, or habits, it didn't really matter. What did was the law of averages. Sydney would have to determine the ages of the men in the photo, guess from looking at her father just how long ago it was taken, then work from there.

The face ages in a fairly specific manner, and from looking at the photo, the deepening of the eyes, the early signs of creasing at the outer corners, and the very slight fleshiness

beneath the jaw, she put the men in their early thirties, figured that would be right around the time period when all this
first started. Twenty-two years ago was right when Robert
Orozco fled to Baja, and since he was in this picture, she figured that was two years before her father was killed . . . She
drew her gaze from her father's face, instead concentrated
on the one unidentified man, his dark skin, high forehead,
which probably foretold even thinner hair on the crown than
the norm, more than likely gray.

In her mind she went over the aging process, because
she'd have to add all the steps to age the face properly. At
forty-five, he'd be dealing with the forming of crow's-feet
wrinkles at the outer eye, and the area beneath the chin
would start to look fleshy, less firm. At fifty, thinner hair,
upper lids starting to sag, deeper set eyes, and the pouch
beneath them becoming more noticeable. It was here where
the definitive signs of aging often sent people scurrying for
Botox and facelifts. This was the age when they noticed the
wrinkles appearing mid-forehead, the flesh sagging in the
cheeks and along the jawline.

At fifty-five the pouch beneath the eyes was more decisive,
the zygomatic arch and the cheekbone more apparent, the
temporal wall and the brow corner more pronounced. This
was what she needed to add to bring this man, this stranger,
to age, and she couldn't help but look at her father in the
photo, try to imagine him the same way, that somehow if she
drew his face, progressed his age, he would seem . . . more
real. Not just a memory.

She shook the thought from her mind, worked on the age
progression sketch of the black man. Finished him so that he
was now a man in his fifties, guessing that he'd have a conservative haircut, a somewhat high forehead, with thinning
hair. When she finished, she looked at him, knew right away
where she'd seen him before. Well, not him, but someone
who looked very much like him.

In prison. He was a dead ringer for Johnnie Wheeler.

35

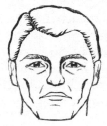

Jared Dunning sipped at his coffee and eyed the
side mirror before turning his attention back to the house. It
was one of those beautiful mornings in the city, the sort that
made you want to pick up, move here, the rest of the world
be damned. Well, he'd certainly be damned. His pregnant
wife would shoot him, was close to it now, though whether
that had something to do with him being gone so long, or
her screwing their next-door neighbor these past couple of
years, he wasn't sure. He wasn't even sure the kid was his.
But he wanted kids. And he wanted this one, so damn his
neighbor. And damn his wife, too.

How the hell anyone working for the Agency stayed married was beyond him. At least anyone working covert ops,
and it was moments like this that made him wish he'd chosen to go into something like encryption analysis, or some
support staff position, where he would have a nice cozy little
office in the basement of the Puzzle Palace in Virginia, getting off at five, instead of peeing in a fucking bottle because
they didn't dare leave for a moment. Not after the near di-
saster the other night when Sydney Fuck-You-Guys-I'll-Do-

What-I-Want Fitzpatrick decided to take off in the middle of the night on a motorcycle, then disappear for two days.

Whatever it was she'd done, it sure had the brass scrambling for cover. He'd give his eyeteeth to know the whole story. All his other teeth were reserved for offerings to whatever gods were watching over him the night McKnight ended up dead—fifteen minutes before Jared's watch started. As thin as the ice he was currently skating on seemed to be these days, he was damned lucky. So were the agents who had the misfortune of sitting on McKnight's house at that inopportune time. For the moment it was listed as suicide. The good hits usually were, and right now they didn't even know if it might have been a hit.

He looked over at Mel, sucking down a Diet Coke, trying to stay awake. Their relief shift should've taken over a couple of hours ago. God only knew where the hell they were, and how the hell he and Mel were going to get any sleep as wired as they were, all so they could be back by ten tonight. "I've been thinking."

"About what?" Mel said, not daring to take his eyes off the Fitzpatrick place, not after their reaming for losing her.

"About the McKnight suicide. You really think it was one?"

Mel shrugged. "I heard that guy had so much shit in his background, it could've been suicide. Public humiliation would've done the guy in."

"But it could've been a hit."

Mel drained the last bit out of his Coke, then tossed the empty can in the back. "I can't even begin to guess what the hell this is about, but whatever the Bureau dug up on McKnight when they were doing his background, it sure as hell had our guys on Mahogany Row scrambling to cover some serious ass."

"Sometimes it's nice to be a peon. Hard to fall far when you're already at the fucking bottom," Jared said as a Lincoln Town Car turned the corner.

He glanced at the driver, his senses going into overdrive as he grabbed the radio, while Mel said, "Oh shit."

"Gnoble's car just pulled onto the street," he radioed.

"I see it."
"Can you move in on foot, without being seen?"
"We've got it."
To Mel, he said, "Get Scotty on the phone. Now."

Sydney stared in shock at the sketch, telling herself she should have seen it earlier, but knowing precisely why she hadn't. One didn't look at Johnnie Wheeler and see past the scar that cut across his face, or the cloudy white eye that saw nothing. Clearly this man *wasn't* Johnnie Wheeler. But remove Johnnie's scar, his blind eye, and it certainly resembled him in every sense of the word. She tried to think of the conversation she'd had with him in the jail. Why her father had decided to take him in; his "church project," Wheeler had called it. Something about Wheeler's father being in the army, getting killed—that her father knew what it was like.

And there was something about Wheeler having a new baby at the time . . .

The endless possibilities swept through her, kept her rooted to the spot. Her father knew Johnnie Wheeler's father. Johnnie Wheeler was in prison for murdering her father.

He said he was innocent.

She wasn't sure which was worse. That he was or that he wasn't.

If he was guilty, it was the worst sort of irony.

If he wasn't, then someone out there knew so much more about this. McKnight. His suicide. The note he'd mailed to her with the photo.

Before she had a chance to contemplate what any of that meant, she heard someone on the steps.

She glanced toward the door. A bit too early for Carillo with their lunch. Scotty probably. She got up to look.

Topper gave a low growl, and she hesitated.

He'd never been wrong yet.

36

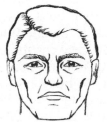

She knew better than to ignore Topper's instincts and she walked over to the door, peered through the peephole.

Donovan Gnoble and his aide walked up the steps, Donovan carrying flowers.

Her breath caught. She stepped away, thinking this couldn't be good. Where the hell were the spooks, the guys who were supposed to be watching her place?

She looked around, saw her things, the drawing, the notes, the photo. Okay. Stop, think. Not the time to panic. Surely, if what Scotty said was true, that Gnoble or someone in his office was really trying to kill her, they wouldn't do it in broad daylight.

Like she was going to sit around and find out?

She grabbed her gun from the counter, shoved it in the waist of her jeans at the small of her back, then pulled her sweatshirt over it.

A sharp rap on the door sent her pulse racing. Topper barked.

She glanced around, saw her sketch, shoved everything inside the briefcase, dropping the lid on it, snapping the clasps closed. And then she grabbed her cell phone, stuck that in her pocket.

Now or never. They tried anything, she'd blast them.

She clipped Topper's leash to his collar, then opened the door, holding the dog tight with one hand, while the other was placed casually on her hip, just inches from her weapon.

She tried for a pleasant look of surprise. The surprise part was easy. The pleasant part another matter entirely. "I was just leaving. What on earth are you doing here, Uncle Don?"

"We heard about your accident last night, and I called your office." He held up a very large bouquet of mixed flowers, arranged in a cut-glass vase. He smiled, stood there, no doubt waiting to be invited in.

She came to her senses. "They're lovely. But you caught me at a really bad time. I need to take Topper for his walk."

His aide said, "We'll just be a little while."

"Wish I could, but he gets very cranky when he's been cooped up all morning."

"It's a beautiful morning," Donovan said. "Why don't we put the flowers inside. We could walk with you. I actually came here to talk to you about something important."

"Perfect." She stepped aside, let them in, making sure the front door was wide open, and she was standing well within it and view of the street.

Donovan set the flowers on the coffee table, stood, took a look around, his gaze catching on the painting of flames. "*What* on earth is that?"

Prescott stepped in to look as well, crossing his arms, a perplexed look on his face. "It's very . . . unusual."

"Just an abstract I'm working on."

"Do you have others?" Prescott asked. "I'm a closet painter myself."

"I didn't know you painted," Gnoble said.

"I have a lot of interests."

Sydney glanced out the door, saw a man walking up the sidewalk, his casual glance toward her apartment giving her a semblance of hope he was someone from the surveillance team, and not some neighbor out for a walk. "Against the wall in the kitchen. But really, I need to get this dog on his walk."

Gnoble slowly reached out toward Topper. "Does he bite?"

"Never bit me," Sydney said, watching as Topper eyed the back of Gnoble's hand with an unusual amount of wariness. Just in case, Sydney reached down, grabbed Topper's collar, and scratched him behind his ears with her other hand. "Good boy. He's okay." Not.

Topper allowed Gnoble to pet him, and she was vaguely aware when Prescott stepped around the corner to look at the paintings. "Ready?" she said, uncomfortable that he'd left her sight.

"Some of these are good," Prescott called out from the kitchen.

"The dog?" she said, jiggling Topper's leash. "He really needs to go out."

"Oh, sorry." Prescott popped out from the kitchen, walked toward them, making kissing noises. "Hey, puppy."

Topper growled, and Prescott yanked his hand back.

"Easy, boy." Sydney patted the dog's head. "Like I said, he gets cranky when he hasn't been on his walk." She held out her hand, indicating they should precede her out the door. When they did, she grabbed her keys and was about to step out, when she thought of the way Prescott had walked into the kitchen. Since the two men were halfway down the steps, she quickly walked into the kitchen, looked around, but didn't see anything but her paintings stacked against the wall beneath the kitchen window. No bombs hidden beneath the table, and he certainly didn't have enough time to get into her fridge, poison her food.

Deciding she was right, if they were up to something, they weren't going to try it now, she followed them out the door, stopping only long enough to lock it behind her before heading down the steps. Gnoble's driver, a tall burly man with a crooked nose, got out, started walking around to open the door for him, but Gnoble waved him off. "We're going for a walk," he said, just as a Siamese cat sauntered past and Topper strained at the leash, wanting to give chase.

"Stay," Sydney ordered, waiting until the cat was past before starting up the hill. The sidewalk was a bit crowded and Gnoble walked beside her, while Prescott walked in the street. Though a thin fog layer usually shrouded her neighborhood, today the sun shone down, which made it a bit surreal to think that she might be walking with someone who had placed, or was going to place, a hit on her. Then again, perhaps she had nothing to fear. People who paid someone else to do the killing didn't want to get their hands dirty, which meant she probably had less to fear from them at the moment. And now that they were outside, she felt fairly certain Scotty's surveillance team was on top of things. Surely they wouldn't have let the senator get up to her door if they thought there was any danger?

A car drove past and Sydney glanced at it, wondering if it was one of the men. She told herself to relax. Pretend as though she didn't know a thing, which only made the silence as they walked all the more noticeable. "So, how goes the election?" she asked, when they came to Topper's favorite fire hydrant.

Gnoble sighed. "Too busy. This time of year always makes me wish I'd listened to my mother and gone to work with my father. Of course, if I lose, I might just want to step into the family business."

Prescott gave an exaggerated shudder. "Bite your tongue. You do not want to leave politics."

Like many politicians, Donovan Gnoble came from old money, which begat more money. His father had owned a very successful chain of convenience stores in the Midwest, probably the largest, the fortune making Gnoble the fourth richest senator on Capitol Hill. Having that to fall back on wasn't a terrible thing, and it certainly came in handy when it came time to seed campaigns or cull political favors where needed.

"That day may come, when I have to leave," he said, staring at the ground. He looked up at Sydney, smiled, then said, "Not that you care about that. You're probably wondering why I really came."

"It crossed my mind." Topper tugged on the leash and they continued up the hill.

"I've been thinking about what you said regarding the man who killed your father."

She tried to keep her voice casual. "Have you?"

"About your thoughts that he might be innocent. I can't help thinking that what if he is, and that's what I built my platform on, then I'm committing the most grievous of injustices."

She looked toward Prescott, wondering what he thought of all this. And Gnoble, apparently reading her look, said, "I've already spoken to him about it. As far as Prescott's concerned, what's done is done, and looking into the matter will only hurt my campaign, not help it. But, to his regret, I'm sure, this isn't his decision to make."

"If you want my opinion," Prescott said, "drop the whole ball of wax on the governor's lap. Let him deal with it."

Gnoble said, "He's right in that sense. We do need to take it to the governor. But before I do, I need to know everything about the case." He stopped, put his hand on Sydney's arm, and asked, "What, exactly, do you remember about that night?"

She thought of the sketch in her briefcase, wondering if that was truly Wheeler's father, and if this had something to do with Gnoble's interest.

Whether she trusted Donovan or not, she couldn't help but think about that night. Perhaps it was the warmth of the sun on her back that helped spur the memories, but they came to her in a flash. She wasn't even supposed to be there that night, but her mother had been called into work at the hospital, to cover another nurse's shift. Sydney had been thrilled, since it meant video games galore, until it was time for bed. And bed consisted of the loveseat tucked behind the door in her father's small office. That's where she'd been when her father was killed. And all she really remembered about that night was when her father came to check on her long after he'd sent her in to sleep, kissed her, pulled the blanket up over her shoulders, saying they'd be going home soon. Just a few more things to finish . . .

She decided it couldn't hurt to tell Gnoble that much, and so she related a short version of this.

"And after that?" Gnoble asked.

She looked over at him as they walked, tried to determine

if this was mere curiosity on his part, or something more, but his gray gaze told her nothing. "Flames. That was pretty much it."

"You woke up to the fire?" he asked. "Not before?"

She closed her eyes, tried to remember, and realized something else woke her, made her notice the fire . . . "I remember the couch was behind the office door, which was open, and I looked through the crack in the door, saw the flames . . . and the front door closing."

"Someone was leaving?" Prescott asked.

She was sure of it, and she couldn't say why. Nor did she want to say why. "I have no idea," she lied. "Who knows what it was. I was thirteen, for God's sake. I don't remember a thing."

"It must have been Wheeler," Gnoble said. "Right after he broke in through the storeroom, then killed your father."

For twenty years she'd kept the past at bay, and allowing it finally to intrude tired her mentally and physically. She didn't want to think about what had happened anymore, and she gave the leash a slight tug. "Let's go home, Topper."

But once they rounded the block, she became acutely aware that she did not want either of these men in her apartment. Thankfully they seemed to have other plans, because as they neared the Town Car, Gnoble told Prescott, "I'll be there in a minute. I'd like to have a word alone with Sydney."

37

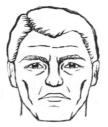

Prescott eyed Sydney, gave her something close to a smile, and said, "I'm sorry about your accident." He left the two of them alone, walked back to the car.

When Prescott disappeared inside the Lincoln, Gnoble turned to her, his hand on her shoulder. "I know what this seems like, my coming to you at this late date. But your father meant something to me. And the fact you feel that the man imprisoned for killing him might not be guilty, well, *that* means something to me. Prescott's going to have a shit fit if he knew I was telling you this. But I'm going to look into it, even if it does cost me the election."

She wasn't quite sure what to think of his little speech, considering that in two days it would all be too late for Wheeler. "I appreciate it."

He squeezed her shoulder, gave a nod of what she believed was reassurance, then walked to the Town Car. It took off just as Carillo pulled up.

"I got a call from Scotty to get my ass over here," he said, watching the senator's car drive off. "He's tied up on something, and couldn't leave."

Sydney didn't move at first, thinking about what Gnoble

said, about looking into Wheeler's case. She eyed Carillo.
"Do you know why politicians get elected? Because they
make you *want* to believe in them. Always be sincere, even
if you don't mean it."

"Sort of the point, I think. Maybe my good news will coun-
teract the crap he just fed you. First thing is that our DOJ guy
is making progress with the photos. He's hoping to finish up,
get them out to us maybe as early as this evening."

"Any indication on what he found?"

"Like I could even understand the guy? Positive to negative something or other, Gaussian, Fourier analysis, noise
reduction. I have no idea what the hell he was saying. He
was talking math, music, and God knows what else. But if
you ever need someone to sit on the stand and impress a jury,
he's the man. More importantly, I got word that Jazmine
Wheeler's out at the clinic, so we should take a run out there,
but *only* after we go pay a visit to Becky Lynn McKnight up
north. We know Jazmine's going to be at the clinic for the
rest of the day. No guarantees on the ex–Mrs. McKnight."

"Becky Lynn? You found something more on her?"

"When I was digging through that file box in the back of
Scotty's car at the hospital, I ran across some of his notes on
the BICTT banking scandal, which, coincidentally or not,
sort of came to a head about twenty-two years ago. That
would be right around the time Robert 'Boston' Orozco fled
to Baja."

"But this we already knew. So, other than the timing
. . . ?"

"There were also some copies of phone records, showing
calls to Baja."

"Whose?"

"One Becky Lynn McKnight, which is why I'd like to pay
her a visit. She's got a nice house in Sausalito, where she's
apparently lived ever since her divorce from McKnight."

"He must have been paying her some hefty alimony."

"Not exactly, which might be part of the reason her
name's popping up in our data banks. They weren't married that long, she signed a prenup, and the moment they
were divorced, she hightailed it back here to the Bay Area.

She's been wheeling and dealing *something* to maintain that lifestyle."

"Orozco did mention that his only contact was playing both sides of the fence."

"She certainly fits that bill, especially since it turns out McKnight did testify about BICTT, and, if the calls are any indication, she's been feeding info to a guy who was *supposed* to testify but fled." He glanced up, then down the street. "How about we talk in the car on the way over? A little more private that way. Well, as private as we can be with a couple guys shadowing us."

"Let me put Topper in the house, then go get that age progression drawing."

"Ah, bring the sheep." He opened the back door, and Topper hopped in.

She sighed. "Sorry, Topper. Your daddy's coming home soon, and he won't be happy if you're not here."

The dog hesitated, but jumped down when she clapped and called his name. "Come on, Top. You can wait upstairs until he gets home." She locked the dog inside Arturo's place, then retrieved her briefcase from her own apartment.

Back in the car, she pulled out the sketch, holding it up. "You're never going to guess who this is."

"Okay, a middle-aged guy named Frank White?"

"Yes. But guess who he resembles? I didn't really see it when I first looked at the photo McKnight sent, but then I wasn't really looking for it, either."

"Looking for what?" he asked, inserting the key into the ignition.

"A resemblance to Johnnie Wheeler."

Carillo eyed the sketch. "The guy in prison?"

"The same."

"*This* is him?"

"No. But they might be related. Father, uncle, who knows? You can't go by the name, but you definitely can go by the resemblance. We should show it to Jazmine Wheeler and see."

"I'm gonna have to take your word on it, since I've never seen the guy. Question is, what the hell does it mean?"

"Maybe that Wheeler *is* telling the truth. Someone set him up."

"Question is, did they set him up on purpose, or was he just a convenient patsy?" He looked at his watch. "We gotta get moving, or your shadows are going to raise all sorts of hell, and I'd like to make sure they don't do it before we make both contacts. Since I told Dixon I was going to stop by and make sure you were okay, *then* go to lunch, we could stop at the Taco Bell near the methadone clinic where Jazmine works."

"You don't think we should stop by the clinic before we go to Becky Lynn's?"

"Just the opposite. It'll put me back in town when Dixon starts chomping at the bit, wondering where I've gone off to. And by the time we drive up north, see Becky Lynn, then come back down and hit the drive-through before we make our stop at the clinic, it'll be too late for your shadows to do much about it." He started up the car, looked over at her. "Of course, you'll have to deal with Scotty and whatever repercussions come out of that, because you know these guys are gonna blow a gasket when they figure out what we're doing."

"Him I can deal with. Dixon, on the other hand . . ."

"Least of our worries," he said as he pulled up alongside Jared Dunning's car. He rolled down his window, waited for Dunning to lower his as well. "We're heading to Taco Bell. One down in Bayview–Hunters Point."

"Why down there?" Dunning asked, looking tired and annoyed.

"You are clearly not a Taco Bell connoisseur. The ones around here suck. But first we gotta make a stop up in Sausalito. Drop off some paperwork. You're welcome to follow."

"Isn't Sausalito *north* of the Golden Gate Bridge?"

"As a matter of fact it is. We'll only be a few minutes, if you want to wait here for us before we head back down to lunch." Dunning uttered a few choice swearwords as Carillo rolled up his window, then politely waited for Dunning to pull out after him before he took off. "Don't think he's real happy."

"I don't think he believes you. Now, where were we? Something about McKnight testifying?"

"Right. Sort of like the story Orozco told you. McKnight testified that he believed he was an innocent patsy. That the BICTT board of directors, that would be the international guys who couldn't legally open a bank in our country, used his all-American name to secure investors, and to cover the foreign paper trail for the real investors. He says he knew nothing about it. The involvement of BICTT was merely as an advisory capacity, for international banking matters, and that he had no idea they were actually shareholders, or that everything under the sun was going through their office before he attached his signature."

"With a scandal of that magnitude, how the hell did McKnight survive to have his name suggested as the federal procurement czar?"

"First of all, because he was cleared. Utterly and completely, *and* even though the Senate subcommittee report *seems* to indicate his story is dirtier than hell. Might have stayed buried had the president not tried to appoint him, thereby setting a chain of events into motion. When Scotty's friend Hatcher walked in to do a background, it was the one thing that apparently no one else really bothered to do before then. Or maybe hoped no one would do."

"Which is?"

"Sit down and actually read a copy of the subcommittee report. All umpteen-million pages of it. It seems McKnight and his BICTT investors were purchasing shares just below the five percent that would trigger the requirement of SEC disclosure—an obvious violation of SEC law, and one that McKnight, with his banking background, would have known about."

"So how the hell did he skate on this?"

"Could be that a certain fairly new senator was sitting in on those hearings."

"Donovan Gnoble?"

"None other. At no time did Gnoble ever mention that he

knew McKnight, shared any business holdings with him, or
that McKnight served under him during his years in the service, whether enlisted, special ops, or black ops. Of course,
if it was black ops, no way would Gnoble mention it. And
that would certainly explain why he'd overlook some serious
flaws in the hearings and let McKnight skate. He can't tell
on McKnight, and McKnight can't tell on him."

"So Gnoble is dirty."

"The question is, is it government-sanctioned black ops
dirt, or *un*sanctioned black ops dirt?"

"Or a little of both."

"Either way, if this were ever made public, it could poten-
tially fuck up a really nice lead in the polls if, oh, the opposing candidate found out and put the proper spin on it. And
Gnoble's not the only party who'd like it kept under wraps.
CIA sure as hell doesn't want any of this festering history
back out in the open. Not if, as Orozco told you, the BICTT
scandal is just the tip of a very large iceberg that's still floating around out there."

"I can see where it might look particularly bad, especially
from where we're sitting, but other than our own suspicions,
and a bit of circumstantial evidence, showing Gnoble's name
on a report . . ." She glanced over at him. "The bank pouch
from Baja. Orozco said that the guys that came after us were
probably a team of black ops. They were sent to get that
pouch."

"It makes sense. When you look at the whole picture.
The background on McKnight, the upcoming election. That
photo suddenly showing up in your mail. If it's all related,
then whatever got stirred up twenty years ago involving your
father and Wheeler, it's rearing its ugly head again. And if
that's what got your father killed . . ."

He shrugged, left it hanging there. As if to say: *What
chance did she have?*

38

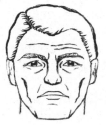

Becky Lynn McKnight did not live in the nicest part
of Sausalito, though Sydney wasn't sure there was a bad part.
Perhaps a more apt description was that Becky Lynn didn't
have a commanding bay view, which probably knocked off
a cool million or so from the price of her home. Its very location, however, made the otherwise quaint, but pedestrian,
single-story, stucco-sided home worth a veritable fortune.

"You sure this is the right place?" Sydney asked, as Carillo slowed near the listed address. "Pretty damned nice,
considering."

"Considering we have her flagged for OC, it fits. You don't
live in houses this nice if you've got no job and no income.
It's the one listed on our files, and the DMV shows that white
Lexus in the driveway is registered to her."

"What's that old saying . . . ?" Sydney asked. "You've
come a long way, baby?"

"She wasn't always a white-bread girl?"

"I was pretty young at the time, but looking back, she had
all the earmarks of a con. Sort of just breezed in one day, and
next thing I knew, she was running the pizza parlor and my

dad was helping her move her things from some dive bar to a nicer apartment."

"So she was a bad stray? Or just went bad?"

"Who knows? I mean, if she's flagged by our guys, what did my father really know about her?" And what did Sydney really know about her father . . . ?

They walked up the porch steps, and Carillo nodded in approval. "You know, government salary aside, if I got transferred to, like, Idaho, I could afford a little place like this *and* a Lexus."

"Even paying alimony to Sheila?"

"Okay, maybe just the Lexus, but I bet the seats stretch out nice."

They stood to either side of the door, and Sydney knocked. A moment later, it was opened by Becky Lynn, now middle-aged, but looking very elegant in her navy slacks and white sweater that seemed so . . . country club chic. Definitely not the blue-jean, sweatshirt-wearing woman who had come into the east-side pizza parlor each night when Sydney was a kid. Her shoulder-length, once-bleached-blond hair was now dyed a dark auburn, and her face was expertly made up. Perhaps she was on her way to a lunch date. She'd aged, of course, with the telltale crow's-feet around her brown eyes, and the over-forty laugh lines and hint of jowls haunting her mouth, which pressed together with tension, before turning up into a strained smile on seeing and no doubt recognizing Sydney. "Oh my gosh. *Little* Sydney?" She smiled, looked a bit too cheerful. "What a wonderful surprise!"

She did not, however, invite them in.

"Hi, Becky Lynn," Sydney said, trying to keep things casual. "I was hoping I might ask you a couple questions about my father."

"I was on my way to a lunch date. Can it wait?"

"Actually, no. May we come in?"

Becky Lynn glanced at Carillo, and Sydney figured she was trying to determine his part in all this. "I guess. If it doesn't take too long." She stepped aside and allowed them entry. The gleaming hardwood floor was covered by a large

Oriental rug that muted their steps as she led them into the front room decorated in light cherry. The decor was exquisite, and quite different from the Becky Lynn that Sydney remembered, a woman who thought that red flocked wallpaper would be perfect for the ladies' room, until Sydney's mother put the nix on that idea.

"What is it I can help you with?" Becky Lynn folded her hands in her lap, attempting, no doubt, to look calmer than she felt—a fact easy to discern from the strong and fast pulse in her carotid. She never asked who Carillo was, something Sydney found a bit odd. Maybe she knew Sydney's profession and didn't need to ask. Either way, they weren't about to pull out their creds and make this an official visit.

"I have some questions about my father . . . money he might have demanded from your late ex-husband. And a photograph I'd like you to look at."

"Oh? Is that all?" Her smile grew so relaxed at that point, Sydney figured she'd somehow missed something very big, something else she was worried about. "I do vaguely recall him contacting Will about money. It could have something to do with some irregularities I remember seeing in your father's books, but those were destroyed in the fire."

"What sort of irregularities?"

"He seemed to be in the habit of ordering large quantities of goods, goods that weren't delivered, or were delivered damaged and were returned for a refund. Odd things like that. I needed the money, so I wasn't about to rock the boat and let on I saw anything."

"Can you name any specific examples?"

"It's been so long, and really I put it from my mind once he died. I didn't think it was the thing to do, pointing my finger at . . . your father, after his death."

"And I appreciate your concern," Sydney said. Not. "But if you could try to remember anyway."

"Well, there was all that hamburger he ordered. I'm pretty sure we didn't serve hamburgers," she offered, and Sydney refrained from commenting that she was only thirteen, wasn't there every day, and could have told her the same.

"There may have even been some orders for liquor, where some whiskey or gin came in damaged, but maybe I'm remembering another place."

And that did send alarm bells ringing. Beer and wine were all her father's liquor license allowed. Hard liquor being delivered, damaged, smacked of organized crime. But was this her father's business, or was this Becky Lynn's doing? She was, after all, the one currently being looked at for organized crime dealings. But Sydney kept her expression as neutral as she could, as though none of this meant anything to her. "Any visitors, anyone who came by that shouldn't have been there?"

"Heavens, Sydney. It was a pizza place just off the freeway. There were always people dropping by we didn't know."

"Did you and my father have an affair?"

She seemed slightly surprised by the question, but not overly so. "Did your mother say that? What a horrid thing to do. I'd think she'd want you to remember—"

"I'm quite sure she has no idea I suspect a thing," Sydney said, in her mother's defense. "Did you?"

"Not with your father. No."

Sydney took that to mean she'd had an affair with someone. "Robert Orozco, perhaps?"

"I'm sure I never met the man."

"And yet you've been calling him down in Baja"—she turned to Carillo—"for how many years now?"

"A lot," he said.

Sydney eyed Becky Lynn. "If I'm not mistaken, the most recent calls were right before your ex-husband killed himself, then right after . . ." She had no idea on the times, but figured it was a safe guess. Someone had contacted Orozco about the suicide, and he'd made it no secret that Becky Lynn was his contact.

When Becky Lynn shifted uncomfortably, Sydney figured she'd guessed right on. "He was a friend of Will's. I thought he should know that Will was having problems."

"But you don't know him personally?"

"No. I helped him out years ago by getting him some fake

ID to leave the country." She gave a saccharine smile, then glanced at her watch. "Now if you have no further questions?" she said, glancing at her watch.

"Just a photo I need you to look at."

Sydney had tucked it in her purse; took it out of the envelope and handed it to Becky Lynn, who raised her brows, and immediately began shaking her head. "No . . . no. Except for your father, and my ex, I really don't see *anyone* in there I know."

"How about the guy in uniform?"

"Sorry."

"You don't recognize Senator Gnoble?"

"*That's* Senator Gnoble? I guess I didn't recognize him without that goatee. Or in uniform, for that matter. He looks so much younger than the pictures I've seen of him in the paper. Are we finished?"

Sydney pointed to Orozco. "And Robert?"

"So that's what he looks like. He's always just been a voice on the phone."

Right. "And this man," she said, pointing to who they thought was Wheeler's father. "Frank White?"

"No. Name doesn't ring a bell, and I can't say I've ever met him. Really, is there a point to any of this?"

"Just trying to figure the connection between my father, your ex, and the restaurant," Sydney said, now just fishing for answers, because, frankly, she'd gotten nothing. "Especially any references to *Cisco's Kid*."

Becky Lynn's face paled. She sat up, brushed at her slacks, then crossed her legs, as though trying to appear far more relaxed than she was. "Cisco's Kid?" she said, sounding, or trying to sound, confused. "What on earth are you talking about?"

"My father's boat?"

The woman narrowed her gaze. "A boat?" And then she smiled, truly relaxed, and Sydney realized she'd missed something critical. "You're asking me about a boat? I've never seen your father's boat. I'm sure I didn't even know he had one." Becky Lynn reached across and grasped her hand, and Sydney could smell the alcohol on her breath, see that her eyes were somewhat bloodshot. That brought a vague recollection of the woman making drunken phone calls periodically to Sydney's mother. What they talked about, why her mother never discussed it, Sydney didn't know. Becky Lynn gave a sigh, exaggerated for her benefit, no doubt, and said, "I really wish I could stay and chat some more, but I've got to go, or I'll be late. It was *so* good to see you again, Sydney. I hope your mother is doing well."

Carillo and Sydney stood, and she walked them to the door, holding it open for them. Sydney paused on the threshold, looked out at the Lexus, and thought how much Becky Lynn had changed since the days of the pizza place . . .

"You know," Sydney said, her foot against the door. "I forgot to mention how sorry I was that your husband died."

"That's right," Carillo said. "We wanted to pass on our condolences."

"Thank you," Becky Lynn replied, her saccharine smile back in place.

And Sydney said, "You don't happen to know what he was so upset about? I heard they found something in his background."

"I have no idea."

"Something to do with . . ." She looked at Carillo. "What was it again?"

"That old banking scandal."

"That's right. BICTT. Isn't that the one where the guys all got together, and if something happened to one of them, they had all these safeguards set up? Sort of as protection? Like that photo being mailed to me."

"Makes you wonder what the other safeguards were . . . Who else will get implicated," Carillo said.

They both turned toward Becky Lynn, who gripped the door, and clearly looked like she would've shut it on them if she could have somehow dislodged Sydney's foot. "Whatever my husband was involved in, I have no idea. And if that's why he killed himself, then so be it. Between him and his business ventures, they nearly bankrupted me."

Sydney gave a pointed look to the house. "Seems you recovered quite nicely. But thanks for your time," she said, as she followed Carillo down the steps. And Becky Lynn looked vastly relieved, until Sydney added, "You've been more of a help than you realize."

They continued their way down the sidewalk, hearing the door shut firmly behind them. When they walked past the Lexus, Sydney looked down the long driveway that led to the back of the house, a deep and narrow lot, like many Bay Area properties. "You think she looked a little rattled when we left?"

"Rattled? Why, Pollyanna. You're not thinking anything untoward, are you?"

"Of course not. I'm simply concerned enough to make sure she doesn't faint, maybe need medical attention when she calls whoever she calls?"

Carillo smiled. "I'm starting to like you more and more. Let's just hope your damned shadows don't get all antsy."

Sydney glanced down the street, gave a cheery wave to the men, hoping they'd stay put in the car, just before she and Carillo casually walked down the drive, until they were out of sight. She noticed the blinds were still closed, then moved up alongside the house, wedging herself between a camellia bush and the brick porch, just beneath the window on the side yard. Carillo went farther down, standing beneath another window. Their efforts paid off, because Sydney could just make out her voice, shrill enough to be overheard through the closed window, which, on this older house, was not double-paned. Apparently they had more than rattled her cage. Sydney could hear her pacing on the subflooring, since she was standing beside a vent, but caught only parts, as Becky Lynn wouldn't stand still. ". . . Do you know who . . ." Then, "Yes. Here. And she had your . . ."

Your what? Sydney wanted to shout. Apparently she was on her cell phone, because suddenly Sydney heard the back door unlocking. Sydney glanced at Carillo, who was on the other side of the porch. They ducked. The camellia branches scraped her neck and face on one side as she went down, wedged herself between the bush and the much rougher brick siding on the porch. She only hoped Becky Lynn was so involved in her conversation that she wasn't looking around her. The back door swung open. "Goddamn, Robert. She was here. And I will not— Damn it, my keys."

She turned, retraced her steps, leaving the back door open. Sydney hunkered down farther, tried to become one with the bush. A moment later she heard Becky Lynn's returning footsteps, just before she stepped out onto the porch. Slammed her back door shut. "No, you shut up and listen," she said, hurrying down the three porch steps. "I'm not sitting in some goddamned jail cell because your head is too far up your ass to see what's going on, you bastard. You told me you had it all under control. I've got a life here and I want to keep it."

She walked past Sydney, cell phone to her ear, purse over her arm, and keys and remote in her other hand. She strode up the driveway to the Lexus, and Sydney heard the sound of the car door unlocking by remote. ". . . All I can say is you better deal with it. And now."

Even after she got in her car and drove off, Sydney and Carillo didn't move until they were absolutely certain she wasn't returning for something else forgotten in her haste to get out of there. Finally they emerged from either side of the porch, Sydney brushing the cobwebs and dust from her clothes. "You get the feeling that we're overlooking something really, really obvious?"

"Yeah. She looked ready to puke when you brought up your father's boat. And then a second later, she knew we didn't know whatever the hell it was we were supposed to know about it."

They walked to their car, waved at Scotty's men parked farther down the street. And Sydney said, "Do you think she was talking to Robert or about Robert?"

"Could've been either. But whoever it was, she wasn't happy. Time to head back to the city, hit that Taco Bell before we visit Wheeler's aunt, so I can at least say I went to lunch."

39

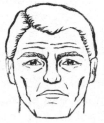

Without the San Francisco hills, the momentarily perfect weather, and the light breeze tinged with salt from the bay, the clinic where Jazmine Wheeler worked could be lifted up and dropped into any large and depressed area of any metropolitan city. The buildings were old and in disrepair, wrought-iron bars covered nearly every window or door on the ground floor, and graffiti caught the eye wherever one glanced.

Bayview–Hunters Point was not the San Francisco pictured in the tourist books. This was the San Francisco of the downtrodden, the drug-addicted, the homeless, and the dealers who preyed on them. As Carillo turned the unmarked vehicle onto the street, slowed to check the address on the building, Sydney saw a group of men, some black, some white, watching them, their collective gazes filled with suspicion, no doubt making the pair for cops. This was one of those areas that most law enforcement types didn't drive into unless they had their hands on their guns and the holsters unsnapped. A glance in the side mirror told her their tail was still on them, and she figured having an extra car with two armed agents behind them came in mighty handy.

They found the clinic, as well as a parking spot in a loading zone that was remarkably empty and in sight of the windows of the building they were about to enter, a plus when hoping to keep the car intact while conducting business in such a neighborhood. The two got out of the car just as Jared Dunning pulled up, opened his door. "What the hell are we doing here?"

"Just need to stop by and have a chat with someone about renewing a prescription," Sydney said.

"Birth control pills," Carillo added.

Jared looked up at the sign. "It's a methadone clinic."

"Damn, Carillo. We are so not sleeping together tonight."

"Way to go," Carillo told Dunning as they walked past him, toward the door. "I was this close."

She waved at the two agents, then entered the building, as Jared Dunning pulled out his cell phone.

The clinic was busy, and while Sydney walked up to the front desk, Carillo stood watch at the door, crossing his arms, taking a don't-fuck-with-me-or-mine stance, something totally wasted on the receptionist, who sat reading a tabloid magazine while sipping a soda, her half-eaten hamburger sitting on the wrapper next to the phone.

"Yeah," she said, barely sparing them a glance.

Sydney held out her credentials. "I'm here to see Jazmine Wheeler."

By rote, the woman reached for a stack of clipboards with patient information forms clipped on them, handed Sydney one, never removing her gaze from the magazine's pages. "Fill this out, take a seat."

Sydney slipped her credentials on top of the magazine so there was no doubt the woman would see them and the badge. "You mind checking to see if she's in?"

"You're not here for methadone?"

"We tend to avoid that sort of thing in the FBI."

R. Ashton, according to her name tag, gave a clueless shrug, picked up the phone, and made a call. "FBI here to see you . . ." She hung up, then, "Jazz'll be out in a minute."

"Thank you."

Sydney stood back, eyeing the gaunt-faced patients who

were now eyeing her with even more distrust as they stood in line, waiting for their doses. She kept her back to the wall, her expression neutral, and waited. Five minutes later, a short, trim woman stepped into the waiting room. She was dressed in dark brown slacks, a tan cable knit sweater, a white lab coat, and a beaded necklace of amber. Her flawless skin was the color of dark chocolate, and despite the gray peppered in her close-cropped hair, she looked much younger than the fifty-some-odd years Sydney had figured as her age.

"You're from the FBI?" she said, fingering the beads of her long necklace, her glance looking past Sydney to Carillo.

"Yes, ma'am." Sydney showed the nurse her ID. "I'm here about your nephew, Johnnie Wheeler."

"What for?" she asked, with a tinge of wariness.

"I have questions about his homicide conviction."

She said nothing for several seconds, merely looked Sydney in the eye as though trying to read her. Then, "And what is it you want from me?"

"I was hoping you might be able to put me in touch with any friends of his, relatives, anyone who might, unknowingly even, have a lead as to what really happened."

"What really happened?" Jazmine said, her voice strained. "Johnnie was stupid enough to cooperate with the detectives who came out and said they were only there to find out what *really* happened. A good show. Said they were going to help him, and they did, right into the back of their car. He was railroaded."

"What do you mean railroaded?"

"By the cops. A scapegoat. Black man in a white town. He didn't do it. There is no justice," she said, stepping back into the hallway. "That's more than I should've told you, and all I'm saying. Anything else, talk to Johnnie's attorney."

Sydney started to follow her down the hall. "Can you at least look at a photo?" she called out as a couple of the resident addicts moved in.

One of them, a tall black man, came within a foot of Sydney, saying, "You heard the lady. Go."

Jazmine Wheeler stopped midflight, spun on her heel, and stalked toward the man, pinning her gaze on him. "Get your ass back in line, Trey, or you'll be drying it out in detox, faster'n you can say where's my methadone? Hear me?"

He put up his hands, edged back. "I'm cool. Just want to make sure you was okay, Miss Jazz, you hear me?"

"I hear you. Now get." She waited until he was back in line before she faced Sydney. "Give me one good reason why I should look at this damned photo of yours."

"Because I'm the daughter of the man your nephew says he didn't kill. And if he didn't do it, I want to know who did, before they stick that needle in his arm two days from now."

Several seconds passed as Jazmine searched Sydney's eyes, perhaps trying to judge her sincerity, and then she said, "My office is the third door on the left. We can talk in there."

She led Sydney down the hall into a small room, cluttered and filled with hanging plants. A yellow school bus photo frame was filled with twelve pictures of a young boy, showing his progression from kindergarten until graduation from high school. Sydney thought she saw a bit of Johnnie Wheeler in the boy, and wondered if it might be his son, the baby he'd talked about having when he was arrested. They were the only photos in the room. A large padlocked file cabinet filled one corner of the office, its side covered with magnets from various destinations around the U.S. The remainder of the space was taken up by a metal desk, buried beneath stacks of medical folders.

Jazmine moved behind the desk, but didn't sit. "I have a lot of patients I have to get through. And when they don't get their methadone, things can get ugly very fast, so make this quick."

Sydney opened her folder and set the photo on her desk. "Do you know any of these men?"

Jazmine gave a dismissive glance toward the picture, then did a double take. "What does Frank have to do with this?"

"You know him?"

"Frank White. Johnnie's father."

"You've seen this photo before?"

"No. But that's definitely him. And he died well before Johnnie was ever arrested."

"Do you know what he did for a living?"

Jazmine hesitated. "There's what he said he did, and then there's what I really think he did. He *said* he was a contract civilian employee doing electrical work for the army. Seemed his services were in demand. All over the world."

"And you didn't believe him? That he was a contract electrician?"

She gave a cynical laugh. "I know the government tosses money around like there's no tomorrow, *except* when it comes to helping out places like this clinic, but how many times do they need to send out emergency electricians to change lightbulbs in places like Pakistan, Chile, or Honduras?" She started stacking folders, rote action to occupy her hands. "You name a political hotspot in the world twenty-two years ago, or some country that bordered one, and my sister's ex-boyfriend was sent there. Usually taking off on a flight that left in the middle of the night. I told her something else was going on, but she didn't believe me, nor did she care. In fact, what I remembered her saying was that since she never married the guy, he could take all the trips he wanted to wherever he wanted, as long as the child support checks came in."

Sydney thought about her father, and his sudden trips to far-off locales to take his alleged photographs for recruitment posters and pamphlets. "Exactly when did he die?"

"Two years before my nephew was arrested for murder." Right around the same time as her own father's accident, she thought, just as Jazmine added, "Faulty wiring, was what I was told. Sparked some explosion."

Explosion . . . ? So many pieces fell into place with that simple statement. The time her father had come home from one of his photography trips with an injury that caused him to lose two fingers. Someone "accidentally" setting off "real" charges instead of the fake ones they were supposed to use for photography. Her father forced into retirement, and their subsequent move from Red Springs, North Carolina, to California. It made her wonder how she'd ever believed her father's story about his accident and his retiring. What had he told her at the time . . . ? Because he couldn't hold a camera steady anymore.

It was *never* about holding a camera; she knew that now. It was about holding a gun.

"Is there something I should know about this?" Jazmine asked, watching Sydney carefully.

Sydney slid the photo closer to her. "Are you sure you don't know the rest of these men? Have you ever seen any of them before?"

Jazmine picked up the photo this time, looked at it for quite a while, but then shook her head. "The one here, with the curly blond hair," she said, indicating Robert Orozco. "Maybe once when Frank came out to visit Johnnie for Christmas. Well, stopped by on his way out of the country, was more like it. But I couldn't say for sure, because the other guy waited in the car."

"Do you ever remember the detectives questioning you about Johnnie's statement, that my father had befriended him?"

"Of course. Johnnie came to me that night because of his burned hands. He'd gone there to get some money to get to this job that your father had arranged for him. Johnnie told me that someone killed him, then set the fire, all while he was hiding in the back."

"Did he say how it was he got burned?"

"Yes." And yet she hesitated, as though trying to decide what to tell Sydney. Finally, "He said he went to help your father. When Johnnie realized he was dead, he fled out the window." She took a frustrated breath, glanced off to the side, before continuing. "*I'm* the one who convinced him to call, tell them just what he told me . . ."

"And Johnnie never questioned how it was that Kevin found him?"

"What was there to question? He'd just had a new baby, was trying to kick the drugs, and when your father told Johnnie that someone at some church had submitted his name, who was he to discount his good fortune that at last things were going his way? The cops said he made it up, an excuse for being in the restaurant that night to steal the money. But why? What could it possibly matter now how your father found him?"

Sydney pointed to her father. "That man standing behind Frank White. That was my father. Kevin Fitzpatrick."

This time it was Jazmine's turn to stare, and Sydney could tell the moment she started to understand just what was going on, the dawning of realization. "Your father?"

"Yes."

"The man my nephew said befriended him, but that everyone said was impossible that they even knew each other?"

"Yes."

"Oh my God . . ." She sank into her chair. "Johnnie was telling the truth. He didn't do it. This proves it."

"No, but it goes a long way in validating his story. It does *not* mean he didn't kill him." Jazmine started to protest, and Sydney said, "I'm not saying he did. Just what we can or can't prove. And just because my father knew Johnnie Wheeler's father, that does not mean that Johnnie didn't kill him. But that's not what I'm worried about," Sydney continued. "My father lost two fingers in an explosion around the same time Johnnie's father was killed. My father was *also* allegedly a contract employee for the army, but his story was that he took photographs for recruitment posters and pamphlets."

"Then why wouldn't your father have told Johnnie that they knew each other?"

"Maybe because of what they really did for the army. A friend of mine saw this photo and suggested that the men in it were obviously Delta Force, an elite group of highly trained special operators. It's been suggested to me that they were working some sort of black ops assignments."

"What does that mean?"

"It means that whatever they were assigned to, especially if it was dealing with anything associated with national security, the government denies their involvement or association, and they could not discuss it with *anyone* outside of their unit. Period. And that would include the sons and daughters of former members."

"Then what good does any of this do for Johnnie if you can't prove it? They're going to execute him on Tuesday." She brought her hand up to her mouth as the reality of it all hit her. "My God. That's in two days . . ."

"It gives us a starting point. Just yesterday I had no idea that my father knew Johnnie Wheeler's father, or that they might have worked together. Now that I do, I have a whole new direction to look in." And not much time to find the answers, she reminded herself.

Sydney returned her photo to the folder, then wrote her cell phone number on one of her business cards, telling Jazmine to call day or night if she thought of anything. As she started out the door, she remembered the suicide note, the nicknames used within it, and she asked, "Do you have any idea if Johnnie's father went by any nicknames? Heard any of his friends call him anything different by chance?"

"Well, Frank was sort of a shortened version of his name. Does that count?"

"Short for what?"

"Francisco. He hated that name."

40

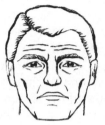

"It's not the boat," she told Carillo after she left
Jazmine Wheeler's office. "It was never about the boat."

He pushed open the door, held it for her. "I thought we'd
determined that when we were at Becky Lynn's and she
blew us off."

"But we didn't determine why."

"And you're going to tell me, when?"

She merely smiled.

"You know that whole anticipation thing, Pollyanna? It
only works for sex."

"Frank is really Francisco."

Carillo stopped midstep. "You're telling me that the Cisco
Kid referenced in the notes is Johnnie Wheeler?"

"Has to be. And it makes perfect sense. Francisco's official story was that he was a contract electrician for the
army. Jazmine Wheeler thinks that unofficially he was doing
something more, since they sent him all over the world. And
get this, he was killed in an explosion right around the same
time my father lost a couple fingers in an explosion."

"There's a coincidence that would be hard to explain," he
said, pausing to answer his cell phone. He mouthed, "Let-

tie," listened for a bit more, then said, "Yeah. We're on our way. Just stopped off to get something to eat." He disconnected, said, "Lettie says that Dixon's looking for us."

"Us? I'm not even here."

"If I had to hazard a guess, your babysitters snitched you off."

"Great."

"Don't stress," he said, as they walked out the door and to their car. "That's why I picked up the extra nachos. Bribe the boss."

"What are they? Gold-plated?"

"Just soggy from sitting in the car for the last twenty minutes. So tell me what else she told you."

Sydney related the rest of her conversation with Jazmine as they drove back.

"So, what you're saying," he said, as he parked in the front of the federal building, placed his placard in the window that would ensure the parking vultures left his car alone, "is that all these guys were working an operation together, some black ops thing, and Wheeler's father gets killed, your father's hurt, forced to quit, and that's where this all begins?"

"It has to be. Orozco said they tried to kill him in the past. Maybe they missed and killed Wheeler's father by mistake. More importantly, Orozco said my father believed the explosion was no accident, and he blamed McKnight."

"And this church connection is how your father found Wheeler?"

"My father didn't attend church. I'm guessing he made up that whole connection, because it seemed believable, and would completely eliminate any mention of just how and why he sought out Wheeler, and why he contacted the others for money for Cisco's Kid, AKA Francisco's kid, Johnnie Wheeler."

"Which means it could've been blackmail?"

"Or just the prodding of someone's conscience."

"In some circles, that means the same thing." Their surveillance team pulled into a space behind them, but didn't follow them up, no doubt figuring that in the confines of the federal building, little could happen. Sydney, however, couldn't help but recall the face of the man from the elevator, especially when they got on, rode it up to the Bureau office. She wasn't about to let down her guard, even in the relative safety of the building.

They headed straight to Dixon's office, neither of them expecting to see SAC Terrence Sheffield in with him. Sheffield was taller than Dixon by a couple of inches, and older by at least a decade. His lined face was permanently etched with that better-not-find-out-you're-doing-something-you're-not-supposed-to-be-doing look, which was mirrored by Dixon's less permanent don't-drag-me-into-what-you-were-doing-or-there'll-be-hell-to-pay look. Choosing between the two, Sydney would have to say Dixon was the one they wanted to placate, but she wasn't sure just how, especially when Schermer walked up, saw them, said, "I got that info on BIC—"

"Later," Carillo said, holding up the Taco Bell bag with what seemed more confidence than Sydney felt. "Got your lunch, boss," he said to Dixon. Schermer backed off, apparently reading the tension.

Dixon, who hadn't ordered lunch, said nothing. SAC Sheffield asked, "What took you so long?"

"Traffic," Carillo said, at the precise same time Sydney said, "Long lines."

Sheffield narrowed his gaze at them. "There's a Taco Bell five minutes from here. How much traffic can there be?"

Carillo handed the lunch bag to Dixon. "They shred their cheese funny. *This* Taco Bell is best."

Dixon took the bag, eyed Sydney, no doubt seeing the dust and cobwebs on her clothes, and said, "I need you both in my office now."

Carillo was smart enough to realize when it was time to quit, and they followed him and SAC Sheffield back to Dixon's office. Dixon closed the door behind them, and she thought, *This can't be good, he knows we were at the methadone clinic*, especially after the look he gave her as he set his Taco Bell bag onto his desk, and said, "We have some problems, Fitzpatrick."

Sheffield's phone rang, and he told Dixon, "You haven't

eaten all day. Better get started." He took his call, and she forced herself not to look at Carillo as Dixon attempted to pull a nacho from the container, only to have it disintegrate into mush and fall onto his desk. The glare he threw their way before he opened his desk drawer and pulled out a plastic fork did not bode well for them, nor the hesitation after his first bite of what must surely have been ice-cold congealed beans and nacho cheese. Not surprisingly, he took several bites to make it look good, a sure sign that once the SAC left, he was going to have their asses.

Dixon would not say a thing before then. To do so meant he did not have control of his subordinates, something he would never admit to in front of his boss. Which meant the problems he'd mentioned were nothing to do with their foray into Hunters Point and the methadone clinic, because clearly neither he nor Sheffield was aware of it . . . yet.

She figured Carillo came to the same thought at the same time, because he met her gaze, gave a shrug, figured he was good for now, then relaxed back into his chair, probably secure in the knowledge that it was her name specifically mentioned in concert with the word *problems*.

She patiently waited, not an easy thing to do when she saw Dixon eyeing the Taco Bell bag, then pulling out the receipt, glancing at it, then the two of them, which made her wonder what he was gleaning from the location no doubt printed upon it. She was almost grateful when Sheffield ended his call and said, "Okay. Let's get this over with. Fitzpatrick, as of now, you're off the case."

She almost asked, *What case?* since technically she couldn't work until the doctor released her. Her next thought was that they knew about her trip to Baja, which meant she was destined to spend the next five years in the basement filing fingerprint cards.

"That was Behavioral Analysis," Sheffield continued, oblivious to her inner turmoil. "They agree with our assessment on the death threat we received this afternoon. It doesn't fit their profile, but for whatever reason, the killer has targeted you, Fitzpatrick, and we're not taking any chances."

"Killer?" she asked. "You're talking about the alleged hit from the senator's office?"

"No. The serial killer the task force is working on. The one suspected in your Jane Doe sketch."

"A *separate* death threat?" Sydney echoed. With this many people lined up to kill her, maybe spending the next five years in the basement filing cards wasn't such a bad idea after all.

Dixon said, "I got this call on my voice mail maybe twenty minutes ago." He punched his access code, then the speaker function of his phone.

"Read about your girl in the news today," came a voice that was low, muffled. Something in the background sounded like car traffic. "Almost got run over . . . You don't want her to end up like the other women, you might want to keep her out of the way."

"It's not *specifically* a death threat," Sydney said, hoping to defuse whatever it was her bosses were contemplating. She did not like that she was being made the center of attention on several fronts. This killer's, the Bureau's, and anyone else who was reading the news.

"She's right," Carillo said. "It could be interpreted as an I-just-want-to-hurt-you-really-bad threat." Sydney threw him her best shut-up look, but all he did was ask her, "That the same voice you heard that first time?"

"My gut says no, but it's more muffled than before. Hard to say."

"Did you record it?" SAC Sheffield asked. "That first call?"

"Unfortunately no." Because by the time she realized it wasn't a prank call, he'd hung up.

"At least we have this one recorded," he said. "Let the techno geeks analyze it. But with this new threat, we can't let you remain in San Francisco."

Sydney froze. Shoving her down in the basement, well, in this case, a back office, was one thing. Relocation was quite another. She glanced at Carillo, who looked as shocked as she did, and it was a moment before she realized the SAC was informing her of her choices for relocation. ". . . to the following offices." He dropped a paper onto Dixon's desk. "If not, the director is willing to make a direct placement to Quantico, since your specialty in forensic art can be utilized there, either at the academy, or on assignments. You have forty-eight hours to decide." Sydney's mouth dropped open. Before she could utter a word, he said, "For your safety. I don't want my agents running around as bait. Not an efficient use of manpower." Sheffield glanced at his watch, said, "We're in agreement, then. Right now, I'm late, so I'll let Dave handle the rest."

He left, but the tension in the room didn't lessen any.

"A transfer?" Sydney said again.

Carillo craned his neck to read the list Sheffield had left behind. "Arkansas, Tennessee, and . . . Missouri. Could be worse."

Sydney felt sick as she looked at the list. She liked being on this side of the country near her family, near her sister. She was even beginning to really like working with Carillo, a fresh change of pace from the staid hours she put in at her old office, and she glanced over at him, saw a spark of concern as he looked at Dixon, waiting for some sort of explanation.

"My guess," Dixon said, eyeing the two of them, "is that someone doesn't think Fitzpatrick should be involving herself in whatever it is she's involving herself in. So you might want to ask yourself who has that kind of connection to pull those strings?" He looked right at her, as though he knew the answer.

And he probably did. Because they all knew that Scotty had those sorts of connections, she'd certainly seen examples of that just in the past few days. She couldn't forget how quickly he'd shaken things up, even as far as the coast guard and getting her off that cutter. And in his misguided— or otherwise—belief that Sydney shouldn't be doing what she was doing, he merely had to make a couple more convincing calls.

And that was assuming it really was Scotty pulling the strings, which was a far sight better than the other possibilities. That one of the *other* government organizations was

behind it bothered her much, much more. There were no
checks and balances for that sort of thing. What they tried to
do to her in Baja was a perfect example. People disappeared,
or were killed, and you didn't find out about it until decades
down the road because of some fluke, some presidential appointment and an astute FBI agent, who took the time to read
some Senate subcommittee report.

Forty-eight hours to decide . . . Wheeler would be executed, and she'd be in some other state too far away to do
a thing. "Do you"—her gaze flicked to the list, and she felt
ill—"think there's any chance it might go through?"

Dixon said, "The way Sheffield was talking just before the
pair of you got here, I'd say yes." He held up the receipt from
the Taco Bell, read aloud, "1610 Jerrold Avenue. That's in
Bayview–Hunters Point."

"Better cheese," Carillo said.

"Cut the crap. What's going on?"

"It's my fault," Sydney said. "He just happened to be in
the car." She glanced at Carillo, who was pretending to pull
a noose around his neck and string it up. "I've been asking questions about my father's case, because . . . I want to
know why he was murdered, and if the suspect about to be
executed is really guilty."

"Whose jurisdiction does the murder belong to?"

"Santa Arleta's," Sydney said, even though they both knew
the answer.

"Then let them handle it."

"She is," Carillo replied. "She was just helping them do a
little legwork is all."

"Then use their legs. And their cars. And their manpower."
Dixon opened his bottle of Tums, shook out a few. "Is there
anything else you've forgotten to inform me of?"

"Can't think of anything," Sydney said. Carillo gave a
shrug, as though to agree.

Dixon eyed the two of them. "You," he said to Sydney,
"have forty-eight hours to decide on where it is you want to
go. I'd suggest you use the time wisely. And Carillo. Keep in
mind we have our second task force sting tonight."

"Finished all the paperwork on it this morning."

Dixon weighed the Tums in his hand. "Have the op plan on my desk before you step out again. And make sure Fitz-patrick's name does *not* appear anywhere on it." They started toward the door, then stopped as he stressed, "*And*, what-ever it is you're *not* working on, try to remember that the ASAC and the SAC do not have the same sense of humor and compassion that I *used* to have before I came to work here and somehow made the mistake of pairing you two up. *Capice?*"

"*Capice*," they both said.

"Tonight, we concentrate on *only* our current case."

To which Carillo said, "Scout's honor."

Dixon looked down at his nachos, then dropped them into the trash where they landed with a thud. "Next time, no ja-lapeños, okay?"

"Told you he didn't like jalapeños," Carillo said, as they walked out the door.

Outside his office, she said, "Do you ever know when to shut up?"

He grinned. "Occasionally. More important question you should be asking is why do you think it was not the same caller?"

"Because the first guy was very specific about adding de-tails of the crime. This second caller said he read about it in the paper. And he called Dixon's phone. Why not my voice mail, since that's the number the first caller used?"

"Good point. So, what's up with Scotty? You think he's dirty?"

"I used to think he was so clean he squeaked. Now I'm not so sure. At least about the transfer."

"So, what're you going to do about it?"

"Only one thing to do. Find Scotty and talk to him about it."

"And if that doesn't work?"

She pulled out her phone, punched in Scotty's number. "I haven't quite decided, but I'm fairly certain that if I have my way, being transferred will be the least of my concerns."

41

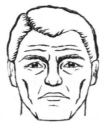

Scotty's cell phone went straight to voice mail. She saw Schermer walk past. "You haven't seen Scotty around, have you?"

"Matter of fact, he was standing just outside the front doors of the building as I was walking in. Looked like he was waiting for a ride or something."

"Thanks." Sydney raced to the elevator, took it down, then ran out front. Her phone rang, and figuring it was Scotty returning her call, she answered it.

It was not Scotty. It was her mother, making sure Sydney remembered her upcoming trip to Bodega Bay with Jake. Sydney walked around the building, hoping to see Scotty, while her mother talked about the trip. She just happened to look up at that moment, and there he was across the street, standing beside a black sedan about half a block up, speaking to someone through an open window. She kept an eye on him, started hurrying in that direction. "Are you listening to me, Sydney?"

"Yes, Mom. Just a bad cell phone connection." Whatever Scotty was discussing, he didn't look happy, she thought. In fact, it looked like he was yelling, and just as suddenly, he glanced her way. Though she couldn't be certain he saw her, he started walking off in the opposite direction.

". . . Jake and I want to leave a couple hours earlier," her mother continued, "and were wondering if we could drop off Angela early."

Sydney stopped in her tracks. "Drop off Angie? At *my* place?"

"You said you could watch her."

"Yes, but that was days ago." Her heart skipped a beat at the very thought. "I—I don't know how to tell you this, but I absolutely cannot watch her. You *can't* bring her over."

"Fine," her mother said, sounding peeved, and she wondered how long her mother would hold this latest travesty over her head. "I'll find someone else. But a call letting me know *would* have been nice."

"Look Mom, I'm sorry. There's just a lot going on right now. I wish I could explain, but you know this job." Scotty quickened his pace, and Sydney covered up the receiver portion, calling out his name. She was losing him. Wherever he was off to, he was in one hell of a hurry. "I need to go. Love you." She flipped the phone closed, then raced after him. "Scotty!"

He turned, stopped when he saw it was she, crossed the street, and met her on the sidewalk.

"We need to talk," she said.

"About what?"

"My transfer, among other things."

He waited.

"Then you knew about it?"

"I heard."

"You don't think that's a problem?"

"What I think is a problem is that someone is trying to kill you, and the Bureau is doing the best it can under the circumstances."

"Circumstances *you're* manipulating, perhaps?"

"I might be adding my views, but no, I'm not the one making the decisions." He shifted, gave a quick look around. "What else did you want to discuss?"

"My father's case. I have some questions about it."

"Sydney—"

"If you can't help me, I'll find someone who can."

"We'll talk over dinner," he said, taking her arm as though they were still lovers, then guiding her toward the building's entrance. "I'll meet you at your desk in about an hour."

"An hour? I'm not even supposed to be at work."

"You're here, aren't you?"

"I want answers, Scotty."

"If I can," he said, walking her up the ramp toward the doors. "Do me a favor? Go up, wait in your office, and give the surveillance team a little break until I get back?"

Certain something else was going on, she smiled. "See you in a bit," she said, then entered, walked past the guards at the metal detectors, and on to the elevator banks. She pressed the button for her elevator, looked up, saw he had turned away, and she decided to follow. She waited inside the glass doors for several moments, but he didn't turn around, apparently satisfied she was heading up to the office. When he seemed to be walking toward the same area she saw him earlier, she figured she could run out the back of the building, come up that direction, perhaps see who it was he was talking to.

She raced through the building, pushed out the door, then ran down the street to the corner. Sure enough, she saw Scotty standing by the same vehicle, parked across the street, the only place allowed. She waited, figured that since it was a one-way street, the car would eventually have to drive past, and she could get a plate, run it, see who it belonged to. Assuming they didn't talk too long. It was damned cold out; the offshore wind ripped down the side of the building. She wasn't wearing a coat, and tucked her hands beneath her arms trying to keep warm.

Fortunately she didn't have to wait long. Scotty stepped away from the car, slapped the door with a bit of familiarity, then crossed the street toward the federal building. Sydney remained where she was as the car pulled out, drove in her direction, then changed lanes to turn the corner right beside her. She focused on the plate, but as the car neared, she realized she didn't need to see the plate at all to see who the car belonged to. She recognized the driver, his crooked nose.

He'd driven Gnoble and Prescott to her house that afternoon. So what the hell was Scotty doing talking to Gnoble's driver? Any logical explanation eluded her, and as the car passed, she peered into the back windows, tried to see if there was someone there, but couldn't tell because of the tinting.

She didn't move until the car turned the corner up the block, and only then hurried to the back entrance of the federal building and up to her office, rubbing her hands together, trying to warm them.

Scotty, apparently, didn't return to the building, not that she was expecting him to. But she didn't have time to worry about it, because the moment she stepped into the Bureau offices, she was caught up in the preparation for the next Operation Barfly task force as the agents assigned to go out were gearing up. Doc Schermer saw her, handed her a stack of papers. "Since you're stuck in the office, any chance I can get you to run a bunch of license plates for me? We're about ready to head out, but these look promising—license numbers that were taken from older model white Dodge vans from the area our hookers saw the guy who looked like your sketch."

"Not like I have anything better to do."

"Thanks," he said, then rushed off. Suddenly he stopped, turned, looked at her. "I heard about the transfer."

"No big."

"Yeah, it is. Carillo's been moping around the last six months, ever since Sheila asked him for a divorce. I don't know if it's this Jane Doe case, or just being partnered up with you, but he's like his old self again."

She crossed her arms, couldn't help but smile. "You saying that guy will miss me?"

"Carillo? No. *I'll* miss you, because *he's* almost pleasant to be around again." He winked at her, walked off. "Let me know when you get those plates run."

She took the papers to her desk, realized that in some ways Schermer was right. Carillo was definitely easier to be around, though she wasn't sure that she had anything to do with it. Her case maybe. Not her.

A few minutes later, she saw Carillo walking to his desk. He looked up. "You're back," he said.

"Waiting for Scotty. We're going to catch a bite, while I grill him about what he knows."

"Good luck with that. Everything that comes out of his mouth these days is like a piece of disinformation, which makes me think the other government agency he's working with? Gotta be CIA. By the way. We got a call from SFPD, who said that one of their undercovers talked to a couple hookers who said that the guy in your sketch was definitely hanging around the past couple nights. So, pretty good chance he's the one who knocked you in front of the car." He picked up a stack of folders on his desk, looked around for whatever else he needed. "Here's to hoping we get him tonight."

"Try not to have too much fun out there without me, okay?"

"Not a chance," he said, grabbing his keys, then walking out. He paused at the door, looked back at her. "Maybe the transfer won't go through."

"Maybe," she said, but with little faith. After he left, she stared at her computer screen, thought about her fate as the voices of the agents walking down the hall toward the conference room drifted back to her. There was one thing she could do to avoid a transfer, avoid being dragged to some outpost where she would no doubt be relegated to working paper crimes.

Resign.

She hoped it wouldn't come to that . . . She loved her job—well, most aspects of it—but she had to be realistic. Right now she needed answers, and if necessary, she'd walk out of the Bureau, end her career, if that was what it took to get them.

She finished running the plates, printed them up, then carried them into the conference room, where the task force briefing was taking place. Doc Schermer and Jeff Timmons were introduced to everyone as the agents working relief. They'd make the rounds, taking the place of any agents or officers needing breaks. Ren Pham-Peck was assigned to replace Sydney's position, working with Carillo as they barhopped. They were quite the combination, Carillo, the tall

Italian, and Ren, a petite Vietnamese woman with dark hair and dark eyes, a big smile, and a vivacious personality. One would never guess by looking at her that she was an FBI agent, which made her perfect for the part.

Twenty minutes later, everyone was filing out the door of the briefing room, leaving Sydney alone, until Schermer and Timmons walked in with Scotty about an hour later.

"Not a lot going on out there," Schermer was telling Scotty.

"That's a good thing, isn't it?"

"For now. So, what are you two up to?"

"Just going to get a bite to eat." Scotty looked at Sydney. "Where to?"

"Chinese." She dropped her radio in her purse, then followed Scotty out.

As they walked down the hall, she heard Timmons say to Schermer, "Why is it the girls always get the free meals?"

"What? You want to be a girl now?" she heard just as they stepped out the door.

Scotty seemed lost in thought as they rode the elevator down, and Sydney wondered about the senator's car, and just who Scotty had been talking to down there. "Something on your mind?" she asked.

"Everything," he said.

Amen to that, Sydney thought, but figured she'd let it go for now, not sure it was the right time to go into specifics.

"Of course," he continued, "I assume you want to know if I had anything to do with the transfer?"

So much for letting it go. "Did you?"

"The truth is that I suggested it up front when I informed them of our joint investigation. Apparently they changed their mind, until you asked to assist. This recent talk has nothing to do with me."

"Joint investigation? As in OGA?" she said, referring to *the* other government agency. The one he wouldn't name.

And sure enough, he looked over at her, didn't answer.

She waited until they were in his car and he was pulling out of the garage. "Why is it that I sense a bit of discomfort in talking about who exactly is involved with this case?"

"There was a time when rules and regulations meant something to you."

"They still do. I've just learned to interpret them a little differently than I used to."

He glanced over at her, gave a tired sigh, then asked, "Which restaurant?"

She specifically chose one on the outer perimeter of the bars that Carillo and Ren were going to be walking through. Scotty drove around, found a parking spot just a few doors down from the restaurant—courtesy of the official FBI placard he placed on the dash, and the red curb signifying No Parking at the corner. The perks in this job were few and far between. Had to take them where they could. Inside, they ordered, then sat at an empty table, waiting for their food, keeping one ear trained on the radio, while Scotty occupied himself by reading a takeout menu.

After several minutes, Scotty reached over, touched her hand, and she nearly jumped. As it was, her pulse started racing, not in a good way, and she told herself this was out of character for him. He was usually so formal in public places, and it was with great effort that she managed to appear calm on the outside, as he said, "What do you want to know?"

As his gaze met hers, Sydney realized that in a way, she was afraid. Afraid that he might be holding back some very important information, information that could help her. "Who were you talking to when I saw you outside the building this afternoon? You seemed upset."

He stiffened. "Upset? I don't recall being upset with anyone."

"Someone in Senator Gnoble's car? I recognized his driver."

When Scotty relaxed, leaned into his seat, she wondered if she'd somehow misread the situation. But then he said, "You know, his driver used to be a cop, up until a few years ago when he took the job with the senator."

"You know him?" Scotty shrugged, glanced at the menu, and then it hit her. "*He's* your informant?"

"We should have ordered Mongolian beef."

"Is there any aspect of this case you can discuss with me?"

He studied the menu. "Pot stickers. I can never find good pot stickers in D.C."

So clearly he'd only taken her to dinner to temporarily placate her. But maybe she could get info another way. "Did your surveillance team mention to you that I took a little drive this afternoon?"

"They did," he said, flipping the page, running his finger down the list of entrees.

"I spoke with Wheeler's aunt. She works at the clinic that Carillo and I visited. Turns out that one of the men in that photo that McKnight sent to me just so happens to be Wheeler's father."

"That right?"

"And, coincidence of coincidences, he was killed in an explosion right around the same time my father happened to lose a couple fingers in an explosion and had to retire from his *freelance* army job."

He glanced at her, but otherwise remained impassive.

"That would probably be right around the time that Robert Orozco fled to Baja."

That got his attention. He lowered the menu, as well as his voice. "If you do nothing else, Sydney, leave that photo alone. And that case. And any mention of what happened in Baja."

"Why?"

"It has nothing to do with anything."

"I think it has something to do with my father's murder."

"You're wrong."

"I think Wheeler was framed. I think my father was friends with Wheeler's father, and that's why he was helping out Wheeler, until Gnoble put the kibosh on it, because *he* didn't want to leave a paper trail to this BICTT thing. My father blamed McKnight for the explosion that injured him and killed Wheeler's father. And I think that when your buddy Hatcher started digging into McKnight's past, this all came out, and McKnight couldn't live with the guilt so he wrote an explosive suicide note that sure as hell pissed someone off, and started a chain reaction somehow. And therein lies the answers to some questions the *Bureau* was searching for twenty years ago, when Senator Gnoble sat on a subcommittee on the biggest banking scandal in history that *he* happened to be part of. BICTT, to be exact."

He shook his head. "Maybe you're right about part of that, that your father sought Wheeler out because of a past association, but *Wheeler* killed him. There is proof. Photos. Surveillance photos."

"As I'm well aware of." Which reminded her that Carillo said they'd probably be in tonight. "But what about all this stuff my father was involved in with McKnight and the senator? The work they did for the government?"

"I don't know all your father's secrets. But I can tell you this much. I don't believe that Wheeler is as innocent as he claims. I told you, I have the—"

"Was my father involved in the BICTT banking scandal?"

He was quiet for so long, at first Sydney thought he might refuse to answer. But then, "Dig too deep, and you might not like the answers."

"I'm fairly certain I won't like them. I already don't like them—at least those I've been allowed to discover. You show up at my apartment, try to hide information that proves my father might be involved in illicit activities, twenty years *after* the fact, and for what? To protect my sensibilities? Or because of some elaborate subterfuge and cover-up?"

"And what if it's a little of both?"

His blue eyes were unreadable. And she remembered what Carillo said, that they didn't know where Scotty stood in all this, but she also knew she couldn't just let things slide, and so she decided to be very direct. "Then I want the truth. I don't believe that Wheeler killed my father in some simple robbery gone bad. If there was something else going on, I want to know what it was, and I don't give a rat's ass if it's an election year and your boss doesn't want to stir up a pat, high-profile case that involves my life. Because if it takes me going to the press to get answers, I will."

"You can't be serious."

"From where I'm sitting, it seems like the prudent thing to do. Someone in Gnoble's office still wants to kill me—over

what? I think the voters have a right to know about his past.
He'll lose, and then there's no more threat. Because that's
what this is all about, isn't it?"

"You're assuming it's about the election, Sydney."

"Well, isn't it?"

"What if it's something else, something that doesn't go
away after the votes are in? That's why we're investigating.
That's why you're being transferred. That's why we haven't
made an arrest, because we don't *know* what it's about."

"Oh bullshit, Scotty. This is a classic case of one arm of
the government not telling the other what the hell is going
on. CIA keeping secrets from FBI. Army intelligence refusing to share with either of you. Those black ops guys that
came after Robert Orozco in Baja, and then me, had to have
been working for some branch. If not ours, then theirs. Special Forces? SAD?" she asked, referring to Special Activities Division, the CIA's covert paramilitary operations, used
when the U.S. wants to ensure there are no connections to tie
the government to the covert mission.

"They were after Orozco and the bank pouch."

"I don't care who they were after. They were shooting at
me. And just because I happened to make it back, and the CIA
and the FBI and the goddamned army decided to compare
notes and finally let me walk out of there, it doesn't mean it's
okay. It means they're still trying to cover up another lie that
covers up another lie, and I'm getting in the way, because
I want to know which one of those goddamned lies has to
do with why my father died. If Wheeler is guilty, so be it. If
he's innocent, then someone out there killed my father, and
I want to know who and why and get him. They're going to
execute that man in less than forty-eight hours if I don't do
something. And if that picture that McKnight mailed to me
has something to do with it, and you know the answers, so
help me—"

Scotty took a frustrated breath. "In the past ten years,
every time we turn around with some banking or lobbying
scandal, some political contribution for contracts scandal,
Gnoble seems to have his fingers in it. He's got to be guilty
of something, and then the few times we actually get him

on something, he gets off with a slap on his hand, makes his pretty speech about how he can understand how his actions were misconstrued and that he only had the best of intentions, then apologizes. The Senate Ethics Committee issues a mild rebuke, and then he's right back at it."

"So he's the Kevlar King. Does that make him any different from any other politician?"

"It does if we know he's doing it, then look the other way. As usual, he's the frontrunner in the polls, because he's smart enough to keep his nose clean the year before elections, and no one can remember just what it was he was being rebuked for. They see the war hero, the get-tough-on-crime guy. He rolls up his shirtsleeves, washes a few dishes in some soup kitchen so you can see his battle scars, and you'd never guess that just a year ago, he was being investigated for taking illegal political contributions from well-greased lobbyists."

Scotty leaned back in his seat, held up his hand, his thumb and forefinger an inch apart. "We finally got an informant who is that close to getting us in on some of his charitable organizations that we're certain are front companies—"

"His driver."

"Yes. And then he overhears a phone conversation Gnoble's aide is having about who they should hire to take you out, only he can't tell who the guy is talking to."

"When was this?"

"A couple days before I showed up at your door." Scotty glanced up, eyed the waiter pouring water a few tables away, making sure he still couldn't be overheard before continuing. "And, as much as one would like to think that your life being endangered was the impetus for all this, the truth is that three days before that, our informant overheard Gnoble telling someone on the phone that McKnight is being considered to oversee the federal budget, and if they don't hide the BICTT money, he'll never get approved. The moment that happened, the investigation was ripped from our hands faster than you could say CYA."

"Then how is it you're still on it?"

"Quite simply I pointed out that they needed me. With our

history together, I was the only one who could get close to you without any questions from Gnoble or anyone else."

"Great."

"No different from you using me to get what you wanted, Syd. A chance to stay on the case."

"Okay, so we're both lowlifes," she said, just as Schermer's voice came on the radio, announcing he'd found a white van with a missing taillight and a woman's purse on the front floorboard. Several agents called in that they were heading that way, and she turned her attention back to Scotty. "So why is the CIA so interested in Gnoble to begin with?"

"Because a lot of the stuff Gnoble's involved in has to do with national security. Always has, even before he was elected to the Senate."

"Starting with when he was the U.S. Army's liaison to the Senate? Back when my father worked for him?"

"Yes. And as a result, every scrap of info we get in our investigation has to be vetted through the CIA first. There are aspects to this case that you or I will *never* be allowed to know about, including some of what involved your father. You can choose to dig for the truth, Sydney, but I'm here to tell you that some things are best left buried, and sometimes it's better the devil you know, than the one you don't."

The devil you know . . . Something about the phrasing struck her, reminded her of something, something important, but before she could figure out what, the radio squawked to life, and Carillo was calling out that he needed help.

42

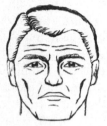

"Your food!"

They ignored the waitress. Ran from the restaurant to the car. Got in. Scotty started it. Stabbed the gas pedal, pulled out of the lot. Carillo's voice came across the radio, in that breathy jolting way it did when someone was running, trying to talk at the same time. "We're . . . chasing . . . him . . . down . . . Mission. Same . . . direction."

"Same guy?" Sydney heard someone ask.

"Hooker . . . think . . . so."

Scotty flicked the emergency switch, and the rearview mirror lowered into a flashing red light, as he gunned it toward the Purple Moon.

Within two minutes, they were there. Scotty parked on the same corner where Sydney was hit. They got out, saw Carillo and Ren running toward them, chasing a man, midtwenties, their direction.

"FBI!" Sydney called out.

He hesitated, glanced behind him, then darted to one side.

His hands were empty. Suddenly there were twenty other agents and officers. The guy was surrounded. Scotty and Sydney must have looked like the path of least resistance.

He ran straight for them. They both grabbed an arm. His shirt started ripping. They were going to lose him. And then Carillo and Ren came flying at him. All three went tumbling to the ground.

For a moment no one moved, and then Carillo reached around the guy, grabbed his hand, brought it back. "Cuffs," he said. Ren produced a pair, and Carillo slapped one cuff over the man's wrist, brought his other hand around, cuffed it, and then he turned the guy over. "We . . . got him," he said to Sydney between breaths.

If he was the guy she'd drawn, she didn't recognize him at all. His nose was broken, bloody, his lips cut from landing on the sidewalk. More importantly, he was now missing several teeth. "*This* is our Jane Doe killer?"

"Purse snatcher," Carillo said.

"What?"

"Stole Ren's purse. That's who we were chasing."

Sydney got down, looked in the guy's eyes. "You push me into a moving car the other night?"

Their UnSub didn't answer, probably too busy spitting out blood and tccth onto the ground. Carillo lifted the guy to his feet.

"Where's the purse?" Sydney asked.

Ren held it up. "Hc tosscd it when we started chasing him."

One of the bystanders looked around, saw all the manpower. "You sure bring out the big guns for just a purse." Which is when Carillo stopped, looked around. There were dozens of law enforcement officers standing around, never mind the half-dozen undercover cars parked helter-skelter at the curb, emergency lights flashing. Carillo's gaze moved from the agents to all the citizens watching the goings-on with interest, realizing in that moment just what had happened to their operation.

"This is clearly an oh-shit moment," he said.

"On the bright side," Sydney said, "maybe you all get off earlier."

He looked down at the teeth the guy had spit out, then at Ren Pham-Peck.

Ren shook her head. "I don't think so. You knocked 'em

out, you pick 'em up. If he's lucky, they can put 'em back in, well, except for the broken ones."

Back at the office Dixon was not pleased by this turn of events—though Sydney thought he did an admirable job of not chewing out Carillo's and Ren's butts in front of the assisting outside agencies who had given up their night for the task force operation. "We'll contact everyone tomorrow afternoon," Dixon said. "Once we assess our *next* plan of action."

And, cops being cops, those from the outside agencies decided to hit the local cop bar in their newfound off-duty status—a bar in an area far from their operation. Scotty walked up to her as they were discussing where they were all going drinking. "You are *not* going out for a drink."

"Fitzpatrick!" Dixon's voice carried down the hall.

"What'd you do?" she asked. "Snitch me off before I even get a chance to try for one?"

Scotty held her gaze for a second too long. "I just want to keep you safe."

"Or keep your surveillance team from being jealous?"

He actually smiled. "That, too."

She smiled back, then started toward Dixon's office, thinking about what Scotty had told her in the restaurant, and ignoring the tiny bit of suspicion as to just why it was he was being so helpful, so forthcoming. Especially considering he'd done nothing but hide things from her from day one.

She glanced back, saw him watching her, and she wondered if things had been different, would they still be together? But then, if things had been different, her father would still be alive, Scotty would be in Washington, D.C., making political career moves, and Sydney might never have gone into the FBI.

She put him from her mind and walked into Dixon's office. Carillo was seated next to Ren—which pretty much told her they were in for an ass chewing.

"A purse snatcher?" Dixon said. "Was it beyond anyone's ability to differentiate between what class of felony we were investigating?"

Ren said, "The hooker thought it was the same suspect as the other night."

"And did anyone check to see if *that* suspect was the right suspect?"

Carillo shrugged. "The other night?" he said. "Like I was supposed to stop and ask him? I got two hookers pointing him out, saying, That's the guy. So I took off after him."

"And did we check with those hookers later?"

"Them? No. I was busy scraping Fitzpatrick off the street corner if you recall. But if it's any consolation, Fitz did ask *this* guy if he pushed her into the street the other night."

"He didn't get a chance to answer. He was a bit indisposed," Sydney added helpfully.

Dixon opened his drawer, reached for his bottle of Tums. "*That* makes me feel a whole lot better." He shook several into his mouth, chewed, and they wisely remained silent. When he finished, he said, "Fitzpatrick, go home. You two, get your asses to the jail, book that son of a bitch, and get in a car and find me our killer."

Sydney started to walk out, then stopped. "Did anyone check with Schermer on that white van?"

"Yeah," Carillo said. "Van was empty, and the purse was empty. Nothing to tie it to anyone, including our purse snatcher."

"Worth a try." About to turn away, she stopped again, tried not to look at Dixon, who was looking slightly annoyed that she was even present in the building when she was supposed to be home recuperating. "You know, the more I think about it, the more I think he could be the guy. He bears a slight resemblance to the sketch, though it's hard to say with his face all banged up. But that's the second time a couple hookers pointed him out as being our man."

"Meaning what?" Dixon said.

"Meaning, don't you find it odd that this whole purse snatching thing started up around the time that our Jane Doe case and Tara Brown cases started taking off? I seem to remember Maggie dragging out an empty purse from Stow Lake, where I found bits of taillight, and Schermer finds a white van with a missing taillight, and an empty purse in it, *and* our Jane Doe was last seen complaining about some creep in a white van."

Carillo leaned back in his chair. "Now that would've been nice to know before we knocked out all his teeth."

"I only just thought of it. And at least you collected the teeth."

Dixon gave a tired sigh. "Ren, check the purse from Stow Lake, and the one found in the van. See if it belongs to any of SFPD's purse snatch victims, or better yet, any rape victims. Carillo, impound that van, and get the ERT on it for any trace evidence."

"The teeth," Sydney pointed out.

Dixon said, "And see if the guy will agree to letting us get an impression of his teeth. If not, write a warrant. Take the impressions and the broken teeth to Dr. Armand. See if he can put it together and determine if we have a match. Thank you, and good night, Fitzpatrick."

Sydney opened her mouth to protest, and Dixon said, "Don't even try. You've been ordered off the case. Get a ride home from Scotty. The rest of us will regroup tomorrow."

Scotty walked her downstairs, but instead of driving her home, passed her off to Jared Dunning. "I, uh, have a couple errands," he said.

She was a bit surprised he wasn't taking her home, but brushed it off. She was about to climb into the backseat when Jared said, "Shit, Mel. Don't make her sit back there with all the trash."

Mel looked back. "Oh. Yeah. Sorry." He got out, let her take the front.

Sydney slid in, buckled up, and as they drove off, said, "So, what's it like working for the Agency?"

"Not bad," Mel said.

Jared shook his head. "Mel, you're a fucking idiot." To Sydney, he said, "Do me a favor. You didn't ask, and he didn't say."

"Ask what?" she said. That, however, was the extent of their conversation. So they were CIA, and were under orders not to say who they worked for.

When they arrived at her place, there were no lights on upstairs, but plenty on downstairs at Rainie's. The car pulled into the driveway, and Sydney saw a little face peeking out. Her heart constricted. "Oh my God. Did you guys know my sister was here?"

Jared looked into the window, saw Angie staring at their car. "She must have been dropped off when we were out watching you and Scotty. But unless she's a threat, the guys wouldn't have stopped her from coming."

"A threat? What about being in danger?" How the hell had this happened? She'd told her mother specifically not to bring Angie here. God, this was all her fault. She'd been so damned preoccupied when her mother had called . . .

She took out her cell phone, phoned Jake before she even got out of the car.

"It's Syd. Where are you?"

"Bodega Bay with your mother. What's going on?"

"I told Mom not to bring Angie here. You dropped her off at Rainie's."

"Well, your mother called Rainie and asked if she could watch her. She said it was okay."

"Oh my God . . . Look, I can't go into any details, Jake. But there are armed men watching my apartment as a safety precaution. Please come get her."

A moment of silence, then, "I'm on my way. Do *not* let anything happen to my little girl."

"How long until you're here?"

"Maybe an hour."

Sydney relayed the info to Jared.

"We'll be watching for him when he gets here," he said. "I'll pass on the info to the other guys."

Sydney knocked on Rainie's door, and Rainie answered, holding a spoon that looked like it was covered in chocolate sauce. "Hey, you just missed out on the sundaes," she said, letting her in.

Angie was seated at the couch, scraping every last bit of ice cream from her bowl. "Hey, Syd! Mom said you had to work tonight or something."

"Yeah, well, I did, and, um, I was talking to your dad on

the phone. Their trip got canceled, and they're on their way to pick you up," she said, trying to sound casual.

Rainie flicked her a glance, said nothing, and Angie's smile faded. "He can't come! Mom said I could stay here. I don't have school tomorrow. It's fall break."

Rainie said, "Who can keep track of these new school schedules?"

"Jake will be here in an hour. Maybe you and Rainie can watch the Disney Channel until he gets here."

"What about you?"

The last place she needed to be was here, near her sister and Rainie. She thought of her imminent transfer, the men watching her outside, everything that was going on in her life right now. Maybe, just maybe, moving far away wasn't a bad thing. "Tonight's not good. I have this horrible sore throat. *And* I feel like I'm going to be sick to my stomach." That much, at least, was true. "I don't want to get you or Rainie sick."

Angie stared into her sundae cup as Sydney walked to the door. Rainie remained silent, probably figuring Sydney would fill her in tomorrow.

"You know what we could do?" Sydney said, pausing by the door. "Watch the Disney Channel together. Like we used to do when I lived in Washington? You can do it down here at Rainie's, and I'll do it upstairs."

Angie gave a slight shrug, noncommittal. "I thought you didn't feel good."

"But that always makes me feel better. Please," Sydney asked.

"Yeah. Okay." She even smiled slightly.

Sydney blew Angie a kiss, told them to lock the doors, then walked up the stairs to her own apartment. On the landing, she heard Topper sniffing at Arturo's door, then settle down, no doubt figuring it was only she. One smart dog, she thought as she unlocked her door, let herself in, before locking it up tight, then glancing out her window. A dark-colored sedan cruised slowly past, and she thought she recognized Scotty at the wheel.

It didn't comfort her in the least, and she turned on all the lights, kicked off her shoes by the door, then made herself a cup of tea, chamomile. It was supposed to be relaxing. Sydney was far from relaxed, and she pulled out that photo that was supposed to be of her father on his last mission . . .

She stared at it, ran her finger along his shoulder, feeling only cold slick paper. This was not the father she'd loved, the father from her fishing trip. Not the father she wanted to remember. This was another man . . .

With a sigh, she looked at the photo again, tried to see if there was something, *anything* that would tell her what she was missing. There was nothing different. Just the same four men in their black, unmarked fatigues, and Gnoble in his uniform. The same rings they all wore. She remembered her father wearing one. Robert Orozco still wore his, she thought, glancing up at the painting . . .

Sydney's phone rang, startling her. Angie calling from downstairs. "Do you have the TV on yet?"

"I'm turning it on now," she said.

"The one in your bedroom. You have to be under the covers, just like when you were in Washington."

Sydney smiled as she walked down the hall, the phone at her ear. "In the bedroom now," she said, then switched on the set. She hit the guide. There was more than one Disney Channel. "What show is on?"

"*Kim Possible.*"

She turned to that channel, then climbed into the bed. "Okay. I'm here and the TV's on."

"Are you under the covers?"

"I'm under the covers."

"No, you're not."

Sydney pulled the quilt from the foot of the bed over her. "I am too."

"What's on your TV screen?"

"The same as yours, imp. Kim Possible is kicking butt on Dr. Drakken."

"I love Dr. Drakken," Angie said. "He's such an idiot."

They watched the TV in silence for a few seconds, and finally Sydney said, "Okay. I'm hanging up now."

"Don't turn off your TV."

"You either."

" 'Night."

" 'Night." Sydney hung up the phone, thinking about Angie, how many times they'd done this when she lived halfway across the world from her . . . Her gaze fixed on the cartoon characters jumping across her set, she relaxed for the first time in days, smiling at the thought that her sister was checking up on her to make sure she really was watching TV. And for some reason it struck Sydney, her sister's name, what her mother had told her it meant, why she'd chosen it. Angela. Messenger from God . . . She closed her eyes, feeling warm beneath the comforter, sleepy even, wondering if Angie was a messenger, what message was she bringing? An odd thought, but Sydney was too tired to figure out why . . .

She wasn't sure if it was the strange dreams that woke her, or the flickering of the TV set. Since it was the latter that bothered her more, she blindly felt for the remote control, then gave up when she couldn't find it. But the flickering continued, penetrated her consciousness . . .

Let it be a dream. . .

Of course it was a dream. She'd had them before . . . The sort where she thought she was awake, but she wasn't, then she dreamed she'd awakened . . .

But the hallway glowed orange. Sydney could see straight down it to the kitchen. To her painting of the flames. A painting that was engulfed. And that red eye winking at her . . .

But it wasn't an eye . . .

And her pulse thundered.

She couldn't move. She'd seen that eye. On the hand of the man who closed the door. The door that closed the night her father was killed.

She could even smell the smoke from the fire . . .

All she wanted to do was close her eyes, move back in time, see her father once more, but now the damned fire alarm was going off.

She felt so sleepy.

"*Sydney!*"

The crash that followed jarred her. She saw the flames

down the hall. Flames that shot to the ceiling with the rush of air. Someone running toward her.

She bolted up, cried, "Angie!"

Someone was racing toward her. Her gun. Where'd she put her gun?

"Sydney!" Scotty appeared in front of her.

She tried to clear her head. Her gun was in her purse.

"You need to get out."

"Where's Angie?"

"*Angie? She's here*?"

Relief flooded her. "Downstairs," she said, then reached for the phone.

"It's called in. Let's go!"

She dropped the phone, allowed Scotty to pull her from the room.

She didn't know what made her stop. Dig in her heels at the door. The sight of the flames engulfing her painting in the kitchen. The thought that Scotty was there so quickly. She pulled her hand from his. Ran back. Got her purse. All she could think was she needed a gun. She was not going out there without her gun.

43

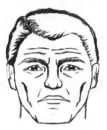

Sydney took one last look at the flames shooting
up in her kitchen, and with a death grip on her purse, ran for
the door. Scotty stood on the porch, waiting, watching. Sirens blared in the distance. Topper barked sharply from behind Arturo's door. A moment later it opened. Arturo stood
there, his expression one of someone who has awoken, and
wasn't sure what was going on. Topper raced out, barked
again, then tried to herd Sydney down the steps.

Arturo's gaze widened. "What the—?"

"Fire. You need to get out."

"Oh my God."

He looked back inside, his expression filled with that mo-
mentary panic of what he should try to save. Sydney grabbed
his arm. "Now."

The cement was cold beneath her bare feet as she raced
down the steps to the damp grass, where Rainie and the others were standing. Angie was in Rainie's arms, and she broke
free, ran to Sydney the moment she saw her. Jake hadn't yet
gotten there, apparently.

"What happened?" Rainie asked.

"I don't know." Sydney held Angie tight, stroked her soft

hair as she looked up at her apartment, the flames through the kitchen window. All her art supplies. "I don't know . . ." she repeated, vaguely aware that Scotty had walked up to her. She pinned her gaze on him. He seemed so calm. "What *did* happen?"

At first he didn't look at her, and she saw the reflection of the fire dancing on his face. He watched the kitchen, then scanned the stairway and around the house, before finally meeting her gaze. "I couldn't sleep, so I thought I'd drive by. To see if you were still up . . . To—" His glance flicked down toward Angie before giving Sydney one of those read-between-the-lines looks. "To see if you were still up. That's when I saw the fire."

And Arturo said, "Well, thank God for small miracles. Good thing you came by."

Though she wanted to demand that Scotty explain how anyone got past the surveillance team or how they failed to see the flames, she couldn't right then, for the obvious reasons.

Within moments sirens echoed off the buildings as two engines turned the corner, stopping in front of the house, their three-sixties lighting the neighborhood like a red and white flashing disco. Soon the neighbors were out on their lawns and, judging from the size of the growing crowd, a number who weren't neighbors and didn't have a life in the middle of the night. Sydney pulled Angie close as they made way for the firemen, who were dragging a hose up the steps. Topper barked at them, and Arturo held tight to his collar.

She couldn't even look up at the apartment. All she could do was bury her face in Angie's hair. It seemed like forever before they got the water on it, an eternity before they got the fire out. "I need to call Jake," Sydney said, pulling her cell phone from her purse.

She punched in his cell number. When he answered, she said, "I thought you'd be here by now."

"We're about fifteen minutes away. There was an accident, and the roads were blocked—" He stopped talking suddenly, perhaps taking in the background noises. "What's happened?"

"We're fine," Sydney said. "But there's been a fire at my apartment."

"Oh my God. Angie?"

"Fine. Right here with me."

She heard him give a loud sigh. "I'll be right there. You're both okay, though?"

"Yes, Jake. We're fine."

"How did it start?" he asked.

"The fire department's checking it out now," she said. "It was contained in the kitchen. It, um, probably started in my painting supplies." No sense in getting him any more worried than he was.

"Let me talk to Angie," he said, just as the phone beeped with an incoming call—not that Sydney was about to interrupt Jake to answer it.

"Your dad wants to talk to you."

Angie took the phone. "Hi, Dad!" she said. "You should see all the cool things going on right now. There's like two fire trucks outside and flames shooting—" She looked up at Sydney, who waved at her, then put her finger to her lips. "Well, maybe it's not *that* cool. A bunch of firefighters, and, like, hundreds and hundreds of neighbors standing around watching. You'd think the whole *block* caught on fire. It's just in the kitchen. And I was downstairs at Rainie's anyway. But I'm okay. Really." She listened to whatever it was Jake told her, then said, "Do I have to?" She gave an exaggerated sigh, then, "Promise. Love you."

She hit the off button, then handed the phone to Sydney. "Dad says I have to go home as soon as he gets here."

"Dads," Sydney said, giving her another hug. She knew she should call Dixon, let him know what was going on, but right now, she was more worried about keeping a calm and collected facade in front of her sister, and so she dropped her phone into her purse, figuring she could call him after Jake arrived. But Angie refused to go sit inside Scotty's car and wait for him, worried that she'd miss the excitement, and when she started shivering, Scotty draped his jacket over her shoulders.

Sydney wasn't sure how much time passed before one

of the firefighters finally walked down the stairs and asked whose apartment it was.

"Mine," she said.

"What happened?"

"I have no idea. I was asleep in bed. Special Agent Ryan woke us. He said he drove by and saw the fire."

Scotty nodded.

"What agency are you with?" he asked Scotty.

"FBI. Same as her."

The firefighter looked like he was about to say something, until his gaze lit on Angie. Clearly these men were having an issue with Angie's presence, and that scared Sydney. "You have somewhere we can talk?" he said. "I need to ask you a few questions."

Rainie said, "I'll take Angie into my place—I can go in, can't I?"

"Yes, ma'am. We'll be up there awhile, but the fire's out. No real structural damage to your part of the house. Her kitchen's toast, though, and I might think twice about parking in the garage until it's fixed."

"Come on, Angie," Rainie said.

Sydney gently propelled her sister toward Rainie, but Angie stopped to give Scotty his jacket. "Thank you," she said, then looked at Sydney.

"I'll be just a few minutes," Sydney told her, waiting until they disappeared, her heart doing a little flip-flop when Rainie's porch light lit up Angie's blond hair like a halo before the door closed behind them.

When they were out of earshot, the firefighter introduced himself as Captain Wyatt, and said, "Most of the damage is centralized in the kitchen. Burned pretty hot. Like there was some sort of accelerant."

Her mind went over all the possibilities. Her door was locked. There had to be some other explanation. "I had a lot of art supplies in there. Brush cleaner, turpentine. That sort of thing." And of course, she told herself, that was probably it. When they'd lived together, Scotty was always telling her that her paint supplies were going to burst into flames one day because of the volatile chemicals.

Captain Wyatt seemed to confirm it. "That explains a lot."
Until he asked, "Is it possible you spilled any of it?"

She felt a dull thudding in her head, tried to think if she'd
left anything open. Maybe Topper had knocked something
over, when she'd been watching him. But surely Sydney
would've smelled it? "I don't think so," she said. "Why?"

He asked her to follow him up the steps. Before they
stepped in, he said, "Any reason someone would want to
torch your place?"

"You really think it was arson?"

"Unless you twisted off the top to your turpentine can and
splashed it across your kitchen table."

They walked into the apartment. The place smelled like
someone had lit a campfire, then doused it with water. Her
braided rug was soaked, felt like a sponge beneath her bare
feet, but at least it was still intact. The walls in the living
room and on down the hall looked as though someone had
tried to paint them gray with a really bad roller brush. No
wonder she'd had such a difficult time trying to rouse herself, and she wondered how much carbon monoxide she'd
sucked in.

She was almost afraid to look in the kitchen, but she followed Captain Wyatt to the edge, realized she couldn't walk
in there in bare feet. The shoes she wore to work were by the
door, where she'd kicked them off, and she slipped those on,
then walked into the once-yellow kitchen. The wall where
her abstracts had leaned was now black, the paint bubbling
up to the ceiling where flames had licked, fueled by the can-
vases that were now nothing more than a blackened pile of
soggy ash. The painting from hell was no more than a piece
of curled blackened remnant on the sodden floor, merely
a fifth of its size, and Sydney reached down, picked it up,
watched the gray water drip down onto the charred remnants
of what had once been her easel. With one hand, she brushed
at the soot, and saw a bit of orange red showing through.
Devil's eye, she thought, dropping it. She turned away, looking from there into her living room, then on down the hall,
into her open bedroom door. Saw the bed where just a short

while ago, she had been curled up, watching the Disney Channel, in concert with her sister below. . .

And that's when Sydney started to shake. She was so wrapped up in her father's murder, dreaming about the flames at the restaurant that night that she had unwittingly endangered her beloved sister, because she couldn't, wouldn't wake up . . .

And because she'd allowed her to stay there, even if in the apartment below.

Her knees felt like they were going to buckle, and somehow she managed to traverse the hallway to her bedroom. And there she tossed her purse onto the nightstand and dropped onto the mattress. She could hear the slight buzz as her phone vibrated another call, but at the moment all she wanted to do was hide from the world, and she pulled her pillow to her face, smelled the stench of smoke on the casing . . . She'd tried so hard to be strong. All these years. Thinking her father was this good person, that he didn't deserve to die. And now she was faced with the reality that he wasn't good, that he'd lived a double life. That maybe he was killed because of it. That she had stirred something up, and brought her sister into the fray, endangered her.

She took a breath, knew that she was feeling really, really sorry for herself, but couldn't help the tear that slid down her cheek. Scotty walked down the hallway to check on her then. He stood there, in her doorway, not moving.

"You okay?" he asked.

She wasn't. She wanted nothing more than to have someone hold her, tell her that everything was going to be fine. "Yes," she said, though she didn't know what she was saying yes to. Him being the one to hold her, or just her need for something more, an escape from all that seemed so wrong in her life right then.

He took a step in, just as one of the firefighters dropped something in the kitchen, and Scotty hesitated on the threshold of her room, his hand on the doorframe. Sydney glanced behind him, saw the firefighters working in her kitchen. One of them was snapping photographs, and Sydney knew they wouldn't be bothering if they didn't think it was an arson.

"Who would do this?" Sydney asked, slamming her fist into the mattress. "You're supposed to have people watching this place. How the *hell* did this happen?"

Scotty didn't answer. He just looked at her.

The flash of the camera went off behind him again, this time reflecting off the ring Scotty wore.

His red National Academy ring.

Her gaze fixed on it. There where his hand rested. On the doorframe.

She closed her eyes. Saw her painting as it was in the kitchen before the fire. The red eye. Not an eye at all. A ring. That's what she'd been reminded of earlier tonight when she'd looked at the painting. She'd seen that ring, or rather one very much like it . . . The night her father was killed . . .

She realized then what she hadn't realized all these years. What she'd refused to recognize—because it was too painful? The person who had killed her father, the person she'd seen leaving the restaurant that night after the arson, had been someone in her father's group. His Posse, her mother called it.

There was no other explanation.

She couldn't look away from that ring of Scotty's, and he lowered his hand and took another step in.

44

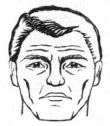

"Sydney?"

Sydney looked up, slid back on the bed, her heart pounding as she stared at Scotty's ring.

"Sydney?"

She grasped for her purse, her gun, but he was on her, and before she could move, he pulled her to her feet, was holding her by her shoulders, and then she heard, "Ma'am?"

It was Captain Wyatt. He'd come up behind Scotty, was looking at them.

"What's going on?" Wyatt asked.

Scotty held on to her for a second or two, his gaze burning into hers. When she didn't answer, he let go, said, "Good question."

"I—I need to call work," Sydney said, her mind racing, because she still hadn't put everything together, and desperately needed to. What if she was wrong? "I need to let Dixon know. I—"

Scotty said, "He's on his way. I called him."

And Sydney figured that was probably Dixon who had called while she was talking to Jake. Sydney looked at Wyatt. "Was there something you wanted?"

"Just letting you know that our own arson investigator arrived."

"Thanks."

He nodded, glanced at Scotty, then returned to the kitchen.

"What did Dixon say?" Sydney asked Scotty.

"He's sending a team out. Just to be sure."

A team. Even Dixon suspected arson, and Sydney looked past Scotty, into her kitchen, feeling her shoulders tense at the thought.

"You should sit down," Scotty said. "Clear your head . . ."

She wanted to, but when she closed her eyes, all she could see was the devil's eye looking at her, and she knew no one was going to make this go away. Not even Scotty. Not until she found the truth. "You were supposed to be watching me."

"This looks bad, I—"

"Looks bad! You have two goddamned teams out there. My sister was downstairs!"

"And that's why it happened. I just talked with Jared Dunning. They knew Jake was coming by to pick her up. They figured in how long it would take him to get there, the time was right . . . They thought it was him, Syd. He must have gotten away when I drove up to check with them. That's when I saw the flames and ran up."

His story was believable. It didn't make it any better, but it was certainly believable. Finally, reluctantly, she said, "I need to get some things together, change."

He held her gaze a moment longer, then stepped away. "I'll be outside if you need me."

"Thanks."

He walked to the end of the hall, hesitated, looked back, and then he was gone, and Sydney closed her eyes, stood there for several seconds, not moving, thinking about that ring he wore. Was that what had compelled her to paint a red jewel on her canvas?

She looked up at the ceiling, wondering what would have happened if she'd just ignored the envelope McKnight had sent, let Scotty take it, not started this. And not cared about finding answers to things she had no control over.

If she'd ignored it all, she could have remembered her father as she always had. A good man . . . Sinking to the bed, she grabbed her purse, felt the weight of the gun within it, admitted weariness, as though she'd been running for hours. If someone were to come in right then, she wasn't sure she'd have enough energy to lift up the gun and fire.

Finally she forced herself up, threw some clothes that were washable into a duffel bag. Tonight, though, it was jeans and a sweatshirt, and she packed her holster, then tucked her gun into her waistband. She walked out, but because she was feeling particularly vulnerable, turned back around, opened her gun safe, pulled out a small .22 semi and ankle holster, and tucked that into her purse.

She left her room, walked down the hall, emerged into the living room, pausing at the kitchen, the mess, wondering how long it would take to fix it, and if she could remain here while the work was being done . . .

Because she realized she didn't want to leave the city. She'd fight that transfer. She was staying here, she thought, stepping out onto the porch, eyeing Rainie's door below her, where her half sister was safely ensconced.

And then there was Scotty. Sydney couldn't deny the attraction to him, even though they had broken up, believed it was over. Maybe it was simply the stress of her world, the need to desperately recapture a time in her life she thought was happier. But now there was this chasm of distrust between them.

She wasn't sure why that thought came to her just then. She wanted to trust him, but something struck her as she walked out of her apartment. Something that made her go back in.

Stop. Look at the coffee table. *The photo she'd left there.* Gone. The photo of her father, taken the night he left on that black ops mission. The photo that McKnight mailed to her.

She looked around. Couldn't find it anywhere.

She supposed it could've gotten lost in the fire.

But she could've sworn she'd seen it . . . Yes. *She'd noticed the rings, looked up at the painting.*

She tore apart the couch, got on her hands and knees, felt beneath the furniture.

Nowhere.

Everything else in her living room seemed intact, considering.

She went back in the bedroom, to see if she'd taken it there. Then returned to the kitchen, certain a clean photo would've stood out, assuming the photo had blown into the kitchen *after* the fire. It was entirely possible that the photo had been left in the kitchen, burned, and was now nothing but soggy ash.

She was fairly certain that was not where she'd left it.

And then Sydney wondered if perhaps she'd left it down at Rainie's. She grabbed her keys, then ran down the steps. Scotty called out to her.

She turned her gaze on him, feeling pretty damned safe with the half-dozen firefighters milling about, never mind the couple dozen neighbors and strangers across the street who didn't have the sense to get in out of the cold. "You haven't seen that photo, have you?"

"Why?" He didn't even pretend not to know what she was talking about, but then neither did he deny taking it.

"It's missing. I find it strange that we have a conversation about it earlier tonight, you just happened to be driving by later, see a fire, happen to rescue me just in time, all when this photo turns up missing. What's so damned special about it? What did it reveal that I wasn't seeing?"

He slipped the photo from his jacket pocket, handing it to her. "I see you made a copy. I found it on the ground outside, *after* the fire was put out. Maybe it blew outside, with all the firemen rushing in, or when we ran out." She looked down at the photo, saw a footprint across the face of it, some water marks, figured it could have fallen before all this started. And who *would* notice it, racing from the fire? "Maybe it's not as important as we thought," he said, as a couple of cars pulled up. One was Jake's. The other Sydney couldn't tell, but definitely an unmarked cop car. "Your father was involved in something that we may never know the complete truth about. Gnoble, McKnight, Wheeler's father, Orozco. That's what the government does, Sydney," he said, keeping his voice down low. "The good citizens of this country don't care that there are things going on in this world that might not be perfectly black and white or stand up to intense scrutiny, as long as *their* world as *they* know it continues to be. So, yes, sometimes things happen that the rest of us in government must look the other way about. Secrets with foreign governments. Bank accounts in corrupt banks. Arms sold to factions that you don't want to look at too closely. That's the way government works." He stepped closer, took her hand in his. "But all that aside, Sydney, sometimes things are just what they seem. No tricks. No mirrors. No government conspiracies involved. Like your father's murder. It was just that. Wheeler broke in. Robbed him, killed him, and left."

Carillo was in the unmarked car, and Sydney saw him walk up, shake Jake's hand, then the two of them walked toward her. Jake, however, continued on to Rainie's, not saying anything to Sydney, which told her he was doing his level best to keep his temper in check. Sydney wasn't having such luck, and told Scotty, "I don't believe it."

"I told you there were pictures, Syd."

"Which prove what?"

Though Carillo stood a polite distance away, he was listening to the conversation, because he walked toward her and said, "The photos, Fitz. The enhancements. They came back. They prove that Wheeler was there that night, before *and* after the fire was set. It's a clean case, Fitz. I looked into it just like you asked. And like you, I had my doubts, until Schermer brought me the enhanced photos from the surveillance cameras, that proved Wheeler returned to steal the money from the restaurant."

"When did he show them to you?"

"Right before we went out on Operation Barfly . . . You mean you haven't seen them?" He looked at Scotty. "Jesus. You didn't show them to her?"

"Why would Scotty have them?" she demanded.

"I was rushing out, Fitz," Carillo said. "He was with me when Schermer brought them in. And with what they contained, I thought someone ought to sit down with you. Not just throw them at you and leave."

Scotty said, "I brought them to the restaurant to show you, but we were interrupted. By a purse snatcher. And then a fire."

"*You* have the photos?" Sydney asked.

Scotty pulled several photographs from his jacket pocket. "*This* is why I came by here tonight," he said, handing the first to her. "I knew this was important to you."

"The photos from the surveillance camera?"

"Yes."

She shoved away the hurt she felt that Carillo would have given them to Scotty, but then reconciled that with the knowledge that he *was* busy, and he *had* tried to get them to her. With trepidation, she eyed the photo, recognized the back of the strip mall where her father's restaurant used to be. Someone climbing through a window. Too grainy to use. The person climbing in was wearing dark clothing, nothing identifiable.

And then Scotty showed her a second photo. "This one was digitally enhanced," he said. "From the original."

It was a close-up of what was undoubtedly a very young Johnnie Wheeler, looking toward the camera. The same scar ran down his cheek, and Sydney remembered the feeling when she'd drawn Tara's rapist, the scar she thought she saw . . . Was that why she'd had such a strange feeling when she'd drawn it?

She put it from her head. That meant nothing. Nothing, she told herself again, looking at the third photo, of him disappearing into the window.

"So he broke in," Sydney said.

"About four minutes before the first nine-one-one call. The rest of the surveillance photos show him leaving out the same window right after the call was made reporting the fire. And he has the burns on his hands in this photo, and there are no burns on the entry."

She stared in disbelief. "There has to be a mistake. The time's wrong. Something."

"No mistake. He lied to you, Sydney. He didn't walk in the front door like he told you. He climbed in through the window. This proves he was there when your father was killed. Wheeler killed him. There's no other explanation."

45

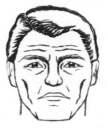

Sydney looked away from the photos, away from Scotty and Carillo, their looks of sympathy, unable to believe that she had let Wheeler dupe her. She'd *believed* him. Believed her father had asked him there, was trying to help him. "What about Jazmine Wheeler and what she said about the church organization?"

"Perhaps," Carillo said, "it *was* just a coincidence. Your father really did search him out to help out the son of an old friend. But that son was too far gone, too into drugs. Couldn't keep himself clean long enough."

Sydney looked down at the photos again, tried to make sense of it, but a loud crash from upstairs startled her.

Maggie Winters had dropped her aluminum clipboard, and papers went flying. "Somebody grab that," Maggie asked one of the other agents as she shone her flashlight on the window, then peered closer at it. "Looks like someone opened the window and dropped in some matches. There's a stick here that he probably used to reach in and knock over the turpentine."

"Great," Sydney said.

"You okay?" Carillo asked.

She nodded, took a deep breath, as Scotty said, "I'd say it's looking like a lot of ugly coincidences all the way around. It happens."

She looked up at her apartment. "If Wheeler's guilty, then who did this?" she asked, pointing. "And why?"

Carillo followed her gaze. "Assuming it wasn't accidental—"

"With a sliced screen?"

"Rules out the accident theory," he continued. "So unless some arsonist just picked you at random—and I think that's taking this coincidence theory too far—I'd say that leaves whoever it is Scotty is investigating on our good senator."

The only thing Sydney could concentrate on right then was that she'd unwittingly brought Angie into danger. "I can't believe this," she whispered to herself.

Carillo put his arm around her shoulder. "First things first," he said. "You need somewhere to stay."

"I'm sure I'll figure something out," Sydney said, trying not to watch Scotty as he moved off a few feet to make a call. A chasm had definitely opened between them. She told herself it didn't matter. He hadn't been completely open with her—and she ignored the thought that she most definitely hadn't been open with him. This had been her father's life. Her life. Not Scotty's.

Carillo saw her watching Scotty. "As hard as it is, you gotta cut him some slack. You know he's only worried about you."

"Yeah, thanks," she said, and Carillo drew her away, diverting her attention, his arm still around her, and she realized that she felt safe there. She could trust him.

They stood like that for several minutes, not talking, until he finally said, "Did I tell you Sheila called me today?"

"No."

"Seems she wants to work things out."

"Boyfriend dump her?"

"Probably. You know she's got six letters in her first name? Say Sheila three times, it's like saying six, six, six. Kinda fits. She-devil Sheila."

She glanced at his face, but he was looking up at her apartment, not really seeing anything, if she had to hazard a guess. "So," she said. "You tell her you're getting used to the thought of paying alimony?"

"I should have. What I did say was that I'd have to think about it. Working it out, that is. Man, that fire really did a number on your kitchen."

They stared up into the window, the burned interior brightly lit as Maggie worked her magic. "And did you?" Sydney finally asked. "Think about it?"

"Still thinking." He flashed a grin. "I was getting used to the idea of living in my car."

"Makes it convenient when you're hungry. Drive right through the Taco Bells. Unless you end up getting transferred . . ."

"Speaking of transfers to out-of-the-way places, Dixon left you a voice mail."

"I am *not* getting transferred," she said, taking out her phone. Sydney flipped it open and punched in the code to access the voice mail. Two messages. "Syd? It's Dixon. Just checking to see if you're okay . . . if you need anything before I get out there. I'm sending a team to investigate. Just in case. Call me."

"Nothing about a transfer," Sydney said, deleting that call. Sydney put the phone to her ear to listen to the next message, and heard, "Things should be getting a little *hot* for you." The same muffled, raspy voice as she'd heard on Dixon's phone earlier. "Oh, by the way," the voice continued, "*you're* next."

And then nothing.

"What is it?" Carillo asked, no doubt seeing the look of shock on her face. Sydney couldn't help but glance around, at everyone across the street, wondering if any of them had called while watching the fire, watching her.

"Someone who thinks I should be next," she said, pressing the button to prompt a repeat, then handing the phone to Carillo.

He listened, eyed the crowd across the street just as she'd done. "Our Jane Doe killer?" he said, handing her the phone.

She checked the incoming number that showed up on her

cell phone screen. Restricted. No number listed. Sydney showed the screen to Carillo. "What the hell is going on? How would he get my number?"

"One possibility," Carillo said. "It isn't the Jane Doe killer. Whoever this caller is, he already knew you. He's the hit that Scotty is investigating."

"Great. This can't get any worse."

Scotty asked, "What's wrong?"

She repeated to him what the caller had said, just as Dixon pulled up. Scotty also looked across the street. "You see anyone who doesn't belong?"

"I see a lot of people who don't belong. It's not like I know all my neighbors here."

Scotty nodded to Carillo. "Let's go take some names."

They crossed the street just as Dixon walked over. He glanced up at her apartment and wasted no time saying, "This have anything to do with your unofficial investigation that you're not investigating?"

"Depends on who you ask," Sydney said, unable to deal with much more tonight. Sydney glanced at Rainie's window, saw Angie glued to the glass, watching everything, Jake standing behind her, his arms crossed, clearly waiting for her to come in and discuss the situation with him. Her mother wasn't with him, and she wondered where she was, what he'd told her. "Carillo can fill you in. I think my stepfather wants to see me."

She left him and walked into Rainie's house.

Angie barely spared her a glance, intent on watching Maggie walking down the steps. "She's the one who collects all the evidence. That's what I want to do!"

"College first," Jake said, no doubt now, more than ever, dead set against her going into law enforcement. He wanted her to be a doctor.

"Where's Rainie?" Sydney asked.

"In the kitchen," Angie said. "Making coffee and hot chocolate."

Sydney glanced at Jake, who nodded toward the kitchen, indicating he wanted to talk to her in there, alone.

They walked into the kitchen, and Rainie handed her a

cup of coffee. The warm mug felt wonderful in her hands. "How're you holding up?" she asked, stirring some chocolate on the stove.

"Not bad, considering."

Rainie glanced behind her to Jake. "Would you like some coffee?"

"No, thank you."

She poured the cocoa into two cups and took a can of whipped cream from the fridge, crowning the top of each cup with a generous portion. "We'll be in the living room. Just close the kitchen door."

She took the mugs, walked out, and Sydney closed the door, then faced Jake.

To say that he was angry was an understatement. "She could've been killed," he said, trying to keep his voice low. "What the hell is going on? You have no idea what went through my—"

"Daddy? You're not mad at Sydney, are you?"

He caught his breath, and Angie pushed through the kitchen door, ran into his arms, and he held her for several seconds, saying nothing, his eyes tightly closed, then just whispered her name. Finally he looked down at her, holding her face. "No, sweetheart. Just scared. You have your stuff?"

Rainie moved into the doorway, threw Sydney an apologetic look, then held up Angie's little purple backpack. "Got it right here," she said, handing it to Jake.

"Kiss your sister good-bye. We have to go."

"But Daddy, I'm not done with—" Apparently Angie thought better of trying to cajole him, and she walked up, gave Sydney a hug and a kiss, and said, "I'm sorry about your kitchen."

"Yeah, well, it needed repainting anyway."

"The fire engines were so cool," she said, with a quick smile, then glanced at her father, who nodded toward Rainie. "Thanks for the sundaes, Rainie."

"You're welcome, Angie."

Jake gave her one last look, then guided Angie out the

door, and Sydney heard her ask him, "Did Sydney do something wrong, Daddy?"

"We need to hurry. You're mother's waiting for us at home."

Sydney watched them walk out, Angie's hand clasped in his, and as they passed the men standing out front, Angie gave a wave to Carillo, and he winked at her. Scotty said something to Jake, who hesitated, then apparently sent Angie to the car by herself. "I'll be right back," Sydney told Rainie.

Dixon pinned his gaze on her as she walked out, and asked, "What's this about the Jane Doe killer calling you?"

She glanced toward Jake and Scotty, who seemed deep in conversation, and said, "I have no idea who it was. Didn't Carillo tell you?"

"I'd like to hear it from you."

She gave him a quick rundown of the call. "Only problem I see is that it doesn't fit the killer's profile."

"So it would seem," Dixon replied. "Unless you recall during your sketch interview of Tara Brown that she mentioned her attacker smelled like fire. That was why you ran off to Houston, wasn't it?"

"Smoke from a fire," Sydney said, recalling her excuse to get to Houston. "I think Tara's case was the anomaly. Reno. Maybe he stopped and lit a campfire between here and there—"

Dixon gave her a stern look, and Sydney clamped her mouth shut, feeling Jake's gaze burn into her. "I think Scotty needs to expand the surveillance to your parents' and sister's house as well."

To which Jake said, "I don't need anyone watching my family."

Carillo asked, "Why would you want to take a chance?"

"I can handle my own family." His gaze lit on Sydney as he added, "At least *most* of my family." And then he walked off, got into the car with Angie, and drove away.

Carillo watched his car disappear around the corner, no doubt checking to see if he was being followed—because Sydney was doing the same.

Scotty looked at her and said, "I'll get a team out to keep an eye on your mother's house."

Carillo said, "Don't worry, Fitz, he won't even know we're doing it."

Dixon nodded. "Probably best. Don't want anyone walking into any surprises." He looked at his watch. "Carillo, take Sydney to a hotel. You and Ren sit with her tonight. Scotty, I assume you're taking this to the next level? We're done playing games?"

Scotty took a deep breath, glanced at Sydney, and she thought she saw the weight of the world on his shoulders as he said, "I just talked to HQ. They want us to go in, make the arrest tonight. We still don't know if Gnoble was part of it, but maybe after we interrogate that slimy aide of his, put the fear of God in him . . ."

He walked off, pulling out his phone.

Sydney turned to Carillo. "Before we go, I need to talk to you. Privately." She drew Carillo away.

"What's up?" Carillo asked.

"I'm going to talk to Wheeler again. I want to show him those photos."

"Why bother? The guy's not worth your time."

"For my own peace of mind? The bastard lied to me. Here I am, busting my butt to help him, putting my job on the line—"

"Before you get worked up, think about who you were really doing it for."

"Okay. Maybe I was being selfish, but he certainly would have benefited. I can't believe I believed him . . ."

"What do they teach you at Basic?"

She met Carillo's gaze. "*Everybody* lies."

"Not that you can blame the guy. They're gonna flip the switch in what? Two days?"

"A little over one. But I still need to hear it from his mouth. I want him to admit it. To quit lying and—and I want him to know I know."

"Okay. Do it. But I'm going with you. Surveillance in case you're being followed."

"Like some dipshit's going to follow me to San Quentin? This is one interview I need to do on my own."

"So I sit and drink a cup in the guard's office. By tomorrow, I'll be in serious need of caffeine anyway. Do me a favor when I get to the hotel. Since I'm going to be up watching you all night, try to get some sleep, so *you* can drive in the morning."

46

The next morning, Carillo rode shotgun while Syd-
ney drove to San Quentin, because she had to hear it from
Wheeler before she could let it go. Hear that he was lying
about this. She'd thought he was this innocent man, that her
father had befriended him because of the relationship with
Wheeler's father, Francisco . . . But once again it occurred to
her, what did she really know about her father anyway?

And therein lay the crux of the matter. She'd been so distracted about her father's secret life and that damned photo
that McKnight sent that apparently she'd grasped at any little thing that might turn it around, prove it was wrong, even
Wheeler's lies, even though his lies didn't prove everything
else was wrong. In fact, Sydney was still distracted by it all,
still upset, so much so that she wasn't even aware that Carillo was talking to Dixon on the phone. "I'll let her know,"
he said, then disconnected.

He tucked his phone on his belt, looked over at her, and
said, "Not sure if it's a good news, bad news, good news
thing."

"Okay . . ."

"They arrested Gnoble's aide, Prescott. Interrogated the

shit out of him, got the big deny, deny, deny, until the moment they walked in with his cell phone and pulled up your cell phone number and the time of your threatening call. That was all it took. He admitted to leaving that voice mail on Dixon's phone, too, and then he confessed to starting the fire. Said he'd unlocked your window, then set up the can of turpentine the day before, when he and Gnoble went out to bring you flowers, so that he could come back, slide the window open, then light it on fire."

"The bad news?"

"He says that Gnoble didn't know a thing. Prescott hired a hit man without Gnoble's knowledge, but decided to do it on his own when the guy kept missing you. So we got Prescott, but Gnoble's untouchable. Bet you'll never guess who Prescott did give up. Mrs. Gnoble."

"Mrs. Gnoble?"

"The one and only. Seems she was worried about McKnight sending you this photo and opening up a big can of worms involving your father, McKnight, and Gnoble. The BICTT scandal. Thought it might interfere with her chances of becoming first lady, so she got Prescott to hire a hit man. They arrested her this morning."

"Then what's the good news?"

"The hit man that Prescott hired? Richard Blackwell. Supposed to be the best in the business? Well, just might be. Only he works for CIA. The guy you saw in court, then out on the street? That's him. He's the one who made that first phone call to you, pretending to be the Jane Doe killer in order to make Prescott think it was legit. His job was to prevent Prescott from killing you, by pretending to be the one who was going to take you out."

Cute Guy from the elevator, she thought. How fitting. She glanced over at him, then back at the road, figuring that was why Scotty had gone along with them and not informed her of what was going on at first. She didn't like it any better, but at least she understood. "Anything else?"

"No. He'll call us the moment something comes up."

"So, what exactly did you tell him we were doing?"

"Going out to breakfast." He leaned his head back, closed

his eyes. "Just don't wake me until it's over. Long night."

All too soon, Sydney was seated opposite Wheeler in an interview room. Again.

She was hating this place. Hating that she'd ever walked in here.

"Yeah," he said. "You got news?"

"I got news," she replied, watching his face carefully. "I got news that a photo was taken of you climbing in the back of the pizza place, during your *second* visit, just before you ripped it off."

He didn't answer, and Sydney found her gaze drawn to his white eye, the one that couldn't see, but seemed to see right through her. He looked away. "Don't know what you're talkin' about."

"They've made great strides with technology. They can enhance things that might not have been useful twenty years ago."

"Yeah, they showed those photos in court. Couldn't prove it was me. Couldn't even prove it was the pizza deliveryman."

"Oh, *very* funny. Did you go back in to take the money from the safe?"

He refused to look at her, and she realized that he had done that very thing.

"I don't believe it. I broke every rule I held sacred, put my career on the line investigating this thing, trying to help you, and you lied to me."

"I didn't lie. I never said a thing. I didn't steal nothing. Don't even know what you're talking about."

"I'm talking about this." Sydney laid the photos on the table. He looked at them, his gaze widening at the face shot that DOJ was able to enhance, his hand on the window frame, uninjured, unburned.

"So I went in the back way. That don't make me a killer."

"You ripped him off. That makes you highly suspect when you said that he gave you the money."

"And he did. The money from the till. Never touched the safe."

"But you went back for more."

"No, I didn't. Those pictures don't prove shit."

"They'll speak pretty loudly when the governor is looking at your case for clemency. When's the big day? Tomorrow? The next?"

He was quiet, looking like he was wrestling with something. His life, no doubt. And Sydney thought about the little things he told her, the things that he couldn't have known unless her father had told him. Was she wrong? "You told me my father said that you could pay him back on Tuesday."

"I don't remember what day he said. I just said Tuesday, 'cause you asked, and it was the day after he was killed."

And her heart sank. She supposed she'd been so eager to believe him, because by doing so, it meant her father was good, altruistic . . . She'd put her hopes in that he, Wheeler, had the most incentive to tell the truth. How was it that she'd overlooked that he also had the most incentive to lie?

"Why? You went back to steal the money from the god-damned safe! What happened? Did he catch you?"

"Just 'cause I'm a thief, don't make me no murderer. No, he didn't catch me. He was too busy talking to someone else."

"There was someone else there?" Sydney said. "How convenient."

"And true."

"You forget to mention that to the cops? Sort of when you forgot to mention that you climbed into the back of the building after he'd already given you money?"

"I told them I saw that guy there. Probably the same guy I saw sitting out in the car when I show to get my green. They did that Identikit thing. I just didn't say *when* I saw him, or *where* I was when I saw him that second time."

"Why not?"

"You saying I was s'posed to tell them? Hey, by the way, while I was breakin' in the back way to rob the place? That guy in the parking lot came in and blew away the owner? You nuts? I got my black ass breaking into a white man's business in a rich white man's town. I can't go tellin' them I was rippin' the place off. They convict me for sure, I say that. 'Specially I say that after the fact. Like I'm makin' it up, or somethin'."

She simply stared at him. Couldn't believe what she was

hearing. She got up, slapped her hand on the door to be let out. "Do you know how many people *suffered* because you lied?"

"I didn't lie. I just didn't tell 'em everything. I told 'em what they needed to know. Ain't my fault they ain't listening. And I didn't kill him."

The guard opened the door. "You done?"

"Yeah," she said, then turned back to Wheeler, trying so hard not to say something smart-assed. "I'm done."

"You gotta understand!" He rose, placed both shackled hands on the table. "If I told you right off, you wouldn't help me! You know that's true!"

She ignored him, walked out, her footsteps echoing down the long concrete corridor, trying not to think about how much time and energy—and emotion—she'd wasted on this case, how she'd so wanted to believe him, because that meant her father's life was worth something . . . And she couldn't help but wonder if she hadn't been distracted by Wheeler's lies, would Prescott have ever gotten close enough to her to set her apartment on fire? Endanger her sister? Maybe she would've foreseen some of the events, been smart enough not to think that everything about her father and his death was a big government conspiracy to cover up the truth, that they weren't out there manufacturing evidence, that her father wasn't trying to blackmail someone to pay off a boat. That the photo meant nothing—

She stopped in her tracks. Realized what she'd failed to see there the whole time. Of course it wasn't about the photo. Not in the sense they'd been looking at. It was the timing. Cisco's Kid . . . "Oh my God," she whispered.

She pivoted, strode back to the interview room where the guard was leading Wheeler back to his cell. "Give me just a couple more minutes," she said.

The guard nodded, and Wheeler sat back down and Sydney thought of him climbing through that window. "If my father gave you money to get to this job, why would you come back and rip him off?"

"Gotta understand. That was a long time ago. Me being young. Stupid. I got mad at my girlfriend 'cause she was taking off, leaving me with a new baby. My aunt's all over my ass, gotta grow up, kick the drugs, 'cause I gotta be a father. We got in a fight over it. What kinda man's gotta beg for a double-saw from his aunt? That's why I called your father. I ain't never heard of this church, and I'm starting to think maybe they're like some kind of cult, I mean, what they doin' pickin' some loser like me from the streets, gonna make me their project? Aunt Jazz tells me to be careful, but maybe this is my chance, and I think, yeah, this is my chance. I think if I had enough green, I wouldn't have to borrow nothing to get no job in San Mateo. I could maybe buy a couple bricks, turn it over real quick."

She was fascinated by the novelty of what Wheeler was saying, the fact it seemed more the unvarnished truth of a young kid who sees opportunity knocking, and is too mixed up to make the right decisions. "So what *really* happened?"

"I show up just like he says, get this gas money to drive down to San Mateo, and he's busy washin' glasses. He tells me to look in that little can but there's only some change, then tells me there's a twenty under the till. And then I leave."

"And?" Sydney asked, leaning against the door.

He hesitated. "So I park around the corner, and I climb in through the back window. A storeroom. Lots of cans of stuff. That's when I hear your old man, 'cause he asked, 'How'd *you* get in?' Thought he was talkin' to me. Like he knew. I froze. Then I realize he ain't talkin' to me. He talkin' to someone else."

"Who?"

"Don't know. Like I told the cops. Mighta been this guy I saw sittin' in the parking lot when I first got there. He's the one watchin' me, but I figure, you know, he's waitin' for someone. But whoever this guy was inside, your father didn't like him none. Least not him bein' there right then. In his face about it."

"Arguing?"

"Yeah. Words. What'd the guy think he was doin' back there."

"Back where?"

"Just back, like he came back for somethin'. That's why

I'm thinkin' he's that guy I saw outside. You know. Already been there."

"Then what?"

"They got in each other's face."

"About what?"

"The other guy's saying, you do what you plannin', you gonna lead 'em all right back to him, and he worked too hard to get where he was. Your old man, he says, get over it, he ain't changin' his mind.' And the guy says he ain't gonna lose it all just 'cause of him. No way."

"Lose what?"

"Don't know. So I'm thinking, time to go. I turn around, gonna climb back out, and *boom*."

She closed her eyes, not wanting to imagine her father being shot . . . It took her a moment to shake it off, force herself to look at him. "You saw him pull the trigger?"

"No, but who coulda done it? Next thing I know, I hear this clinking from behind the bar, like someone pulling bottles out, then I hear splashing, and someone lights a fire."

"And what did you do?"

"What else? Guy's gotta gun. I'm thinkin' he's shootin' me next, so I ain't moving until I'm sure he's gone. And then I got the hell out, same way I got in."

She glanced at the twisted scars on his hands. "How did you get burned, then?"

"What was I s'posed to do? I went to see if your old man was dead, but the flames shot up and I knew I had to get out of there."

She wasn't sure if she believed him. But she knew one way to find out. She pulled out her cell phone, called Carillo, and told him to bring her briefcase from his car. He brought it to her a few minutes later, and the guard let him in. "You want me to wait here?" he asked.

"No."

Carillo left without further comment.

She took out her sketch pad, wondering if she even had a chance of success, because there were two things against her. One, she wasn't even sure he was telling the truth. Two, she'd never elicited a sketch from someone for a crime that had occurred that long ago. Usually it was a matter of hours from when the crime occurred, though she'd done some sketches months, even a couple of years after. But not twenty years . . . Cognitive recall worked under normal circumstances. Would it work for a case that happened two decades before?

"Do you think you could identify the man you saw?" Sydney asked him.

"Back then, yeah. Now? How am I s'posed to know?"

"Pretend twenty years hasn't gone by. We have pictures of all these people, how they looked. Could you identify him?"

"I been in this cage every night seein' his face, knowin' his ass should be here, not mine. Yeah. I can do it. You got pictures for me to see?"

"No. We're going to make one."

He looked dubious. "I already described him."

"But not to me." She took out her sketchbook, a pencil, and set them on the table. Then, with a prayer for the truth at last, Sydney said, "What I want you to do is go back about an hour before you broke in. What were you doing?"

"Leaving JJ with Aunt Jazz and driving up to Santa Arleta."

"What was the weather like?"

"Why you askin'?"

"Humor me."

"Cold. Windy. And there's stars out, when I drove over the bridge. I remember the stars, 'cause Aunt Jazz always told me to make a wish. Like they ever come true, you know? So, yeah. I remember the stars."

She simply nodded. More important to let him talk, remember the little details, even if they were innocuous thoughts, anything to retrieve the tiniest slivers of memories that would help him remember what she needed for the drawing . . .

He continued to ramble for a bit, then said, "And I park around the corner and wait, figuring your old man gotta be gone by then, you know? He was just 'bout ready to leave when I saw him that first time, maybe that's who was waitin' for him in the parking lot. His ride. And I decide to walk up the back, see the windows. And I figure, you know, the place is closed up for the night, so I can just climb in the back. No one's gonna be back there."

"Do you remember hearing any noises?"

"Nothing. Quiet. Figure it's closed. Quiet's good."

"So you break in. What was the room like around you?"

"Dark. Lots of cans. Stuff around. And then I hear, 'What are *you* doing here?'"

"Okay. You hear that and you . . ."

"I look out the door."

"At what point did you see the other guy's face? The killer?"

"When he tells your father he ain't gonna lose it all. It's like he was lookin' right at me. Like he saw me, *knew* I was there. That's when I turn to leave. That's when I'm thinkin', yeah, he's that same guy sittin' in that parking lot when I walk in. Ain't no customer. He's waiting for your old man. Waitin' to kill him. That's why I think he set me up."

"I want you to look at that face, that moment when he looked right at you. What was the shape, the outline of the head?"

He drew a circle in the air. And so it began. He described, Sydney drew. If he hesitated, she would bring him back to that moment. The moment she didn't want to relive, but had to over and over. Look at his face. Tell her what he saw. All to get a sketch, a sketch that may or may not be the face of the man who killed her father.

And as Sydney sketched, she wondered how she would know. How would she know if he was telling the truth? How would she know *this* was the face of a killer?

She needed to keep her mind open. Needed to not prejudice the drawing with her own beliefs, because she didn't yet know the truth. And eventually she saw it begin to take shape.

And her heart skipped a beat.

Had she drawn this, or was it his sketch?

Was it something she wanted to believe, or was it the truth?

She had to be sure. And so, on purpose, she lengthened and squared the chin, made it different. She had to know that this was coming from his mind, not hers.

"Yeah," he said, and her heart sank. Her drawing, she

thought. Not his. Why should she be surprised he had lied? This was his last shot at freedom. Tomorrow was his last day on this earth. "Yeah," he said again, nodding. "That's the man that killed your father."

She'd witnessed numbers of false sketches over the years, someone trying to conjure a suspect in their mind to clear themselves, agreeing that the sketch she'd done was "perfect." Another dead end, she thought, and, to prove her point, asked him, "Is there anything you'd do to make it look more like the man you saw? Any changes?"

She expected none, and sure enough he shook his head, saying, "Nothing. Looks just like him . . ." She gave a perfunctory smile, started to put the sketchbook away, when he said, "Except the chin ain't his. Wasn't square. Like, maybe shorter and more round, like this," he said, taking his finger and tracing it where he thought it should be.

"You're sure?"

"Yeah. Didn't want you to think, you know, that you're a bad artist, but that ain't his chin," he said, and her heart started pounding.

His drawing after all . . .

She changed the sketch. Showed it to him.

He nodded. "Yeah. That's him. That's the man that killed your father."

Gnoble.

Back before he'd ever grown that trademark goatee.

His wife had just been arrested. And if she knew his secrets, he had to be worried. Desperate. And he lived in the same town as her mother. Her sister.

She called for the guard, grabbed her sketchbook, then took out her phone, punched in Dixon's number. "You know that case I wasn't investigating . . . ?"

47

"You know," Carillo said, keeping pace with her as they crossed the parking lot, "this is the second time you've tried convincing me this guy is innocent."

"He is."

"He was guilty when we drove in this morning. You sure he's not yanking your chain?"

Sydney stopped suddenly, and Carillo nearly ran into her. "No," she said, handing him her sketchbook, so she could dig her keys and her cell phone from her purse.

"It's Gnoble?"

"Before he grew his goatee. How many people do you know who could describe him like that? What I think is that he grew it after Wheeler saw him there. Gnoble framed him from the get-go. I think Gnoble was waiting out front to kill my father for helping Wheeler, because it was going to re-open all sorts of nasty things."

"Like how Wheeler's father was killed during an unsanctioned black op that may have ties to BICTT?"

"Exactly. And I think that when he saw Wheeler walk in there that night, he figured he'd be leaving prints, knew he had a record, so why not set him up to take the fall for my father's murder? It just worked out better than he planned, because Wheeler broke in to rip off the place anyway. That's what I think," she said, unlocking the car doors. They both got in and Sydney said, "No one would've been the wiser, until I showed up here to talk to Wheeler. And that's what started all this. Not McKnight and his photo and his suicide because of his damned guilty conscience about running the country's budget when he's got millions of stolen black funds tucked away. It started the moment my mother called Senator Gnoble, and told him I was thinking about going to the prison."

"Pretty elaborate setup, don't you think?"

"Look at Gnoble's background. They were all working special ops. Everything they did was elaborate. A man like Gnoble doesn't get where he is by doing something half-assed." Sydney flipped open her phone to call Jake. "He gets there by taking advantage of any opportunity. Wheeler's presence that night twenty years ago was the perfect opportunity."

"So what's the story with this photo McKnight sent to you?"

Jake didn't answer the phone. She started the car, let it idle. "That by itself was really nothing. Had the suicide note been included with it . . . The note sure as hell shook up the CIA. They jumped on that quick, cleaned it up so nothing could come back to haunt them. Gnoble might have been worried, but he was smart enough to know that the CIA was not going to let any of that information out, because his wasn't the only reputation that could be harmed. It had nothing to do with why Gnoble wanted me dead. It was only when I showed up in Baja, started stirring up a hornet's nest that the CIA got worried."

"They're trying to sanitize the past, and you're trying to bring it out in the open."

"Which means that Scotty was right in one respect. It wasn't about the photo. Never had been. At least as far as Gnoble was concerned."

"I'm not sure I entirely understand . . . ?"

"It *was* about Cisco's Kid. Wheeler. Not the boat. And my deciding to go to San Quentin and interview him, find out why he did what he did, that shook up Gnoble, and no doubt his wife. Cisco, Frank White, was probably killed on an unsanctioned black op that Gnoble was responsible for. One that ties Gnoble, and a lot of top government officials and businesses, into the BICTT scandal, some of which could still be operating today, assuming Orozco's information proves correct. And Orozco said my father probably would've been killed later if he hadn't been killed in the robbery. Why? Because he's a tie to Gnoble's involvement. Gnoble's cover-up of Cisco's death. My father's threats of exposing them. All of which Gnoble eliminates by killing him. And the pure genius is that Gnoble sets it up to look like a robbery, which keeps the safeguards that he and Orozco put in place in case of their suspicious deaths."

"Which makes you a target because . . ."

"I am the only witness who might be able to verify that Wheeler was really telling the truth. The moment I walked into San Quentin, and faced the only other witness, Gnoble had no guarantee that I wouldn't remember what really happened the night my father was killed. He needed Wheeler's execution to go through. The Innocence Project stepped in for a brief moment, and suddenly Gnoble's entire future balanced on his knowledge that he'd committed one crime with absolutely *no* statute of limitations. Murder. One more day, half that equation is gone, executed. That makes me his biggest threat to him and his wife's chances of making it to the White House," she said, backing from her space, then shifting to drive.

"You think Prescott knew all this?"

"I doubt he knows the entire story, only what Mrs. Gnoble told him. Maybe all she needed to do was point out that if I told some big secret having to do with my father's past, there goes the election. Prescott probably agreed to set up the hit to save his own damned job, because if Gnoble's not reelected, Prescott's out."

No answer at her mother's. Not even the machine picked up, which meant someone was on the other line, not paying attention to the call-waiting beep. Probably Angie. Sydney disconnected. "Gnoble or his wife had to have given Prescott my cell number to make that call. Had to be Gnoble. Gnoble could call my mom to get it. Prescott couldn't," she said, driving up to the guard tower to get their guns.

They checked their weapons, and Sydney holstered her primary, then strapped her backup pistol on her ankle holster, before driving out the gates, then pausing at the end of the road to call Jake's cell phone, listening to it ring.

Carillo snapped his holster, saying, "Maybe that's why he stayed in touch all these years. Good ol' Uncle Don. Conveniently there should you happen to remember what really happened. Ready to take action."

"At his wife's urging, no doubt." Jake's phone went to voice mail, and Sydney punched in her number, followed by a 9–1–1, hoping he'd get right back to her. She drove down the street that led away from the prison, then followed it around to the freeway, just as Jake called back. She flipped open the phone, took a breath, and said, "I have some bad news . . ."

"Is it any worse than the news that your boss just finished telling me?"

"If it's about Gnoble, then no. Where are you?"

"A better question is where are you?"

"Just leaving San Quentin," Sydney said.

"Then do us both a favor and drive straight to your office."

"But—"

"For God's sake, Sydney, shut up and listen to me, and pretend just this once that I know what I'm talking about. *We* are not the threat, and if you come here, and Gnoble's foolish enough to go after you, because he thinks you can testify against him, then you are putting *everyone* in this house at risk."

She was just pulling onto the freeway, thinking about what he said, wishing she could say something in return. But Sydney knew he was right. Her first instinct was to go there, protect her sister, her mother. Even Jake.

"Sydney?"

"I'm here," she said, glancing into the rearview mirror, then moving into the fast lane.

"Look. We'll be fine. I'm going to take your mother and sister out of town until he's caught. Your mother is upstairs putting a few things together."

"Okay."

"Be careful. We'll call you."

And he disconnected.

She stared out at the car in the lane ahead of her for several seconds, almost on autopilot, and finally Carillo said, "What's wrong?"

She told him what Jake had said.

"Okay, so we go back to the office instead of Santa Arleta. Dixon sort of ordered us back there anyway, didn't he?"

"If you interpret that we're not to be involved in Gnoble's arrest, then yes, but what if Gnoble goes to my mother's?"

"Like Jake said, why would he? They're no threat to him. If Gnoble's smart, he'll be hightailing it out of here."

The car in front of her slowed, and Sydney snapped out of her stupor, went around it, then stepped on the gas. "This guy's a stone-cold psychopath. It's clear he has no conscience."

"Our advantage is that he doesn't know he's cornered, *yet*, assuming he doesn't think his wife's going to start singing, and he hasn't figured you've been out to the prison, so maybe if we think like him . . ."

She glanced at Carillo, tried to see things as he was seeing them, before turning her attention back to the road. "Clearly he's very logical. Very methodical."

"Okay. So logically and methodically even if he knew you'd come here, done this sketch, he's got to realize that the word of a convicted killer isn't going to mean shit. There is no way that sketch is going to exonerate Wheeler *or* convict Gnoble."

"Not unless someone other than Wheeler can place him at the scene."

"You *are* the only other witness."

"I can place a hand with a ring on it." She scoffed. "That'll fly."

"One more link in the case," Carillo said. "And clearly if his wife tried to put a hit on you, they don't know that's all you can remember, or they're worried you'll start remembering."

"There's got to be something we've been missing . . ."

"A bigger threat than you?"

She thought about everything she'd learned, all the pieces that were now fitting neatly together. And all those that, until now, seemed at odds . . . She glanced toward Carillo. "It just occurred to me that we've overlooked one very important part of all this. Someone who's stayed in touch with all the players. The go-to girl if you want to leave the country and start a new life. Becky Lynn."

"Probably the only organized crime that woman is running is bleeding Gnoble, Orozco, and McKnight for hush money. Talk about your gravy train. So, what're you thinking?"

"I'm thinking that Dixon ordered us off Gnoble, but he didn't say a thing about Becky Lynn."

"And being *good* agents, we should take the initiative."

She hit the gas, disregarding all speed laws, redlighting anyone who didn't move out of her way fast enough. About the point they neared their freeway exit, it occurred to her that there was a serious flaw or two in their plan. Apparently Carillo sensed this, because he said, "You have that look . . ."

"We know this case. Dixon doesn't. Do we depend on Scotty thinking of her? Or do we call Dixon, let him know. And if we do, and *you* were Dixon, discovered that we were sitting on a key player *after* he ordered us off . . ."

"Good point. You think it's too early to pick up an order of nachos?"

She smiled. "Not in my book."

48

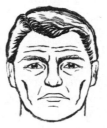

They pulled onto Becky Lynn's street, parked a few houses down, just as they'd done the first time they'd been there. This time, they checked the street both directions just in case Gnoble was there. They didn't see his car, but Becky Lynn's white Lexus was in the drive and the trunk lid was open.

"Loading or unloading?" Carillo asked.

But before Sydney could decide, Becky Lynn stepped out of the door with a suitcase and a tote bag—maybe tripped out was a more apt description—then on down the porch steps, righted herself, walked to the car, threw both items in the trunk. She walked back to the house, navigated the steps, gave a thorough perusal in both directions, then shut the door. "Apparently going somewhere."

"Looking a little tipsy. Not sure I like the timing. Why now?"

"And where to?" Sydney said as she hit redial, calling Dixon.

He answered on the second ring. No greeting, just "You two better be heading back to the office."

"Our car is pointed south as we speak." The left side, at least. "I'm calling because it occurred to us that there's a witness you might not know of." Sydney told him about Becky Lynn, her importance to the case, and their worry that Gnoble might try to take her out.

"Gnoble hasn't left his house yet," Dixon said. "His car is still parked there. If it moves, we'll know. Scotty's team is sitting on it, until we can get SWAT out there."

Santa Arleta wasn't that big of a town, but she wasn't sure she could find Gnoble's place on her own, since the last time her mother and Jake had taken her there, she was probably fifteen. "You wouldn't happen to know Gnoble's address . . . ?" she asked.

"I do."

"Just curious," Sydney said, watching as their mark finally emerged, locked her door, then threw one last and apparently very heavy suitcase in her trunk before slamming it shut. "But seeing as how Becky Lynn might be the *only* witness who can tie all these players together, *including* Gnoble, and she's loaded enough suitcases into her car that it looks like she's not coming back anytime soon—"

"And you would know this because . . . ?"

"We . . . stopped for lunch, and just happened to see her?"

Carillo said, "Ask him if he wants us to pick him up something."

"Let me guess," Dixon said, clearly not amused. "Taco Bell and you can see her from the drive-through line?"

"Supervisors . . . It's like you're *here*," Sydney said, just as Becky Lynn backed out of her driveway, then took off. "Uh, food's ready. Gotta go." Sydney shifted to drive, pulled out after her.

"I'm *ordering* you," Dixon said, and Sydney was fairly certain she heard him shaking Tums from his bottle, "to stay away. If she stops somewhere, even *looks* like she's getting on a plane, taxi, or goddamned magic carpet, you will *not* pull her over, you will *not* make contact. What you *will* do is get on the radio and notify Scotty. Clear?"

"As a plastic lid over a plate of steaming nachos."

She flipped the phone shut, tossed it in the center console, then turned her attention to Becky Lynn's Lexus, about to make a right turn at the end of the street.

"So," Carillo asked, checking the radio to make sure they were on the proper frequency—just in case—"he have any special lunch requests?"

"If I had to guess, a new bottle of antacid, hold the jalapeños. He did mention that Scotty's team is sitting on Gnoble's house, and that Gnoble hasn't moved yet." Even so, Sydney kept an eye on the mirrors. This wasn't the time to take chances. They weren't dealing with some namby-pamby politician from Capitol Hill. Gnoble's training made him extremely dangerous.

"It'd be nice to know where he lives. You think she's heading his way?"

"He lives in the same town as my mom, so I hope not," Sydney said, but she had a sinking feeling as Becky Lynn pulled onto the freeway, then got off the exit to Santa Arleta. Becky Lynn turned a corner, swerved, narrowly missing the curb, and then overcorrecting, only just missing a burgundy minivan in the oncoming lane.

"The way she's driving," Carillo said, "we might not have to worry."

"Unless she kills us all . . ." But Becky Lynn did not turn onto the main road in the direction Sydney thought was toward Gnoble's house. Instead, she turned left on Acacia, then right when it dead-ended on Conifer. Her stomach clenched. "I don't like the looks of this."

"Looks of what?"

"The direction she's heading." And Sydney sent up a prayer. *Please don't let her turn left at the next street. Please, please.*

She did.

"Son of a bitch." Sydney gunned it, not caring whether Becky Lynn saw them, not caring that she was defying orders by turning on the red light to pull her over.

But Becky Lynn did not stop.

And the street she'd turned on led right to her mother's house.

49

Becky Lynn drove up the winding road at a speed
only a drunk or someone with an agenda would dare.

"What the hell would she be coming here for?" Carillo
asked, leaning as Sydney braked at a curve, then accelerated
out of it.

"When she gets drunk, she calls my mom, crying. Has for
years, and I have no idea why. What I do know is that she's
never come here. Drunk, sober, or otherwise."

"Isn't there supposed to be a team on this place?"

Sydney looked up the road, just where it curved, and she
could see the front end of a Crown Vic up at the top of the
hill. "They might be too far back. We should call and tell
them to move up a few feet."

Becky Lynn pulled into the drive, sideswiping the hedge,
her car blocking Jake's extended-cab pickup. Sydney pulled
in after her, only then noticing Jake was just getting into the
pickup. He stopped, looked at them. Her mother was holding
the passenger door open for Angie, who was climbing in, her
puppy held tightly in her arms. Sydney picked up her phone
from the center console, tucked it on her belt, told Carillo,
"Grab the radio. Call Dixon."

She got out, shouted, "Becky Lynn!" as she raced after her. Carillo followed, radio in hand.

Becky Lynn stumbled, turned back, saw them.

Jake stepped away from the truck. "What the *hell* is going on?"

Sydney grabbed at Becky Lynn. "She drove over here. We tried to stop her."

Becky Lynn brushed at her hand. "Look. I'm shorry I got your father killed. I dint know he'd get so mad when I told him . . . I dint know that creep was gonna shoot him."

And suddenly her focus was completely on Becky Lynn. "What creep?"

"He got mad, 'cause your father wanted payback. My fault. I told him . . ."

"Told who?"

Sydney heard a sharp yap from the puppy. She scrambled out of the car, and Angie screamed. "Sarge! Come back here!"

Before her mother could stop Angie, she was out of the car, racing after the puppy.

"Angela!"

"I have to get Sarge."

Becky Lynn struggled with Sydney. They needed to get her out of there. "Carillo!"

"Mary . . . my fault . . . Have to shpeak to Mary."

Sydney put her in a wrist lock, pulled up. She wanted her out of there. Away from her family. Carillo ran over, took her other arm. "Let's go," he said.

They spun her around, started marching her down the long drive. The dog darted from the lawn to the driveway, cutting in front of them. Angie raced past, trying to cut Sarge off before she made it to the street.

"Angie!" Jake shouted. She swooped down, just behind Becky Lynn's car, came up with the dog in her hand, then stopped short, her mouth fixed in a little oh.

Gnoble stepped from behind the hedge, his gun pointed right at her before they could move. Or draw their weapons. Before they could shout out for Angie to run, he grabbed her. Wrapped one arm around her neck, held the gun to her head.

Carillo and Sydney froze. She judged the distance, the time it would take her to draw. Gnoble's gun was already out. Pressed against her sister's temple . . . Her heart thudded in her chest. And that puppy started squirming, but Angie wouldn't let go.

Becky Lynn tried to free herself. Sydney worried she'd say something stupid and get Angie killed. Sydney yanked up on her wrist.

The woman cried out, but Gnoble ignored her. "Convenient," he said. "Everyone I need, and then some."

Becky Lynn quit struggling. "I dint tell them."

"Shut up, Becky Lynn," he said. Tears streamed down Angie's tiny face, but she didn't cry out. "All you had to do was drive one block from your house, meet me at the gas station, and give me the goddamned envelope, and I wouldn't have to leave a bunch of corpses behind."

Becky Lynn sniffed. "I dint tell them about Cisco."

"You'll be dead before they figure it out," he said, pointing his gun at Sydney and Carillo. "You two, let her go, then hold up your hands."

Carillo and Sydney let go of Becky Lynn. She fell to the ground, sobbing, rubbing at her wrist.

"We need to talk about this," Sydney said.

"Talk about how your father tried to bleed me dry, because I sent him and Cisco on a suicide mission? Or talk about how you forced my hand by following Becky Lynn?" he replied, and Sydney swore she could feel Jake's gaze burning into her. "That time's over."

"Look," Sydney said. "Every agent and officer in the area's looking for you right now. You stay here, you'll be caught for sure."

He smiled. "Which is why I paid cash for a less obvious car right after they arrested my lovely wife, then paid someone to drive off in mine just a short while ago. They should be following it down the freeway right about now. Besides, if they thought I was here, wouldn't they be here as well?"

And of course, he was right. They'd be all over this place. Or maybe they were, she realized. But with him holding Angie that way—unless they were sharpshooters—their hands were tied. "Let my sister go," she said.

He held tight to Angie, but pointed his weapon at her and then Carillo. "Your guns," he said. "We'll start with you, Sydney. Don't forget who I'm holding."

She slid back her jacket.

"Now real careful. Gun from the holster. Two fingers."

She reached down, unsnapped her holster. Gripped the gun, until she could draw it with thumb and forefinger. Her heart raced. "You need a hostage," she said, holding out the gun so the barrel hung down. "Take me."

"Toss it on the ground. Right there in front of Becky Lynn."

She tossed it slightly behind Becky Lynn.

"Now drop your jacket, and make a slow turn. Hands in the air."

Sydney shrugged out of her jacket. Let it fall. And then she turned. Slow. Saw Jake by the open driver's door. Inching closer to it. Had to be a gun in there. Saw her mother on the other side, face pale, tears streaming. A fleeting glimpse of the house, the lawn. The scent of the eucalyptus.

When she came full circle, she saw her sister, watching her. Her lower lip trembling. The puppy squirming against her.

Sydney met Gnoble's gaze once more. "Pants legs," he said. "Lift them."

She pulled up on each side.

"Dump the gun. Nice and careful."

And briefly Sydney thought she could draw it, fire as she came up.

Except her sister was in the way.

And Sydney knew he knew.

She pulled at the Velcro, held out the ankle holster, and tossed it by her semiauto. Heard him tell Carillo, "Now you. Same thing." And Sydney knew he wasn't bothering with hostages. They meant nothing to him. Just a hindrance. He was caught. Needed the envelope Becky Lynn spoke of. Something important. A new ID and fake passport. A quick getaway . . .

Sydney pretended to look at Carillo. Saw Jake near the truck door. And she realized then what she needed to do. Even if it meant her own life.

She looked at Angie. Willed her sister to look at her again.

She did. Sydney dropped her gaze to the ground, trying to tell her to get down. Gave a slight nod. Saw her brows raise.

How to get the message? Sydney needed her out of the way . . .

Angie hugged the puppy tighter. Protected it.

Sarge.

The *police* dog.

Sydney wiggled her fingers on her right hand. Saw Angie's gaze flick over. Sydney lifted her palm. Gave the signal for stop.

Angie bit her lip. Kept her gaze on her hand.

Good girl.

She waited until she heard Carillo being ordered to turn around. Sydney knew he'd see Jake, see him edging toward that truck door. Sydney took the chance. Said, "Slowly, Carillo."

"Shut up!" Gnoble yelled.

"Trying to be helpful. Don't want anyone hurt by flying bullets."

Gnoble kept his gaze fixed on Carillo. She pretended to do the same. Saw Jake. Nearer. Nearer.

She took a breath. Please God . . .

And then, waited until Carillo was back around.

Sydney stood with her palm still out. Turned it. Slowly. Until it faced the sky. Then jerked it up. The sign for sit.

Angie bit Gnoble and dropped to the ground.

Gnoble started to grab her.

"Donovan!" Jake shouted.

Carillo and Sydney dove.

Shots rang out.

Her mother screamed.

"Daddy!"

Sydney grabbed her gun. Rolled to her right. Fired at Gnoble. Again and again. Something hit her. Burned her chest.

"*Daddy!*"

Gnoble slumped to the ground. Becky Lynn gathered herself up. "No . . . No!" she cried, stumbling over to him.

Angie ran past them, her puppy forgotten, and Sydney forced herself up. Ignored the burning in her chest. Kept her gun trained on Gnoble. Carillo was at her side, doing the same. They rushed forward, just as Jared Dunning and three other men burst onto the driveway, their guns drawn, one of them saying they couldn't get a shot, because of the kid.

Carillo pulled Becky Lynn back, shoved Gnoble with his foot.

He was not going anywhere. And the truth was, Sydney wanted to shoot him again. Just to make sure.

Breathe, she told herself. *It's over. Just breathe.*

"You okay?" Carillo asked her.

"Something hurts." Sydney felt her chest, realized one of Carillo's casings had landed in the little hollow between her bra and her skin. "Damned things are hot," Sydney said, reaching down, digging it out.

"I can get it for you."

She was about to quip something really smart-assed, just as she turned back, saw her mother. Saw Angie.

Saw Jake on the ground.

Her heart thudded.

She'd done this. She'd brought all this on.

"Oh my God . . ."

"Go," Carillo said, holstering his weapon, then pulling out his cell phone. "I've got her."

Sydney ran over, knelt beside them. Saw Jake's gun on the seat of his car. He'd never even reached it. Just diverted Gnoble's attention to save Angie.

She couldn't see through the blur of her tears. Couldn't see anything but the growing red stain in his gut as her mom applied pressure. "Mom. I'm sorry. I'm sorry."

Angie was sobbing. "He's okay, right, Mommy?"

"Ambulance en route, Fitz," Carillo shouted.

Her mother pressed down harder, and Sydney put her hand over hers, tried to help. Her mother looked her right in the eye, her voice calm. "He'll be fine. Get me a towel, Angela."

Angie ran into the house, just as Jake opened his eyes. Tried to take a breath. "God . . . it hurts."

"I'm sorry. Jake. I'm sorry . . ."

He closed his eyes again, and Sydney wondered if he'd ever forgive her. If any of them would forgive her . . .

The sirens grew louder, echoed off the house. Scotty arrived first, saying something about a neighbor walking over, telling them that Gnoble had taken off in a different car just before they'd gotten there. Two radio cars pulled up. Officers got out, ran up. Carillo with his creds out, holding Becky Lynn. "FBI. Two down. This one in custody."

But it seemed an eternity before the ambulance came. Angie ran out with a towel, gave it to her mom, who placed it over Jake's wound, pressed down, her voice calm, soothing, urging Jake to be still.

And then they came to put him in the ambulance, this man who had raised Sydney after her father had died.

And Sydney watched them working on him, afraid to say anything. Afraid to move.

Her mother came over to her, took Sydney's hand in hers, while her gaze remained on Jake. "This is not your fault."

"I—"

"Becky Lynn came to see me. You didn't bring her."

"Why?"

"Because this morning when she called, I told her not to call again. Every year around the anniversary, she'd get drunk and call to apologize about the explosion that injured your father, and then his murder. I guess this time . . . I just wanted to move on."

Her mother looked at her, tried to smile, failed. She reached out, brushed a bit of something from Sydney's cheek, dirt, grass, who knows, and said, "Call your aunt and uncle. Watch Angela."

"I will."

She kissed Sydney, walked over to the EMTs as they put Jake on the gurney. Efficient. Just another body to them.

The next thing Sydney knew, they were wheeling Jake toward the ambulance, her mother walking beside them, holding Jake's hand. Sydney looked down at him, still as death on that gurney, and all Sydney could whisper was "I'm sorry, Jake," over and over as she walked on the other side.

Just as they were getting ready to lift him into the ambulance, he opened his eyes, looked at her. "Syd . . ."

His voice was quiet. Sydney leaned over, not sure what to say, what to do.

"If Angie . . . grows up to be a goddamned cop . . . I want . . . want her . . . to be . . . like you."

Sydney squeezed his hand, and he looked at the EMT and said, "How . . . fast . . . can you drive this thing?"

50

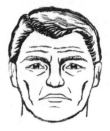

Two days later, Sydney picked up a file folder con-taining her Jane Doe sketch. The tentative ID was verified, and they now had a name to put on her headstone. Delia Jones. The forensic odontologist had positively identified her killer from a reconstruction of the bite made from the broken teeth of the purse snatcher Carillo had arrested a few nights ago. "You'll turn this in for me?" she asked Carillo, handing the file folder to him.

"Yeah, sure." He was quiet, watching her place the last few odds and ends in the box on her desk. "You could fight this transfer. Wasn't that the plan?"

"It was. Until the moment I saw Gnoble with a gun to my sister's head. Maybe even before that moment. I don't ever want to put my family through that again. I'm not sure I could go through that again."

"Just when I was getting used to working with you."

"You'll find another naïve agent to torture, Carillo."

"Not like you. I mean, look at what you've done. The Democrats would roll out the red carpet for you anywhere you went in this state. You single-handedly took out their candidate's biggest contender for senator."

"Funny," she said, throwing him a dark look. "But I've made up my mind."

"But Quantico?"

"Why not?"

"Because *nothing* happens there. You're walking down hallways filled with recruits and marines and cops. It's evidence and paperwork and teaching. Boring."

"After the past week I've had," she said, "boring sounds perfect."

"Yeah, yeah. But just remember. Once you come to the dark side, Pollyanna, it's hard to go back."

Doc Schermer walked up, eyed the boxes on her desk, then gave an overly bright smile as he stuck out his hand. "Good working with you, Fitzpatrick."

"You, too, Doc," she said, shaking his hand. "And keep Carillo in line."

"Always. So, what's the good word on Wheeler? He out, yet?"

"Soon," she said. "Apparently there's a lot of red tape to clear up a man wrongly accused."

And Carillo said, "Especially when they can't publicly release ninety percent of what Gnoble was involved in that led up to that false accusation. It'll be interesting to see how this plays out in the press."

"Won't it," Schermer said. "You think they'll go public on Mrs. Gnoble's involvement?"

"They might," Sydney replied. "Only because Prescott managed to tape a few of their conversations, particularly one very incriminating statement in which she said that once Wheeler was executed, the only thing standing between her and becoming first lady was my repressed memories."

"And Becky Lynn?" Schermer asked Sydney.

"I have a feeling she's going to make a deal."

"A deal?" Carillo said. "I'll bet she asks for witness protection and a new identity. She was sitting on millions upon millions of missing BICTT funds that the Black Network wouldn't hesitate to kill over."

"Okay," Schermer said. "I'm a little confused. If she had

the money in the offshore accounts all this time, then why'd Gnoble kill your father?"

"To cover for the black op, the one where Wheeler's father was killed and mine was injured. That was how they acquired the BICTT funds. Not only wasn't it sanctioned, the government didn't even know about it. Gnoble was after the money, plain and simple."

"Your father, too?"

"You mean was he in it for the money? I'd like to think he didn't know it wasn't a government op. But I do know he felt guilty enough to try to make it up to Wheeler for the loss of his father. The only problem was that Gnoble couldn't risk moving any of that money, beause of the paper trial he was worried would follow."

Carillo nodded in agreement. "Something that had less to do with his political career, and more to do with BICTT's Black Network, who had taken lives for less."

He was right about that, she thought. It was that same paper trail that the CIA wasn't willing to divulge to the American public, citing national security issues, as they were either still hunting down BICTT's Black Network, or they were covering for their own involvement in using the bank. Hence the hush-hush about the real story. For now, Sydney could live with that. She knew the truth, and in a sense some form of justice had been done. For Wheeler at least. She still had questions about her father's involvement, still wondered how the man she'd known and loved could have been involved in something so wrong. Perhaps one day she might come to understand him, learn to accept he wasn't the man she thought he was. For now, she was going to have to accept her mother's mantra, tell herself it was time to move on—no matter how much it hurt. She had her mother, and sister, and Jake, she thought, looking from Schermer to Carillo, then at the boxes on her now empty desk. "I think that's everything. Any last words of wisdom?"

"Actually," Carillo said, lifting one of the boxes to help her carry it down to her car, "I was hoping for some from you, since you know Dixon so well. He's, uh, not going to keep watching me close, is he? I can't even turn around without him wondering what the hell I'm doing."

"He'll get over it. He's probably more upset about you having corrupted me than anything else," she said with a smile. "And even if he's not happy with you, his boss is."

"Only because he got to go on live TV, stand next to the governor, and state that the FBI was *instrumental* in solving the twenty-year-old wrongful conviction of Johnnie Wheeler, who was falsely accused of murder."

Which of course got the governor good exposure, because he got to overturn a conviction with lots of fanfare, and the trickle-down effect was noticeable—until it came to a screeching halt at Dixon's desk.

If it didn't get him to Tahiti any faster, he wasn't impressed.

She looked around, grabbed her briefcase and the smaller box left on the desktop. "Ready when you are." She'd already said her good-byes to Dixon and Lettie. Now all she needed to do was go home, finish packing her things there.

When they got to the elevator, Carillo asked, "How's your mom taking all this?"

"I think she's finally finding peace."

"You finding any?"

"Only if I don't think about it too much," she said, reminding herself what her mother had told her, that her father had loved her, and she should just remember him before that time. "Jake gets out of the hospital tomorrow," she said, changing the subject somewhat. "Angie keeps asking when she can take a photo of his scar, so she can brag about it to her little friend whose daddy works for the sheriff's office. She's one up on him, you know. His dad's never been shot."

"That kid is one tough cookie."

"If Angie ever becomes a cop, watch out for the bad guy."

The elevator door slid open, they stepped on, and Carillo pressed the down button. As the door swished closed and they started their descent, he said, "So. About the copies of the bank numbers we kept. I'm not sure I buy that they only belong to a few offshore accounts, but then it's certainly none of our business if they're still hiding something, still in operation . . . Of course, now that you're heading to your nice, safe, and, I might add, boring job in Quantico, maybe we should turn them in."

"Yeah, maybe we should," she replied as the lift came to a stop, the door opening to the parking garage. She looked over at him and smiled. "But then, what fun would that be?"

Author's Note: Fact or Fiction

While the body of this novel, and each character within, is a work of fiction, many of the events were inspired not only from my own experiences working as a forensic artist and police officer, but also from documented history, some of it decades old, just as the book portrays.

Although my fictional bank is known as BICTT, the inspiration for this international financial institution came from the real life Bank of Credit and Commerce International (BCCI), which was known in federal law enforcement circles as the Bank of Crooks and Criminals. BCCI was a major international bank founded in Pakistan in 1972, which eventually operated four hundred branches in more than seventy countries, with dozens of shell companies, and offshore banks with assets totaling more than twenty-five billion dollars.

In 1991 BCCI became the focus of the biggest banking scandal in history, with thirteen billion dollars still unaccounted for, and allegations of a "black network" division—still in operation after the bank's closure—responsible for mafia-like tactics, be it extortion, kidnapping, and, by some accounts, even murder. Investigators found that BCCI was set up specifically as a conduit for a number of illegal operations, such as terrorism funding, arms trafficking, drug money laundering, sale of nuclear technology, bribery of public officials (which explains how the bank managed to stay under the radar for so many years), and tax evasion.

Buying and selling global intelligence through the bank was a natural by-product, because the bank held the skimmed national treasuries and funds of some of the world's most notorious leaders, such as Saddam Hussein and Manuel Noriega, as well as funds from numerous countries' intelligence agencies. The National Security Council used BCCI to funnel money for the Iran-Contra deals, and the CIA maintained accounts in BCCI for covert operations. Investigators were told that the Defense Intelligence Agency maintained a slush-fund account with BCCI, apparently to pay for clandestine activities.

BCCI attempted to infiltrate the U.S. banking industry by secretly buying three U.S. banks, including First American Bankshares, whose chairman was former U.S. Defense Secretary Clark Clifford. BCCI's de facto ownership and "nominee" shareholder arrangement meant that BCCI itself remained invisible to U.S. banking regulators.

For a time, perhaps.

That much money can't be moved without raising some questions, and eventually the New York District Attorney's office pressed an investigation, as did Senator John Kerry's Subcommittee on Terrorism, Narcotics and International Operations. But Kerry's probe into BCCI was hindered at every turn by the Justice Department, who refused to turn over documents and even blocked the deposition of a key witness. Some believe the bribes and intelligence connections of BCCI were one reason that the Justice Department seemed less than cooperative. Others speculate that the Justice Department was merely covering up for various U.S. governmental agencies' ties to BCCI, especially with the allegations that BCCI had funneled millions to bribe top U.S. officials (for at least ten years before the bank's downfall).

Imagine running across a little black book that held all the records showing which U.S. officials and major corporation heads were bribed to facilitate the bank in its operations. That would certainly shake up a few individuals, and send them running to cover their tracks. And who knows what happened to all the money still unaccounted for, or if some other enterprising crook has pocketed some of that money, or opened up a new bank to fill the void left by BCCI's departure. Whatever the real truth is, Senator Kerry's subcommittee report and other scholarly articles and books on BCCI make for some interesting reading. It certainly fueled my imagination.